THE FOUNTAINHEAD OF CHINESE EROTICA

The Fountainhead of Chinese Erotica

The Lord of Perfect Satisfaction
(*Ruyijun zhuan*)

with a translation and critical edition

CHARLES R. STONE

University of Hawai'i Press
Honolulu

Library of Congress Cataloging-in-Publication Data
Ruyijun zhuan. English
   The fountainhead of Chinese erotica : the lord of perfect satisfaction
(Ruyijun zhuan) / with a translation and critical edition, Charles R. Stone.
      p.   cm.
   ISBN 0-8248-2412-1
   I. Title: Lord of perfect satisfaction.   II. Stone, Charles R.   III. Title.

PL2694.5. .R8913 2003
895.1'346—dc21

                                              2002010917

Designed by inari

Printed by The Maple-Vail Book Manufacturing Group

Contents

Acknowledgments

It was for a seminar on the *Jin Ping Mei* taught by David Roy a few years ago that I first wrote about the *Ruyijun zhuan*, a work that has been a source of entertainment, education, and vexation ever since. I thought I had just enough material to write a paper—not so much that I could scarcely fit it into this book. I hope the reader will conclude that the *Ruyijun zhuan* deserves the attention. It is adamantly serious, even when brilliantly comical, and fastidiously erudite even when implacably vulgar. It is an unprecedented little work that is clearly unlike the misconceptions of it that have flourished since it was written over four and a half centuries ago.

David Roy has lent invaluable assistance from the beginning. Without his guidance, this book and its author might have turned out quite differently. When I first proposed to write about this topic, Anthony Yu also offered valuable advice. His *Rereading the Stone* and Martin Huang's *Desire and Fictional Narrative in Late Imperial China*, moreover, contributed significantly to my understanding of human desire in the Chinese context. Patrick Hanan offered timely advice at an early stage; editorial assistance and critical comments were provided by Richard Wang, Keith McMahon, Katherine Carlitz, Catherine Swatek, Judith Zeitlin, Laura Wu, James Copeland, and Ellen Widmer. Judge Richard Posner offered criticism of an early outline, and Robert Hegel generously lent me his personal copy of the rare *Sui Tang liangchao shizhuan*. Dale Hoiberg has over the years procured all manner of out-of-print titles, without which the completion of this work would have been much more difficult. I am particularly grateful to James Cahill for providing, upon extremely short notice, a copy of the painting reproduced on the cover of this book. Although I have benefited from much assistance in the completion of this project, and am particularly grateful for the deft editorial suggestions made by Patricia Crosby and Don Yoder, some infelicities doubtless remain, and for those I must take credit myself.

To my wife, Lucy, and five-year-old son, Bertrand, I owe a debt of gratitude that I do not know how to repay. The completion of this book was not easier than I had anticipated; without their continuous support and encouragement, it would have been impossible.

But David Roy must get the last word. As everyone who has been one of his students already knows, his own work would have been completed long ago were it not for the attention that he lavishes on everyone else's. He has recently calculated that if he is able to devote his undivided attention to the completion of his monumental annotated translation of the *Jin Ping Mei*, he should be able to complete it within the next two decades; this assumes, of course, that he continues to work six days per week, which he undoubtedly will. This daunting task he happily styles his retirement. I eagerly anticipate, as all of his students and colleagues eagerly anticipate, the successful completion of his life's work.

Introduction

Even Derrida can claim that he is misunderstood, though
his principles should prevent his saying so.

—Frank Kermode, "The Men on the Dump," p. 104

The *Ruyijun zhuan* (Lord of perfect satisfaction) is a short work of fiction written in classical Chinese by an unidentified author at a time uncertain.[1] It purports to tell the story of Empress Wu Zetian's (r. 690–705) controversial rise to power during the late seventh century and her irregular conduct and administration thereafter.[2]

At the beginning of the *Ruyijun zhuan* the beauty of fourteen-year-old Wu Zetian catches the eye of Emperor Tang Taizong (r. 626–649).[3] She is transported to the imperial palace and appointed lady of talents (*cairen*), one of the emperor's numerous minor consorts.[4] Her activities as a minor consort are unremarkable, and standard historical sources contain few descriptions of this stage in her career. Twelve years later, however, fate presents the opportunity that Wu Zetian requires. Emperor Taizong falls seriously ill. Wu Zetian waits upon him at his bedside where the crown prince, soon to become Tang Gaozong (r. 649–683), often administers medicines to his father.[5] As imperial consorts are usually denied association with men other than the emperor — and often lose status or are removed from the palace when the new emperor assumes the throne — Wu Zetian recognizes that a unique opportunity is at hand. When Gaozong initiates an adulterous and incestuous relationship with her, literally at the foot of the dying emperor's bed, Wu Zetian does not affect to resist. Nor does she fail to make explicit the tacit consideration upon which her favors have been conferred. As soon as Gaozong ascends the throne, she is to be appointed empress.

Upon Taizong's death, however, Wu Zetian and many other imperial

1

consorts are removed from the palace, their heads are shaved, and they are made nuns in a Buddhist temple. After only a year, in a tearful encounter with Gaozong as he offers incense to the spirit of his father in the temple Wu Zetian now inhabits, she persuades him by the usual means to allow her to return to court even though she had served the previous emperor. Against the advice of numerous advisers, she now becomes an official consort. Wu Zetian flatters her supporters, liquidates her rivals, and undermines the influence of the current empress. At length she governs Gaozong himself with the insolent fidelity of a servant whose charms have become indispensable. Then, seven years after Gaozong's death, she demotes her son the crown prince and becomes the first and only woman emperor of China.[6]

A reign of terror follows. Normal judicial procedures are suspended. A system of informing on rivals directly to the empress is instituted. The Tang imperial family is persecuted almost to the point of extinction, and the establishment of a new Zhou dynasty (690–705) is officially proclaimed. After her political opponents have been tortured, murdered, or exiled, Wu Zetian recognizes it is time to apply a powerful religious sedative. If she reveals that she is, in fact, a reincarnation of Maitreya, the Buddhist messiah, she knows the hearts of the pious masses can be won to the new dynasty. Thus she instructs her adherents to produce a Buddhist text disclosing a version of her true spirit that had not been conspicuous. Copies of this text are then deposited in new temples in every county in China.[7] In the first year of the Perfect Satisfaction reign period (Ruyi 692), after the last vestiges of overt opposition have been eliminated, Wu Zetian proclaims that all of China, in accordance with Buddhist principles, is henceforth to be strictly vegetarian. It is illegal for those who have survived the period of terror to slaughter a pig or disturb even the whisker of a shrimp.[8] Despite numerous famines, Wu Zetian cannot be persuaded to rescind this edict for another eight years.[9]

Such is the tenor of the reign of Wu Zetian—or at least how it is commonly caricatured in standard historical sources. The *Ruyijun zhuan* describes many of the major political events of her reign, particularly the controversies surrounding her demotion of the crown prince. It also focuses on more personal aspects of her life and motivation—upon her relations with lovers and rivals after she reenters the imperial palace. Her insatiable appetite for power and sex increases steadily as she acquires full dominion over an emperor, his court, and eventually the entire country. The book is written in a style that resembles a genre of history called *yeshi*, a variant of standard historical sources that focuses on minor personal events that would not normally merit the attention of an official historian.

The *Ruyijun zhuan* is not, however, known for its depiction of minor historical events. Nor is it known for shedding new light on the personal motivations of Wu Zetian. It is known for the sex. The descriptions of sex in the *Ruyijun zhuan* are explicit and unprecedented in Chinese fiction. Indeed the work invented a new vocabulary of obscenity that would set the standard for a new genre of erotic fiction that proliferated during the remainder of the sixteenth century. Many of the sexual situations and much of the unique vocabulary found in the landmark sixteenth-century novel *Jin Ping Mei* (The plum in the golden vase), for example, come from scenes in the *Ruyijun zhuan*.[10] Several works of fiction whose artistic achievements are of conspicuously lesser merit also appear to have found a kind of inspiration within its pages. The *Sengni niehai* (Monks and nuns in a sea of iniquity), *Xiuta yeshi* (Unofficial history of the embroidered couch), and *Nongqing kuaishi* (Heart-throbbing history of powerful passions), to name but three examples, use much of its vocabulary and often copy fragments of sentences or entire pages verbatim.[11]

The *Ruyijun zhuan* was, in short, a new departure for Chinese fiction. Contemporaries recognized that it was a new way of writing about human sexuality and they immediately copied it. Most Chinese erotic fiction written during the next hundred years was ultimately inspired by the *Ruyijun zhuan* or borrowed from its vocabulary. Some scholars have therefore concluded that the *Ruyijun zhuan*'s use of Tang-dynasty (618–907) history is merely a pretext for telling a dirty story.[12] Wu Zetian's scandalous conduct is legendary. Her ruthless rise to power, her subversion of the Tang judicial system, and her controversial relations with several men are standard topics of later histories. It is not surprising that a work like the *Ruyijun zhuan,* which focuses on some of the more sordid details of Wu Zetian's reign, does not enjoy the best of reputations. And when its graphic descriptions of Wu Zetian's sexual inclinations are considered, its fate could scarcely be in doubt. The *Ruyijun zhuan* is invariably placed among the basest examples of Chinese fiction, remarkable only because it founded a new genre that was offensive to an unprecedented degree.

It is therefore curious that the earliest appraisals of the *Ruyijun zhuan* argue, or affect to argue, that it illustrates an important moral. The contemporary sixteenth-century scholar Huang Xun (1490–c. 1540) protests in his "Du *Ruyijun zhuan*" (Reading the *Ruyijun zhuan*) that it could not even be discussed without polluting one's mouth; yet he finds that it nevertheless illustrates the dangers of immoral conduct infecting the highest levels of government.[13] He also concludes that Wu Zetian is not responsible for the debauchery and decline of the Tang dynasty—her actions, rather, are the direct result of the immoral behavior of the founding emperor Tang Taizong. It is almost superfluous to note that this reckoning is not in accord with standard interpretations of the reigns of Taizong and Wu Zetian. Moreover,

Taizong is only briefly mentioned at the beginning of the work. And although Huang Xun thinks the *Ruyijun zhuan* is fit to be burned, he curiously proceeds to compare its moral to a poem about the Tang dynasty written by the famous Neo-Confucian scholar Zhu Xi (1130-1200).[14] In short, Huang Xun contends that a book in which Wu Zetian appears on every page is actually about a previous emperor who is barely mentioned and maintains that its message, although delivered in an unspeakably vulgar fashion, somehow bears comparison to the august pronouncements of a great Neo-Confucian scholar. Huang Xun, I think, is suggesting that this peculiar work is not what it seems.

Another early interpretation of the *Ruyijun zhuan* is found in Huayang Sanren's preface dated 1634.[15] Like Huang Xun, Huayang Sanren argues that it is an obscene story told in an offensive manner. Yet he too claims that the *Ruyijun zhuan* contains an important moral and could "serve as an admonitory example."[16] The male protagonist, Xue Aocao, the paramour of Wu Zetian at the center of its most graphic descriptions, is in fact compared to Zhang Liang (d. 189 B.C.), a renowned minister of the Han dynasty (206 B.C.–A.D. 220).[17] Like Zhang Liang, Xue Aocao helps the ruler resolve a serious problem concerning the status of the crown prince. Although Xue Aocao personally takes part in lascivious conduct, Huayang Sanren notes that he is faithful to the state and in fact persuades the empress to act in a moral fashion when the arguments of her senior advisers fail. The moral is illustrated with a quotation from the *Yi jing* (Book of changes) which argues that in difficult circumstances, remonstration may be forced to take unusual forms.

Huang Xun and Huayang Sanren admit that the moral of the *Ruyijun zhuan* is delivered in an offensive fashion and is, moreover, highly unconventional. Nevertheless, even though they wrote the earliest interpretations of this work and appear to take it seriously, some scholars have concluded that what they have to say about this book is simply not plausible.[18] A preliminary investigation of the text, however, reveals that rejecting their arguments creates more problems than it solves. The *Ruyijun zhuan* does indeed describe human sexual activity in unprecedented detail, but it places many such descriptions in an overtly political, ironic, or indeed moral context. When the text is examined dispassionately, we see that most of the *Ruyijun zhuan* is devoted to political machinations of the seventh century: the rise to power of Wu Zetian, her demotion of the crown prince, his eventual reinstatement, and historical details and personalities that seem to have nothing to do with the erotic part of the story. No explicit descriptions appear in the first half of the work. And when they do appear, they are most often accompanied by protracted discussions of morality as it relates to good government, considerations of the remonstrations that may be used when the time is not propitious for traditional methods, and an unusual amount of historical detail that not only seems pointless, but sabotages the erotic ambiance. Unlike the "typical" pornographic novel, which begins with a small cast of characters that dwindles as the plot becomes irrelevant, the cast in the *Ruyijun zhuan* is enormous and continues to expand throughout the work.[19] Despite its short length, there are some twenty main characters, twenty minor characters, and twenty-five additional allusions to historical persons, almost all of which are historically accurate. If the plot of the *Ruyijun zhuan* is compared to virtually any pornographic novel, the difference is striking.

The author of the *Ruyijun zhuan* not only creates an unnecessarily complex plot, he also invents a new and influential vocabulary of obscenity. He conspicuously avoids the use of euphemistic and poetic descriptions of sex that are commonly found in poetry, medical texts, and earlier erotic stories. If the purpose of the *Ruyijun zhuan* were to raise the standard of the dirty book to new heights, one might have expected it to build upon the foundation prepared by famous erotic tales like the *Han Wudi neizhuan* (Intimate biography of Emperor Wu of the Han), the *Zhao Feiyan waizhuan* (The outer story of Empress Zhao Feiyan), or even parts of the *Xixiang ji* (Romance of the western chamber).[20] Or one might have expected quotations from a collection of erotic poems like the *Yutai xinyong* (New songs from a jade terrace).[21] Yet I have not discovered a single instance in which the author of the *Ruyijun zhuan* refers to an earlier erotic work. When he does refer to earlier works, it is most often to cite standard interpretations of the reign of Wu Zetian found in the *Jiu Tang shu* (Old history of the Tang dynasty), the *Xin Tang shu* (New history of the Tang dynasty), the *Zizhi tongjian* (Comprehensive mirror for aid in government), or their sources.[22] Moreover, the author uses a wide variety of historical sources; he does not merely open the *Zizhi tongjian* to the reign of Wu Zetian and copy down the history, as is often the case with authors of historical novels. And if he wishes to create a context for a sexual scene by incorporating a famous allusion, he quotes, of all things, the Confucian classics: in pivotal scenes of the *Ruyijun zhuan* there are allusions to incidents found in the *Shi ji* (Historical records), *Zuo zhuan* (Zuo documentary), and *Han shu* (History of the Former Han dynasty) and at least a dozen actual quotations from the *Shi jing* (Book of poetry), *Yi jing* (Book of changes), *Mengzi* (Works of Mencius), and *Lunyu* (Analects).[23] Some of the allusions found in the poetry are, in fact, from obscure Tang historical sources. If the author were simply writing a sex book, why would he consciously avoid referring to earlier erotic fiction and instead litter his text with references to some of the most unerotic and moralistic passages found in the Chinese histories and classics?

Certainly authors of later erotic fiction saw contradictions in the way the *Ruyijun zhuan* is written. While the new vocabulary coined by the *Ruyijun zhuan* quickly became the standard for the Chinese erotic novel and some of the most infamous pornographic novels use its vocabulary for purely prurient purposes, it is also evident that authors of later erotic works ignore the fact that many of these terms are introduced to Chinese fiction in a conspicuously ironic context—that the *Ruyijun zhuan* uses a wide range of historical materials to undermine many of the sexual situations it describes. Perhaps the clearest example is in the *Nongqing kuaishi*.[24] The bulk of the *Ruyijun zhuan* is copied verbatim into the *Nongqing kuaishi*. But dissonant references to the historical record are deleted; references to the Confucian classics are excised; and inappropriate references that detract from the portrayal of sex are cut—especially, it seems, if in the *Ruyijun zhuan* they call the reader's attention to the impropriety of the characters' actions.

Even the very first graphic description in the *Ruyijun zhuan* is, upon closer examination, not what it might seem to be. At about the midpoint of the work its naked hero Xue Aocao is presented to Wu Zetian. Nature had been profligate in her gifts, particularly those of which the empress was expert in the art of appraising. As she had recently become so dissatisfied with her other lovers that she ordered one of them beaten to death, she is unable to forbear the object of her desire in its meridian splendor. But she then declares her perfect satisfaction in a most curious fashion:

> The empress held it fast in both hands as if she had just received a treasure and said: "How monumental! It is not of this world. I have known many men, but there has never been one like this. In the past, Wang Yifu had a chowry with a handle of white jade; it was uniquely transparent and lustrous. For this reason I name it 'chowry handle': the ultimate of beauty."[25]

This is the locus classicus of the term "chowry handle" (*zhubing*), the famous euphemism. What is most significant about this term is not, however, that it paints an irresistible erotic picture. Indeed, some might find that a piece of cold, translucent white jade is not the most sensuous of objects. The term "*zhubing*" is significant because it is named after the chowry owned by Wang Yan (255–311), one of the most famous politicians of the Western Jin dynasty (265–317).[26] He held many government positions, was considered an arbiter of taste for his age, and ended his career as chief minister. His conduct during crises of state, however, was inadequate, and his negative moral example was thought to have precipitated the fall of the dynasty. Thus when Wu Zetian coins the term "chowry handle," the author of the *Ruyijun zhuan* has her utter succinct, ironic criticism of her own actions. Because of Wang Yan's example, "people felt ashamed to talk about the Moral Teaching . . . and from clerks in the Imperial Secretariat on down, everybody admired the principle of folding his hands in silence, and took the neglect of duty for their ideal. Although all was still at peace within the Four Seas, those who understood the true state of affairs realized that they were on the verge of ruin."[27]

Is this concise historical allusion meant to place the first graphic scene of the *Ruyijun zhuan* in an ironic light? There are numerous references of this sort; some should be evident to every educated reader, others are indirect, a few are quite obscure. One thing, however, is clear: while authors of later pornographic novels turn to the *Ruyijun zhuan* for a new vocabulary of sex, they implicitly recognize that the *Ruyijun zhuan* cannot be quoted promiscuously—it must be quoted selectively if it is to be included in a work that is primarily about sex. Although the term "*zhubing*" is found in many novels written after the *Ruyijun zhuan* and many writers are familiar with this particular passage, I cannot think of a single erotic novel that does not delete the ironic reference to Wang Yan.[28]

And then there is the role played by its nominal hero Xue Aocao. As Hua-yang Sanren notes in his preface, it is Xue Aocao who is ultimately responsible for restoring the legitimate crown prince—a result that even the repeated re-monstrations of Wu Zetian's senior ministers could not effect. Although Xue Aocao's arguments are based on traditional moral principles, although he voices them with great passion, and although he places his life in danger by criticizing an empress who casually liquidates senior officials who dare to offer similar criticisms, the manner in which he displays his loyalty to the state is unconventional: he offers his most effective remonstrations while commit-ting lewd acts with the empress. When authors of later erotic novels refer to the *Ruyijun zhuan* they assiduously remove these odd remonstrations. The *Nongqing kuaishi* quotes the rest of this work almost verbatim, for example, yet it eliminates virtually every trace of Xue Aocao's ridiculous moral pretensions and turns him into a vulgar plaything of the empress.

Not only does the author of the *Ruyijun zhuan* dwell upon unusual expres-sions of traditional morality, avoid referring to earlier erotic literature, and in-clude much material that later erotic novels would choose to eliminate; he also skips periods of Wu Zetian's life that would have been quite appropriate for inclusion in an erotic work. When she is first conveyed to the palace at the age of fourteen—by all accounts a ravishing beauty—there is no direct descrip-tion of her sexual relations with the crown prince. The graphic description of Wu Zetian's amorous adventures is postponed until she is in her seventies, when such descriptions are, for an erotic work at least, untimely. And as the tale progresses, the erotic subject matter becomes nearly unimaginable. Near the end of the *Ruyijun zhuan* we find one of the first explicit descriptions of masochistic sex found in the Chinese language, but by this stage the empress is in her eighties.

Yet for the past few centuries the prevailing interpretation of the *Ruyi-jun zhuan* has projected it as little more than a sensational tribute to Wu Zetian's sexual perversions that does not require, or deserve, further comment. Virtually nothing has been written about its humor, its irony, its erudite references to classical texts, or the effect of its rhetorical technique on later works like the *Jin Ping Mei*. And while it might be tempting to conclude that the *Ruyijun zhuan* is just a precursor of later erotic novels like the *Rou putuan* (The carnal prayer mat), one of the more famous examples of this genre, the *Ruyijun zhuan*, I think, is ultimately in a class by itself.[29] While the *Ruyijun zhuan* is on one level a parody of the hackneyed tale of a ruler who is ruined by a favorite concubine, on the whole its tone is dark, even bleak, and its purported moral seems contradictory if not ludicrous. The manner in which it incorporates references to earlier texts also seems unnecessarily obscure: my discussion of the connotations that lurk behind the various names and nicknames of its hero Xue Aocao, for example, a shallow creature whose character would not seem to merit serious attention, occupies over ten pages and invokes a surprising array of historical texts. While works like the *Rou putuan* may refer to classical texts, such references tend to be obvious. They also tend to be openly facetious. They simply augment the novel's levity as the author ridicules the social and moral conventions of his day. The *Rou putuan* is ultimately a parody of the moral seriousness, political relevance, and even the sexual descriptions found in the *Ruyijun zhuan:* as its protagonist Vesperus does not possess the prodigal natural endowment of Xue Aocao, his drooping spirits require that he be augmented with a surgical implant of canine origin.

Considering how little is currently known about the *Ruyijun zhuan*, unqualified pronouncements about its meaning are clearly premature. Its date of composition and the author's identity are unknown. There are conflicting speculations about the authors of the preface and postscript, and the significance of these brief analyses has not been adequately assessed. The earliest appraisal of the *Ruyijun zhuan* by a contemporary has not been analyzed carefully. Most of the ironic or dissonant material quoted by the *Ruyijun zhuan* has not been identified or analyzed. Its depiction of Tang history has not been compared to original source materials. And although the *Ruyijun zhuan* invented a new genre for Chinese fiction and numerous works quote fragments or entire pages verbatim, what later authors learned from this work and chose to ignore has scarcely been mentioned. Moreover, even the best modern edition of the *Ruyijun zhuan* contains numerous errors. Surely the answers to these basic questions about its author, its earliest commentators, and the text itself might influence the way in which it is read.

Part Two of this book presents an annotated and corrected edition of the

Ruyijun zhuan and an annotated translation. But correcting the text of the *Ruyijun zhuan*, translating it, and identifying its sources are merely the first steps in its interpretation. It is also necessary to place it in historical context—to compare its unique descriptions to traditional Chinese conceptions of human sexuality. While the *Ruyijun zhuan* might at first seem to be unprecedented, its treatment of human sexuality has, in fact, much in common with the major fiction of sixteenth-century China. And while it might seem to be a precursor of radical late-Ming reevaluations of human desire, just beneath the surface is an improbable notion of human desire that is, as we shall see, obstinately conservative.

After citing a likely candidate for the author of the *Ruyijun zhuan* and comparing his most urgent concerns to the philosophical and political controversies of his day, I conclude that he might well have been inspired by contemporary events. Is it simply a coincidence that most of the *Ruyijun zhuan* describes the succession of the crown prince and the legitimacy of the sovereign in a way that also applies to the most destructive succession scandal of the Ming dynasty? It would be a mistake, however, to claim that a controversial work of art like the *Ruyijun zhuan* is nothing but an allegory for something else. While I think the *Ruyijun zhuan* is much more than a dirty book, it did not acquire its reputation by accident. Nor can it be denied that even its most sympathetic contemporary critic condemned it and was, in turn, himself condemned for having condescended to read it.

But even if all ironic references to the historical record and the Confucian classics were removed from the *Ruyijun zhuan* and only the graphic sex were left, it still should not be considered pornographic—unlike the countless novels that drew their inspiration directly from it. This argument leads ineluctably to a paradox that will require nearly the rest of this book to explain: the *Ruyijun zhuan* is not an example of the genre it invented.

PART ONE

Context and Analysis

1

Pornography and the West

None of them was aware that a certain decorum is essential
even to voluptuousness, that drapery may be more alluring
than exposure, and that the imagination may be far more
powerfully moved by delicate hints which impel it to exert
itself, than by gross descriptions which it takes in passively.

—Thomas Babington Macaulay, *The History of England*, 1.304

The *Ruyijun zhuan* contains explicit descriptions of sexual activity that are
unprecedented in Chinese fiction. This much is not in dispute. What these
descriptions may ultimately signify, if anything, and whether their meaning
is transformed by the brief, ironic references to the historical record that
often accompany them, however, are questions that may occasion some debate. This is particularly the case when one considers that few readers could
be expected to identify many of the recondite references found in this work,
much less comprehend their significance. After examining a single poem
that reveals the sophistication of these historical references, I will then ignore this aspect for the moment and explore what is left. But first we must
address the question of pornography.

Is the *Ruyijun zhuan* Pornographic?

The mere existence of explicit sexual descriptions in the *Ruyijun zhuan* has
caused some to conclude that it is the first pornographic work in the Chinese language. Earlier works like the *Han Wudi neizhuan* and the *Zhao Feiyan
waizhuan* do contain some erotic descriptions; but as they are not very detailed, they are not usually considered pornographic. Early medical texts
sometimes describe sex in great detail; but as their descriptions are related
to Daoist physiological alchemy and tend to be technical, they do not approach the threshold of pornography either. If the mere existence of

explicit descriptions were sufficient to cause a work to be labeled porno-graphic, then the *Ruyijun zhuan* would certainly deserve that label. But por-nography is not just the description of sex. It is a rhetorical technique that is inseparable from the manner in which a story is narrated. This is the case in both Eastern and Western examples of this genre.

In this book I avoid the term "pornography" whenever possible. It is mis-leading and imprecise and unusually difficult to define. (Perhaps it would be more correct to say that the word is not so difficult to define, it is just that no two definitions are the same, many are mutually exclusive, and most are of little practical value in evaluating a work of literature.) When I do use the word "pornography," it describes a narrative technique and nothing more. It does not address the legal or moral status of works that contain descrip-tions of sex, although I do mention these issues in the notes.

Pornographic technique is the union of banality, obscenity, and repeti-tion. Pornographic works almost always contain just the rudiments of plot and characterization. These are not necessary. Style, structure, and every-thing else that does not directly stimulate the reader's libido are avoided. Further investigation of the term's origins reveals there is much more to it than just the description of sex.

Although the word "pornography" was born in ancient Greece, the mod-ern sense of the term did not exist before the middle of the nineteenth cen-tury.[1] At that time, excavations at Pompeii unearthed artifacts that shocked and distressed the curators of the National Museum of Naples. Much of what they had excavated, they thought, was obscene. There were statues, frescoes, pottery, even images adorning the outside walls of dwellings, that were graph-ically sexual in nature.[2] Perhaps the volcanic eruption that suffocated the city and its inhabitants was a form of divine retribution. In any event, the curators decided they could not place obscene objects on display, even objects from re-mote antiquity. Innocent minds—of women, children, and those who did not possess the proper education—would be corrupted. The solution was to cre-ate a secret museum to house the offensive materials; only a handful of edu-cated men was allowed access for the purpose of scholarly research. These materials were labeled "pornography," which literally means "writing about prostitutes." Despite the ubiquity of such artifacts in Pompeii, it was argued that they were obviously the products of the lowest classes of society. No other explanation could be imagined. Thus when the term "pornography" was used during the nineteenth century, it described the obscene products of an un-desirable element of society from which normal people could not be trusted to protect themselves.

Even today, sexually explicit materials are considered particularly sinis-ter because some people are spontaneously attracted to them in a way they find difficult to forbear. To the extent that such materials excite the flesh, the higher rational faculties are debilitated. And thus we inevitably find that new technologies pregnant with great promise for the improvement of the human condition quickly degenerate into vehicles for the dissemination of sexually graphic materials that are ever more explicit. The prevalence of salacious sites on the Internet is merely one recent example. Although some believe that the Internet is an indispensable resource for the education of every primary school student, and although political candidates vie to provide universal access at taxpayer expense, it cannot be denied that the Internet has become the most efficient mechanism of distribution that pornography has ever known—a fact that, no doubt, is not lost on the grateful students for whose benefit this access has been facilitated.

In *Pornography and the Law,* Eberhard and Phyllis Kronhausen study the question of pornography dispassionately.[3] As theirs is one of the more rational and useful discussions of this topic, it has become something of a classic. They define the term "pornography" by comparing works that are thought to be pornographic to those that are not. They argue that, by itself, the presence of sex in a work of fiction tells us very little about it. They argue instead that there is a distinction between pornography and a kind of writing they call "erotic realism" which may also contain descriptions of sex. While their definition is dated and is weakened by numerous fallacies, I think it remains a useful tool for analyzing a work of fiction—in any event more useful than certain recent discussions of this topic.[4] And, with some qualification, I believe it also tells us something worth knowing about explicit materials written during the sixteenth century in China:

> Both the technique and the aim of pornography (hard core obscenity) are diametrically opposed to those of erotic realism, and even when, by the accident of context, the effects are at times identical, it is well to keep in mind that the overall intent is very different. . . . *In pornography* (hard core obscenity) *the main purpose is to stimulate erotic response* in the reader. And that is all. *In erotic realism, truthful description of the basic realities of life, as the individual experiences it, is of the essence,* even if such portrayals (whether by reason of humor, or revulsion, or any other cause) have a decidedly anti-erotic effect.[5]

Pornography includes descriptions that are in bad taste. The most private relations are treated with flagrant disregard for any sense of moderation or decorum. But most important, the purpose of a pornographic work is to arouse the reader. This is accomplished through simple, direct stimulation provided by a series of sexual images that the reader is invited to witness as a voyeur. The Kronhausens note that the same type of physiological response produced by pornography may also be elicited by works they consider "erotic realism." But this is not its primary purpose. Erotic realism attempts to portray the basic realities of human life; it does not shrink from details that make some readers uncomfortable. Many of the world's greatest novels, in fact, incorporate frank descriptions that could at times be considered crude or even obscene; *Gargantua and Pantagruel, Ulysses,* and the *Jin Ping Mei* are but three famous examples.[6]

But erotic realism, as Bakhtin has observed of novels in general, functions dialogically.[7] Such novels are symphonies of many distinct, individual voices; they use many different types of language and description; and they often resort to parody, crude humor, and laughter. The reader must interpret continually the world that is presented to him. Even when such novels include descriptions of sexual activity, they are often deflated with humorous details or lead to ironic consequences that are quite unerotic. The comedy of the human situation is close to the heart of such novels: "Laughter destroyed epic distance; it began to investigate man freely and familiarly, to turn him inside out, expose the disparity between his surface and his center, between his potential and his reality."[8]

This is what is missing in pornography. There is no crowd of voices echoing the full complexity of the world; there is just one voice, or one point of view masquerading as many voices, whose ultimate purpose is to simplify. In pornography there should be no distractions. It avoids details that could undermine the erotic effect.[9] It is not about exposing comic disparities; it is about exposure of a more literal sort. It reduces a lewd story to a series of prurient descriptions that provide stimulation. As the purpose of pornographic works is simple and uniform, so the style tends to be simple and uniform as well:

> The *basic structure* or organization of "obscene" books remains fairly constant, regardless of their outward shape, size, and individual style. . . . *A book which is designed to act upon the reader as an erotic psychological stimulant ("aphrodisiac") must constantly keep before the reader's mind a succession of erotic scenes.* It must not tire him with superfluous non-erotic descriptions of scenery, character portrayals, or lengthy philosophical expositions. All these are unnecessary trimmings for the writer of "obscene" books. The idea is to focus the reader's attention on erotic word-images, and not to distract him with side issues and tangents of one kind or another. . . . The characteristic feature in the structure of "obscene" books is the *buildup of erotic excitement* in the course of the text. An "obscene" book may start out with a scene which is only mildly erotic and not highly stimulating. In progression, it will then become "hotter" and "hotter" until the story culminates in the description of the most sensual scenes, which are highly conducive to the arousal of erotic desires.[10]

The *Ruyijun zhuan* has little in common with these definitions. Its style and structure are of a different nature entirely. It is not an endless stream of erotic scenes, but a history of Empress Wu Zetian's personal life based on an unexpectedly broad selection of historical sources. A close examination of its use of these sources reveals that its portrayal of the history of the Tang dynasty is far more complex than may at first be apparent. Above all, such passages also undermine the erotic aspect of the story.

Consider a poem found near the very beginning. Emperor Gaozong has just decided to elevate his favorite consort Wu Zetian to the rank of empress, a step that will require the demotion of the current empress. But as the current empress has never committed a transgression, a suitable justification is needed. Gaozong, however, is not up to the task. He thinks a simple mandate is sufficient and merely babbles a pretext that strains even the feigned civilities of the most slavish court parasites. Wu Zetian, he notes, has a son. The current empress does not. It would therefore be advantageous for the state if he demoted the legitimate empress and elevated Wu Zetian, an impostor, in her stead. None of his senior advisers are disposed to grant such a dispensation. They remind the emperor that Empress Wang was formally married to him.[11] When Taizong was on his deathbed, he grasped Gaozong's hand in the presence of these same advisers and solemnly instructed them to assist and protect his son and daughter-in-law. The advisers cannot forget such a sacred commitment. Wu Zetian, they also note, is not the daughter of one of the more illustrious families of the realm and indeed had entered the imperial palace as a minor consort. She soon attracted the attention of Emperor Taizong who was persuaded to indulge her with his imperial favor. Upon his death, she was removed to a temple and was made a nun. The advisers conclude it would be difficult to find a more controversial candidate to replace the current empress. Gaozong's relations with Wu Zetian are not only improper but incestuous. Everyone knows this. It will be impossible to avoid devastating criticism. Gaozong, typically, punishes the advisers whose recommendations he has just solicited. He then proclaims Wu Zetian empress. At this point we find the following poem:

> Despite all obstacles the emperor's loyal servant
>   did not regard his own welfare;
> His direct remonstrances were truly
>   in the manner of Bi Gan.
> The official tablet was returned on the imperial steps,
>   in the end his heart was red-blooded;
> His forehead kowtowed on the palace steps
>   until the columns were red with blood.
> If the majestic phoenix lacks the heart
>   to establish the ordinances of the state,

> Incestuous hinds will have something to say
>   that may confuse the imperial intelligence.
> The present dynasty has generously instituted
>   spring and autumn sacrifices in his honor
> Which for all eternity again make manifest
>   his loyalty to the altars of earth and grain.[12]

Readers who have studied Tang history will recognize that a photographic memory would be of some assistance here. This poem contains many phrases describing the reigns of Gaozong and Wu Zetian that are found in standard historical sources. Even a brief summary of such references reveals the poem to be unexpectedly erudite. The first line, "Despite all obstacles the emperor's loyal servant," is a slightly modified quotation from the *Yi jing* that occurs at least twice in the Tang histories; it describes a situation in which an official must confront danger in the service of a higher cause. The second line contains a reference to Bi Gan, paternal uncle of the infamous King Zhou (r. 1086–1045 B.C.), the last emperor of the Shang dynasty (c. 1600–1045 B.C.), who was licentious and would not listen to counsel. Bi Gan remonstrated with him with great candor and sincerity, but his tenacity only earned him a horrific death. This reference to Bi Gan, in turn, is most likely an allusion to a loyal Tang official named Zhou Jing who was implicated in a plot to kill Wu Sansi (d. 707), the nephew of Wu Zetian; variations of this line are found in the Tang histories. Variations of the fourth line are found in the Tang histories as well. The fifth line contains an obscure reference to an official named Zhangsun Wuji (d. 659); the "majestic phoenix" is the name of a rhapsody written by Emperor Taizong that describes the tenacity of his minister's virtue. After Taizong died, however, Zhangsun Wuji's virtue wavered: initially he voiced concerns about Gaozong's plan to elevate Wu Zetian, but after intense pressure was brought to bear and bribes were delivered by the cartload, he no longer found it necessary to voice his opinion. The sixth line contains the erudite term "incestuous hinds"; the earliest occurrence of this phrase is found in the *Li ji* (Book of rites), where it refers to a father and son committing incest by sharing the same woman. In this instance it refers to Gaozong's incestuous relationship with Wu Zetian; this same term is used to describe their relationship in the Tang histories.

The story of Emperor Gaozong and Wu Zetian is perfect material for a pornographic work: it is the story of an illicit love born of irrepressible desire. Gaozong is attracted to Wu Zetian the instant he lays eyes upon her, and he initiates an affair even though their love is proscribed by law and his father is dying in an adjacent room. He elevates her to empress although he is warned of the dire consequences. He is unable to contain his desire, however, and over the course of several years he exhausts his vital essence, his vision fails, and he is debilitated. But their physical relationship is never described. Instead the text is littered with historical passages and poems illustrating the immorality of their relationship. The poem about Gaozong's elevation of Wu Zetian, for example, does not describe the sweetness of forbidden fruit. It argues that senior advisers must be courageous and resolute when an emperor acts in an immoral fashion, even if they have to pay with their lives. And almost every line illustrates this point with an erudite allusion. It is difficult to imagine a less erotic description of the consequences of Gaozong's relationship with Wu Zetian. Pornographic works are not known for their erudite portrayal of historical events. Nor do they generally include poems constructed of references to the historical record that portray uncompromising fidelity to moral principles. Pornography usually ignores history, and extended discussions of morality are rare. Such materials simply do not contribute to the erotic potential of the story.

Officials who flourish in the *Ruyijun zhuan* are, to say the least, not of the highest moral caliber. Unlike the virtuous statesmen of the past, they pander to the emperor's every whim, no matter how immoral. It is precisely in the most trying of circumstances that the advice of an honest official is of most value. But few officials possess the tenacity to resist the emperor's demands, and the rest are terrified into submission. And after Wu Zetian has proclaimed herself emperor, it is too late; any officials courageous enough to offer advice are cashiered. At length she grows weary of remonstration of any description; virtuous officials are simply refused admission to the imperial presence. In such circumstances, moral remonstrations with one's ruler can be expected to assume unusual forms. This is the case in the *Ruyijun zhuan*. As anything that resembles the bitter pill of morality is rejected before it can be administered, it is necessary to disguise morality with an outward display that may at first appear to be its opposite. This is similar to the technique that many Han-dynasty authors of erotic rhapsodies claim to have used: the description of sensuous situations paradoxically facilitates the delivery of an austere moral message that would otherwise never be heard (see Chapter 2).

Critics who have not examined the manner in which the *Ruyijun zhuan* portrays the history of the Tang dynasty—and who have thus failed to identify its numerous references—are the first to claim that the history found in the *Ruyijun zhuan* is merely a pretext for telling a dirty story.[13] If the allusions found in the poem quoted here were disclosed to them, they might argue that it is just a coincidence. But at some point the accumulation of such coincidences may give rise to doubt and cause the reader to suspect that the author may, in fact, be incorporating such materials on purpose. It seems possible, therefore, that critics of the *Ruyijun zhuan* have got it backwards:

perhaps the history is not a pretext for telling a dirty story; perhaps the dirty story is a pretext for telling an unusual tale about history and morality.

An obvious objection to this suggestion is that the references found in the *Ruyijun zhuan* are too obscure for the average reader to identify. And what kind of reader would think of turning to the histories of the Tang dynasty to verify the significance of such a poem contained in such a text? But to admit that many of these references are indeed difficult to identify does not mean they are not significant. There is an abundance of erudite references in the *Ruyijun zhuan,* and they are almost always scrupulously accurate. It seems unlikely, then, that they found their way into this work by accident.

In addition to the passages containing historical allusions, the *Ruyijun zhuan* also contains a great deal of material that distracts the reader's attention at the most inopportune moments. Just when the text begins to describe sexual situations, for example, it interrupts them with lengthy moral remonstrations that are obviously out of place. These remonstrations do not depend on the recognition of obscure references. Moreover, they are spoken by major characters in language that is not hard to understand, though they may remain hard to believe. Xue Aocao, Wu Zetian's well-endowed favorite, is determined to correct the faults of his ruler. The path of duty is plain before him, but he has not chosen an easy task. With some reluctance he submits to the imperial pleasure, and before, during, and after a long series of lewd acts they commit in the second half he repeatedly lectures the empress on the impropriety of demoting the crown prince without sufficient justification—paraphrasing historical figures who have offered the same remonstrations to no avail. His labor of love is of long duration. It takes him years to convince Wu Zetian that she should restore the legitimate crown prince. But in the end he succeeds.

Even when the explicit descriptions are examined out of context and all historical references are ignored, there is still reason to doubt that the *Ruyijun zhuan* is pornographic. Pornographic works are structured to increase erotic excitement. Although they often begin with innocuous scenes, they inevitably become more explicit and stimulating. Thus the culmination of the story is more conducive to the elicitation of an erotic response than the beginning. As the plot of the *Ruyijun zhuan* progresses, however, there is not a crescendo but a decrescendo of explicit detail. The most lengthy description of a sexual encounter is found at the midpoint; from that point forward, such accounts gradually become shorter and less detailed. By the end, encounters between the empress and her favorite are often dispatched in a summary fashion. Some are only a few lines long. Xue Aocao's moral remonstrations, however, become longer and more emphatic. I can think of no pornographic work whose structure is even remotely similar to that of the *Ruyijun zhuan.*

And then there are the descriptions themselves. Pornographic works are supposed to titillate the reader. But the *Ruyijun zhuan,* upon closer examination, does not focus the reader's attention on the erotic potential of the details. It distracts his attention with observations that are unerotic, weird, or even overtly moralistic. The first graphic passage is a description of Xue Aocao's unique endowment. A talented young man of eighteen, he is widely read in the classics and histories and excels at calligraphy and painting. But his physical endowment is such that every time he has a drink with friends, they pressure him to expose himself. They find the spectacle quite entertaining and have a good laugh at his expense. Xue Aocao, however, is troubled by the cause of his renown. He is particularly troubled by the fact that he is still a virgin. He is so large that, once aroused, even veteran prostitutes are unable to accommodate him. Girls are constantly falling in love with such a talented and handsome youth, but when they learn of his unique endowment, they flee his presence. His life is ruined. No one is willing to marry him. He sighs constantly and suffers from feelings of anguish. What is the root of his problem? Behold:

> When it became engorged its veins stood out and its head had four or five sunken furrows. When it became excited, the flesh in the furrows protruded like a snail oozing forth. From the tip to the base the sinews vigorously rippled like an earthworm. From head to tail it had more than twenty striations. It was red and lustrous, clear and unblemished. These characteristics were, no doubt, due to the fact that it had not yet been tainted by women. When the youths saw it they were all amazed and tested it by hanging a peck of grain from its head. It stayed erect with strength to spare. Everyone guffawed uncontrollably and fell into a heap.[14]

The magnitude of a man's physical endowment is often said to parallel the intensity of his desire. But this is not the case with Xue Aocao. He is not known for his lechery. Indeed, he is depressed, alienated, and still a virgin. The author of the *Ruyijun zhuan* has endowed this young man with the kind of physique that conventionally leads to disaster, but Xue Aocao does not seem susceptible to uncontrollable desires. And then there is the description itself.

Images of nature are preludes to the stimulation of desire. Love poems in the *Shi jing,* for example, often describe the beauty of a natural setting and gradually shift the focus to the features of a beautiful woman who has become the object of desire. Later poems describe feminine beauty in more detail and expand upon the correlations between beauty, desire, and nature. Descriptions of flowers, songbirds, luscious fruits, and various natural phenomena are metaphors of the body; they also suggest the intensity of one's passion. But such metaphors are almost always used to describe the woman, not the man. And in the case of the *Ruyijun zhuan,* the choice of metaphors is unprecedented. Xue Aocao's manhood is compared to slithering snails and earthworms.

Unlike a typical pornographic work, this description, while graphic, does not appear to be conducive to the stimulation of lewd desires. It is vivid, yet it is treated as a joke by Xue's friends who derive no erotic stimulation whatever from this spectacle. The reader is not drawn into a solemn and solitary sensual reverie but is instead confronted with dirty images and the laughter of a crowd of juvenile clowns. It is not easy to imagine that the primary purpose here is titillation.

The most detailed description of Wu Zetian's sexual organs is similar. After the story of Xue Aocao's life has been told, he curiously remains a virgin for twelve more years. But, of course, he is eventually summoned to the imperial palace in the expectation that his special endowments, which have never been put to use, will be of service to the empress. By this time Xue Aocao is in his thirties and Wu Zetian is in her seventies. Like other women, she finds Xue difficult to accommodate, but her past history has not left her completely unprepared. Near the end of the first graphic description of sexual relations, we encounter the following passage:

> Aocao did not listen and penetrated about two more inches. The empress could not prohibit him, so she let Aocao come and go, thrust and retract, to the point where his sperm was about to ejaculate. At first Aocao did not know that he was going to ejaculate, and he thrust forward until his chowry handle penetrated all the way to her cervix. The cervix is the innermost recess of a woman and its flesh is like a flower pistil enveloped by a calyx beginning to frondesce. When the head of the man's stalk penetrates to this point, he will feel a melting sensation the pleasure of which is indescribable.[15]

As in his description of Xue Aocao, the author is intent upon describing in bizarre detail what has never before been described in Chinese literature. At what should be the moment of maximum excitement, however, we are confronted with this line: "The cervix is the innermost recess of a woman and its flesh is like a flower pistil enveloped by a calyx beginning to frondesce." It is an image from nature, true, but unlike any of its predecessors. Flowers are often used to describe a woman's sexual organs, but not like this. It is as if the author is conducting a gynecological examination; then, in a moment of weird inspiration, he describes what he has not seen with a vivid visual metaphor whose technical precision would not disappoint a botanist. This description, like that of Xue Aocao, does not contribute to the creation of an erotic mood; it contributes to its deflation.

The *Ruyijun zhuan* has little in common with the Kronhausens' definition of pornography. If the main purpose of a pornographic work is to stimulate an erotic response in the reader, it is difficult to explain the bulk of the *Ruyijun zhuan*. It has too much history. The history is far too accurate. There is too much moral remonstration. The plot is too complicated. There are too many characters. There is no crescendo effect. And most of all, it interrupts even the most explicit descriptions with ironic references and odd observations that almost always detract from the erotic ambiance. The *Ruyijun zhuan* has more in common with what the Kronhausens call erotic realism — though one might be tempted to call the *Ruyijun zhuan* an example of "unerotic surrealism" instead. Certainly its descriptions are more offensive than erotic and are pushed to limits that can scarcely be considered realistic. In any event, if the *Ruyijun zhuan* is to be considered pornographic, it is first necessary to explain how such a variety of unerotic passages and sophisticated allusions found their way into it.

Theoretical Considerations

Human sexuality may also be examined from a theoretical perspective. In *The History of Sexuality,* Michel Foucault examines it in light of the historical emergence of discourses of modern life. As in his discussions of medicine, psychology, and prisons, Foucault argues that sexuality should be viewed as the product of new forms of regulation and new attempts at acquiring knowledge. Sexuality is not a stubborn and dark desire but "an especially dense transfer point for relations of power."[16] It is not something to be ignored but "an obscure speech that has to be ferreted out and listened to."[17] Although he occasionally refers to the works of the Marquis de Sade and other controversial writers, he is not primarily concerned with the question of pornography or its place in history.

In the past few years, serious attention has been focused on the history of pornography in the West. Lynn Hunt has edited two books which reserve for pornography an unexpected place in the major movements that followed the invention of the printing press: the Renaissance, Scientific Revolution, Enlightenment, and French Revolution.[18] She argues: "Early modern pornography reveals some of the most important nascent characteristics of modern culture. It was linked to free-thinking and heresy, to science and natural philosophy, and to attacks on absolutist political authority. It was especially revealing about the gender differentiations being developed within the culture of modernity."[19] In pornography, she says, one can witness a transition between worldviews, and she notes that pornography appears at a time of great fictional experimentation. She also argues that until approximately 1800 pornography was almost always an adjunct to something else: an ally of subversive materialist philosophy, criticism of the source of political power, or examination of the changing roles of women in a society whose economic development had allowed them new freedoms. Pornography tends to argue that civil laws are contrary to human nature and that conventional morality is absurd. During the Enlightenment, dangerous works of pornography, politics, and philosophy all belonged to the same category: *livres philosophiques*.[20] Famous *philosophes* like Diderot did indeed write controversial books, but his conception of sexually explicit description is quite different from what we think of as pornography today.[21] Although Hunt claims that pornography "seems to be an especially Western idea" and Foucault's examination of sexuality concerns only the West, the application of their ideas in the Chinese context is more useful than many another discussion of sexually explicit materials.[22]

The *Ruyijun zhuan* and Its Readers

Erotic works are most effective when they destroy the normal mechanisms of reading.[23] In an erotic work, the author provides everything the reader needs to know in a fashion that does not require interpretation. There is little reason to examine the motivation of central characters, for example, as the reader's job is simply to watch what they do. If any imagination is required it consists in visualizing each scene as vividly as possible to enhance the process of self-seduction.

Although the *Ruyijun zhuan* sometimes pretends to destroy the normal mechanisms of reading, in most cases it simultaneously inserts an odd observation, a recondite reference, or a dose of conventional morality. There are no uninterrupted passages of explicit description designed to lull the reader into a mindless state of sensual bliss. The reader, if he is paying attention, is more likely to wonder why the author has inserted so many strange and unexpected things in the story. At first the reader might think he should respond to the *Ruyijun zhuan* as if he were reading a typical erotic novel, but he would not be reading it carefully if he did.

The author knows that his descriptions of sex will compromise the rational faculties of his reader and weaken his ability to comprehend everything else. He punctuates his tale with weird observations and moral allusions that the majority of readers would miss even if they were not thoroughly distracted. Thus while parts of the *Ruyijun zhuan* might be considered offensive, it cannot be considered pornographic unless its descriptions are taken out of the context into which its author has so carefully placed them.

2

Precursors

> The chaste severity of the fathers in whatever related to the com-
> merce of the two sexes flowed from the same principle — their ab-
> horrence of every enjoyment which might gratify the sensual and
> degrade the spiritual nature of man. It was their favorite opinion,
> that if Adam had preserved his obedience to the Creator, he
> would have lived for ever in a state of virgin purity, and that some
> harmless mode of vegetation might have peopled paradise with a
> race of innocent and immortal beings.
>
> —Edward Gibbon, *The Decline and Fall of the Roman Empire*, 2.120

The peculiar combination of love, politics, history, and moral remonstration
found in the *Ruyijun zhuan* is not unique to this work or to the fiction of the
late Ming dynasty. This combination is found, as well, in early Chinese poetry
like the *Shi jing* (Book of poetry).

It is perhaps more accurate to say that many of the poems found in the
Shi jing are about love and that later commentators find, or add, the politics,
history, and morals. In the Mao commentary to the *Shi jing*, the earliest extant
systematic interpretation of that text, even simple love poems contained in
the *Airs of the States* (*Guofeng*) are interpreted as illustrations of court intrigue.[1]
The commentary asserts that the songs are about politics and relate to specific
historical persons or events. Poems that express satisfaction and social order
are about a good ruler; poems that express the opposite are about a bad ruler.
In poems of dissatisfaction, the ruler is often an absent lover, and his minister,
the poet, an abandoned woman. Such poems, the commentary says, are metaphors for an unappreciated official who is remonstrating with an immoral
ruler. Descriptions of love, courtship, and feminine beauty are interpreted in
political terms and ultimately seen as criticism of the ruler.

Such allegorical or metaphorical readings of *Shi jing* love poems are
sometimes hard to accept.[2] Traditional commentators often ignore a poem's
literal meaning and seem oblivious to its beauty. Even if there is no reference
to history in a poem, they try to set it in a specific historical context — and when
it is mentioned in an early history like the *Zuo zhuan*, they argue that it should
be read as a historical document. Sometimes traditional commentaries read

groups of poems as if they were miniature histories of the states in which they originated.[3] Although allegorical interpretations of *Shi jing* love poems might seem unnatural to a modern reader, there is ample evidence that these poems were commonly interpreted in such a fashion long before the Mao commentary. In time the poems of the *Shi jing,* particularly the love poems, acquired a set of political connotations and these formed the basis of Mao's interpretations.[4] When a ruler or an official quotes a line from a *Shi jing* poem in the *Zuo zhuan,* it is a means of expressing an opinion with diplomatic discretion. A meeting of a ruler and his senior advisers can hinge on brief allusions to love poetry; the poems are quoted out of context and mobilized to express ideas about politics, morality, and history that are quite foreign to the original poem.[5] Huang Xun's "Du *Ruyijun zhuan*" quotes the *Shi jing* in such a fashion, as does the *Ruyijun zhuan* itself.

The combination of love, politics, history, and morals contained in *fu* poetry is not, however, the product of later commentators. *Fu* poetry, which dates to approximately the middle of the second century B.C., is known for its ornate style, hyperbole, and rich description. Many of the descriptive Han *fu* were written by court poets and submitted directly to the emperor. Although the beautiful language and attractive scenes were meant to delight the emperor, some authors claim that the *fu* could also contain elements of indirect remonstration (*fengjian*). But such a claim, when made about a genre that appears totally devoted to the pleasure of the reader, gives rise to deep suspicions; there is a discrepancy between the professed moral content and the sensuous manner in which it is delivered. Contemporaries sometimes describe the *fu* as seduction under the guise of moral instruction.[6] An interesting example of a sensuous situation leading directly to thoughts of politics and morality occurs in the "Shanglin fu" (Rhapsody on Shanglin Park) by Sima Xiangru (179-117 B.C.), the most famous author of *fu* poetry and the model for many later imitators. The prospect of feminine beauty is seductive, but it also elicits an unexpected response from the emperor:

> Shiny white teeth
> Glow through lovely smiles,
> Eyebrows arch gracefully
> Over eyes casting tender glances.
> The soul surrenders itself to beauty so inviting,
> To its side the heart joyfully hastens.

And thus, when wine and music are at their most intoxicating, the Son of Heaven becomes bemused and thoughtful, as if overcome by a sense of loss. He cries, "Alas! this is gross extravagance! Lest the leisure from government be spent in idleness, I have followed the way of heaven through hunting and killing; time and again I rest in this park. But I fear those who come after me will indulge in wasteful extravagance, become lost in the pursuit of pleasure, and fail to return. This is not the way to continue the imperial legacy, to establish and pass on the way of government for one's progeny!"[7]

To paraphrase Wai-Yee Li: the apotheosis of pleasure is a prelude to the compunctions of conscience.[8] The emperor relishes the accumulation of sensuous details—the predictable, gradual progression of alluring attributes that reveals he is an accomplice to his own seduction. But when his soul and heart are moved and he sinks into a world of sensual pleasure, he is overcome by a sense of loss. Inexplicably he returns to a world in which government, morality, and his imperial legacy are of primary importance. For the remainder of the "Shanglin fu," the emperor understands the hunt in proper allegorical terms. His delectation of sensual pleasure paradoxically prepares him for moral and spiritual self-cultivation. His moral example becomes so persuasive, in fact, that all society is transformed; the legal code is no longer required because there are no more criminals.[9]

But it is not clear how the prospect of divine maidens with shiny white teeth and arching eyebrows, at the moment of the most intense pleasure, could elicit a moral response that leads the emperor to consider his political future. The emperor seems suddenly to have understood, and perhaps risen above, the problem of sensuality. At first it might appear that he has come to this realization by himself. But it is the *fu* that provided moral remonstration which paradoxically took the form of sensual enticement. Thus the emperor can have it both ways: he does not have to reject sensuality in favor of the contemplation of good government. Who would read a *fu* poem about good government? So long as the contemplation of sensuous situations brings about the desired result, it is acceptable. In the case of some emperors, it may paradoxically be more persuasive than overt moral remonstration that would simply be ignored.[10]

The *Ruyijun zhuan* takes the combination of love, politics, morality, and history found in Han *fu* and commentaries on the *Shi jing* to a new level. Everything is direct. The descriptions of sex are explicit. Politics is discussed on virtually every page. The hero Xue Aocao remonstrates with the empress almost every time they are together. And the text is full of overt references to the historical record. The services of a commentator are not needed to explain that the descriptions of love are about politics and morality. Thus the *Ruyijun zhuan* seems related to earlier examples of paradoxical moral instruction, at least superficially. But the descriptions can be so distracting that the other elements are in danger of being overshadowed. Nevertheless, when viewed from this perspective, it becomes more difficult to reject Huayang

Sanren's assertion that the activities of Xue Aocao are a unique form of moral exhortation. The *Ruyijun zhuan* develops the tension between morality and sensuality to an extreme, perhaps to the point of absurdity. There is also a prolonged delay between the delectation of sensual pleasure and the ultimate compunctions of conscience: it takes Wu Zetian years before she agrees that the needs of the state must be fulfilled and the crown prince restored. But like the emperor in the Han *fu*, she does in fact draw the correct conclusion from remonstrations that are sensual in nature.

Early Chinese Erotic Fiction

The descriptions of love in the *Ruyijun zhuan* are set in a context that is not naturally conducive to the seduction of the reader. Its style and subject matter are closer to a kind of early erotic story that focuses on emperors, imperial settings, and the problems that stem from the emperor's uncontrollable urges. Physical love in these works is not so much about seduction as it is about infatuation and excess. Sex in these texts is problematic even before it is introduced into the story.

One of the most famous examples of such stories is the putative Han text *Zhao Feiyan waizhuan*.[11] It tells how the empress captivates the Han-dynasty emperor Cheng Di (r. 33–7 B.C.), gradually depletes his vital energies, and then administers a fatal overdose of aphrodisiacs that causes him to ejaculate to death.[12] Compared to the *Ruyijun zhuan*, however, there is little explicit description. At one point the emperor plays the part of a voyeur and observes the flicker of candlelight on Zhao Feiyan's supple flesh as she takes a bath at night, but such scenes pass in the blink of an eye. The only part of Zhao Feiyan described is her skin. The emperor does no more than peek through a curtain. The author does not dwell on erotic situations. His descriptions are condensed and to the point. The emperor's death from excessive love-making, certainly one of the most bizarre deaths in classical Chinese fiction, is described in only three lines. His semen flows without interruption until his bedding is saturated, his body is drained, and then he expires. Sex is not dirty; but it is dangerous if it leads to excess, which it often does.

The *Han Wudi neizhuan*, too, describes the destruction of an emperor due to his uncontrollable sensual infatuation.[13] This mystical Daoist text details the visit of the Queen Mother of the Western Paradise to Han Emperor Wu (r. 141–87 B.C.) on the seventh day of the seventh month of 110 B.C.[14] Emperor Wu, engaged in the pursuit of immortality through Daoist alchemy, is instructed by the Queen Mother in the art of physiological cultivation. As in the *Zhao Feiyan waizhuan*, few passages in this work are explicit.

Most of the text describes mystical Daoism, and the most direct portrayals of sex concern the physiological process through which the emperor can become an immortal. He is told that he must love his vital essence, conserve it, perform breathing exercises, and swallow his saliva in a ritualistic Daoist fashion. The Queen Mother informs him that if he does these things, his *qi* will be transformed into blood, his blood into vital essence, the vital essence into spirit, the spirit into liquid, and the liquid into bone. Additional transformations will occur each year for the next nine years; then his form will change and he will become an immortal. Near the end of the *Han Wudi neizhuan,* the Queen Mother presents a rare text of Daoist sexual alchemy to the emperor, a text that is transmitted only once every four thousand years. But he ignores her instructions and dies of a sensual overdose.

Tang works like the *Daye shiyi ji* (Gathering remaining accounts of the Daye reign period) and the *Milou ji* (Tale of the tower of enchantment) describe the sensual entanglements of the infamous Sui Yangdi (r. 604-618); other works like the *Yang Taizhen waizhuan* (The outer story of Yang Taizhen) describe the disastrous consequences of Tang Xuanzong's (r. 712-756) incestuous relationship with Yang Guifei (719-756).[15] As in the *Ruyijun zhuan,* at least a skeleton of these stories is found in standard historical sources.

The author of the *Ruyijun zhuan* also draws on the *Shi ji* for a significant and controversial historical allusion: the story of Lao Ai (d. 238 B.C.).[16] Lao Ai was a libertine of the third century B.C. whose prodigal natural endowment was mated to an insatiable appetite. In one of the more scandalous episodes related in the *Shi ji,* the famous businessman, politician, and prime minister Lü Buwei (d. 235 B.C.) connived to smuggle this personage into the private chambers of the empress dowager (d. 228 B.C.), the mother of Emperor Qin Shihuangdi (r. 221-210 B.C.).[17] She had been carrying on a secret affair with Lü Buwei for years, but Lü Buwei feared that his continued involvement with her would not redound to his credit after her son reached maturity. As it was not in the empress dowager's nature to restrain herself, Lü Buwei endeavored to call a suitable replacement to her attention. When he made the acquaintance of Lao Ai, he knew he had his man. Lao Ai was made a retainer in Lü Buwei's household and an occasion to stimulate the lewd imagination of the empress dowager was devised. Lü Buwei had suggestive music performed at a gathering and instructed Lao Ai to hang the wheel of a cart on his erect penis. He then instructed Lao Ai to parade about the room so that his prowess might be displayed for all to see, knowing that word would soon get back to the empress dowager. It was not difficult to persuade the empress dowager to favor Lao Ai with an audience. And she did not find him unworthy. Lü Buwei then devised a scheme whereby Lao Ai would be assured easy access to her private quarters in the future: he contrived to have Lao Ai falsely convicted of a crime for which the sentence was castration. But while the official in charge of inflicting this abject punishment did pluck Lao Ai's beard—marking him as a eunuch—through bribery the empress dowager persuaded the official that there was no need to complete the task.

Lao Ai soon discovered that he could gratify his ruling passion in the discharge of his duty, and the empress dowager fell hopelessly in love. An entourage of several thousand servants waited upon him and over a thousand sycophants vied for his recommendation. Lao Ai had become inordinately rich and powerful. But it was not in the best interests of a vulgar eunuch impostor to excite the envy of the masses. Earlier suspicions were confirmed when it was learned that Lao Ai had fathered two sons with the empress dowager. It was furthermore rumored that they were plotting to insinuate these sons into the normal line of succession upon the death of the emperor. Lao Ai was apprehended for usurping the official powers of the empress dowager in the commission of treasonous acts. The emperor ordered carriages to tear the limbs from his body. His children were thrown into sacks and beaten to death with clubs.[18] His clan was exterminated to the third degree. And Lü Buwei, faced with the prospect of an ever-escalating series of humiliations inflicted at the direction of the emperor himself, committed suicide. Once Lao Ai and Lü Buwei were dead, the emperor was persuaded to mend his relations with his mother (who, it appears, had neglected to inform him that Lü Buwei was in fact his real father).[19]

The "Du *Ruyijun zhuan*" by Huang Xun, the earliest interpretation of this work, compares its hero Xue Aocao to Lao Ai. Their most conspicuous attributes are, of course, their extraordinary physical endowments. But the similarities do not end there. Both are concerned with the status of the crown prince: Lao Ai with elevating his own illegitimate progeny to that position, Xue Aocao with restoring the legitimate crown prince. Both are men of scandalously low social status, and both exercise inordinate influence over their much older imperial lovers. Traditional gender roles have been reversed as well, as the women have the upper hand in these relationships and command a great deal of political power. The manner in which Xue Aocao and Lao Ai are called to the attention of their new lovers is also analogous: Wu Zetian knows she has found what she is looking for as soon as a court parasite whispers that a promising candidate has been identified in the capital. In the case of Xue Aocao it is, however, a peck of grain and not the wheel of a cart whose ponderous weight is suspended from his person to assess his stamina.

Another allusion to the story of Lao Ai, I suspect, is Xue Aocao's improbable attempt to castrate himself. While it first appears that Xue Aocao has inflicted a grievous wound, the magnitude of his task is such that he does not have time to complete it before Wu Zetian rushes to his side to offer solace and succor. Xue Aocao's attempt to castrate himself, it would appear, should be read at least as seriously as Lao Ai's counterfeit castration.[20] In any event, the story of Lao Ai's sexual impropriety, cynical manipulation, and attempt to pervert the proper line of succession is particularly applicable to the story of Wu Zetian told in the *Ruyijun zhuan*.

In the standard histories, circumlocutions are of course employed to describe the salacious details (when such details are described at all). The depiction of sex found in the type of early Chinese erotic fiction that influenced the *Ruyijun zhuan* is similarly condensed and uninspired. The narrative stops when sex is introduced. Neither author nor characters entice the reader with extended descriptions of sensuous situations; they usually mention only one or two aspects of such situations and then move on to something else.

Many thematic aspects of the *Ruyijun zhuan* derive from the early erotic stories about emperors and life in the imperial city. Such works contain a fair amount of history derived from standard sources, and they often focus on problems of state, particularly the status of the crown prince. Most emperors lose control when faced with sensual enticements they are unable to withstand, in each instance creating a crisis for their government.

The *Ruyijun zhuan* develops to an extreme many of the features found in this type of early erotic story. Its descriptions of sex are, of course, far more graphic than those found in its predecessors, and it contains much more history than most earlier stories. Moreover, it contains not one ruler but four. As in the earlier stories, the narrator focuses on each ruler when imperial power is lost because of an unnatural infatuation that disturbs relations within the imperial family. In the *Ruyijun zhuan*, the relationship between promiscuous infatuation and the loss of power is direct, and the time period between historical events is condensed to illustrate this point. Emperor Taizong dies soon after he becomes enamored of Wu Zetian. His son Emperor Gaozong becomes ill and dies after committing incest with her. And Wu Zetian herself becomes ill and loses the throne after becoming infatuated with Xue Aocao.

Perhaps erotic fiction about emperors is not really about the sensual dimensions of beauty. By the end of the *Ruyijun zhuan* Wu Zetian is in her eighties. Because it would not have been appropriate to use traditional descriptions of feminine beauty at this point—her hair had turned white and some of her teeth had fallen out—the author intentionally makes the description of beauty irrelevant. As in the earlier stories, power (or the loss of it) is ultimately behind the portrayal of sex. In the *Ruyijun zhuan*, beauty has not only lost its seductive allure, it has been replaced with descriptions that are offensive and aggressive. Characters find themselves inexplicably attracted to dirty images, pain, even violence.

Daoist Sexuality and Chinese Medicine

The descriptions of sexual activity found in Chinese erotic novels can be properly evaluated only when placed in historical context. Even when the purpose of explicit descriptions is the erotic stimulation of the reader, in traditional China the consequences are quite different than in modern China or the West. In traditional China, sex was theoretically regarded as an art. It contributed to physical health, it increased vitality, and in the case of a Daoist practitioner it could even give rise to the production of an inner elixir (*neidan*) that could stop or even reverse the aging process, resulting in physical immortality.[21] The effects produced by human sexual activity were related to those produced by various respiratory exercises, gymnastic drills, massage, and techniques for conserving bodily secretions.[22] As early as the second century B.C., illustrated sex manuals were in general use that emphasized the careful regulation of sexual pleasure so that tranquillity of the spirit and longevity of the body would result.[23] Celibacy was dangerous; in fact, early Daoist practice encouraged sexual relations with several partners, sometimes in a group context.[24] But if sexual activity was not accompanied by the proper restraint, or if vital essences were not conserved, the result could be illness, debilitation, and death.

Joseph Needham argues that for some purposes sexual cultivation was indispensable:

> Taoist sexuality was neither sensual nor guilt-ridden, neither antinomian nor irreligious; for Taoism as for Tantrism the operations of physical love were a powerful aid to the mystical apprehension of the divine power within the universe—"one Yang and one Yin together make the Tao." They were a natural amplification of the meditational and other exercises, a further form, as it were, of the contemplative life, though also in China a technical procedure of preparing the "elixir within," the anablastemic enchymoma, for which no other process could substitute.[25]

Thus it is not surprising that the "Meiren fu," a work that on one level concerns pure seduction, ends with explicit references to the Daoist tradition. After the protagonists have consummated their relationship, the man notes that "the blood in my veins had settled, and my heart had become steadied in my bosom."[26] The author has not depicted sensuality for its own sake; he has demonstrated that sexual relations are a way to nurture life and vitality.[27] This is not to say that traditional Chinese culture did not contain significant groups who looked upon such activities with skepticism, disapprobation, or even hostility. Daoist conceptions of human sexuality nevertheless became an integral part of traditional Chinese medicine, greatly influenced the manner in which sex was portrayed in early handbooks, and set the standard by which the functioning of the human body was understood for many centuries, an understanding that is influential to this day.

One of the earliest references to Chinese sex manuals is found in the bibliographic section of the *Han shu*.[28] Eight works are listed in a section titled "Fang zhong," or "In the Bedchamber," where they are given ponderous names such as *Yao Shun yindao* (The way of sex of the sage-rulers Yao and Shun). Although none of these texts has survived, the *Han shu* compiler wrote a brief appraisal of these works at the end of the list. Attention, he says, must be given to the proper way of engaging in sexual activity:

> The Art of the Bedchamber constitutes the climax of human emotions, it encompasses the Supreme Way (Tao). Therefore the Saint Kings of antiquity regulated man's outer pleasures in order to restrain his inner passions and made detailed rules for sexual intercourse. An old record says: "The ancients created sexual pleasure thereby to regulate all human affairs." If one regulates sexual pleasure he will feel at peace and attain a high age. If, on the other hand, one abandons himself to its pleasure disregarding the rules set forth in the above-mentioned treatises one will fall ill and harm one's very life.[29]

There is no hint of sarcasm, no suggestion that these texts should be taken lightly. Indeed, a few of the titles even contain the names of sage-rulers from remote antiquity. Good rulers, it would appear, recognized that sexual urges could at once be regulated and stimulated—not only for the pleasure and longevity of the individual but for the proper regulation of the state.

The study of ancient Chinese sex manuals broke new ground in 1973. Archaeological excavations at tomb three of Mawangdui in Hunan province unearthed a cache of rare manuscripts written on silk rolls and bamboo slips. Several of the manuscripts were ancient medical texts, and a few of these appear to be the kind of sex manual described in the *Han shu* bibliography.[30] As this tomb dates to 168 B.C., these are the earliest extant Chinese sex manuals. Like the later manuals mentioned in the *Han shu,* the manuals found at Mawangdui appear to have been considered medical texts. Of the fifteen medical manuscripts found in tomb three, four are sex manuals. Donald Harper argues that of these four, the text *He yinyang* (Joining yin and yang) provides "the most concise yet thorough account of sexual practice in the ancient 'nurturing life' tradition."[31] It comprises sections of verse and prose: the verse contains cryptic rhyming metaphors that allude to esoteric sexual techniques; the prose sections then explain what has been alluded to in the verse. As this text was written for an audience intimately acquainted with its esoteric terminology, it is difficult to make sense of it today:

1. The recipe for whenever one will be conjoining Yin and Yang.
2. Grip the hands, spit on the Yang side of the wrists.
3. Stroke the elbow chambers.
4. Go under the side of the armpits.
5. Ascend the stove frame.
6. Go under the neck zone.
7. Stroke the receiving canister.
8. Cover the encircling ring.
9. Descend the broken basin.
10. Cross over the syrupy-liquor ford.
11. Skim the Spurting Sea.
12. Ascend Mount Constancy.
13. Enter the dark gate.
14. Ride the coital sinew.
15. Suck the essence and spirit upwards.
16. Then one can have enduring vision and exist in unison with
    heaven and earth.[32]

And this is just the opening verse of *He yinyang*. It begins with a metaphorical description of foreplay, and by the end of the verse the goal of sexual cultivation has been reached. But everything in between is open to interpretation. It is hard to imagine what many of the metaphors denote. But clearly they refer to the female body and clearly the text is written from the male point of view. The text is a symbolic Daoist landscape of the body; it describes what is happening inside the body while its functions are set in a larger metaphorical context.[33] Although the ultimate meaning of these metaphors must remain opaque to the uninitiated, they are placed in a context that is similar to later sex manuals. Above all, energy and essences must be conserved. Yet there is no trace of asceticism: the regulation of sensuality is perfected through its stimulation. The absence of stimulation leads to the same depletion of vital energies that is caused by sensual excess.

Before the Mawangdui medical texts were unearthed, the most important Chinese sexual handbooks were found in the *Ishimpō* (Essence of medical prescriptions), a Japanese collection of Chinese medical texts compiled by Tamba Yasuyori (911–995) in 984 in Japan.[34] The *Ishimpō* is particularly important because it preserves fragments from a wide range of medical texts from the Han dynasty through the Sui dynasty that were later lost. Chapter twenty-eight, titled "Fang nei," or "In the Bedchamber," is subdivided into twenty-nine parts with titles such as "Shi dong," or "The Ten Movements"; each part comprises numerous quotations from earlier medical texts.[35] Earlier in the twentieth century, Ye Dehui (1864–1927) noted that many of the titles mentioned in chapter twenty-eight resembled titles found in the bibliographic section of the *Sui shu;* he then reconstructed several sex manuals from the fragments in the *Ishimpō.*[36]

One of the most famous manuals Ye Dehui reconstructed was the *Sunü jing* (The classic of the plain girl). The nature of sexual activity is explored through dialogues between the mythological ruler Huangdi and the Plain Girl. The pleasurable nature of sexual activity, which also contributes to health and longevity, is counterbalanced by the danger that excess could lead to depletion, illness, and even death—themes often repeated in erotic fiction. As in the Mawangdui literature, the sex manuals found in the *Ishimpō* are primarily for men. Even parts that are ostensibly for the benefit of women are written from the male point of view. These texts are clearly descendants of the Mawangdui texts, but they are not nearly so cryptic. They do not contain the dense metaphorical verse found in *He yinyang*, for example, and most of their descriptions resemble the prose parts of the Mawangdui texts. In style they are similar to chapters devoted to physiological cultivation found in Tang-dynasty medical classics like the *Beiji qianjin yaofang* (Prescriptions worth a thousand pieces of gold for emergencies) by Sun Simiao (581-682).[37] Sun Simiao describes physiological alchemy in great detail. He claims, in fact, that if a man can have sex with ninety-three women while maintaining control of his vital energies, he will live for ten thousand years.[38] His descriptions of the beneficial aspects of regulated sexual activity, and the manner in which it is regulated, are clearly related to earlier Daoist theories and practices.[39]

Daoist theories of sexual cultivation, however, are systematically undermined in the *Ruyijun zhuan*—or at least shown to be impracticable when applied to real human beings. The notion that real people could dispassionately engage in sexual cultivation is greeted with derision by the author of the *Ruyijun zhuan*. When his characters are stimulated, they almost immediately lose self-control. There is no tranquillity of the spirit; indeed, sexual encounters lead to confusion and dissatisfaction. There is no regulation of the body; indeed, most encounters are pushed to new limits. There is no conservation of vital essences; there is, instead, a deliberate escalation of waste and excess. And there is no hope of immortality; Emperors Taizong and Gaozong die after becoming infatuated with Wu Zetian, and she herself becomes ill. Only Xue Aocao seems to have benefited from his sexual experiences. By the end, in fact, he has become an immortal. And yet he violates every conceivable Daoist precept in the most egregious manner possible. During a period of great mental turmoil he even attempts to castrate himself, an act that would irrevocably sever this route to immortality. His transformation into an immortal, like the depiction of sex, is not a sympathetic portrayal of the Daoist tradition but a parody of it.

The depiction of Daoist views of sexuality is not even consistent from one page to the next. At one point Wu Zetian feels debilitated because of her sexual excesses, but later she is rejuvenated although nothing has changed: her white hair regains its color and some of the teeth that have fallen out begin to grow back. Similarly Xue Aocao is weakened because of his relationship with the empress, but he too is rejuvenated and eventually becomes an immortal. Yet at no point in the *Ruyijun zhuan* do the characters engage in anything even remotely related to Daoist sexual cultivation. Their sexual relationships work in a mechanical and predictable fashion: the passions are engaged and sexual activity occurs; then the passions increase and sexual activity increases; then self-control is lost and sexual activity becomes excessive. The ultimate result is self-destruction. Emperors Taizong and Gaozong die. And except for Xue Aocao, all of Wu Zetian's lovers are murdered or die because their vital energies have been depleted.

The *Ruyijun zhuan* was one of the first Chinese works to depict human sexuality in such a graphically skeptical fashion. By the middle of the sixteenth century, such skepticism had become commonplace. Van Gulik notes that by this time the degeneration of the once therapeutic art of Daoist sexual cultivation was clearly visible in popular novels and short stories that "stressed repulsive physical details of the sexual act, so that many passages in their stories are mere scatology."[40] These writers are often fascinated by the prospect of the liberation of human emotion, but they simultaneously lament the chaos it causes. Human sexuality has become a problem.

The *Jin Ping Mei* contains one of the most infamous critiques of Daoist theories of sexuality found in a sixteenth-century novel. In chapter twenty-seven, Ximen Qing, the male protagonist, ties his wife Pan Jinlian to a grape trellis and sexually abuses her for an extended period of time. But as in the *Ruyijun zhuan*, this scene in the *Jin Ping Mei* is interrupted with descriptions of seemingly irrelevant details that do not contribute to the erotic ambiance. Ximen Qing halts his tryst to play various games, get drunk, chase the maidservant Chunmei up and down an artificial mountain, fall asleep, and engage in extended discussions. At length he returns to Jinlian, who is now at the brink of unconsciousness. But when Ximen Qing and Jinlian finally engage in sexual battle, Chunmei appears with a flagon of wine and the description of sex comes to an abrupt end yet once again:

> Just as they were approaching the height of bliss, who should appear but Ch'un-mei, who had come with the heated wine. As soon as she saw what was happening, she put down the wine flagon and fled straight to the top of the artificial hill, the highest point in the garden, where she leaned over a chess table in the Cloud Repose Pavilion and toyed with the chess pieces.
>
> When Hsi-men Ch'ing looked up and saw where she had gone, he beckoned to her with his hand but was unable to induce her to come down.

"Little oily mouth!" he exclaimed. "If I can't get you down here, I might as well give up."

Thereupon, abandoning the woman, he set off in pursuit, but by the time he had run up the stone steps in great strides, all the way to the pavilion on the summit, Ch'un-mei had come down by way of a winding "sheep's-gut" path on the right side of the hill, passed through the whitewashed "snow cave" of Hidden Spring Grotto, and arrived at the Dripping Emerald Cavern halfway down in the "waist" of the hill, where the flowering vegetation was at its thickest.

Just as she was in the act of hiding there, Hsi-men Ch'ing unexpectedly caught sight of her and, embracing her around the waist as she stood in the shadows, said, "Little oily mouth! I've got you after all."[41]

Chunmei and Ximen Qing are scampering up and down a metaphorical Daoist landscape of the human body: it describes an esoteric technique of physiological alchemy called "making the vital energies return to augment the brain" (*huanjing bunao*), a process said to produce a kind of enlightenment and long life bordering on immortality.[42] This technique reverses the normal flow of vital essences during sexual intercourse; they ascend from the genitals, flow along the dorsal column, and are finally deposited in a spot on the top of the head. At the top of the head, the union of male and female principles is visualized as a sun and a moon.[43] Ximen Qing's race up and down the hill traces the flow of vital energies in his body. But when he reaches the summit, supposedly the pinnacle of the vital force, he does not find the illumination symbolized by the sun and moon—instead he finds the Cloud Repose Pavilion, clouds being a traditional symbol of ignorance. As Ximen Qing is ignorant of the proper methods of physiological cultivation, he scampers right back down the hill and exhausts his vital essence on Pan Jinlian.

In the *Jin Ping Mei*, as in the *Ruyijun zhuan*, all thought of regulating sexual activity vanishes when characters are physically aroused. They do not follow any of the techniques described in medical literature. They do not seem capable of placing themselves in the proper, tranquil state of mind. They do just the opposite. The technique of *huanjing bunao* is supposed to be practiced only in carefully regulated situations: when the partners have refrained from drinking wine or eating rich foods, when they are able to exert strict control over their emotions. Perhaps the author is skeptical of this Daoist procedure. After all, a man's desire to have sexual relations with scores of women may represent something other than the dispassionate pursuit of immortality. But perhaps the ultimate point is that normal humans simply cannot exert self-control once their sensual natures have been aroused—even if it is in their best interests to do so. The authors of the *Ruyijun zhuan* and *Jin Ping Mei* call attention to such difficulties by inserting parodic, inappropriate, and unexpected

material that disrupts their most provocative descriptions of sexual activity—
a technique that is new to erotic literature.

This change in the erotic novel's focus can be attributed, in part, to
shifts in outlook that occurred during the late Ming dynasty. These changes
are not limited to the erotic novel, however, as many of the features found
in the *Ruyijun zhuan* occur in other types of fiction as well. The pursuit of individual desire becomes more prevalent in late-Ming fiction: central characters come to realize that their desires require gratification, but these desires
are usually portrayed in an ambivalent fashion. Characters often respond to
innocuous sensuous situations in an inexplicably exaggerated fashion, causing them to destroy their families and themselves. What was it in the late
Ming dynasty that made the depiction of human desire so problematic?

3

Desire in the Ming Dynasty

> Now, nature is that which is formed by Heaven; the
> disposition is the substance of nature; and desire is
> the proper response of the disposition. To seek what
> desire deems attainable is that which the disposition
> certainly cannot avoid.
>
> —Xunzi, "The Rectification of Names," 22.694

Is the *Ruyijun zhuan* a precursor of radical philosophies that appeared during the latter part of the sixteenth century? Writers like Li Zhi (1527–1602), the most famous exponent of the iconoclastic style associated with the Taizhou school of Neo-Confucianism, argue that spontaneous, individual experience is more important than the pronouncements of sages or the study of books.[1] Traditional conceptions of the self are too rational, conservative, and constrained. Human desires, even sexual satisfaction, no longer impede the pursuit of enlightenment: the exploration of human sexuality now happily assists in that pursuit. While the graphic descriptions found in the *Ruyijun zhuan* might at first seem to celebrate the unfettered expression of human desire, there is reason to be skeptical. And while we cannot assess the purpose of these descriptions merely by examining the intellectual history of the era, tracing contemporary developments in philosophy and fiction will help us to place them in a larger context that contributes significantly to their appraisal.

New Developments in Contemporary Philosophy

In the first few decades of the sixteenth century, just before the *Ruyijun zhuan* was written, a revolution in Chinese philosophical thought began. The rationalistic Neo-Confucianism of Cheng Yi (Cheng Yichuan, 1033–1107) and Zhu Xi—thinking that had dominated the Chinese intellectual landscape since the twelfth century—had, in the opinion of many, deteriorated into frivolous scholasticism. Since 1313 their interpretations of the classics had been considered official state doctrine, and in 1415 their commentaries on the Four Books and the Five Classics were made the basis of the official examination system.[2] But their philosophy had been regarded as official state doctrine for hundreds of years and its original character had become obscured. To its critics, the Neo-Confucianism of Cheng Yi and Zhu Xi was no longer a standard for moral action but a tool for obtaining power, prestige, and wealth through the examination system. Far from being a method of attaining enlightenment, it had become an obstacle.

Neo-Confucianism during the sixteenth century shifted the focus from the study of ancient texts and external phenomena to examination of the self. Society and the world were to be understood through an investigation of human nature and one's own mind. In a way that sometimes borders on tautology, the mind was also considered the ultimate authority. The school of Wang Yangming (Wang Shouren, 1472-1529) dominated the debate during his lifetime and remained influential for at least a century thereafter.[3] Wang Yangming attacked the philosophy of Cheng Yi and Zhu Xi. He questioned whether their emphasis on textual criticism and the study of external phenomena contributed to the moral foundation of the individual. In Wang Yangming's opinion, education had degenerated into a ritual of memorization, recitation, flowery composition, and argumentation. Contemporary philosophy was devoted to useless superficialities, he charged, its eloquence disguising the fact that it was empty, false, and unnatural.[4]

Wang Yangming brought new vitality to the philosophical debate. The task of the individual, he contended, was not to study external phenomena or classical texts but to identify with the innate principle of nature found in one's self. Zhu Xi's objective investigation of things (*gewu*) was inverted: the mind was not to be devoted to external things; the study of external phenomena results in the fragmentation of thought. The pursuit of true knowledge must be an internal search that depends on the extension of individual moral consciousness (*liangzhi*). Truth is not a set of doctrines but a personal experience. As many have noted, Wang Yangming's philosophy is not the investigation of things (*gewu*) but the investigation of the mind (*gexin*).[5] Often he was pressed by his students to provide further detail, but Wang Yangming usually turned the question back upon the student: for each person it is different and thus impossible for another to explain. Wang Yangming's emphasis on the role of personal intuition and experience makes his philosophy highly subjective. But this is not to say it is without standards or that everyone is expected to rely on his own understanding of morality. Ideally an individual's personal experience reveals that traditional moral values are part of his true nature.[6] In the normal course of life, one's true nature is inevitably obscured—and the best way to restore its original brilliance is through scrupulous self-examination.

At the heart of Wang Yangming's philosophy is the pursuit of sagehood. But the criteria used to interpret this pursuit differ from previous models: "How can the signs of sagehood be recognized? . . . If one clearly perceives one's own innate knowledge, then one recognizes that the signs of sagehood do not exist in the sage but in oneself."[7] The pursuit of sagehood occurred in an intellectual atmosphere that encouraged the syncretic examination of concepts borrowed from Buddhism and Daoism. And social relations too were changing rapidly as social mobility and economic prosperity reached new heights.[8] The sage was not merely an ancient ideal; sagehood had become a practical goal that would benefit a normal person who thought about it. Individual development and self-expression were being emphasized in an entirely new way.

The importance of individual behavior during the late Ming dynasty is well documented.[9] It is visible in the proliferation of morality books (*shanshu*) and registers of good and evil (*gongguo ge*). Writers of vernacular fiction examine an expanded range of themes and characters in unprecedented detail. The pursuit of self-cultivation, the examination of the consequences of moral action, the interpretation of individual desire—all are central concerns.

When the human mind is aroused by desire or distracted by selfish pursuits, however, the practice of self-cultivation becomes next to impossible. Wang Yangming addresses this problem at the very beginning of his celebrated *Daxue wen* (Inquiry on the great learning):

Although the mind of the small man is divided and narrow, yet his humanity that forms one body can remain free from darkness to this degree. This is due to the fact that his mind has not yet been aroused by desires and obscured by selfishness. When it is aroused by desires and obscured by selfishness, compelled by greed for gain and fear of harm, and stirred by anger, he will destroy things, kill members of his own species, and will do everything. In extreme cases he will even slaughter his own brothers, and the humanity that forms one body will disappear completely. Hence, if it is not obscured by selfish desires, even the mind of the small man has the humanity that forms one body with all as does the mind of the great man. As soon as it is obscured by selfish desires, even the mind of the great man will be divided and narrow like that of the small man. Thus the learning of the great man consists entirely in getting rid of the obscuration of selfish desires in order by his own efforts to make manifest his clear character, so as to restore the condition of forming one body with Heaven, Earth, and the myriad things, a condition that is originally so, that is all. It is not that outside of the original substance something can be added.[10]

It is significant that the learning of the great man can be said to consist "entirely" in the abolition of selfishness and desires that obscure his original character. But it is not immediately evident how these desires are to be resisted or uprooted. Nor is it clear what should be done when one's selfish desires have already been stimulated, or one has acquired a taste for them, or they have become deeply ingrained. One thing, however, is clear: desires are dangerous. They can lead to anger, destruction, murder, fratricide, and the complete disruption of social order. The term Wang Yangming generally uses to describe human desires, "*renyu*," may also include the pursuit of fame and wealth, not just the stimulation of emotions related to a person's physical constitution. But there is little doubt that physical appetites precipitate some of the most serious disturbances of the tranquillity of the spirit. Indeed, the needs of the body are taken to be the most intractable obstacles to the fulfillment of the mind.

Many novels and short story collections of the sixteenth century examine aspects of Neo-Confucian individuality that had become part of contemporary discourse. It is not surprising that the pursuit of individual autonomy and enlightenment is problematic—that the importance of individual autonomy is often overshadowed by the complications inherent in its pursuit. This is particularly the case when selfish and sensual desires enter the picture. The *Ruyijun zhuan* and other fiction of the period have more in common than might at first be apparent.

The Sensual Impulse in the Four Masterworks

The desires of ordinary people are, on the whole, described in much more detail in the sixteenth century than in earlier fiction. The individual affirmation that one might have expected, however, does not materialize. Instead of unfettered enlightenment and the emancipation from emotional and moral restraints, major fiction of the sixteenth century tends to describe people who are confused. And the more they think, the more confused they become.

The magnitude of the problem becomes clear in the Four Masterworks of the Ming novel: the *Xiyou ji* (Journey to the west), *Shuihu zhuan* (Outlaws of the marsh), *Jin Ping Mei,* and *Sanguo yanyi* (Romance of the Three Kingdoms).[11] When the Four Masterworks turn to the primary human motives, they almost invariably describe a mind that has been destabilized. Often the ultimate motive is weakness of will, which leads to the pursuit of a deluded image of the self, obsessive preoccupation, and loss of control. In sixteenth-century fiction, the destruction of inner equilibrium parallels a similar breakdown in the social order. And one of the most problematic and potentially destructive forces—which can be said to reflect the central conflicts of the Four Masterworks as well as other fiction of the sixteenth century—is human sexuality.

In the *Xiyou ji,* for example, Pigsy is an allegorical depiction of human appetite. His foibles provide the occasion for much of the novel's broad satire. But a more profound examination of the role of sensuality involves the hero of the novel, Tripitika. His pursuit of enlightenment is equivocal: constantly plagued by peevish worries about his physical comfort, he is unusually concerned with his appetites, often loses his temper, and repeatedly lets sensuality cloud his vision. The sensual aspect becomes most insistent when it is least expected—and therefore most significant. In chapter sixty-four, for example, Tripitika is bathed in images of classical enlightenment as he lectures four aged immortals on the nature of perfect wisdom. The immortals are delighted by the instructions they receive. They discuss quiescence, sincerity of mind, and the unity of substance and function. But as the moonlight grows brighter and the display of Tripitika's wisdom becomes more brilliant, the entrance of a flirtatious young girl twirling a sprig of apricot blossoms reduces him to a state of paralyzed anger and trepidation. When she suggests that they take advantage of the beautiful night to celebrate their physical natures, he is so disturbed that he is not even capable of repulsing her. He bursts into tears, wails helplessly, and is finally extricated by his attendants.[12] The four aged immortals are, of course, fiends in disguise. Their purpose is not to elicit a description of perfect wisdom but to tempt Tripitika into violating his purity. Although technically he passes this test, his reactions to sensual stimuli are so exaggerated that his devotion to quiescence and tranquillity of mind must ultimately remain in doubt. We are not told why Tripitika acts in this fashion. Nor is it clear whether the brilliance of his enlightenment has been diminished by this fiendishly simple test.

In the *Shuihu zhuan,* minor characters always find time to engage in juvenile pranks, drink too much, boast, rob people, pick fights, commit the occasional murder, and evade the authorities. On the surface it depicts the kind of trouble that outlaw bands cause when the central government is feckless. Not far beneath the surface, however, is a serious portrayal of the sensual impulse as it affects characters like the outlaw leader Song Jiang, the nominal hero of the novel, and Li Kui, his temperamental alter ego. Song Jiang's purported aim is to restore order to a country that has been torn by civil strife, but his heroic pretensions are seriously compromised by his complicated relations with women and his thinly veiled lust for power. In chapter seventy-two, for example, when he travels to the capital and meets with the famous courtesan Li Shishi, he becomes intoxicated and writes a poem that exposes his ambition to translate his successes as a bandit leader into substantial power in the imperial capital. Just as he is about to reveal his true identity, he is interrupted by the emperor himself, who has arrived to see Li Shishi. Song Jiang realizes that this is the unique opportunity he has been awaiting for most of the novel: finally he may petition the emperor for an amnesty so that his band can obtain official recognition. But at this point Li Kui inexplicably goes on a rampage after being subjected to the sight of Song Jiang's boastful flirting with the courtesan, and they are compelled to beat a hasty retreat. When Song Jiang is placed in a setting that casts his ultimate motivations in an ambiguous light, his legendary mastery of the strategic situation is shown to be impotent when it is most needed.[13] Other characters too are inexplicably violent at critical junctures. Wu Song, an impetuous hero who once beat a tiger to death with his bare hands while intoxicated, attacks and kills a Daoist priest simply because he is seen embracing a girl.[14] When major characters in the *Shuihu zhuan* encounter situations that arouse their senses, they lose their heads. Often their loss of control is accompanied by heroic drinking, but inebriation is ultimately like any other sensual stimulus that threatens to take control of any character who dares to partake of it.[15]

The *Jin Ping Mei* is an intricate tapestry into which the full complexity of human sensuality is woven. Sensuality is visible in the delectation of fine foods, rare wines, and elegant clothing; it is apparent in the appreciation of diverse genres of poetry, various types of drama, exquisite furniture, expensive art, and contemporary song; it reveals itself in the attention paid to nature, architecture, religious rituals, and, of course, sex. Indeed it has been argued that entire chapters are little more than scenes of "total sensual involvement, of all kinds, having little action other than a wide spectrum of responses to highly varied sensory stimuli."[16] The hero of the novel, an upwardly mobile businessman named Ximen Qing, is known more for the intensity of his appetites than for the delicacy with which he satisfies them. Even though his storerooms are overflowing with the finest of everything, he is incapable of appreciating it. His polymorphic vulgarianism is not, however, as revealing as the novel's examination of the sensual impetus.

One of the most significant examples occurs near the very end of the novel. Again the question of sensuality intrudes into the narrative when it is least expected. In this case, Ximen Qing's ostentatiously pious first wife Wu Yueniang decides to end her family line by giving up her only son to become the adept of a mysterious monk named Pujing. Years previously, this monk had rescued Yueniang from an attempted rape while she was on a religious pilgrimage. As payment for saving her, he made the unusual demand that she give him her child after he grew up. Years later, Pujing returns and demands that Yueniang live up to her end of the bargain. That night she has a nightmare, perhaps planted in her head by Pujing himself, portraying violent sexual advances upon her and ending with the death of her son and her imminent rape. At this point the reader is informed that Yueniang has attained enlightenment because of the dream. Yueniang herself, however, does not know if she is confused, enlightened, or indeed fully awake. Confronted by a strong and troubling sensual situation, she is immobilized. She then reacts without thinking and makes the crucial decision: she gives up her only son. Although the attainment of enlightenment during the latter part of the sixteenth century is often described as a spontaneous and unpredictable affair, it is safe to assume that the reader is not meant to conclude that Yueniang actually achieves enlightenment because she dreams of her own rape and destroys what is left of her family. In fact, her dream causes her to lose composure and undermines her ability to think rationally.

Instability of mind and confused motives are evident in the earliest of the Four Masterworks, the *Sanguo yanyi*, as well. Even the heroic protagonists Liu Bei (161–223) and Cao Cao (155–220) lose self control and are surprisingly weak in the face of sexual temptation.[17] At the end of chapter fifty-four, for example, when Liu Bei has decided to enter into a strategic marriage alliance with the warlike Lady Sun, he comes across a large stone in his path and decides to make it a symbol of his determination and strength. Borrowing the sword of an attendant, he raises his head to heaven and swears that if he is able to cleave the stone in two he will return to Jingzhou as undisputed ruler of the realm. He lifts the blade, he strikes, the stone is split in two. After this heroic display, Liu Bei is supposed to consummate his marriage with Lady Sun. But for several days, for reasons unspecified, he is unusually concerned for his safety. Finally there is a banquet and he is taken to the bridal chamber. Two rows of red candles lead to the entrance. In the flicker of the candlelight he sees that Lady Sun's female attendants, who are arrayed to each side, are wearing swords. Liu Bei turns so pale that the woman in charge of the ceremony offers to allay his fears by instructing Lady Sun to disarm her attendants. Lady Sun, of course, is shocked that such a famous hero could be made so apprehensive with so little justification. Although Liu Bei overcomes his initial apprehension and does consummate the marriage, his excessive anxiety is transformed into a state that borders on stupefaction. He loses his sense of time and place. Sending word back to Jingzhou that he has been married, he then partakes in a celebration that lasts several days. He is so immersed in the pursuit of pleasure, in fact, that he forgets his dramatic oath to return to Jingzhou in triumph.

Liu Bei has fallen into a trap. The conspirators who led him into it boast in a letter how this "stratagem of the beautiful woman" has worked to perfection: Liu Bei and his home territory are now vulnerable. When the issue of sensuality arises, Liu Bei's display of power and ambition melts into a shameful display of self-indulgence. With his cause now in grave danger, one of Liu Bei's lieutenants reminds him that they must return to Jingzhou immediately. Cao Cao, his implacable enemy, always quick to sense weakness in a rival, can attack at any time. Liu Bei, however, says he must first ask his wife for permission. He stalls and tries to mislead her, but she is too smart for that; he bursts into tears, falls to his knees, and protests that he did not mean to mislead her. She calmly replies that she knows the situation in Jingzhou is perilous and he must return at once. Ironically it is Lady Sun who comforts Liu Bei, and he is finally persuaded to return home.

If self-examination and the attainment of sagehood were held to be important in the Four Masterworks, one might have expected them to be celebrated in the *Sanguo yanyi*. A major character like Guan Yu (d. 219) is not only known in the historical sources for sagacity and bravery but had indeed become apotheosized as the god of war. Yet at one of the most critical moments in the novel, when Cao Cao's troops are retreating from the Battle of the Red Cliffs in a particularly vulnerable position, Guan Yu recalls Cao Cao's former generosity and is frozen in his tracks. Instead of seizing the opportunity to change the course of history, Guan Yu vacillates: his "heart is moved" and he allows Cao Cao to escape.[18]

In the middle of the sixteenth century, the issue of destabilization and its relation to sensual impulses is distinctive in the short story as well. In what Patrick Hanan calls the Middle Period of the Chinese vernacular short story, the lives of the merchant and shopkeeper often take center stage.[19] Many of these stories revolve around domestic stability, a state that is often threatened. In the Middle Period stories that Hanan calls the "folly and consequences" type, most focus on sex as the principal danger.[20] In stories like "Wenjing yuanyang hui" (Fatal attraction), a man's sexual drive makes him vulnerable and unfaithful.[21] Indeed men may be drained completely of their vital energy, causing illness, death, and the family's ruin. There is no squeamishness concerning the depiction of sordid detail, yet the narrator's implicit vantage point is always moral and expresses no vicarious delight in the depravity of the subject.

In the fiction of sixteenth-century China, the liberation of the common man is compromised when a character's instincts conflict with the tenets of established morality. The sensual dimension is alluring and powerful, but it is above all dangerous and confusing. The manner in which human desire is portrayed in the realm of fiction is related to its depiction in contemporary philosophy. On first consideration, the invention of the Chinese erotic novella might appear to be a manifestation of a new appreciation of the sensual dimension of human nature. But in fact the first erotic novella in the Chinese language, the *Ruyijun zhuan*, portrays an understanding of human nature that is much closer to traditional Neo-Confucianism than to the radical reappraisals that appear later in the sixteenth century. Characters who give free reign to their passions meet with disastrous ends. The implied narrator appears to be arguing, paradoxically, that the most useful guidance regarding desire is to be found in traditional sources that stress the importance of constraint and regulation.

Desire in the Late Ming Dynasty

To classical philosophers like Xunzi (c. 310–c. 219 B.C.), as well as many orthodox Confucian philosophers, desires are an inextricable part of the human disposition:

> Now, nature (*xing*) is that which is formed by Heaven; the disposition (*qing*) is the substance (*zhi*) of nature; and desire (*yu*) is the proper response (*ying*) of the disposition. To seek what desire deems attainable is that which the disposition certainly cannot avoid.[22]

Desire cannot be ignored, and Xunzi does not even entertain the thought that it can be eradicated or uprooted. Desire is a perfectly natural human response. But desires are not a stable force. They may become subversive and hence must be controlled. This is where rituals become important. Ritual principles and regulations were established so that human nature could be ordered and rectified; one's natural appetites are not merely to be indulged. Indeed, Xunzi argues that a person who follows such a course of action "will inevitably begin with strife and pillage, grow into transgressing limits and violating principles, and end up as a criminal."[23] Rituals and regulations provide a channel in which desires may be constrained, moderated, and ultimately transformed.[24]

During the sixteenth century, however, traditional interpretations of human nature were being reexamined with increasing skepticism. By the end of the century an outspoken minority of writers like Li Zhi are arguing that even the pursuit of sexual satisfaction for its own sake might be regarded as a positive undertaking: a person's ability to express his own desires spontaneously contributed to his authenticity and could even lead to enlightenment in a way that is wholly unrelated to earlier Daoist theories of physiological alchemy. Self-expression had displaced self-restraint. Li Zhi was attacked as decadent, of course, and his ideas were not nearly so influential as those of traditional Neo-Confucianism. Yet as Maram Epstein notes: "His positive treatment of the term desire (*yü*) foreshadowed its wider usage by several mainstream Ch'ing philosophers."[25]

Careful readers do not generally assume that a work of fiction affirms everything it describes. When a work of fiction contains graphic descriptions of sexual activity, however, it is often supposed that there is little difference between its content and its style. But simply because a work contains descriptions of sexual activity, the likes of which are not found in previous literature, does not necessarily mean that it is a tribute to lubricity. The *Ruyijun zhuan*'s portrayal of human desire can be assessed more accurately by examining traditional descriptions of desire and comparing them to controversial reappraisals in contemporary philosophy. Human desire in the Chinese context has been investigated recently by Anthony Yu in his *Rereading the Stone: Desire and the Making of Fiction in Dream of the Red Chamber.*[26] Agreeing with D. C. Lau that "the notion of desires is at the heart of most of Chinese thought," Yu traces definitions of the term "*qing*" back to classical texts as early as the third century B.C., examines how the dialectic of nature and disposition developed in traditional Chinese philosophy, analyzes the role of rituals and regulations that were promulgated by philosophers like Xunzi in order to rectify human nature, discusses literary theories that examine the outer manifestation of inner disposition in poetry as old as the *Shi jing* and fiction as late as the *Hongloumeng,* and shows that the "reception history of many literary works of the Ming-Qing period can thus appear as one long crisis of the containment of desire."[27] In short, Yu describes how human emotions have been interpreted in traditional Chinese thought: their origins, their depiction throughout much of Chinese history, the proper response when one's emotions have been stimulated, and important examples of Chinese philosophy, poetry, and fiction over the course of two thousand years.

It is not easy to add to such an erudite and comprehensive discussion. It is, however, possible to examine the specific context in which the *Ruyijun zhuan* was written and see how developments in philosophy might have influenced the portrayal of desire in this controversial work. The *Ruyijun zhuan* presents a graphic description of what happens when traditional methods of controlling human desire are ignored, when they have lost their persuasive power, or when the fulfillment of individual desire takes precedence over social responsibility. The improper regulation of human desire produces a crisis for the individual—a crisis that the author of the *Ruyijun zhuan* implies should be solved through the proper application of traditional methods designed to contain it.

Huang Xun, who might well have been the author of the *Ruyijun zhuan* (see Chapter 4), appears to have been influenced greatly by the thought of Zhu Xi. He attended a school that was closely associated with Zhu Xi, wrote appraisals of passages found in his collected works, read Zhu Xi's historical writings with particular interest, and even seems to have agreed with his unconventional interpretation of the history of the Tang dynasty. In the "Du *Ruyi-jun zhuan*" he illustrates the moral with a quotation from a poem about the Tang dynasty written by Zhu Xi. Moreover, Huang Xun discusses Zhu Xi's understanding of human emotions and desires on more than one occasion.[28] As the thought of Zhu Xi seems especially to have influenced the possible author of the *Ruyijun zhuan*, I want to examine Zhu Xi's understanding of a famous classical text on this topic and see how Huang Xun's contemporaries, Wang Yangming in particular, discuss this same text. Thus I want to focus on an aspect of human desire that is particularly relevant to the interpretation of the *Ruyijun zhuan:* what happens when the emotions are aroused and what should be done about it.

When Emotions Are Aroused

One of the most famous descriptions of human emotions is found in the *Zhongyong* (Doctrine of the mean). Zhu Xi—indeed virtually every Chinese philosopher who discusses human emotions—refers to this passage in some way:

> Before the rise (*wei-fa*) of joy, anger, sorrow, and pleasure, [the mind-and-heart] may be said to be in the state of equilibrium (*chung*). When they are arisen and reach due proportion, there is what may be called the state of harmony (*ho*). This equilibrium is the great root of all under heaven; this harmony is the universal Way of all under heaven. Let the states of equilibrium and harmony prevail, and a happy order will reign throughout heaven and earth, and the myriad things will all be nourished.[29]

Emotions are by nature neither good nor evil. When they have not yet been stimulated, there exists a profound equilibrium; but the stimulation of emotions does not necessarily cause disruption. If emotions are kept within certain limits they may contribute to a state of harmony. Emotions are not to be denied, ignored, or suppressed. If they are expressed in a moderate fashion, they are not a problem.

To Zhu Xi, unregulated or selfish emotions must be avoided because they give rise to desire (*yu*). This type of desire is closely allied with impropriety and excess. Because pleasure can easily lead to an excess of desire, it is viewed with particular distrust: "Generally speaking, if one acts because of pleasure, how can he avoid being incorrect?"[30] At one point, Zhu Xi describes the relation between feelings and desire with a water metaphor. The mind is originally like water, and nature is like tranquil water. Feelings are water that has begun to flow, and desire is water animated by waves.[31] There are good waves and there are bad waves; there are good desires and there are bad desires. Bad desires are wild and violent: they are powerful enough to undermine a person's foundation and destroy the principle of heaven. Concerning the relations between the sexes, Zhu Xi thinks it would be dangerous if people indulged their desires or acted solely because of pleasure; in such an instance a man would lose the strength of his character and a woman would forget that her duty is obedience.[32] Through moral and spiritual cultivation, however, the passions can be controlled and people can be protected from excesses that might otherwise lead them astray.[33]

Wang Yangming considers this famous passage from the *Zhongyong* on several occasions. He discusses the "equilibrium before the feelings are aroused" and the "harmony after they are aroused" in a manner that shares many of Zhu Xi's concerns—a fact that has been noted by many commentators.[34] Wang Yangming does not, however, describe human desire in great detail. Although his students frequently press him for a more precise description of the equilibrium that exists before the feelings are aroused, he usually replies with an answer that is meant to encourage the student to arrive at the answer himself. To one direct inquiry, he replies with the following parable: "I cannot tell you any more than a dumb man can tell you about the bitterness of the bitter melon he has just eaten. If you want to know the bitterness, you have to eat a bitter melon yourself."[35] This is a parable from a famous collection of stories called the *Biyan lu* (Blue cliff records), a Zen textbook compiled by the monk Keqin (*hao* Yuanwu, 1064-1136) during the Song dynasty.[36] Although Wang Yangming does not attempt to describe in words the equilibrium before the feelings are aroused, all who are present are said to have attained a certain degree of enlightenment. Wang Yangming would have been the first to argue that in such an instance the use of traditional philosophical disputation cannot produce the kind of enlightenment that is engendered by a parable that stimulates each person to arrive at his own understanding.

At other times, Wang Yangming does discuss both the equilibrium before the feelings are aroused and the harmony after they are aroused. But he does not describe them as Zhu Xi does, though there are superficial similarities. In fact, Wang Yangming thinks the phrase "harmony after the passions are aroused" is an oxymoron if understood in the traditional sense. To the extent that the passions are stimulated, the equilibrium of our original nature is obscured and there is no harmony. If we do not first attempt to reach the state of equilibrium before the feelings are aroused, which he calls the principle of nature (*tianli*), we cannot hope to approach the purity of our original nature. Wang Yangming frequently asserts that the principle of nature is simply to "get rid of selfish human desires."[37] Human desires are one of the most serious threats to the realization of our original nature:

> Take a person sick with intermittent fever. Although at times the illness does not appear, so long as the root of the disease has not been eliminated, the person cannot be said to be free from the disease. Only when all such selfish desires as the love for sex, wealth, fame, and so forth in one's daily life are completely wiped out and cleaned up, so that not the least bit is retained, and the mind becomes broad in its total substance and becomes completely identified with the Principle of Nature, can it be said to have attained the equilibrium before the feelings are aroused and to have acquired the great foundation of virtue.[38]

As one commentator notes, Wang Yangming's discussion of the equilibrium before the feelings are aroused is again reminiscent of Zhu Xi's.[39] But if Zhu Xi's commentary to the passage from the *Zhongyong* uses similar terms to describe the relationship between equilibrium and the principle of nature, Wang Yangming's discussion of desire emphasizes something quite different.[40] Unlike Xunzi, Mencius, and other early philosophers who think that the expression of desire is inevitable and is not necessarily a problem if regulated with rituals—and unlike Zhu Xi, who also recognizes, though perhaps with greater reluctance, that desires are an ineluctable part of our constitution—Wang Yangming describes human desires as a corruption of our original nature. Desire is an intermittent fever that is difficult to diagnose and treat. Desire is not an aspect of our nature that is to be rectified through rituals; it is like a medical condition that requires diagnosis and treatment.

The issue of desire is particularly important if one is to become a sage, which Wang Yangming believes should be the goal of every person. If the equilibrium before the feelings are aroused is the ultimate goal, then desire is an impurity that must be eradicated: "The reason the sage has become a sage is that his mind has become completely identified with the Principle of Nature and is no longer mixed with any impurity of selfish human desires. It is comparable to pure gold, which attains its purity because its golden quality is perfect and is no longer mixed with copper or lead."[41] Selfish human desires are base alloys that adulterate our original nature. Everyone possesses an original nature that is pure and complete but obscured by the contamination caused by the functioning of the mind. At the end of this dialogue, Wang Yangming makes the relationship between selfish human desire and the principle of nature as clear as he can. They are in precise inverse proportion to one another: "If we reduce our selfish human desire a little bit, to that extent we have restored the Principle of Nature."[42] Wang Yangming is not describing the regulation of desire but a systematic process of reduction that will lead to its extinction.

Zhu Xi says that desires are like waves, some good and some bad. To Wang Yangming, however, as soon as a ripple of thought appears in the metaphorical pool of water that is the mind, it leads to excess: "The original substance of pleasure, anger, sorrow, and joy is naturally in the states of equilibrium and harmony. As soon as one attaches a bit of his own idea to them, they will become excessive or deficient; they will be selfish."[43] To Wang Yangming, the state of equilibrium amounts to a state of mindlessness. When the passions have been engaged—when the mind contemplates pleasure, anger, sorrow, or joy—excess is the natural result. Thought itself leads to excess. Thought itself is desire.[44]

Wang Yangming's description of human desire is unlike traditional Neo-Confucianism; in this regard it is much closer to Zen Buddhism. He often describes the mind as a mirror, one of Buddhism's most prevalent metaphors.[45] The goal is to remove the accumulation of dust that obscures its clarity—to return the mirror to its original, spotless condition. The task of the individual in Wang Yangming's philosophy is thus to eliminate the obfuscation caused by selfish desires and to reestablish the lucidity of one's original nature.

Wang Yangming's discussion of the famous passage from the *Zhongyong* quoted earlier is ultimately a paradox. In the *Zhongyong*, the mind is in a state of equilibrium "before the rise of joy, anger, sorrow, and pleasure." When these feelings have been aroused in a moderate fashion, they can exist in a state of harmony. On several occasions, however, Wang Yangming claims that the original substance of pleasure, anger, sorrow, and joy is naturally in the state of equilibrium itself. In other words, he argues that pleasure et al. can exist in the "equilibrium before the feelings are aroused." How a feeling can exist before a person thinks of it is a proposition that his critics, and even some commentators from his own school, have trouble explaining.[46] How the original substance of anger, for example, can exist in the "state of equilibrium before the feelings are aroused" is difficult to imagine if one considers anger to be an arousal of one's feelings occasioned by thought.

Wang Yangming would be the first to admit—or in this case even insist—that the words used to describe his philosophy are incapable of conveying its true spirit. They are, at best, an inadequate approximation: a person must comprehend his philosophy through his own experience and reach his own understanding if it is to have any real value. Even so, if the goal is the diminution and ultimate extinction of desire, instead of its careful regulation, the problem still boils down to this: what is one supposed to do if one's desires have been stimulated? Wang Yangming sidesteps this question. Instead he asserts, with characteristic optimism, that a person will naturally know what to do when the time comes. Pursuing enlightenment is like traveling down a road; when you come to a fork you will realize, by yourself, which path should be taken.[47] In fact, if the goal is to realize your innate nature, there is not much you can do—or at least not much that can be put into words:

> There is no human nature that is not good. Therefore there is no innate knowl-
> edge that is not good. Innate knowledge is the equilibrium before the feelings
> are aroused. It is the state of broadness and extreme impartiality. It is the origi-
> nal substance that is absolutely quiet and inactive. And it is possessed by all men.
> However, people cannot help being darkened and obscured by material desires.
> Hence they must study in order to get rid of the darkness and obscuration. But
> they cannot add or subtract even an iota from the original substance of innate
> knowledge. Innate knowledge is good. The reason why equilibrium, absolute
> quiet, broadness, and impartiality are not complete in it is that darkness and ob-
> scuration have not been entirely eliminated and its state of preservation is not
> yet complete.[48]

A person should try to arrive at a state of innate knowledge—of equilibrium before the feelings are aroused. One cannot actually think about this process, however, because thought itself gives rise to selfish desires. One should study in order to illuminate the darkness, even though no study of any kind can add anything to, or subtract anything from, one's original nature. Wang Yangming is not unclear because he is unwilling to provide the answer but because he believes that such problems do not lend themselves to the type of answer a teacher can utter and a student can then commit to memory and put into practice. The problem, however, remains: he does not offer specific advice about what to do when one's selfish desires have been aroused. Wang Yangming does not emphasize the regulation of desire through rituals as urged by Xunzi, Mencius, Zhu Xi, and other philosophers. We are to turn inward to find the principle of nature that is complete and pure in every person. But precisely how we are to recognize that our true nature has been found—and how we are to know that we have not unwittingly uncovered a deluded or imperfect reflection of our true nature—is a serious question that appears to surpass the limits of language.

In 1567, thirty-eight years after his death and soon after the death of the Jiajing emperor (r. 1522-1567), Wang Yangming was honored with the post-humous title Wencheng, or Completion of Culture. In 1584 it was officially decreed that he would be offered sacrifices in the Confucian temple—the highest honor that could be bestowed upon a scholar, an honor granted to only four other thinkers of the Ming dynasty. His philosophy became dominant in both China and Japan, and since that time the magnitude of his stature has not been in doubt. It is important to remember, however, that his philosophy was considered controversial during the last decades of his life, that his earldom and other hereditary privileges were revoked upon his death, and that his thought was strictly proscribed by officials at the highest levels of government. It was averred that he had criticized the philosophy of Zhu Xi without justification and that he had been improperly influenced by Zen Buddhism. Radical branches of his school, the Taizhou school in particular, were labeled degenerate; passions, desires, and even depravity itself, it was alleged, had become the foundation of their debased interpretations of innate knowledge.

The *Ruyijun zhuan* was written decades before Wang Yangming's philosophy was widely accepted and before it was radically transformed by the Taizhou school. In fact, it was almost certainly written when his philosophy was still controversial and subject to vigorous attack.[49] Was the manner in which the *Ruyijun zhuan* describes human desire—the way it is aroused, the way it takes control of a person, and the way that characters deal with their desires—influenced by discussions of this topic that were raging precisely at the time it was written? I do not wish to imply that the *Ruyijun zhuan* is a philosophical treatise whose ultimate purpose is to critique the thought of Wang Yangming and his school. Nevertheless, the work does detail the destructive consequences that contemporaries feared would be produced by such a radically subjective philosophy. Further examination of its portrayal of human desire demonstrates, if nothing else, that it is not a precursor of the radical reappraisals of human desire that emphasize its beneficial aspects.

The portrayal of human desire in the *Ruyijun zhuan* is not unlike that found in the Four Masterworks. The mere introduction of sensuality in these novels causes central characters to lose control. What these characters lack is the ability to regulate their response to the expression of human desire. They attempt to contain this aspect of their natures through denial, not regulation. At times they are successful, especially if they are merely contending with desires that arise out of their own minds. But when their sensual natures have been stimulated by external forces, there is no hope. There is nothing that Li Kui can do—nothing that any of his band can do—to suppress his uncontrollable rage.

Desire in the *Ruyijun zhuan*

When human desires are aroused in the *Ruyijun zhuan,* the result is even more pronounced than in the Four Masterworks. Except for Xue Aocao, all of Wu Zetian's paramours pursue their desires to their ultimate destruction. Some become ill and die because their vital essences have been depleted; others court danger in a manner they know will lead to their death; still others are murdered because they can no longer provide perfect satisfaction. Their illnesses develop over an extended period of time, their ruin is foretold by contemporaries, and their murders can be predicted by anyone who has witnessed Wu Zetian dispatch loyal ministers who dared to question her prerogatives. Yet they cannot desist. When a character's emotions have been stimulated, particularly those related to the sensual part of his nature, he loses control.[50]

Xue Aocao is the only exception—and the manner in which he ultimately persuades Wu Zetian to reinstate the crown prince is a unique aspect of this work. Wu Zetian is not capable of regulating her desires; she does not even try. Every time she sets foot in a garden, hears the warbling of a songbird, or encounters the beauty of nature, she lapses into a kind of sensuous revery, her emotions are stimulated, and immediate gratification is required. But fortunately for the deposed crown prince, her most capable lover is the only one who possesses any morals. Unlike his predecessors, Xue Aocao is not interested in the material wealth the empress attempts to bestow upon him; nor is he interested in obtaining high office or political power. He is the first to argue that he is undeserving and unqualified. And indeed he is—having attained his current favor solely by committing lewd acts with the empress. He does make one request, however, and it is that Wu Zetian reinstate the crown prince she had improperly demoted. When his request is not well received, he resorts to what appears to be a desperate act: he attempts to castrate himself. I cannot think of an earlier work of Chinese fiction that depicts self-mutilation in such a graphic fashion. Xue does not attempt to regulate the empress' uncontrollable desire. He tries to eradicate it at the source with one bold stroke. He is not committing this rash act for his own benefit, moreover, but claims he is acting for the ultimate benefit of the empress and the state. He is attempting to annihilate the symbol and irreplaceable object of Wu Zetian's desire.

Although Wu Zetian appears to take Xue Aocao's attempt seriously, there is reason to be suspicious. As noted in Chapter 2, Xue Aocao's fake castration is probably an allusion to the counterfeit castration of the famous libertine Lao Ai. Thus Xue Aocao's desperate attempt to mutilate himself in the name of the proper line of succession of the Tang dynasty can be viewed as yet another parody: if Wu Zetian's appetites were insatiable, even monstrous, then any method capable of suppressing them would have to be monstrous as well. In any event, Xue Aocao's desperate gesture captures Wu Zetian's attention as nothing else could. She had ignored the remonstrations of senior ministers for years, but now she suddenly realizes that Xue is right and the crown prince should be reinstated. The root of her desire, however, has not been eradicated. Soon after the crown prince is restored, the senescent empress takes up where she left off. There is no middle ground: either sex is pursued to excess or it is not pursued at all. The sensual impulse leads naturally to excess and exhaustion. Though characters might attempt to deny and expunge this aspect of their natures, it is impossible. If a single ember is left, the sensual appetites rekindle themselves, burst into flames, and consume the person.

The portrayal of human desire in the *Ruyijun zhuan* is so extreme that it must ultimately be regarded as a parody. The longer Wu Zetian lives, the more extreme her desires become. This is not a sympathetic portrait of libertinism or an encomium on the beneficial aspects of human desire. It is the portrayal of a world without standards—the description of an attitude toward human desire that the author thinks is not only immoral but destructive.

4
Authorship

The earliest known appraisal of the *Ruyijun zhuan,* the "Du *Ruyijun zhuan,*"
was written by Huang Xun, a scholar who held several government positions
during the Jiajing reign period (1522-1567). The original text, three pages
long, is found in his *Dushu yide* (Trifles gleaned from reading books), a collection of miscellaneous observations he wrote about a wide variety of texts
over the course of several years.[1] Much of this work was written during the
1530s, not long after he had passed the *jinshi* examination and embarked
on his official career. The *Dushu yide* is not only the earliest work to mention
the *Ruyijun zhuan.* It also contains one of the earliest references to its hero
Xue Aocao, a figure whose name is not found in the Tang histories or, for
that matter, anywhere else.

In the "Du *Ruyijun zhuan*" Huang Xun observes that this work is obscene and fit to be burned; yet he endures his revulsion long enough to write
an erudite appraisal of it. He deplores Wu Zetian's indecency; yet when he
views her conduct in the light of other Tang rulers, he finds it was the inadequate moral standard set by Emperor Taizong, not the immorality of Wu Zetian, that was ultimately responsible for the decline of the Tang. Wu Zetian,
he asserts, was the product of Taizong's immoral example. But the work he
purports to analyze is not the most persuasive illustration of this assertion, as
Wu Zetian acquires her absolute authority through seduction and manipulation and maintains it with an alloy of terror and corruption. Moreover,
Huang Xun compares the moral of this work to a poem about the Tang emperors written by the famous Neo-Confucian scholar Zhu Xi (1130-1200).[2]

But as Huang Xun says the *Ruyijun zhuan* is obscene—even speaking of it pollutes his mouth—it does not seem appropriate to invoke the name of Zhu Xi in this context. Indeed, later authors could not comprehend why Huang Xun would chose to write about the *Ruyijun zhuan* in the first place. If his purpose was to criticize Emperor Taizong's lax moral standards, surely he should have analyzed Zhu Xi's poem, not this lurid work. As Huang Xun is attracted to a work he finds repulsive, as he perceives a moral where others find only depravity, and as he arrives at a conclusion which the work itself does not appear to illustrate, the reader might suspect that Huang Xun has ulterior motives for writing this appraisal.

When we examine Huang Xun's other writings, we find that he knows a great deal about the *Ruyijun zhuan,* the history it purports to portray, and the way it was written. Not only had he read the standard Tang histories and the *Zizhi tongjian,* but it appears that he also consulted original source materials. He discusses the reign of Wu Zetian on several occasions. He even writes about her paramours Zhang Changzong (d. 705) and Zhang Yizhi (d. 705), two vulgar creatures whose frivolous exploits do not deserve to be mentioned in the *Dushu yide* either.[3] The "Du *Ruyijun zhuan*" and some of Huang Xun's other writings also incorporate obscure allusions in a manner that is strangely reminiscent of this work. Indeed, the more one reads Huang Xun's other writings, the more one might suspect that Huang Xun himself could have been the author.

But of all the paradoxes found in the *Ruyijun zhuan,* the possibility that it might have been written by Huang Xun is perhaps the most surprising. Not only was he a respected official, but he appears to have been quite conservative. He was not interested in radical new philosophies or controversial reappraisals of human desire. He was a stubborn disciple of the thought of Zhu Xi and the Cheng brothers. When he analyzes historical texts, he focuses on passages that illustrate traditional moral values. His conception of morality is simple and clear, and contemporary descriptions of his official career emphasize his integrity. He was compassionate, scholarly, and urbane. In short, Huang Xun is the last person whose name one would associate with a work like the *Ruyijun zhuan.* It is difficult to imagine why he would have wanted to read, much less write, a work of this description. As very little has been written about Huang Xun, let us begin by examining his life, career, and literary works.[4]

Who Was Huang Xun?

Perhaps the earliest reference to Huang Xun is found in a local gazetteer published in 1547 to 1549 called *Jiaxing fu tuji* (Illustrated record of Jiaxing prefecture). As most of this work is devoted to maps of local geographical features, its descriptions of officials who served in this region tend to be brief. Its depiction of Huang Xun is no exception:

黃訓、字學古、歙人進士。爲政溫良、不取聲譽、愛民好士、有去後之思。遷兵部主事。[5]

Huang Xun, whose style name was Xuegu, was a *jinshi* from She district.[6] He administered government in a compassionate manner, did not strive for fame, and loved the people and appreciated scholars. Fond thoughts of him remained after he had departed. He was transferred to the post of secretary in the Ministry of War.[7]

Huang Xun's official career began when he was appointed magistrate of Jiaxing district in 1530.[8] As the *Jiaxing fu tuji* was written only a few years after Huang Xun died, it is reasonable to assume that its authors had firsthand knowledge of his career and character. A district magistrate was an all-purpose representative of the emperor and the central government; the ability to work with all classes of society was an indispensable prerequisite. Magistrates were unofficially called "father and mother officials" (*fumu guan*)—expected to care for their subjects with the same compassion and patience that parents would use when taking care of their own children. This appraisal of Huang Xun, though brief, suggests that he conformed to the standard of conduct expected of a district magistrate.

A more detailed description of Huang Xun's career and character is found in a prefectural gazetteer called *Huizhou fu zhi* (Records of Huizhou prefecture), the preface of which is dated 1566. Wang Shangning (*jinshi* 1529), one of the compilers, passed the *jinshi* examination in the same year as Huang Xun, wrote the preface to his *Dushu yide,* and appears to have known him professionally as well as personally.[9] It is not known, however, whether Wang Shangning himself wrote the following appraisal of Huang Xun:

黃訓、字學古、歙潭渡人。從父商所就學;日誦數千言、淹貫經史、以文名。舉進士、試嘉興令。卻兼[10]金三千、繼者至今遂爲例。以政最、召至京。當道故知訓擬掌科。其從者耳知誆索兼金。曰: 是污我一生矣;寧不得耳。從者深啣[11]之。當道中左言。擬授知州秩。文選力爭、竟授郎官。後當道自知失時望、[12]造門引咎謝之。其大節分明如此。陞任道卒。所著有黃潭文集、讀書一得、大學衍義膚見諸書。又撰皇明經濟錄。[13]

Huang Xun, whose style name was Xuegu, was from Tandu in She district. He followed his father to his place of business and pursued his studies there; every day he recited several thousand words, became totally immersed in the classics and histories, and became known for his literary abilities. He passed the *jinshi* examination and was made probationary magistrate of Jiaxing.[14] He declined three thousand pieces of gold, and those who succeeded him have to this day followed his example. As his administration was of the highest caliber, he was summoned to the capital. His superior had formerly known Huang Xun and planned to give him a post in the Office of Scrutiny.[15] When the followers [of his superior] heard of this they attempted to extort gold from him. Said [Huang Xun]: "This would sully my reputation for life; I would rather not accept [the position]." The followers greatly resented this. His superior was criticized by the censors. He had intended to appoint Huang Xun to the position of subprefectural magistrate.[16] The head of the Bureau of Personnel objected to this, and as a result he was appointed bureau director [in the Ministry of War].[17] Afterwards his superior came to realize that he had lost favor with the public, personally went to Huang Xun's door, admitted his own fault, and apologized to him. His moral fortitude was as clear as this. While on the path of promotion he died. His written works include the books *Huang Tan wenji* (Collected works of Mr. Huang Tan [Huang Xun]), *Dushu yide*, and *Daxue yanyi fujian* (Superficial remarks on the *Daxue yanyi*). He also wrote *Huang Ming jingji lu* (Record of the governance and assistance of famous ministers of the imperial Ming).[18]

In addition to possessing a temperament that was eminently suitable for government service, Huang Xun had also acquired a reputation for absolute integrity and was known for his literary abilities. Not only did he write or compile four books but one voluminous work, the *Huang Ming mingchen jingji lu,* appears to have been held in high regard and is available in facsimile reprints to this day. Today his *Dushu yide* is known only for the "Du *Ruyijun zhuan*," and his collected works are consulted only for the biographical information they contain about the author of the first appraisal of this controversial work.

The most detailed information about the life and career of Huang Xun is found in his collected works. Huang Xun writes that he was born in 1490.[19] He failed his examinations three times and did not become a *jinshi* until 1529, when he was almost forty years old.[20] In the following year he was appointed magistrate of Jiaxing district.[21] In 1532 he was recalled to the capital and made a commissioner to Jiangnan.[22] It is not clear precisely what title he held at that time; it might have been *tixing ancha qianshi,* or assistant surveillance commissioner in the Provincial Surveillance Commission, an office responsible for matters relating to judicial inquiries and investigations.[23] At about this time he refers to himself as a *beiyuan sima,* an unofficial reference to an executive official in the Ministry of War.[24] His commission to Jiangnan ended in 1536.[25] It was probably during the next year that he was appointed *bingbu lang*, or bureau director in the Ministry of War.[26] Many of the entries in his collected works are dated; the last is dated 1540.[27] As the preface is dated 1559 and its author states that Huang Xun died about twenty years previously, it is quite likely that Huang Xun died in 1540 or shortly thereafter.[28]

The author of the preface to his collected works states that Huang Xun's character is clearly evident in his own writings—and it is.[29] Huang Xun admired classical literature and obstinately adhered to the simple virtues of the past. His style name, Xuegu, literally means "study the ancient"; it also describes his taste in literature. In the *Dushu yide* he discusses passages found in the *Yi jing, Han shu, Zhuangzi* (Works of Zhuangzi), *Sanguo zhi* (History of the Three Kingdoms), a commentary to the *Yi jing*, the works of Mencius, a history of the Song dynasty, the sayings of Zhu Xi, the *Shi ji*, and various compilations from the Tang dynasty. And these are only some of the works he discusses in the first volume. Most of what he read was old, erudite, and of impeccable reputation. And then there is his appraisal of the *Ruyijun zhuan*. For a scholar who feasted upon the prim scholasticism of Zhu Xi and obscure passages from the dynastic histories illustrating eternal moral truths, his inclusion of a discussion of the *Ruyijun zhuan* is perplexing. If the range of titles he discusses in the *Dushu yide* is any indication, Huang Xun did not even like fiction. He was certainly not attracted to controversial works, much less infamous ones.

Further investigation of Huang Xun's collected works fails to uncover any conspicuous reason why he might have chosen to write about the *Ruyijun zhuan*. In fact, the more one reads about his character, the more curious this choice appears. When he writes about his education and aspirations, he stresses the pursuit of virtue and the cultivation of a pure mind. Candid descriptions of human sexuality are out of the question. When Huang Xun even mentions human desire, a topic he often discusses in relation to the thought of Zhu Xi, he is quick to observe that it must be resisted. The more powerful desires simply require more strenuous resistance. The question is not how desires are to be fulfilled, but how the spiritual pollution that accompanies their inevitable expression is to be precluded.[30]

The manner in which Huang Xun chose his *hao* (literary name) offers the most concise illustration of his personality and aspirations. He attended an academy called the Ziyang Shuyuan.[31] During the Song dynasty Zhu Xi had visited this academy, and it was partially reorganized in accordance with his suggestions. A statue of Zhu Xi was still to be found next to this academy during the late Ming. Two pools of water were on one side; Zhu Xi had described them as a "square mirror pool."[32] Huang Xun often stood next to the pools and sighed: "How can I make my mind like this pool? If my mind were like this pool then it would be pure and devoid of desire. The Way could be known and be put into practice, and the nobility of the ancients could be attained."[33] Huang Xun decided that his *hao* should be "mirror pool" (*jiantang*), an abridgment of Zhu Xi's description. Then he had a seal carved with his new name so it could serve as a constant reminder of his devotion to purity of mind—a goal that, if his collected works are any indication, he would spend the rest of his life striving to attain.

Huang Xun was not attracted to the writings of contemporary philosophers like Wang Yangming. Indeed, to the extent that the thought of Wang Yangming deviated from the philosophies of Zhu Xi and the Cheng brothers, Huang Xun held it to be defective.[34] His response to one of Wang Yangming's central concepts, the extension of individual moral consciousness (*zhi liangzhi*), is characteristically blunt: "Alas, how is this [like] the learning of Zhu Xi?"[35] Furthermore, what Wang Yangming thought was worthy of study "is not what Zhu Xi would have called learning."[36] And should there be any doubt as to his philosophical preferences, Huang Xun says: "I am truly a man from Anhui [as was Zhu Xi's family]. I know of Master Zhu Xi and that is all."[37] This was not the sort of person to be captivated by radical new ideas; he was only interested in classics and traditional philosophies that had stood the test of time.

Huang Xun did, however, wonder whether he was pursuing his goal in the proper fashion.[38] What was most valued in his day, he concluded, was passing the *jinshi* examination, even though this was not the proper purpose of study. When Huang Xun finally became an official, he continued to adhere to the values he had learned through his studies. He believed that the cultivation of personal virtue was the primary purpose of an education, a lesson that some of his colleagues did not seem to have mastered. His refusal to condone bribery, for example, appears to have been greeted with disbelief. It was an eccentricity that deserved special mention in his biographies. His probity nevertheless appears to have made a lasting impression on those who followed him—which may well have confirmed his suspicion that the moral standards of his fellow officials were far from adequate. The inculcation of such standards was the very purpose of the education that had qualified them for government service in the first place.

The "Du *Ruyijun zhuan*"

The "Du *Ruyijun zhuan*" is the earliest extant appraisal of the *Ruyijun zhuan*. It is also the most significant piece of evidence yet discovered that proves this work was written before the middle of the sixteenth century. Although the preface to the *Dushu yide* is dated 1562, internal evidence suggests that much of it was written during the 1530s. Huang Xun dates several entries, the last date being 1538, approximately two years before his death.³⁹

In the *Dushu yide*, Huang Xun usually discusses only one or two aspects of each work he cites. If he is writing about history, one of his favorite topics, he might commence with the title of a voluminous work like the *Han shu*. The entry might be shorter than a single page and mention one incident or historical figure, or it might be several pages in length and discuss a philosophical principle or historical precedent. Huang Xun often uses anecdotes from the histories to illustrate moral truths, and he also discusses historical texts in an effort to understand the problems of his own day. Assuming that his reader is well educated, he dispenses with all introductions of texts, authors, and historical figures. He often quotes obscure lines from rare sources and presumes that his reader will recognize and appreciate them.

The date of composition of the "Du *Ruyijun zhuan*" is not known. An entry on the previous page is dated 1536; an entry fewer than ten pages later is dated 1538. But as most of the *Dushu yide* is not arranged according to order of composition, we cannot assume that the "Du *Ruyijun zhuan*" was written during the 1530s.⁴⁰ Dating this text calls for an analysis of its relation to the novella and to Huang Xun's other works. But first let us examine the text itself:

嗚呼、唐之昏風⁴¹甚哉。太宗淫巢王妃、知有色不知有弟。高宗蒸武才人、知有色不知有父。玄宗淫壽王妃、知有色不知有子。兄不兄、子不子、父不父。可以為人乎？況可以為君乎？況可以為國乎？此三君者一也。太宗蓋英明君也、乃亦知有色、不知有弟。況高宗之下愚、玄宗之中才乎？信色之大惑惑人也哉。朱子曰："晉陽啟唐祚、王明紹巢封、垂統已⁴²如此、繼體宜昏風。"⁴³嗚呼、唐之昏風甚哉。太宗首惡之名不可逭⁴⁴矣。予觀三尤物者、巢王楊妃之於太宗、太宗之淫妃也、非妃之敢淫太宗也。壽王楊妃之於玄宗、玄宗之淫妃也、非妃之敢淫玄宗也。敢淫者、武才人乎？才人年十四事太宗、至高宗以為昭儀時年三十一矣。前年尼感業見高宗之褆⁴⁵而泣。泣雉奴奇貨⁴⁶也、而高宗故悅之、心動焉。心也、陰先陽唱、⁴⁷禽獸行⁴⁸成。敢[淫]者武才人乎？才人而昭儀、而皇后、而皇帝。改唐而周、改李而武。置控鶴、置奉宸。敢淫者、豈惟雉奴外五、六郎⁴⁹已乎？史外誰傳如意君矣？言之污口舌、書之污簡冊、可焚也已。⁵⁰然如意君、薛敖曹其人也？武氏九年改元如意、不知果為敖曹否？敖曹曰如意者、蓋淫之也。武氏果有敖曹其人乎？可讀武氏傳、殆絕幸僧懷義者與？不然。何偉岸淫毒佯狂等語似敖曹也？不曰懷義曰敖曹者、豈謂姿體雄異⁵¹昂藏敖曹與？⁵²於敖曹者、嫪毒⁵³之謂與？嗚呼、傳之者、淫之也、甚之也已。⁵⁴夫武氏敢淫於終、恃勢也、無足怪。予獨怪夫始之淫、高宗也。群焉女比、吾敢泣者愛、⁵⁵厥蒸心動。昔之云：⁵⁶ "如童如也、將何恃乎？" 人謂恃有高宗耳⁵⁷成

之好在。予謂亦恃有太宗家法在。弟死不難於淫其妻、父死豈難於蒸
其妾？不然、鶉之奔奔、[58] 不可道也。何敢思樂聚麀而淫焉如此哉？太
宗首惡之名、固不逭[59] 矣。[60]

Alas, the muddled wind of the Tang dynasty was indeed extreme. Taizong debauched the consort of the prince of Chao; he knew desire but did not know his
younger brother.[61] Gaozong committed incest with Lady of Talents Wu; he knew
desire but did not know his own father.[62] Xuanzong debauched the consort of
the prince of Shou; he knew desire but did not know his own son.[63] An elder
brother was not an elder brother, a son was not a son, and a father was not a
father. How could they have been human? Moreover, how could they have been
rulers? Finally, how could they have governed a country?

These three rulers were as one. Taizong was no doubt a worthy and enlightened ruler, but even he knew desire and did not know his younger brother.
What could have been expected of Gaozong's fatuity or Xuanzong's mediocrity?
Truly "the great delusion of desire does beguile men!"[64] Zhu Xi said: "From its
beginning in Jinyang prefecture the Tang flourished, then the sovereign clearly
succeeded the lord of Chao; when the inheritance is already in such a state, it is
appropriate that the succession become a muddled wind."[65] Alas, the muddled
wind of the Tang dynasty was indeed extreme. Taizong cannot evade the blame
for having begun this depravity.[66]

As I behold those three bewitching women, regarding Consort Yang of the
prince of Chao and Taizong, it was Taizong who debauched the consort, not the
consort who dared to debauch Taizong. Regarding Consort Yang of the prince
of Shou and Xuanzong, it was Xuanzong who debauched the consort, not the
consort who dared to debauch Xuanzong. Was it Lady of Talents Wu who dared
to incite debauchery? When the lady of talents was fourteen she served Taizong;
by the time Gaozong made her lady of bright deportment she was thirty-one.[67]
The previous year, as a nun in Ganye Temple, she beheld Gaozong's beautiful
robes and wept.[68] She wept because she regarded Gaozong as a unique commodity, yet Gaozong took delight in her for that reason and his heart was
moved.[69] As for the heart, if the female comes first and the male sings out, incest
is the result.[70]

Was the one who dared to commit debauchery really Lady of Talents Wu?
She was lady of talents, then lady of bright deportment, then empress, then emperor. She changed the name of the Tang dynasty to Zhou and changed the imperial surname from Li to Wu. She instituted the post of auxiliary to the director
of imperial mounts and instituted the post of director of the palace corral.[71] As
for those with whom she dared to engage in debauchery, how could they have
been limited to Squire Five and Squire Six in addition to Gaozong?[72]

Who wrote the story *The Lord of Perfect Satisfaction*, which is beyond the purview of history? To speak of it is to pollute one's mouth and tongue; to write of it is to pollute the stationery on which it is written; it is fit for burning. As for this Lord of Perfect Satisfaction, what about Xue Aocao? In the ninth year of Wu Zetian's reign she changed the name of the reign period to the First Year of Perfect Satisfaction; could this indeed have been on account of Xue Aocao?[73] Xue Aocao was, no doubt, called the Lord of Perfect Satisfaction because he committed debauchery with her. Did Wu Zetian actually have [a relationship with] this man Xue Aocao? One can read the biographies of Wu Zetian; did she stop at her relationship with the monk Xue Huaiyi?[74] No. Why is the extremely licentious language of total abandon used to describe Xue Aocao [not found in the biographies of Wu Zetian]?[75] He is not called Xue Huaiyi but is called Xue Aocao. Could this be because a physique that is exceptionally masculine, imposing and superior, has been called Aocao?[76] In regard to Xue Aocao, is he a depiction of Lao Ai?[77] Alas, to write of such matters is to be licentious, extremely so.

As for Wu Zetian daring to commit debauchery until the very end, she was relying upon her power and this is not surprising. Who I find particularly blameworthy is the one who first debauched her, Gaozong. In a group the women were compared; the one who dared to weep was loved, and his incestuous heart was moved.[78] In the past it was said: "Like a child, in the future upon whom will you rely?"[79] People say that as for something to rely upon there was Gaozong's freely chosen infatuation. I say that she could have also relied upon the precedent set by the example of Taizong's domestic regulations. When a younger brother died, if it was not difficult to debauch his wife, when a father died, how could it have been difficult to commit incest with his concubine? If this were not the case, the phrase "Boldly faithful in their pairings are quails" could not be spoken.[80] How could they have dared to think of blithely assembling a herd of incestuous hinds and engaging in such debauchery?[81] Taizong certainly cannot escape blame for having begun this depravity.

Huang Xun's appraisal of the *Ruyijun zhuan* describes the systemic corruption of the Tang imperial family and its disastrous effect on the state. By describing events that precede and follow the career of Wu Zetian, Huang Xun demonstrates that the degeneracy of the Tang was not merely the product of her lechery but the ineluctable result of the conduct of previous emperors, Taizong in particular.

Huang Xun first recounts three famous cases of incestuous adultery committed by Tang emperors. Taizong committed adultery with Yang Fei, the consort of his brother Li Yuanji; Gaozong committed adultery with Wu Zetian, Taizong's lady of talents; and Xuanzong committed adultery with Yang Guifei, the consort of his eighteenth son. The affairs of Taizong and Xuanzong are not even mentioned in the *Ruyijun zhuan*, yet to Huang Xun they are part of its moral: "An elder brother was not an elder brother, a son was not a son, and a father was not a father. How could they have been human? Moreover, how could they have been rulers? Finally, how could they have governed a country?"[82] Huang Xun argues that when the foundation of a dynasty is in such disarray, a confused result is inevitable. He quotes part of a poem by Zhu Xi lamenting the immoral behavior of the Tang emperors; the last two lines make the moral perfectly clear: "When the inheritance is already in such a state, it is appropriate that the succession become a muddled wind."[83]

Huang Xun is not impressed with the character of Xue Aocao. He questions whether such a person actually existed, doubts that Wu Zetian changed the name of the reign period to Ruyi because of him, and speculates why he would have been given the name Aocao, which means "filthy," if he were meant to represent a specimen of masculine virility. Huang Xun notes also that Xue Aocao is like Lao Ai, a well-endowed commoner whose dubious career we encountered in Chapter 2.

Although the *Ruyijun zhuan* reminds Huang Xun of the immorality of the Tang emperors, he finds little redeeming value in this story or the way it is told: "To speak of it is to pollute one's mouth and tongue; to write of it is to pollute the stationery on which it is written; it is fit for burning."[84] This sentiment is echoed by a Qing-dynasty (1644-1911) relative of Huang Xun named Huang Zhijun who criticizes Huang Xun's decision to write about this work in the first place. Although he concedes that the majority of Huang Xun's observations about literature and philosophy are valuable, he thinks his remarks about this work are out of place: "As for his essay on reading the *Ruyijun zhuan*, why on earth would one want to read such a book? He quite appropriately discusses a quotation from a poem by Zhu Xi in order to lay the blame upon Taizong for the muddled wind [of the Tang dynasty], but the topic itself should have been changed."[85]

Huang Xun's relationship with the *Ruyijun zhuan* is subtly yet irreversibly transformed when it is read next to his collected works. Often he takes notes on the same historical sources used by the author of the *Ruyijun zhuan*: the *Xin Tang shu, Jiu Tang shu, Zizhi tongjian,* and a host of others. When he writes about Tang sources, he is often interested in Wu Zetian's relationships with Taizong and Gaozong.[86] He even wrote a brief appraisal of Wu Zetian's paramours Zhang Changzong and Zhang Yizhi.[87] He also mentions several historical allusions found in the *Ruyijun zhuan*: the extermination of the Lü clan, the murder of Zhaowang Ruyi, the story of Bi Gan, and the story of Xue Rengao, to name but a few.[88]

But the most significant similarities between the writings of Huang Xun and the text of the *Ruyijun zhuan* are found in a unique poem buried near the end of his collected works. In his "Qibier xing" (Ballad to the little barbarian),

Huang Xun not only proves that he knows a lot about Tang history. He reveals that he is unusually knowledgeable about Wu Zetian's paramours.

Huang Xun's "Ballad to the Little Barbarian"

The close relationship between the "Ballad to the Little Barbarian" and the *Ruyijun zhuan* has not before been noted. In this poem Huang Xun mentions most of Wu Zetian's paramours and even refers to the "*aocao*" of Xue Aocao. Like the historical references found in the *Ruyijun zhuan*, many of those in this poem are fairly erudite:

契苾[89]兒行:

契苾[90]兒武媚娘;天河照影雙鴛鴦。
控鶴庭中恨不早;萬象神宮臥小寶。
小寶何好卻如意;身不可闍頭可剃。
剃盡三千力士頭;金刀遺恨沈 南璆。
春風爭傳鸚鵡聲;喚起大雲驚八紘。
大雲不掩敖曹史;千年蒙面堂堂李。
李花摘盡蓮花開;兒顏不厭娘顏衰。
狄門一老洛州來;白馬寺鬼抱兒哀。
哀聲不到長生殿;摘盡李花猶一片。
一片重開百葉花;上陽老魄落誰家。
龍瞳耽耽顧鳳頸;[91]當世何人回不敏。[92]

Ballad to the Little Barbarian:[93]

The Little Barbarian
    and Fair Flatterer Wu;
The Milky Way illuminated
    this pair of mandarin ducks.[94]
The imperial mount was in her court
    but she regretted they did not meet sooner;
In the Palace of the Spirit of Myriad Forms
    she slept with Feng Xiaobao.[95]
Xiaobao was so fine,
    in fact he was perfect satisfaction;
He could not be castrated,
    but his head could be shaved.[96]
Completely shaved were the heads
    of three thousand mighty men;
But the metal blade had lingering regrets
    for Shen Nanqiu.[97]
The spring zephyrs vied to transmit
    the cries of the parrot;

The *Classic of the Great Cloud* was called into being,
   and it startled all of creation.[98]
But the *Great Cloud* could not conceal
   her filthy history;
For a thousand years the faces will be hidden
   of the illustrious Li clan.[99]
The plum blossoms were plucked to extinction
   as the lotus bloomed;[100]
Youthful beauty was not repulsed
   by a woman in decline.[101]
An old man from the family of Di
   came to the capital Luoyang;
The spirit in the White Horse Temple
   embraced the child and wailed.[102]
His anguished cries did not reach
   the Palace of Long Life;
Plucked to extinction were the plum blossoms,
   yet there was still one bud.[103]
This one bud blossomed again
   as a flower with a hundred leaves;
The old spirit in the Palace of the Upper Yang
   into whose house could she then descend?[104]
Her dragon pupils were brilliant,
   and behold her phoenix neck;
What person of that time
   would have replied that she was not clever?[105]

Almost every line of this poem contains an erudite reference to Tang history. Some lines are, in fact, constructed of idiosyncratic abbreviations of rare terms taken out of context. If the historical trivia found in this poem are identified and provisionally interpreted, it soon becomes apparent that this poem is one of the most important references to the topics found in the *Ruyi-jun zhuan*. If my analysis is correct, this poem is a precursor.

This poem mentions most of Wu Zetian's paramours listed in standard historical sources. But Huang Xun does not simply list their names. He uses the rarest nicknames and the most obsolete titles: the *qibier*, or "Little Barbarian," in the title of this poem is one of Zhang Yizhi's nicknames not often found in the standard histories. Soon after Wu Zetian ascended the throne, a lascivious song by this title became popular in the Eastern Capital. Zhang Yizhi was known to have sung songs of this type in her company, and its scurrilous overtones made this term a particularly appropriate nickname. The poem also contains a reference to one of Zhang Yizhi's official titles, *konghe*, an abbreviation for *konghejian nei gongfeng*, which means something like "auxiliary to the director of imperial mounts." Wu Zetian created this office specifically for Zhang Yizhi in the year 699; within a year, however, she had changed its name to something else. If the reader does not know that this recondite abbreviation refers to Zhang Yizhi, it is difficult to imagine how this line could be interpreted.

In 688 Wu Zetian renamed the Mingtang, or Brilliant Hall, as the Wanxiang shengong, or Palace of the Spirit of Myriad Forms. Its construction was supervised by Xue Huaiyi, one of her famous paramours. Historical sources, however, rarely refer to the Brilliant Hall as the Palace of the Spirit of Myriad Forms. Moreover, the blooming of the lotus refers to Zhang Changzong—also known as Squire Six, or *liulang,* another name for the lotus blossom. Xue Huaiyi's original name Feng Xiaobao is also mentioned. His rival, the imperial physician Shen Nanqiu, is found in this poem, too, although he is mentioned only a few times in the Tang histories.

This poem refers to obsolete versions of the names of the palaces where Wu Zetian's lovers resided and the temples where they were murdered. It refers to the rivalries that developed between her lovers, mentions a fragment of the name of a minister who sought to restrain her sensual excesses, cites a controversial document she forged with a paramour in an effort to legitimize her reign, and ends with another rare allusion that was used to describe Wu Zetian when she was a child. It also includes the phrase the "cries of the parrot," an allusion to a dream mentioned in the *Ruyijun zhuan.* These historical fragments could not have been collected from any single source of which I am aware. And despite some effort, I have still failed to identify a few of this poem's more obscure allusions.

While some of the material found in this poem appears in the *Ruyijun zhuan,* as well, it is clear that neither could have been based solely upon the other, as each text contains uncommon references that are not found in its counterpart. The poem and the novella both demonstrate a familiarity with some of the more arcane details of Wu Zetian's reign. Huang Xun knew Tang history. And like the author, he was clearly interested in some of the more sordid details of Wu Zetian's love life. But why he might have chosen to write a work about the history of Wu Zetian's lubricious exploits with a series of ignoble paramours is a question for which there is no simple answer. It would be useful if we knew the dates of composition of the "Ballad to the Little Barbarian," the *Ruyijun zhuan,* and the "Du *Ruyijun zhuan,*" but these texts are not dated. Nevertheless, internal evidence allows us to speculate on the order in which they might have been composed.

Some Speculations

The "Ballad to the Little Barbarian," the *Ruyijun zhuan,* and the "Du *Ruyijun zhuan*" were probably composed in that order. When the texts are read in this sequence, there seems to be an evolution in the author's approach to the topic. The tone becomes more serious, Wu Zetian's personal conduct is placed in a wider historical context, and Huang Xun's criticism of the immorality of the Tang rulers becomes more strident. Each text builds on the one that precedes it. But while they all ostensibly describe the same history, the ultimate purpose of each is quite different.

The "Ballad to the Little Barbarian" is about Wu Zetian's ignoble paramours. While Huang Xun does not condone her lecherous proclivities, he does find they are good material for a naughty poem. The senescent empress and her vulgarian paramour Zhang Yizhi make a ludicrous pair of mandarin ducks, traditional symbols of lovers. Xue Huaiyi gains access to her private chambers by shaving his head and pretending to be a monk; naturally, Wu Zetian does not find it necessary to castrate such a fine specimen. Shen Nanqiu, the imperial physician, does not have to be castrated either because he already enjoys easy access to her private quarters. One day, while Wu Zetian is in the process of exterminating the Tang imperial family, Zhang Yizhi catches her eye and is not repelled by the prospect of sleeping with an empress who some might have considered decrepit. Although Wu Zetian is in her sixties, it is no secret that she is attracted to every man, however vile, who is still intact. This poem does not mention her relations with Emperors Taizong and Gaozong—more troubling relationships that have overtones of adultery and incest. And while this poem might possibly be viewed as scathing criticism of Wu Zetian's personal conduct, it is written in a rather jocular tone. Thus the reader is not driven to conclude that its ultimate purpose is moral. It is just a frivolous exercise.

The "Ballad to the Little Barbarian" was probably written before the *Ruyijun zhuan*. While many of the events described in the poem appear in the novella, there are some crucial differences. One is found in the following line: "Xiaobao was so fine, in fact he was perfect satisfaction." In the novella, the crucial term "*ruyi*," or perfect satisfaction, is only used in relation to Xue Aocao. It describes Wu Zetian's lewd apotheosis and is never used in relation to Feng Xiaobao, who was quite a disappointment. In the "Du *Ruyijun zhuan*," Huang Xun notes that this term "*ruyi*" describes the perfect satisfaction that only Xue Aocao was capable of providing. Huang Xun also mentions that Wu Zetian changed the name of the reign period to Ruyi because of Xue Aocao. If the poem were written after the novella, it is very unlikely that Huang Xun would have chosen to associate the term "*ruyi*" with Xue Huaiyi instead of Xue Aocao.

There is an even more important difference between the poem and the novella. Xue Aocao is not, in fact, mentioned in this poem. Although it does contain his given name, "*aocao*," in this case it simply means filthy: "But the *Great Cloud* could not conceal her filthy history; For a thousand years the faces will be hidden of the illustrious Li clan." The syntax of this line suggests that the term "*aocao*" is not a person's name; the following line, a parallel construction, uses an adjective in the analogous position. Furthermore, this line is not historically accurate if "*aocao*" is interpreted as a reference to Xue Aocao. The first part of the line mentions the *Classic of the Great Cloud*, a text that had nothing to do with him. In the "Ballad to the Little Barbarian," this reference to the "*aocao*," or filth, of Wu Zetian's reign appears to be the embryo of inspiration that would at length mature into the lewd character of Xue Aocao. If the poem were written after the novella, instead of before, it seems unlikely that Huang Xun would have made the mistake of associating the name Xue Aocao with the *Classic of the Great Cloud*. He almost never gets his history wrong, even when he is writing about trivia. The history presented in the poem, in the novella, and in his appraisal is all surprisingly accurate.

Some of the rare allusions to Wu Zetian's lovers in the "Ballad to the Little Barbarian" appear in the *Ruyijun zhuan*, as well, but the tone and style are quite different. From the very beginning, the novella places Wu Zetian's amorous adventures in a political context. It commences with her relationship with Emperor Taizong and continues with her incestuous affair with Emperor Gaozong. Her relationships with a series of lewd clowns delineate the ever-expanding boundaries of her self-indulgence and poor taste, but these relationships are also a crucial test for her ministers. Some are compromised, and some are murdered, because they dare to intimate disapprobation. The tone of the novella is quite bleak. The imperial family is confused. The proper line of succession is subverted. Wu Zetian demotes the legitimate crown prince, usurps the throne, proclaims herself emperor, and corrupts everything within her grasp. The text is also full of ironic references that place her actions in a dubious light. The reference to Wang Yan's chowry handle when Xue Aocao is first introduced to Wu Zetian is a good example.[106] Right when the reader is led to expect gratuitous lubricity he is administered a dose of conventional morality that deflates the erotic ambiance of the scene. Wu Zetian's activities with her lovers are condemned, but the most severe criticisms are made through dense poems and unidentified allusions to historical sources that are easily missed. And, of course, the novella is full of graphic details that are entirely absent from the poem. While the *Ruyijun zhuan* may at first appear to be a celebration of the wanton expression of human desire, there is a strong undercurrent of moral aversion that makes it a dark portrayal of corruption instead.

The "Du *Ruyijun zhuan*" was, I think, written after the novella. It examines the question of imperial immorality in an even larger historical context than its predecessors. Huang Xun denounces the decadence of the Tang emperors with such passion that one might suspect his motives. His moral indignation is palpable. This story is so offensive, and the manner in which it is told so obnoxious, that it scarcely bears repeating. Yet repeat it he does, and at some length.

I would not be surprised if the "Ballad to the Little Barbarian" was written when Huang Xun was still a student. Although it contains many historical allusions, it is not written in a sophisticated fashion. Once the allusions have been identified, there is not much more to say about it. Some are indeed obscure, but this does not mean they are profound. Reading this poem once is like completing a difficult crossword puzzle. Upon a second reading, the reader might well conclude that once is enough.

I would not be surprised if the *Ruyijun zhuan* was written after Huang Xun had failed his examinations two or three times. He was discouraged. He was angry. He was jealous of those who had passed. And he might have felt that both his scholarship and his morals were superior to those of his rivals. This work incorporates many obscure references, but most appear to have been included for an ulterior purpose. Parts also appear to have been written in an unexpectedly sophisticated fashion. Sometimes the narrator inserts an allusion, Wu Zetian interprets it one way, Xue Aocao interprets it another way, and the reader is free to appraise both of their interpretations, compare them to the source of the allusion, and reach a conclusion of his own.

I would not be surprised if Huang Xun's "Du *Ruyijun zhuan*" was written after he had become an official. Certainly a respected official, known for his probity and scholarship, would have been ashamed of a dirty little book he wrote while a student. When one considers the reputation of the work that Huang Xun has chosen to evaluate, it is apparent that his moral indignation is superfluous. There is Taizong's incest, Gaozong's incest, Xuanzong's incest, the filth of Xue Aocao, the debauchery of Wu Zetian, the vulgarity of her lovers, and more. There are no shades of gray, no mitigating circumstances. It is a very bad book indeed. But he knew this when he first read it, and he curiously fails to explain why he felt compelled to appraise it. Huang Xun's true purpose, I suspect, might have been to address an embarrassing indiscretion of his youth. Yet he does not seem to know what to say about it. His "Du *Ruyijun zhuan*" is an impassioned condemnation of precisely the kind of work that Huang Xun argues he should not have read in the first place. Huang Xun makes his case so clear that it is evident he did not need to make it.

If Huang Xun did indeed write this work, his exaggerated reaction to it makes more sense. He finally passed the *jinshi* examination and had begun to ascend through the bureaucracy, even though he refused to compromise his integrity. He was a compassionate, scholarly, and serious official. He was honest to the point of obstinacy. In addition to his official duties, he had compiled a fifty-three-volume collection of memorials, political tracts, and biographies of outstanding statesmen that dated to the beginning of the Ming dynasty. His colleagues held him in high regard. He was widely read in the classics and flattered himself that he was taking notes on some of the more important passages for posterity.

Huang Xun knew that descriptions of sensuous situations could engage the reader's imagination like nothing else. He also knew that discreet examples were found in texts as respected as the *Shi jing* and Han-dynasty *fu* poetry (see Chapter 1). Many authors and commentators claimed that descriptions of sensuous situations, instead of inducing the reader to sink insensibly into a state of voluptuous depravity, could instead prepare him to overcome these desires. The theory was that such depictions stimulated the most problematic aspect of human nature and could ultimately be used to regulate its expression. But Huang Xun was angry when he wrote the *Ruyijun zhuan* and he went too far. His accounts of sexual activity are too extreme, and the responses they elicit from the reader can be overwhelming. Indeed his descriptions are more extreme than anything that preceded them, and the erudite references that undermine many of them are too obscure, too inappropriate, just too bizarre. In any event, almost everybody missed, or ignored, whatever point he might have been trying to make. They saw only the sex. And instead of viewing these obscene depictions of sexual activity as the apotheosis of filth, excess, and immorality, many perversely welcomed them as a bold new affirmation of precisely those unregulated desires that Huang Xun spent the better part of his adult life trying to eradicate from his own constitution.

This analysis of the relationship between Huang Xun and the *Ruyijun zhuan* is based on circumstantial evidence. Is there any external evidence to support these speculations? Huang Xun's collected works describe in some detail the Tang history cited in the *Ruyijun zhuan*. As we have seen, the *Ruyijun zhuan* spends an inordinate amount of time discussing questions of legitimacy, the status of the crown prince, the moral standing of the ruler, and the proper foundation of the state—themes that are further highlighted by Huayang Sanren's preface. Is it simply a coincidence that Huang Xun considers these topics at some length in his collected works? He discusses controversies about crown princes, questions of succession, legitimacy, and related topics. Moreover, these topics were linked to extremely contentious debates that were raging at precisely the same time Huang Xun might have been writing the *Ruyijun zhuan*. In other words, contemporary events may have caused Huang Xun to turn his ironic little poem into an obnoxious critique of the government. Did Huang Xun expect the reader of the *Ruyijun zhuan* to conclude that he was really writing about current events? This is the topic of the next chapter.

5

Speculations About
Contemporary Events

It is people just like ourselves who are most affected
by passion.

—Wang Yan, *A New Account of Tales of the World*, p. 324

Even if the reader should acquire a taste for the manner in which Huang Xun incorporates obscure allusions, he is still unlikely to find the collected works appetizing. The type of mourning vestments a son should wear at his mother's funeral—to recall one memorable example from the early twelfth century he discusses at length—could become a point of controversy if the mother had previously put the son up for adoption. In such a case it might be more proper for the son to wear the vestments that would normally be worn during the funeral of an aunt, although some precedents suggest that the bond between a natural mother and her son should never be slighted in such a fashion.[1] Sometimes Huang Xun illustrates such controversies with even more obscure precedents that would numb the imagination of most readers.

But it would be a mistake to assume that Huang Xun's allusions are always meant to be obscure or pedantic. In many cases his purpose is quite the opposite. Frequently he assumes that his arguments are transparent and that he can afford to summarize them in a manner the uninitiated might find abrupt and confusing. This is often the case when he is writing about contemporary events. When Huang Xun's observations do not seem to describe the text he is purporting to analyze or he lapses into a protracted digression of questionable relevance, we must examine the larger context in which his observations were written.

Huang Xun's analysis of the *Ruyijun zhuan* is one of these cases. He condemns the immoral example of Emperor Taizong, a character who is mentioned only briefly at the beginning. He then denounces the incest committed

74

by Emperor Xuanzong, an affair that would not even occur until Wu Zetian was long dead. And by the end of the "Du *Ruyijun zhuan*," it is perhaps most surprising that Wu Zetian is granted a special dispensation. Despite her incest, adultery, torture, murder, corruption, and lechery—critical lapses in judgment and personal failures for which she appears to be completely responsible— Huang Xun finds that the blame rests with Emperors Gaozong and Taizong. And although the incestuous affairs of Taizong and Xuanzong are not even mentioned in the *Ruyijun zhuan,* to Huang Xun they are part of its moral: "An elder brother was not an elder brother, a son was not a son, and a father was not a father. How could they have been human? Moreover, how could they have been rulers? Finally, how could they have governed a country?"[2]

One might conclude that Huang Xun does not fully comprehend the text he is purporting to discuss. Yet it is not hard to demonstrate that in fact he knows a great deal about this work, its sources, and the way it incorporates obscure allusions. But why would he have made a series of erudite observations that do not appear to be supported by the text itself? Some of the more arcane passages in Huang Xun's *Dushu yide*—like the passage discussing the rituals that should be used by an adopted son when he attends the funeral of his natural mother—are more significant, and infinitely more interesting, when read in the light of current events. This is the case with Huang Xun's appraisal of the *Ruyijun zhuan* as well. Was this work supposed to be read, in whole or in part, as a description of current events? Before addressing this question we must explore in some detail one of the most famous controversies of Huang Xun's time, an issue that deranged the political climate during the last two decades of his life: the accession of Emperor Shizong.[3]

The Accession of Emperor Shizong

The preceding emperor Ming Wuzong (r. 1506-1522) had just died after a long illness contracted during a freak boating accident.[4] He had not designated an heir apparent and had not left any instructions concerning a possible successor. But Chief Grand Secretary Yang Tinghe (1459-1529) was confident he had the situation under control, and few could have doubted the ultimate success of his proposals.[5] While rumors of an imminent uprising circulated throughout the capital and one of the deceased emperor's favorites was reportedly on the verge of staging a coup, the grand secretary's choice of a successor could make these dangers evaporate as rapidly as they had arisen. Yang Tinghe was one of the most powerful politicians at court. It appeared he would be able to interpret historical precedents in a manner that, while perhaps not satisfying a scholar's appetite for technical precision, would nevertheless have preserved the political continuity of the Ming dynasty. As the empress dowager herself supported his efforts, it seemed certain his substantial powers would only increase by playing such a prominent role in the selection of the next emperor. Indeed, it appeared that his rivals, the court eunuchs in particular, would soon be placed in an unenviably precarious position. But it would have been prudent to put into writing precisely what was expected of the heir to the throne.

The boy chosen by the grand secretary was a thirteen-year-old prince named Zhu Houcong (1507-1567), the future Jiajing emperor, commonly known by his temple name Shizong. Shizong, a cousin of the deceased Emperor Wuzong, had few allies at court. If any unforeseen difficulties should arise, these could be postponed until he ascended the throne. In any event, even the most exorbitant demands of a political neophyte could scarcely have been expected to challenge the political acumen of a chief grand secretary who, at the height of his powers, had personally selected this young man to assume the imperial yellow and reign over all under heaven. It was not unreasonable for Yang Tinghe to presume he could issue an edict that ended with a simple instruction: "Bring him to the capital to inherit the throne."[6] But it did not take long for the grand secretary to perceive that the succession of the new emperor would not proceed according to plan.

What Yang Tinghe had proposed was not as straightforward as he had pretended. Emperor Wuzong had died without an heir, and some unusual, though not unprecedented, arrangements had been made. Shizong was expected to continue the imperial line as Wuzong's adoptive younger brother. For ceremonial and ritual purposes, Shizong's uncle Xiaozong (r. 1488-1506) was to be regarded as his father.[7] His natural mother and father were to be regarded as his aunt and uncle. While such an arrangement was not uncommon, in this instance it appeared to be a necessity if the future Shizong was to become emperor. The problem was not trivial: it was disputable whether Shizong and his line had, in fact, a legitimate claim to the throne. While Shizong's father, Zhu Youyuan (1476-1519), was a son of Emperor Xianzong (r. 1465-1488), his mother was a concubine who had never been elevated to the rank of imperial consort.[8] According to the *Ancestral Instructions* written by the founder of the Ming dynasty, Zhu Yuanzhang (r. 1368-1399), the sons of such concubines and their descendants could not carry on the imperial line in their own right.[9] The future Shizong was thus not in the proper line of succession. But if he agreed to become the adoptive younger brother of the deceased emperor, Yang Tinghe's schemes could have proceeded as planned. A delegation was sent to escort the future Shizong to the capital, and three weeks later he arrived in Liangxiang, about sixty-five miles southwest of the capital Beijing. But as soon as the young prince learned the details of Yang Tinghe's plan, it began to unravel with alarming speed.

Yang Tinghe had instructed the delegation to receive the prince with the rituals appropriate for an heir apparent. The prince, however, claimed he was already a reigning monarch. His argument was not a frivolous one: no mere mortal can bestow the mandate of heaven, and heaven had already bestowed it upon him. As the throne can never be vacant, not even for a single day, the title of emperor had been transferred to him by celestial means upon the death of Wuzong. The chief grand secretary assumed that Shizong would agree to become the adoptive younger brother of the deceased emperor, but this assumption was premature. Wuzong's last testament, drafted by Yang Tinghe, said nothing about becoming heir apparent. Nor did it specifically mention adoption, although adoption was clearly implicit in Yang Tinghe's interpretation of a line he included from the *Ancestral Instructions:* "When the elder brother dies, the younger brother succeeds."[10] But Shizong could not understand how it would have been to his advantage to interpret it in this fashion. Furthermore, if Shizong was to be regarded as an heir apparent or an adopted son, would it not have been proper to make these arrangements before Emperor Wuzong had died? But these arrangements had not been made, so how could the new emperor now be expected to have ritual obligations to the deceased emperor or his line? And how could he have been expected to slight the memory of his own father by failing to offer proper sacrifices to his spirit tablet in the ancestral temple? Shizong had been instructed to succeed to the imperial throne—and that, quite simply, is what he intended to do.

The grand secretary wrote three letters to welcome the prince as heir apparent. Ceremonial protocol required that an heir apparent be petitioned three times. Only upon receipt of the third petition would he condescend to assume the throne with the requisite display of reluctance and humility. But upon viewing one such request, Shizong exclaimed: "The will summoned me to inherit the throne. I am not the heir apparent!"[11] It was then requested that Shizong enter the capital through the Dongan Gate and proceed to the Wenhua Hall where a group of officials would greet him. But Shizong could not be fooled: as this was a procedure used for an heir apparent, he again refused. By now his entourage had arrived outside the walls of Beijing. Still there was no agreement. Yang Tinghe's lieutenants continued to press his case, but Shizong had had enough. He took the initiative and marched straight into the capital through the Daming Gate as reigning emperor. Heaven and earth were notified along with the spirits of the ancestors and the altars of earth and grain. The cosmos is said to have registered its approval of the new emperor in the form of a gentle rain that soon began to fall, relieving a drought that had long parched the region surrounding the capital.

Yang Tinghe had met his match in the unlikely figure of an obscure princeling who had contrived to turn his complete lack of experience and absence of political allies to his own advantage. The future Shizong was, by turns, a filial son, a precocious politician, and an insufferable teenager. The intense pressure brought to bear upon him only strengthened his resolve. Once he had made up his mind, no remonstration could divert him from his chosen path. The grand secretary, exasperated, would remain in power for a few more years importuning the young emperor incessantly to adopt his views concerning historical precedents. And such arguments would continue to fall on deaf ears.

Many felt that Shizong's reign was illegitimate. According to the *Ancestral Instructions,* he had no right to become emperor unless he were adopted into Wuzong's line. But Shizong not only refused to accede to the schemes of the grand secretary but eventually conferred titles upon his parents to which they were not legally entitled. He would also embark on temple-building projects whose ultimate purpose was to elevate his father to the rank of emperor posthumously. This campaign was not welcomed by the bureaucracy either. And just when the controversy seemed to be dying down, the death of an imperial relative would fan the flames of partisanship and the controversy over burial rituals would again consume the court. The argument concerning Shizong's relationship to the previous emperor, his own parents, and the imperial rituals used to express these relationships ineluctably developed into one of the most serious and protracted political controversies of the early sixteenth century. It came to be known as the *Dali yi:* the Great Ritual Debate.[12]

The Great Ritual Debate and Huang Xun

Huang Xun was clearly aware of the Great Ritual Debate. After all, it was the most divisive controversy of Ming Shizong's reign and internecine conflicts were to inflame the court for the last two decades of Huang Xun's life. Yet the manner in which he discusses this debate is characteristically indirect. He does not question the legitimacy of the reigning emperor or the propriety of his actions, but he does examine the implications of the historical precedents cited by both sides of the debate.

The arcane passage about the mourning vestments a son should wear during the funeral of a mother who had put him up for adoption, for example, mentioned earlier in this chapter, contains brief phrases that were closely associated with the Great Ritual Debate. Although Huang Xun is ostensibly discussing a precedent from the early twelfth century, it is perfectly clear he is thinking about current events. One significant phrase that he uses in this passage is from the "Sangfu" (Mourning vestments) chapter of the *Yi li* (Book of rites): "An adopted son recompenses his parents."[13] Although this phrase had been cited over the millennia in many ritual controversies, immediately after Shizong became emperor it began to occur with great frequency in the historical record, as even a cursory examination of a work like the *Ming tongjian* (Comprehensive mirror of the Ming dynasty) will show.[14] This phrase also figures prominently in some of the most famous early petitions to the throne concerning the Great Ritual Debate.[15] As this phrase had become inextricably linked to the controversy surrounding the accession of Shizong, contemporaries could scarcely have thought of anything else whenever they encountered it.

In his collected works, Huang Xun also discusses the phrase "When the elder brother dies, the younger brother succeeds," which had proved crucial to the interpretation, or misinterpretation, of Wuzong's last testament.[16] He considers Shizong's controversial temple rearrangements and construction projects, and he discusses the status of the crown prince on several occasions.[17] Like many other concerned officials of his day, he spends a fair amount of time brooding over the Great Ritual Debate, the historical precedents behind it, and the sometimes expedient, that is to say tortuous, interpretations of these precedents.

The Great Ritual Debate and the *Ruyijun zhuan*

Significantly, a concise summary of the Great Ritual Debate appears at the very beginning of Huang Xun's "Du *Ruyijun zhuan*." While enumerating the improprieties of the Tang emperors, Huang Xun offers an observation that does not seem to be about the work itself: "An elder brother was not an elder brother, a son was not a son, and a father was not a father."[18] Although Huang Xun claims that this phrase describes the relationships between Tang Emperors Taizong, Gaozong, and Xuanzong, clearly it is a better description of the confusion of family relationships caused by the Great Ritual Debate. Emperor Wuzong was supposed to be the elder brother of Shizong, but he was actually his cousin: an elder brother was not an elder brother. Emperor Shizong was supposed to be the son of Xiaozong, but he was actually his nephew: a son was not a son. And Zhu Youyuan was Shizong's natural father, but he was supposed to be regarded as an uncle: a father was not a father. These relationships were at the heart of the Great Ritual Debate, and when Ming historical documents of the period discuss the relations between father, son, and elder brother, they almost always refer to this dispute.[19] When a contemporary encountered Huang Xun's discussion of an elder brother who was not an elder brother, a son who was not a son, and a father who was not a father, all of whom were emperors, he might well have thought about the Great Ritual Debate. But did Huang Xun actually believe the *Ruyijun zhuan* was in some way related to this debate?

When the *Ruyijun zhuan* itself is read next to Ming descriptions of the Great Ritual Debate, significant parallels emerge. Although I do not think the *Ruyijun zhuan* is a roman à clef—that every person and incident is meant to represent a person or incident of this debate—contemporaries could have interpreted parts of it as a critique both of the current emperor, Ming Shizong, and the philosophy upon which he and his adherents ultimately appear to have relied to end the Great Ritual Debate: the philosophy of the school of Wang Yangming.

At the heart of the *Ruyijun zhuan* are succession struggles and the question of legitimacy. Wu Zetian usurps the throne. She disinherits the Li clan. And she exacerbates the problem by further confusing family relationships and the issue of her successor. She changes the imperial surname from Li to Wu, demotes the legitimate crown prince who later becomes Tang Zhongzong (r. 705–710), and tries to replace him with her nephew, Wu Sansi. Several officials in the *Ruyijun zhuan* criticize Wu Zetian at length; even Xue Aocao, while sharing her bed, remonstrates with her on this very question. The work also incorporates several allusions to earlier attempts to subvert the proper order of succession; the story of Jin Xiangong is the most obvious, but succession controversies underlie the story of Lao Ai as well. Even Huayang Sanren's preface avers that the *Ruyijun zhuan* is about succession controversies, and it makes the remarkable claim that Xue Aocao should be compared to the famous Han-dynasty minister Zhang Liang because he provides a crucial service to the state by persuading Wu Zetian to reinstate the legitimate crown prince. Unlikely as it may seem, remonstrations concerning Wu Zetian's legitimacy and the status of the crown prince occupy as much space in this work as its notorious descriptions of sex.

But are the numerous references to illegitimacy and crown princes in the *Ruyijun zhuan* in any way related to the Great Ritual Debate? As it turns out, the crown prince who is demoted by Wu Zetian in the *Ruyijun zhuan,* the future Tang Zhongzong, figured prominently in Emperor Shizong's solution to one part of the Great Ritual Debate. Emperor Shizong insisted that uncle Xiaozong be called uncle and not be regarded as his father. When the title "imperial deceased uncle" was finally conferred upon Xiaozong, this part of the debate was over.[20] The earliest historical precedent for this crucial term was found in the history of the Tang: the term "imperial uncle" was used by Tang Xuanzong (r. 712–756) to describe none other than Tang Zhongzong, the legitimate crown prince in the *Ruyijun zhuan*. The precedent of Tang

Zhongzong was furthermore often cited by the supporters of Ming Shizong.[21] As Huang Xun describes the moral of this work with a line that could easily be interpreted as a reference to the Great Ritual Debate—and as the bulk of the *Ruyijun zhuan* itself is concerned with the succession struggles of Tang Zhongzong, whose precedent offered the solution chosen by Ming Shizong to end a crucial part of the debate—one might be inclined to conclude that this is not a coincidence.

And there is more. In the *Ruyijun zhuan*, the argument that persuades Wu Zetian to reinstate Tang Zhongzong is also reminiscent of the Great Ritual Debate. Officials argue that Wu Zetian's nephew should not be named crown prince: if he were to assume the throne, he would not be able to offer the proper sacrifices to her in the ancestral temple. This is precisely what had happened to Ming Xiaozong. Shizong was supposed to be the son of Xiaozong, but he was actually his nephew; when Shizong refused to become Xiaozong's adopted son, Xiaozong and his son Wuzong, the two previous emperors, were not offered the proper sacrifices in the ancestral temple.

I suspect that readers of the *Ruyijun zhuan* were meant also to see a connection between Zhang Cong (1475-1539)—one of the first men to write a memorial to the throne in support of Emperor Ming Shizong's interpretation of his obligations to the previous emperor—and the Zhang brothers. In the *Ruyijun zhuan*, the Zhang brothers are called academicians of the North Gate, a designation referring to officials charged with drafting imperial pronouncements. The Tang histories do not state that the Zhang brothers were ever appointed to such a post; in fact, they are described as functionally illiterate.[22] This work rarely gets the history wrong; in the few cases in which there are discrepancies, it appears the author has altered the historical record on purpose. In this case, the Zhang brothers could have been given this title to compare them to Zhang Cong, who was in fact a Hanlin academician; an unofficial and archaic version of this title happens to be "academician of the North Gate."[23] When Zhang Cong was named to this post, the entire academy threatened to resign, so unacceptable did they find his level of scholarship.[24] As in the case of the Zhang brothers, high officials complained that Zhang Cong was merely an opportunist who had the imperial ear because of his shameless flattery; he was also accused of abusing his influence.[25] And, of course, these three men all share the same surname. Such speculations could be produced in abundance, but they are only speculations.

This is just a brief outline of the beginning of the Great Ritual Debate—a complicated controversy that lasted from 1521 until Shizong placed his father's spirit tablet in the Ancestral Temple in 1538. While I believe there are reasons to suspect that this debate and the *Ruyijun zhuan* may be more closely related than previously thought, I am hesitant to assign parallels between characters and incidents of this debate and those in the novella. I merely wish to point out a few similarities I noted as I read through some of the more famous historical records of the Ming dynasty. Perhaps contemporaries saw these similarities as well. In any event, there is one parallel that does appear to deserve further scrutiny: the effect that the philosophy of Wang Yangming might have had upon both of them. Huang Xun appears to have been most concerned about the precedent set by the manner in which this debate was conducted. While it would probably be an exaggeration to assert that the *Ruyijun zhuan* is ultimately about the main characters of the Great Ritual Debate, the case can be made that the novella attacks the irregular manner in which this dispute was adjudicated.

Sentiment vs. Precedent

Although Wang Yangming does not appear to have made any public statements about the Great Ritual Debate, his position on the use of intuition as a criterion for moral action appears to have influenced the arguments of Ming Shizong and his adherents.[26] Wang Yangming argued that rituals should accord with human feelings (*renqing*). The bureaucracy argued that rituals must be based on external models, historical texts, and the considered analyses of scholars like Zhu Xi and Cheng Yi. But such remonstrations would be to no avail, as Shizong did not find them to his advantage. Carney Fisher suggests that "in many ways . . . the Great Ritual Debate was in fact the first incursion of the Wang Yangming brand of Confucianism into Chinese political life."[27]

To a scholar like Huang Xun who admired the philosophy of Zhu Xi, the victory of arguments based on intuition must have seemed like the triumph of sentiment and opinion over reason and precedent. If in the course of performing solemn rituals a disagreement should arise, it would be most proper to examine historical precedents and decide the matter based on the facts. While it might be hard to restrain one's personal feelings in some cases, Huang Xun thought that feelings did not contribute to the resolution of such arguments. And it was inconceivable that feelings should have been regarded as the final arbiter of any but the most trivial of controversies. Yet this is what appears to have happened in the Great Ritual Debate. The grand secretaries flattered themselves that arguments based on historical precedent would prevail. They were also comforted by the fact that no one of stature initially took the emperor's side in this debate. Under such circumstances, how long could the young emperor have been expected to hold out? While it was natural for Shizong to have had strong feelings for his real father, no doubt he would eventually yield to their repeated admonitions and officially become the adopted son of his uncle.

A turning point in this dispute came in the middle of 1521 when Zhang Cong wrote a memorial to the throne in support of Shizong's position.[28] Zhang Cong argues that the emperor should not desecrate the bond between parent and child; he had agreed to continue the imperial line, but he had not agreed to become Wuzong's heir. When ritual practice is contrary to a person's inner feelings it should not be followed. Precedent and historical models are not the standard of morality. One should attend instead to individual circumstances, be introspective, and preserve the sanctity of family relationships because this is the most natural and filial course of action. Shizong was elated upon reading Zhang Cong's memorial. He exclaimed: "As soon as I can get this issued, I can then fulfill my filial obligations."[29] Although the court was almost unanimously against the emperor and his new ally Zhang Cong was a novice with almost no political power, this appears to have been all that Shizong needed to shift the terms of the debate.

It is perhaps significant that Emperor Shizong summoned Wang Yangming to court in 1521 and that Yang Tinghe was the one who blocked the move. But while Wang Yangming's philosophy does not appear to contradict Shizong's arguments, it is by no means clear that Wang Yangming would have recognized his own philosophy after it had been applied by some of the emperor's adherents who seem to have appreciated its political utility more than its moral purpose. In any event, it is worthwhile remembering that his thought was strictly proscribed by officials at the highest levels of government and denounced for its radical subjectivity, particularly by the adherents of the school of Zhu Xi.

Huang Xun was from the old school. He was disturbed by new developments in philosophy that seemed to pervert the moral authority of the histories and classics. What Wang Yangming considered worthy of study did not lend itself to serious analysis. And while Ming Shizong's adherents argued that there was an intuitive sense which guided each person to solve questions like the Great Ritual Debate, many must have concluded that this argument amounted to little more than pernicious license.[30] Even after their champions had endeavored to explain them, which was rare enough, these intuitions were vague. As this was a profoundly spontaneous philosophy, precedents, arguments, and indeed words themselves were incapable of transmitting its true essence. Nor did it appear these intuitions were susceptible to efforts to reshape them, except perhaps in those fortunate dispositions in which remedial efforts were already superfluous. It was thus inconceivable that the emperor, or anyone else, should have been allowed to impugn the purity and grandeur of sacred rituals with emotional appeals to an innate sense whose very authority was intimately related to its adherents' inability to describe it.

But there is a more practical problem with relying on internal standards: rulers like Wu Zetian. Few would aver that her intuition could have served as the criterion of moral conduct. That people could reach hitherto unimaginable heights of self-fulfillment if only left to their own devices is a pleasing fiction. The unpleasant truth is this: the world is populated by a weak and degenerate race of creatures that needs to be regulated, not set free.

It is therefore significant that throughout the *Ruyijun zhuan* Wu Zetian's emotional state is described with ironic references to precedents and texts—precisely the traditional tools that the apostles of human sentiment found incapable of expressing the true nature of *renqing*. These allusions do not extol the virtues of passion. Instead they demonstrate that a person who has fallen under its influence is no longer capable of understanding such precedents, even when they are spoken by the characters themselves.

In the *Ruyijun zhuan*, there is scarcely an exception to this rule: when Wu Zetian refers to a *Shi jing* love poem, a standard history, or a classical text, even a cursory examination of her allusion reveals that she is attempting to derive a meaning from it that is particularly ill suited to the original text. When such references are taken into account, it is hard to take the *Ruyijun zhuan* as anything but a parody of the proposition that a ruler like Wu Zetian should be allowed to rely on her own standards. Instead of describing an ultimate justification for moral action that strips away layers of tedious argumentation, making morality more personal, compelling, and relevant, it reveals that Wu Zetian's feelings are indistinguishable from her insatiable appetites. The *Ruyijun zhuan* is an emotional, indeed vulgar, response to the philosophy of the school of Wang Yangming—or at least to what happened after it was applied in a political context. The *Ruyijun zhuan* was written by someone who believed that morality should be based on historical precedent, classical texts, and tradition, not individual intuition. Thus it is full of allusions to immoral stories found in historical sources that illustrate precisely how improper Wu Zetian's actions really were—warnings she should have recognized but did not. She was acting upon her spontaneous desires, and a central assumption of the *Ruyijun zhuan* is that these are not the proper foundation upon which to build a state. Even if this work is not ultimately a caricature of the major personalities of the Great Ritual Debate, it does seem to be critical of the philosophy that played such a prominent role in its resolution.

6

Sources

The learned reader must have observed that in the course of this mighty
work, I have often translated passages out of the best ancient authors,
without quoting the original, or without taking the least notice of the
book from whence they were borrowed. . . . To fill up a work with these
scraps may, indeed, be considered as a downright cheat on the learned
world, who are by such means imposed upon to buy a second time, in
fragments and by retail, what they have already in gross, if not in their
memories, upon their shelves; and it is still more cruel upon the illiterate, who are drawn in to pay for what is of no manner of use to them.

—Henry Fielding, *The History of Tom Jones*, 2.100

Wu Zetian is the only woman to have become emperor of China. Most historians depict her ascent to such heights as an anomaly and criticize her personal conduct with particular asperity. She was an opportunist. She committed
adultery. She committed incest. She cast a spell upon two emperors that no
remonstration could break. Then she usurped the title of emperor and persecuted the heirs of the Tang to the brink of extinction. Although most historians place the blame squarely upon Wu Zetian for wielding her preternatural
charms with such devastating effect, a disinterested observer of the Tang imperial family might just as well conclude that it was always susceptible to distractions of this sort.

The minority view held by Zhu Xi and repeated by Huang Xun in his "Du
Ruyijun zhuan" does not absolve Wu Zetian of her immoral conduct, but it does
transfer much of the blame elsewhere.[1] Wu Zetian entered the imperial compound when she was only fourteen. She was educated in the service of Emperor Taizong. He was an excellent teacher and she a most devoted student.
That Taizong's son did not hesitate to commit incest with her suggests that the
standard of morality maintained in that household was not exceptional. Of
even greater embarrassment to traditional historians were Wu Zetian's irregular relations with a series of men after she became emperor. These are mentioned in virtually all standard histories. After Gaozong died, Wu Zetian
became more promiscuous and sought out ever more ignoble partners. Once

their sordid services were no longer required or their interest in a senescent empress had flagged, they were unceremoniously dismissed, ignored, forgotten, framed, or even murdered. After Wu Zetian became emperor, Feng Xiaobao, a mountebank who plied his trade in the capital, was called to her attention.[2] She shaved his head, changed his name to Xue Huaiyi, and dressed him as a Buddhist priest to facilitate his access to her private chambers. Sunk in voluptuousness and indolence, it did not take long for his special relationship with the empress to go to his head—when Wu Zetian had an affair with an imperial physician named Shen Nanqiu, Xue Huaiyi became a petulant arsonist and she had him murdered.[3]

Later in life Wu Zetian bestowed her favor on a pair of brothers named Zhang Yizhi and Zhang Changzong. Though beautiful and attentive, they amounted to little more than dissolute vulgarians. Historians are particularly embarrassed by the public display to which Wu Zetian subjected her infatuation. Once she adorned Zhang Changzong with bird feathers because she was of the opinion that, so attired, he resembled a famous immortal. To the exasperation of her advisers, she then paraded him about the city on a pretentiously decorated wooden crane. She also bestowed ever more elevated titles upon the Zhang brothers although their illiteracy and frivolity implied they were incapable of completing (or perhaps even fully comprehending) their official duties.[4] It was a complicated story, as most human relationships are, yet Wu Zetian could scarcely have devised a more exquisite torture for their colleagues than to make them perpetual eyewitnesses to such a display of self-indulgence and poor taste. The Zhang brothers remained the beneficiaries of her imperial infatuation until the end of her reign. By this time they had amassed immense fortunes. But when Wu Zetian's ten thousand years were about to expire, officials burst into their living quarters and beheaded them. Many of their relatives and coadjutors were hunted down and similarly executed. When their heads were stuck on poles and put on display, the story goes that neither colleagues nor commoners could disguise the delight they felt upon viewing this horrific spectacle. By dawn of the next day the heads of the Zhang brothers and their cronies had been hacked to bits.

Although the *Ruyijun zhuan* focuses on the more unsavory aspects of Wu Zetian's reign, the notion that its descriptions of sexual misconduct may ultimately stand for political misconduct merits attention. The text recounts Wu Zetian's sexual excess, but it also details the problems caused by immoral conduct—particularly because it is perpetrated by the ruler and involves the confusion of normal lines of succession. When one considers the range of histories to which the *Ruyijun zhuan* alludes, it is reasonable to assume it was written for an educated reader familiar with classical history. But if the erudite references were placed there on purpose—and were meant to engage the intellect of the kind of reader who is equipped to grapple with oblique references in historical texts—it would then appear that the *Ruyijun zhuan* was written for precisely the kind of person who would not be interested in such a story in the first place. Why did the author set such erudite allusions in a context so inappropriate?

The *Ruyijun zhuan* and Tang History

The author of the *Ruyijun zhuan* was something of a historian of the Tang dynasty. He often paraphrases descriptions of the reign of Wu Zetian found in the *Jiu Tang shu,* the *Xin Tang shu,* and the *Zizhi tongjian.* On occasion he also refers to their sources. It is clear that he did not merely open the *Zizhi tongjian* or the *Zizhi tongjian gangmu* (Comprehensive mirror for aid in government in outline and detailed form) to the reign of Wu Zetian and paraphrase a few pages, as is often the case with historical novels.[5] It is also clear that he had a collection of historical texts and incidents in the back of his mind, even when he does not quote them directly.

The author's ostensible purpose was to write a history of Wu Zetian's love life. He refers to all of her lovers mentioned in the historical sources I have consulted, even when they are quite obscure. He describes what is known of their careers in the imperial compound and delineates their ultimate fates. He also accurately summarizes what little is known of Wu Zetian's personal life. The first half of the work is, in fact, full of accurate (though apparently irrelevant) historical details. Some passages are so condensed, and contain so many historical figures, that they seem fragmented. Nevertheless, the chronology of events in the *Ruyijun zhuan* follows standard sources. The right ministers appear at the right time and say the right things; minor characters, even obscure characters, appear out of nowhere, for reasons unknown, and just as quickly pass again into oblivion where they belong.[6] Only after the author dispenses with what amounts to an unexpectedly detailed history does he invent the character Xue Aocao and begin to write fiction in the manner for which this work has become so notorious. But even then he continues to refer to standard historical sources and the classics to describe Wu Zetian's state of mind, to make ironic comments, and to add obscure details whose ultimate purpose is yet to be determined.[7]

Although there is a great deal of history in the *Ruyijun zhuan,* only one passage paraphrases the historical record at some length. Near the beginning, when Emperor Gaozong decides to demote Empress Wang and elevate Wu Zetian, a virtuous minister named Chu Suiliang (596–658) remonstrates that this course of action is unacceptable.[8] He notes that Wu Zetian is not the daughter of an illustrious family of the realm, that she entered the imperial palace as a minor consort in the court of Emperor Taizong, and that he and other senior advisers had promised Taizong to protect and support his son and daughter-in-law. The populace could also be expected to oppose Gaozong's relationship with Wu Zetian. Several sentences of Chu Suiliang's speech are based on passages in the *Jiu Tang shu* and the *Xin Tang shu*.[9] Moreover, this is one of the few instances in which the author of the *Ruyijun zhuan* chooses to alter the historical record. In the standard histories, Chu Suiliang is demoted for his brave remonstrations but is not tortured or ordered to commit suicide as in this work. Chu Suiliang was one of the most famous ministers of the Tang dynasty; such a drastic departure from the historical record would have been obvious to every educated reader. It thus appears that the author alters the adviser's fate at this juncture to indicate that his work will soon enter the realm of fiction.

Apart from this extended paraphrase of the Tang histories there are many fragmentary quotations and partial paraphrases from these sources. One of the more interesting, though brief, paraphrases of the historical record is spoken by Xue Aocao. During one of his remonstrations with Wu Zetian he argues that the legitimate crown prince should be reinstated; he then notes that Wu Zetian should act upon his advice before she loses the support of the populace irrevocably. He says: "The hearts of the people do not yet despise the Tang."[10] This is a paraphrase of a line in the *Xin Tang shu:* "As I see it, neither heaven nor the people have yet come to despise the virtue of the Tang."[11] In the *Xin Tang shu,* this line is spoken by the famous minister Di Renjie (607–700); like Xue Aocao, Di Renjie argued that Wu Zetian should reinstate the legitimate crown prince before the populace became openly rebellious.

Di Renjie's advice to Wu Zetian's lover Zhang Yizhi at this juncture is relevant too. Concerned for his safety, Zhang Yizhi turned to Di Renjie for advice: "Zhang Yizhi often casually asked about strategies that would provide for his personal safety, and Renjie said: 'Only by recommending the return of the prince of Luling can you avoid disaster.'"[12] By recommending the reinstatement of the crown prince, Xue Aocao is doing precisely what Di Renjie had counseled another of Wu Zetian's lovers to do when he found himself in the same predicament. Di Renjie's advice is important because it lends credence to the argument made by Huayang Sanren in his preface to the *Ruyijun zhuan* that moral exhortation in difficult times can take peculiar forms. In this case even Di Renjie, one of the most moral ministers of the Tang dynasty, thought that Zhang Yizhi, a corrupt and frivolous paramour of the empress, could provide a valuable service to the state by calling for the reinstatement of the legitimate crown prince. It is likely, then, that the author of the *Ruyijun zhuan* was aware of this passage in the *Xin Tang shu* and that it inspired the unusual role played by Xue Aocao.

Moreover, some of the poems in the *Ruyijun zhuan* reveal that its author is intimately familiar with obscure aspects of Tang history. The poem that begins "Despite all obstacles the emperor's loyal servant" was discussed in Chapter 1. Other poems found in the *Ruyijun zhuan* are even more difficult to interpret—suggesting that the author is not in the least concerned that the average reader would not be able to comprehend their real significance. One such poem refers to Di Renjie's attempt to persuade Wu Zetian to reinstate the legitimate crown prince. Finally his arguments produce the desired result, and the following poem alludes to his efforts:

> One sentence calls back
> the dream of the parrot;
> Snatched back from the highest heavens
> he returns as a young phoenix.[13]

This poem refers to a dream that Wu Zetian had before she decided to reinstate her son Li Xian (656-710).[14] A few different versions of this dream are found in the Tang histories and their sources. Perhaps the earliest version is found in the *Chaoye qianzai* (Comprehensive record of affairs within and without the court):

> Empress Wu Zetian once had a dream about a parrot; its plumage was magnificent but both of its wings were broken. She asked her senior ministers what it meant, but they all remained silent. Administrator Di Renjie said: "The word parrot is homophonous with Your Majesty's surname; the two broken wings are your two sons, the prince of Luling and the prince of Xiang. If Your Majesty were to elevate these two sons then the two wings would be restored."[15]

Immediately after Wu Zetian hears this explanation she reinstates the crown prince. Even readers who do not recognize the history behind this poem may be able to guess that the return of the young phoenix refers to the reinstatement of the crown prince. For the reader who does know this story, the poem is far more interesting. It not only describes the event but indicates the state of mind of Wu Zetian and the skill of Di Renjie at interpreting her concerns and molding them to his own purpose. It simultaneously provides historical background while furthering the plot. And it does so in an exceptionally concise manner.

An even more erudite poem is used to describe Wu Zetian's lover Zhang Changzong. Wu Zetian is so delighted with him that she pretends he is a reincarnation of a famous immortal named Wang Zijin and turns him into a vulgar spectacle.[16] Such a display of imperial infatuation elicits the derision of every historian who describes this affair. The import of the poem used to describe Zhang Changzong at this juncture, however, is not immediately apparent:

> In the past he encountered Fuqiu Bo;
>   Today he is like Ding Lingwei.
> The palace attendant has talent and demeanor;
>   But his name is not that of the archivist.[17]

The first three lines of this poem are not that difficult to interpret. Fuqiu Bo and Ding Lingwei are famous immortals.[18] The term "palace attendant" (*zhonglang*) was one of Zhang Changzong's titles.[19] The interpretation of the last line, however, requires further investigation. The term "archivist" (*zangshi*) refers to an office once held by the famous philosopher Laozi.[20] Laozi's surname was Li—like that of the Tang ruling house that considered Laozi to be an ancestor. The immortal Wang Zijin, to whom Zhang Changzong was often compared, was the son of Zhou Lingwang and also bore the royal name; but Zhang Changzong did not. This poem may thus be interpreted as criticism of Zhang Changzong. Although he lived a life of luxury as one of Wu Zetian's favorites, he could never have insinuated himself into the line of succession. In other words: this poem intimates that he should enjoy his odious status as Wu Zetian's paramour while he can because this relationship, and the preferment he obtains because of it, are not as immortal as might be thought.

This poem is in fact a fragment of a longer poem written by a contemporary official named Cui Rong (652–705).[21] Although the historical Zhang Changzong may have known of this poem, the historical record implies that his powers of discernment were not sufficient to have enabled him to comprehend it. The four lines quoted in the *Ruyijun zhuan* are also found in the *Jiu Tang shu* and other standard sources.[22] But even if the author was only familiar with these four lines, there is no reason to suspect he did not fully comprehend them. Indeed he places them into precisely the proper context. And when the allusions in such a poem are identified, they contribute more to the story than may at first be apparent.

Who Is Xue Aocao?

Xue Aocao is probably the invention of the author of the *Ruyijun zhuan*. His name does not appear in any of the histories of the Tang dynasty that I have consulted.[23] But this does not mean that his name was not ultimately inspired by a host of historical sources. In the *Ruyijun zhuan*, Xue Aocao is the grandson of a concubine who committed adultery with a servant boy. His parents are dead, as is his only sibling. He moved to the capital when he was only eighteen years old. He was on his own. While the character of Xue Aocao is fictional, the author does trace his lineage to the illustrious Xue family that played a prominent role at the start of the Tang dynasty. A brief but accurate history of a few members of this family is found near the beginning of the work.[24]

The heroes of many Chinese erotic novels are, like Xue Aocao, orphaned at a young age. This is the case with the infamous Ximen Qing in the *Jin Ping Mei*. Such orphans, deprived of the moral guidance provided by an extended family and left to their own devices, can be expected to turn out badly. But Xue Aocao, his lewd activities with Empress Wu Zetian notwithstanding, is the exception to the rule. He sees himself as a moral agent and avails himself of every opportunity to remonstrate with the empress, no matter how incongruous his protests become. But much of the *Ruyijun zhuan*, as Huang Xun notes, is unspeakably filthy. This aspect of the work too is incorporated into the name of Xue Aocao. "Aocao" is a cognate of terms like "*aocao*," "*aozao*," and "*angzang*," all meaning "filthy." Variants of these terms date to at least the Han dynasty.[25] Several examples are found in Song-dynasty texts as well.[26] They are also, of course, used in Ming-dynasty works to describe things that are foul, repulsive, or annoying.[27] Xue Aocao's name therefore means "Filthy Xue"—hardly the name an author would choose for his hero if his purpose were to celebrate his sexuality. Furthermore, there can be little doubt that other authors thought this name referred to Xue Aocao's filthiness; in the *Xiuta yeshi* the term "*aozao*" is used to describe sexual practices that are traditionally considered dirty.[28]

One sentence that Huang Xun uses to describe the name of Xue Aocao reveals yet another, even more obscure, association that no one but the author himself would have made. Huang Xun wonders why Aocao was given this name: "Could this be because a physique that is exceptionally masculine, imposing and superior, has been called Aocao?"[29] To answer this question, it is necessary to examine the biography of a man named Gao Ang (c. 500–538) that is found in the *Bei shi* (History of the northern dynasties).[30] His style name (*zi*) was Aocao, the same as Xue Aocao's given name. As this term usually evokes nasty connotations, it is not surprising that it is rarely used as a name. Nevertheless, the *Bei shi* notes that Gao Ang's father chose this name for his son because he was audacious, courageous, and "imposing and superior" (*angcang aocao*).[31] This is the same phrase that Huang Xun uses when he discusses the name Aocao in the "Du *Ruyijun zhuan*." Furthermore, the *Bei shi* says that Gao Ang possessed "a physique that is exceptionally masculine"; this same phrase is used by Huang Xun as well.[32] Is this correspondence significant?

Although the characters comprising these two brief phrases are certainly not rare, these particular combinations of them are, to my knowledge, found nowhere else in the standard histories. That they are both found verbatim on the same page of the *Bei shi*, are both used to explain the rare name Aocao, and are both found in Huang Xun's "Du *Ruyijun zhuan*" would appear to be a striking coincidence. But perhaps there is a simple explanation. If Huang Xun is in fact the author of the *Ruyijun zhuan,* he might have come across the story of Gao Ang in the *Bei shi,* borrowed his unforgettably incongruous style name for his hero, and used two phrases from this history, perhaps unconsciously, when he later discussed this work in the "Du *Ruyijun zhuan.*" Huang Xun often writes like this—as can been seen on almost every page of his *Dushu yide.* He copies obscure lines from even more obscure sources; sometimes he identifies his allusions, but usually he does not. In many cases the ultimate meaning of his allusions depends on ascertaining their provenance—not always an easy task. This exceptionally condensed way of writing is comparatively rare in vernacular Chinese fiction, but it is relatively common in classical Chinese history: the occurrence of a sentence, a phrase, or even a single rare word can be used to create a context, serve as an argument, or express an opinion.

If this is not how these two lines from the *Bei shi* found their way into Huang Xun's "Du *Ruyijun zhuan,*" we are led to conclude that either it is a sheer coincidence—or else Huang Xun read the work, later found the name Aocao in an irrelevant section of the *Bei shi,* and then used two lines from the biography of Gao Ang to describe the name Aocao in his "Du *Ruyijun zhuan.*" But this seems even more unlikely. Why would Huang Xun refer to Gao Ang's biography in the first place? There is no clear answer. There do not seem to be any similarities between Gao Ang's career and Xue Aocao's. The young Gao Ang was an outlaw who terrorized the countryside; later in life the state came to value his military prowess and made him a general. He was held in high esteem, and no mention is made of any amorous adventures. Furthermore, by the Ming dynasty it does not appear that the term "*aocao*" possessed any positive connotations whatsoever: it simply meant "filthy." Indeed, I have been able to find only one single instance in which this term is discussed in a positive fashion—and that is in the biography of Gao Ang in the *Bei shu.* So when Huang Xun asks: "Could this be because a physique that is exceptionally masculine, imposing and superior, has been called Aocao?" the answer to this question is suggested by the precise wording of the phrases that comprise it. Although the term "*aocao*" almost always means "filthy"—and Huang Xun clearly knows this—he quotes verbatim two brief yet rare phrases from the biography of Gao Ang in which it does not mean "filthy." Perhaps he simply finds this unusual name amusing; perhaps this is meant to pass for a display of his erudition.[33] In any event, there is little doubt that Huang Xun plays such games on a regular basis. He does not care if the reader is incapable of understanding such trivia. As in his poem "The Little Barbarian," he seems most pleased with himself when his allusions are obscure to the point of being almost unintelligible.

There is still more to the various names used to describe Xue Aocao. Immediately after he consummates his relationship with Wu Zetian, she gives him the nickname "Ruyijun," or Lord of Perfect Satisfaction. This is, of course, the title of the work. Wu Zetian gives him this nickname because he is everything she has ever desired in a man, at least physically. But this nickname also possesses a few other connotations that the educated reader could be expected to recognize. When Wu Zetian gives Xue Aocao the nickname "Ruyi" she also changes the name of the calendar year to Ruyi. The first and only year of the Perfect Satisfaction reign period was 692. It lasted for only a few months before Wu Zetian changed it to something else. None of the historical sources I have consulted speculate on the meaning of this name, but the *Ruyijun zhuan* does: it is named after Xue Aocao. Wu Zetian, in fact, changes the name of the reign period to Ruyi even before she gets out of bed, so satisfying is her first encounter with her new lover. In the *Ruyijun zhuan*, the name of the new reign period is adopted and abandoned at the historically correct time. The author has thus provided a comical, and indeed preposterous, explanation for something that historians do not appear to have addressed. But it is also a succinct illustration of Wu Zetian's blind infatuation: she spontaneously expresses her desires without regard to protocol, her advisers, or public opinion.

The term "*ruyi*," which literally means "as you wish," is also the name of a kind of scepter, probably a transliteration of the Buddhist term "*anurubbha*." A *ruyi* is usually from one to three feet long and may be made of bone, horn, steel, bamboo, wood, jade, or stone. Often sutras were written on *ruyi* and served as prompts for Buddhist monks as they recited scriptures. In this context the *ruyi* is a symbol of eloquence; it is, however, likely that it existed as an auspicious object for some time before it became associated with Buddhism. From approximately the Six Dynasties period (420–589), Mañjuśrī, the bodhisattva of wisdom, was often portrayed holding a *ruyi*.[34] Several *ruyi* from the Tang dynasty have survived; the earliest examples suggest that it had not yet become closely associated with Daoism. After the Tang, the *ruyi* became a symbol of good fortune and was often decorated with carvings of mushrooms of immortality (*lingzhi*). By the Ming dynasty the *ruyi* was firmly established as a symbol of erudition and longevity and had become an indispensable fashion accessory for both scholars and immortals. The *ruyi* was also sometimes used as a weapon for self-defense, but its primary role was as an auspicious object. As they serve no practical purpose today, the *ruyi* found in museums are often viewed as ornate backscratchers.

In the *Ruyijun zhuan*, a minister named Yang Zhirou protests when Wu Zetian changes the name of the year to Ruyi.[35] He does not think that naming a new reign period after such an object is appropriate. Little does he know that the term actually refers to Wu Zetian's appraisal of the even more inappropriate services rendered by Xue Aocao. As a *ruyi* is long and thin and can be said to resemble a phallus, it possesses strong erotic connotations. It is the perfect nickname for Xue Aocao. This object is both a symbol of his physical constitution and a reference to the perfect satisfaction he provides. When authors of later novels mention a *ruyi* it is often laden with erotic connotations; indeed, in some cases the *ruyi* evokes such a strong erotic response that it is used as a sexual implement.[36]

There is still more to the term "*ruyi*." One of the more significant connotations of this word is implicit in Huayang Sanren's preface to the *Ruyijun zhuan*. This preface stresses a political interpretation: Huayang Sanren thinks it is a moral drama about the status of the crown prince, the manner in which he is deposed, and his later reinstatement. He makes the unusual claim that Xue Aocao's remonstrations are so important for the state that they could be compared to those of Zhang Liang, one of the key advisers of the founding emperor of the Han dynasty, Liu Bang (256–195 B.C.).[37] Huayang Sanren does not pull his interpretation of the *Ruyijun zhuan* out of thin air. This work spends an inordinate amount of time discussing the status of the crown prince. Xue Aocao repeatedly reminds Wu Zetian that she should reinstate the legitimate crown prince, whom she had demoted to prince of Luling. Huayang Sanren notes there was a similar succession controversy at the beginning of the Han dynasty. A favorite concubine named Qi Ji persuaded Liu Bang that his son Crown Prince Liu Ying (207–189 B.C.) was weak.[38] She proposed that he be demoted and that her own son Zhaowang Ruyi be made crown prince instead.[39] Although Zhaowang Ruyi's father Liu Bang is not mentioned by name, it does contain two allusions to loyal ministers who protected him in moments of danger.[40] And his sadistic wife Empress Lü is mentioned by name.[41] When the *Ruyijun zhuan* is read in light of Huayang Sanren's preface, I think that the "*ruyi*" in the name of Zhaowang Ruyi is one more allusion that could be evoked by Xue Aocao's nickname.[42]

One of the historical references used to describe the character of Xue Aocao is both comic and grotesque. But even when the author describes a comic situation, disaster and political upheaval lurk just beneath the surface. When Xue Aocao is first presented to Wu Zetian, he is given a bath in the Huaqing Palace—which was not built until the year 723 and was not known by that name until 747, long after Wu Zetian had died. Furthermore, it should have been located on Mount Li, not on the palace grounds. The author has inserted this geographically impossible anachronism in order to compare Xue Aocao to the famous imperial consort Yang Guifei.[43] When she was first presented to Emperor Tang Xuanzong, she took a celebrated bath in the Huaqing Palace that aroused his animal spirits. The presentation of Xue Aocao to Wu Zetian possesses erotic potential, too, but it is ruined by the details: the spectacle of a young, obscure, submissive, and unusually well endowed male concubine being presented to the insatiable septuagenarian Wu Zetian is quite absurd. One could not hope to find a more unlikely romantic introduction in Chinese fiction. Furthermore—as in so many references to sensual encounters found in the historical record—this allusion calls to mind the danger an emperor courts when he allows his sensual impulses to cloud his judgment. Yang Guifei meant nothing but obsession and disaster to Tang Xuanzong; she disrupted the court, contributed to the country's instability, and was eventually strangled in a desperate attempt to placate a restless and insubordinate military.

There is more to the character of Xue Aocao than meets the eye. Or perhaps we should say that the connotations elicited by his name—and the allusions to the historical record that are used to describe the situations in which he finds himself—are more complicated than they might at first appear. Xue Aocao's character does not evolve out of a careful examination of his inner motivations; it is merely the occasion of the author's irony. Xue Aocao himself does not suspect what his various names connote. Nor does he appreciate the irony of the situations in which he unwittingly finds himself. Xue Aocao is, in short, the most perverse invention of a work that is devoted to perversity. Every aspect of his character is in direct contradiction to another. He is a handsome, clean, young virgin; yet his name means "filthy." He is like the fickle Xue Huaiyi; yet he is truly faithful and not even slightly jealous. He possesses the endowment of Lao Ai; yet he also possesses the moral sense of Di Renjie. He is the only man capable of providing perfect sexual satisfaction for Wu Zetian; yet he then attempts to castrate himself. He has risen to prominence in Wu Zetian's court for reasons that are not proper; yet he is the one who eventually convinces her it is improper to demote the legitimate crown prince. He is like Yang Guifei; yet instead of bringing the dynasty to the brink of destruction, he saves it. And while the story of Xue Aocao is sometimes considered the first graphic celebration of human sexuality in Chinese literature, the descriptions themselves are more offensive than erotic and many of the most sensual scenes are undermined by allusions that are bizarre, ironic, or, indeed, moralistic. Many readers, simultaneously attracted and repulsed by the graphic and unprecedented descriptions, are too preoccupied to notice that this work actually consists of a relentless series of irreconcilably absurd, and not particularly subtle, contradictions.

The Uses of Irony

Apart from its numerous references to historical texts, the *Ruyijun zhuan* presents brief quotations from classical texts like the *Book of Poetry*, the *Analects* of

Confucius, and the works of Mencius. These references are usually ironic, often inappropriate, and sometimes blasphemous. Many highlight the disparity between a character's conception of himself and what he actually does—a disparity most evident when his sensual nature has been stimulated.

Most of the brief historical allusions in the *Ruyijun zhuan* are left unexplained. One exception is yet another allusion to an improperly demoted crown prince. In one of the most implausible scenes of this implausible work, Wu Zetian mentions the demotion of a famous crown prince from antiquity in a curious attempt to describe the intensity of the love she feels for Xue Aocao. She refers to the story of Jin Xiangong—a bleak illustration of the disaster that meddling with the status of the legitimate crown prince can inflict on both family and state.[44] When Jin Xiangong's favorite concubine Li Ji gave birth to a son named Xiqi, Jin Xiangong's infatuation with her was such that he demoted his own son Crown Prince Shensheng and elevated Li Ji's child in his stead. In a gesture of heroic loyalty, Shensheng committed suicide so that the state might be spared the trauma of a succession controversy. Nevertheless his brothers were estranged from their father, the state was brought to the brink of civil war, and the illegitimate crown prince, Xiqi, was murdered. This, in short, is the story of one of the most destructive elevations of an illegitimate crown prince to be found in the annals of history. As Wu Zetian had just improperly demoted her own son, it is curious that she would cite a story which places her own actions in such an unfavorable light. Even more curious is her claim that this reference to Jin Xiangong illustrates her love for Xue Aocao. In the *Ruyijun zhuan,* there is a direct link between sexual infatuation and the attempt to elevate illegitimate heirs to the status of crown prince. Even the story of Lao Ai, whose physical constitution inspired Xue Aocao's, ended with his effort to promote illegitimate heirs to the status of crown prince. Reasonably we may suspect that Huayang Sanren recognized some, if not all, of these allusions and concluded that the issue of succession is indeed a central aspect of this work. Even if the reader is unable to accept his interpretation, one can see how he might have arrived at it.

The *Ruyijun zhuan* also contains ironic allusions to the *Shi jing*. About a month after Wu Zetian and Xue Aocao separate, she writes him a letter asking him to return. She misses him badly. The nights are now intolerably long and the moon illuminates her loneliness. In the spring they used to cavort in the garden, but now she drinks alone. Her life is a melancholy series of sighs irrigated by pitiful streams of tears. Perhaps he might return if she wrote him a letter describing the maudlin state into which she has sunk:

In the past we hurriedly bid farewell. To think about this carefully, it causes distressing sighs. Every time I drink by myself on a fine spring day, and sleep by myself on a moonlit night, I realize that, though surrounded by beauties, I lack a soul mate and glistening tears appear on my gown and table. The days gone by were so happy, today is so sad. The nights gone by were so short, tonight is so long. In the blink of an eye we were as far apart as heaven and earth, in no time at all we were suddenly as distant as Hu and Yue. What is man's allotted span that he should endure living separation? Today I have sent a letter to communicate that on a night in which there is a full moon, I am sending a small oxcart to convey you through the Gate of Expectant Spring so that you may stay a few days in order to complete our yet unfulfilled fate and furthermore make a tryst to be lovers in the life to come. Do not say "How could there not be other men?" I can see you if I stand on the tips of my toes. The purport of the works I have quoted is such that I need say no more.[45]

This letter is a series of stock descriptions of a lovelorn woman. To emphasize her fidelity while in this pitiful state, Wu Zetian incorporates three lines from *Shi jing* love poems. When she ponders her separation from Xue Aocao she says: "To think about this carefully, it causes distressing sighs."[46] The first half of this line is from a poem describing the sorrow of a faithful wife who has been separated from her husband. At first it appears to be a glimmer of sophistication in a letter that otherwise fails to rise above the level of bathos. But there is more to it than that.

Although Wu Zetian uses this line to describe the kind of sorrow she feels when contemplating her last encounter with Xue Aocao, the reader may recall that their last encounter was hardly reminiscent of a *Shi jing* love poem. Their final meeting was not a pastel portrait but a garish eruption of emotions so intense that the participants were driven to desperate lengths to express them. Wu Zetian could not endure the pain caused by Xue Aocao's imminent departure. The only way she could express it was to inflict pain herself. But she did not have in mind the lover's pinch which hurts and is desired: she burned incense on their sexual organs in a masochistic ritual and then instructed Xue Aocao to reenact every sexual position they had ever tried. Xue Aocao, ever the obedient subject, reenacted each position no fewer than ten times. It took them the entire night to complete this arduous task. As this is the first graphic description of masochistic sex found in Chinese literature — and the most excessive display of carnal endurance found in a work devoted to excess — I think the educated reader is meant to conclude that Wu Zetian's choice of a line from a demure *Shi jing* love poem to describe their final encounter does not exactly capture its most memorable aspects.[47]

Wu Zetian's audacity knows no bounds. If anyone were capable of making such a comparison at this juncture it would be Wu Zetian: if a murderess could become the reincarnation of Maitreya, an insatiable octogenarian masochist could become an icon of connubial fidelity. But is that the point of this passage? Despite Wu Zetian's audacity, perhaps she has actually persuaded herself that this is how she feels. In the *Ruyijun zhuan,* whenever her sensual urges are excited she becomes a fool. In this instance her sentimental identification with the most faithful of women in traditional Chinese poetry concisely portrays how her passions have led her into a state of delusion.

Near the end of her letter, Wu Zetian incorporates two more lines from *Shi jing* love poems. Coquettishly she anticipates that Xue Aocao might resist her request when she says: "Do not say 'How could there not be other men?' I can see you if I stand on the tips of my toes."[48] The first half of this line appears three times in the *Shi jing;* the last half is found once; both phrases are traditionally used to describe a loyal wife lamenting her husband's absence. These fragments do not make much sense if the reader does not recognize that they come from the *Shi jing.* Indeed, Wu Zetian alerts Xue Aocao to the significance of the quoted material when she concludes: "The purport of the works I have quoted is such that I need say no more." She thinks she has made herself perfectly clear. But has she?

This is a rare case in which the author explicitly calls attention to his methods. But while Wu Zetian mentions that her letter contains significant quoted material, she does not identify her sources or explain what these quotations mean. And by claiming that their purpose should be obvious, she is conversely sowing the seed of doubt: the reader is being encouraged to compare her words to her actions. What she thinks, what Xue Aocao thinks, and what the implied narrator expects the reader to think at this point are three very different propositions.

At the end of the letter, Wu Zetian says: "Do not say 'How could there not be other men?'" Again she is identifying with a loyal wife in a *Shi jing* love poem. This line describes a wife's anticipation of the incredulity her husband might express when she informs him that she has indeed remained faithful, even though they have been separated for an extended period of time. Wu Zetian's reference to a *Shi jing* love poem at this juncture, while it may convey the intensity of the love she feels for Xue Aocao, does not tell the whole story. Though her letter is perhaps legally accurate, she does not volunteer information. Indeed, right before she wrote this letter she did have a relationship with the Zhang brothers that was not appropriate—particularly if she wishes to compare her fidelity to some of the most devoted women in Chinese poetry. After Xue Aocao left and the wounds caused by the burning of incense on her sexual organs had healed, Wu Zetian slept with both of the Zhang brothers. She regretted her infidelity only to the extent that they were not capable of gratifying her sexual appetites. The Zhang brothers were both handsome and attentive, and they had entertained the empress for many years. But she now requires the perfect physical satisfaction that only Xue Aocao is capable of providing. She is lonely because she is not content to spend her time with men who do not measure up. She is faithful by default. Her concept of fidelity bears an unmistakable resemblance to frustration and boredom. If Wu Zetian had found a lover whose qualifications surpassed those of Xue Aocao, she would not have been quoting ancient love poems at this juncture.

Xue Aocao weeps when he reads Wu Zetian's letter. He writes a response, sighs, and sums up the situation as follows: "If I enter the palace again I will certainly never leave. When you see an opportunity you should seize it and not wait an entire day, isn't that right?"[49] Wu Zetian summarizes her understanding of the situation with three lines from the *Shi jing* that are scarcely reminiscent of her conduct. Xue Aocao does not appear to have perceived the irony in her quotations. But even if he does, he follows her lead and quotes a famous line from the *Xici zhuan* (Great commentary to the Book of Changes) which summarizes his situation in a manner that is also quite incongruous: "When you see an opportunity you should seize it and not wait an entire day." Like Wu Zetian's allusions to the *Shi jing*, this line must be placed in the proper context:

> The Master said: To know the seeds, that is divine indeed. In his association with those above him, the superior man does not flatter. In his association with those beneath him, he is not arrogant. For he knows the seeds. The seeds are the first imperceptible beginning of movement, the first trace of good fortune (or misfortune) that shows itself. The superior man perceives the seeds and immediately takes action. He does not wait even a whole day.[50]

By the end of the *Ruyijun zhuan* one might almost expect Xue Aocao to appreciate traditional Confucian descriptions of the superior man. His relationship with Wu Zetian is not modeled on such a description, but things are never what they seem in the *Ruyijun zhuan*. Like the superior man of this passage, Xue Aocao has indeed refrained from flattering his superiors; he is in fact the only lover Wu Zetian ever had who did not do so. He has also refrained from acting in an arrogant fashion, although it is an occupational hazard to which many of Wu Zetian's other lovers had proved themselves susceptible. But Xue Aocao is not like her other lovers. In one sense, a very degraded sense indeed, he really is a superior man. He does persuade her to reinstate the legitimate crown prince, and he does resist her attempts to corrupt him utterly, but his virtues are perilously close to what should normally be considered vices. Even if he is the only one capable of persuading the empress to act in a moral fashion, his is not an example that others should follow. His story seems to portray the desperate measures to which ministers must resort when a dynasty has sunk to such depravity. In a world in which virtues are barely distinguishable from vices, the pursuit of virtue may scarcely be worth the effort.

Let me end my examination of the *Ruyijun zhuan*'s use of quoted material with a brief example that is simultaneously erudite, weird, and obscene. Near the end of the story, Wu Zetian and Xue Aocao attempt to express the apotheosis of their love by mechanically completing an aspect of their physical relationship that had remained unfulfilled. As Wu Zetian writhes in discomfort, Xue Aocao remarks: "I'm slowly getting to the best part." This is a proverbial expression that has been attributed to the famous Jin-dynasty (265-420) painter Gu Kaizhi (c. 344-c. 406).[51] He is said to have uttered it when asked why he always ate sugarcane from the top to the bottom: "Whenever Gu Kaizhi ate sugar cane he always proceeded from the tip to the root. Some people found this peculiar. He said: 'I'm slowly getting to the best part.'"[52] The author of the *Ruyijun zhuan* appears to have known the provenance of this expression and includes it at this point for its unusual connotations: as Xue Aocao himself remarks, he is working his way from the tip to the root; he is also getting to the best part. Like other quotations found in scenes that might otherwise seem pregnant with erotic possibilities, this one distracts the reader's attention instead of fortifying it. It is the kind of bizarre observation that is almost never found in lascivious works whose sole purpose is to excite the animal spirits of the reader.

The notes to my translation of the *Ruyijun zhuan* in Part Two contain many more references to the historical record and Confucian classics. Many of the especially significant ones clearly allude to famous works, but others are sometimes exceptionally brief—so brief that the reader might not always agree they are actually quotations. In some instances, skepticism is not unwarranted. Yet I have chosen to examine even the most brief and obscure references because Huang Xun, the possible author of the *Ruyijun zhuan*, can write in a very cryptic fashion indeed.

7

Preface, Postscript, and Colophon

But virtue, as it never will be moved,
Though lewdness court it in a shape of heaven,
So lust, though to a radiant angel linked,
Will sate itself in a celestial bed
And prey on garbage.

—Shakespeare, *Hamlet* I. v

The preface to the *Ruyijun zhuan* was written by a man whose pen name was Huayang Sanren. Scholars have concluded that it was written between 1514 and 1754 by a contemporary of the author, by a precocious hermit of the seventeenth century, by an anonymous Japanese author of the eighteenth century, or even, perhaps, by the author himself.[1] While there is no shortage of candidate authors and dates of composition, the preface itself has attracted little attention. Scarcely a word has been written about its contents, its style, or its relation to the work it purports to introduce.[2] And yet a careful examination of this preface might very well lead to the identification of the person who wrote it.

Preface

While Wu Zetian's lover Xue Aocao is not destitute of personal merit and has happily discovered a manner in which he can gratify his appetites while ministering to the feeble moral sense of his sovereign, it is not proper to compare his rude intrigues to the glorious career of Zhang Liang, one of the most artful statesmen of the Han dynasty. Yet this is precisely what the author of this preface does. But instead of provoking heated debate, his audacity has been greeted with cold indifference: the same scholars who express such a keen interest in the identity of its author do not even mention his ridiculous conclusions. Before addressing questions of authorship and date of composition, therefore, we should first examine the preface itself.

The preface alleges that Xue Aocao has stumbled upon a situation in which even the stratagems of Zhang Liang would have been to no avail. As Zhang Liang's resourcefulness was legendary, this is a remarkable assertion. Qi Ji, one of Emperor Liu Bang's favorite concubines, had persuaded him that his son Crown Prince Liu Ying was weak, effeminate, and not worthy to succeed him. Her own son Zhaowang Ruyi, she said, deserved to be made crown prince in his stead. But she made the fatal mistake of overestimating the stamina of Liu Bang's infatuation and underestimating the licentious fury of her rival Empress Lü. Upon learning of Qi Ji's plot, Empress Lü solicited the advice of Zhang Liang, a trusted adviser who had already rescued the dynasty on more than one occasion. This challenge was an acute test of his political acumen, as Qi Ji had succeeded in persuading the emperor to admit what he already knew in his heart to be true: his son the crown prince was conspicuously deficient in the personal attributes that Liu Bang valued most. As this was also clear to Zhang Liang, he chose to say nothing rather than engage in empty sophistry. Instead he devised an elegant scheme to convince the emperor that deposing the crown prince without sufficient reason would not enjoy the support of his subjects. He persuaded the "four whitebeards" to emerge from their lofty seclusion and appear in the company of the crown prince; as Liu Bang held the four whitebeards in great esteem, their appearance with the crown prince made the thought of deposing him unimaginable. Although Zhang Liang had thwarted the elevation of an illegitimate crown prince with a silence more eloquent than words, it would not take long for Liu Bang's heirs to reap a bloody harvest once the seeds of discord had been sown. And Qi Ji would at length discover that her artless foray into politics was not productive of the most salutary of consequences.

Upon the death of the emperor, Empress Lü's son was indeed invested with the imperial yellow. But her irritated sense of justice did not permit her to let the elevation of her son pass without further comment. She found it necessary to acquaint her vanquished rival with her displeasure in a manner that was consistent with the cruel genius of a monster. She began by poisoning Zhaowang Ruyi. She then proceeded to amputate Qi Ji's hands and feet, gouge out her eyes, burn her ears, tear out her tongue, and throw her mangled yet living remains in a privy. Empress Lü had now been elevated above the necessity of dissimulating her appetite for revenge, which she gratified with inflexible pertinacity. Then she cheerfully observed that she had turned the emperor's favorite into a "human pig." After this pig had become accustomed to foraging for putrid sustenance in its melancholy new environment, Empress Lü summoned her son to behold the horrific spectacle. At first he could not perceive who, or what, was before him. But upon learning that it was his father's favorite concubine, he burst into tears, fell ill, and was unable to rise from bed for over a year. At length he concluded that he could never rule over all under heaven if he allowed his own mother to act in such an inhuman fashion. Not even the consumption of a perilous quantity of aphrodisiacs could revive his drooping spirits. Before long he refused, or perhaps was unable, to govern. Upon his death, Empress Lü usurped the power if not the official title of the new emperor and improperly bestowed feudal princedoms upon members of her own clan. But when her ten thousand years were about to expire she became apprehensive for the fate of her posterity. Her apprehensions were but too well justified, for the revenge she had exacted on the emperor's former favorite would at length be visited upon her own clan. After she died, every man, woman, and child in the realm who bore the surname Lü was exterminated.[3] While Zhang Liang had saved the legitimate crown prince from his enemies, no one could save the young man from his own pusillanimous constitution.

The author of the preface to the *Ruyijun zhuan* is not entirely mistaken when he compares the tale of Wu Zetian to the story of Liu Bang and Empress Lü. Both stories portray the mischief caused to the state when the stimulation of a ruler's sensual nature leads to an attempt to demote a legitimate crown prince. But the succession controversy instigated by Liu Bang's concubine was not as desperate as the one provoked by Wu Zetian. While Liu Bang was seduced into having doubts about his legitimate successor, Wu Zetian usurps the throne and subverts the established order. And even when Liu Bang's duty to the state had been clouded by seductive appeals, he still proved susceptible to traditional methods of moral remonstration. Wu Zetian, by contrast, came to find such remonstrations obnoxious, and the few ministers who dared to criticize her in public were fortunate to pay with their careers when they did not pay with their heads. Under such circumstances her astonished ministers discovered they had no choice but to countenance the irregular methods of Xue Aocao, an object of contempt whose methods had nevertheless proved far more effective than theirs.

If the preface were meant to be nothing but an insincere apology for the graphic detail found in this work, it seems unlikely that its author would have betrayed a familiarity with some of its more subtle rhetorical techniques. If it were meant to be nothing but a feeble excuse, it would probably have resembled the postscript. While we will examine the postscript in more detail near the end of this chapter, at this point it is instructive to note how sharply its tone and contents differ from those of the preface. The postscript is an exercise in affectation. To say that the language of this work is "polished and uniquely colorful" is to reduce its capacity to shock and offend. To say that it is "more pleasurable by far" than earlier erotic works is to ignore that the sensuality in this work inexorably leads to excess, pain, and a profound sense of loss. Nor does the postscript betray any special understanding of this work's rhetorical techniques or the serious subject that lurks just beneath its lewd exterior. Instead it compares the *Ruyijun zhuan* to texts that it quite conspicuously fails to mention. While the *Han Wudi neizhuan* and the *Zhao Feiyan waizhuan* did influence its subject and setting, as noted in Chapter 2, it is significant that rather than referring to these two famous erotic texts, the *Ruyijun zhuan* instead incorporates dozens of allusions to some of the most unerotic passages to be found in the Confucian classics—a fact of which the author of the postscript appears to be blissfully ignorant.

The preface, like the work itself, does not refer to earlier erotic literature. Instead it incorporates brief quotations from the *Shi jing* and the *Yi jing,* texts quoted in the novella as well. And instead of coyly alluding to its "colorful language," it asserts that although this work is told in an offensive fashion, it may still serve as an admonitory example. As the author of the preface refers to relevant succession controversies and to two classical texts in a manner consistent with the way they are quoted in the novella itself, there is reason to suspect that he might have been aware of the author's purpose and appreciated the unusual manner in which he chose to express it.

And then there are the quotations. It is significant that the brief reference to the *Shi jing* found at the very beginning of the preface, "It is the story of the inner chamber," is from a poem traditionally interpreted as criticism of sexual misconduct.[4] It is not difficult to imagine why Huayang Sanren chose this allusion. The reference to the *Yi jing* found in the preface is identified as such, and Huayang Sanren uses it to summarize his point. He avers that even Zhang Liang's masterful stratagems would have failed to persuade a sovereign like Wu Zetian to behave herself. In the *Yi jing,* the line "simply handed in through a window" (*na yue zi you*) describes a dangerous situation in which regular methods of exhortation are inappropriate or impracticable.[5] Huayang Sanren might have appreciated Richard Wilhelm's interpretation of the traditional commentaries to this line:

> In times of danger ceremonious forms are dropped. What matters most is sincerity. Although as a rule it is customary for an official to present certain introductory gifts and recommendations before he is appointed, here everything is simplified to the utmost. The gifts are insignificant, there is no one to sponsor him, he introduces himself; yet all this need not be humiliating if only there is the honest intention of mutual help in danger. . . . The window is the place through which light enters the room. If in difficult times we want to enlighten someone, we must begin with that which is in itself lucid and proceed quite simply from that point on.[6]

Huayang Sanren asserts that "Mr. Aocao used this method." Though Xue Aocao appears to have been sincere, surely his methods were not what the commentators to the *Yi jing* had in mind when they contemplated breaches of ceremony and etiquette that might be unavoidable. Yet even if Xue Aocao's efforts are not unequivocally virtuous, he does possess an intrepid moral sense that helps to compensate for his rude methods.

Who Was Huayang Sanren?

Wang Rumei argues that Huayang Sanren is an alias for a Ming loyalist named Wu Gongchen (c. 1610–c. 1662, *juren* 1636).[7] If he is correct—and I think he is—the date "*jiaxu*" of the preface refers to the year 1634.

Huayang Sanren is listed as the compiler of the early-seventeenth-century work *Yuanyang zhen* (A needle for embroidering mandarin ducks), a collection of four short works of fiction that depict the melancholy decay of the late Ming dynasty.[8] It is not known whether Huayang Sanren wrote the *Yuanyang zhen,* edited the work of others, or merely compiled it. In any event, it describes the geography and customs of localities with which Wu Gongchen would have been intimately familiar.[9] Two poems by Wu Gongchen are found in an early Qing (1644–1911) compilation of poems written by Ming loyalists.[10] His *hao* is listed as Huayang Sanren, and he is said to have died on Mount Mao. Part of the range of Mount Mao contains the Huayang grotto; this locality is also known as Mount Huayang. Wu Gongchen's pen name appears to be a reference to this region. As Wang Rumei notes, Mount Huayang is often associated with hermits and religious figures who have renounced society. There are many famous examples, and some of their unsociable appellations are almost homophonous with that of Huayang Sanren.[11] Wu Gongchen's apparent affinity for the life of a recluse does, however, seem curious because his preface to the *Yuanyang zhen* argues that active engagement with society is necessary in order to cure it of its manifest ills. It seems that Wu Gongchen would have viewed the withdrawal from society as ineffective if not immoral.

But when Huayang Sanren's pen name is interpreted in light of Wu Gongchen's life and writings, we see that it is meant to suggest, not a hermit who has withdrawn from the world, but a world that is incapable of appreciating moral individuals like himself. Wu Gongchen flatters himself that he did not withdraw from the world; the world had withdrawn from him. He does not refer to himself as a *shanren,* or mountain man; he styles himself a *sanren,* a term that in this case describes a person whose talents have not been properly appreciated by society.[12] And this is a central point of the *Yuanyang zhen:* scholars who should have been selected for government service, because of the moral virtues they had acquired after years of laborious study, instead find that their refined scruples are no match for the raw ambition of a new class of merchants who, however unlettered, are fluent in the practical arts of bribery and extortion. After the fall of the Ming, Wu Gongchen finds himself on Mount Huayang. But as he writes at the end of one of his poems, there is no escaping the tumult that doomed the Ming: "Even if there were a peach blossom utopia stretching for thousands of *li,* there would still not be a place to avoid the wind and the waves."[13] While Wu Gongchen has chosen a pen name that superficially resembles the appellation of a hermit, the active commitment to moral action he describes in his prefaces suggests that he is the type of recluse who would rather have been an official.

Other Candidates

Although Wang Rumei has amassed considerable evidence to support his argument that Huayang Sanren is probably a pen name of Wu Gongchen, some have questioned his conclusions. Others have offered conflicting explanations.

The author of the preface to the *Siwuxie huibao* edition of the *Ruyijun zhuan* is skeptical of Wang Rumei's conclusions.[14] If the preface was written in 1634, Wu Gongchen would have been about twenty-four years old at the time—too young to have chosen the pen name of a recluse. Besides, he would have been too busy preparing for the imperial examinations to have written such a preface. These speculations are based on an imperfect understanding of the meaning of the pen name Huayang Sanren. And even if Wu Gongchen had been deeply immersed in study during autumn of the year 1634, is it not possible that after a long and doubtless edifying night spent memorizing Zhu Xi's commentary to the Four Books, he might have found the time to read a short, controversial work and write a few lines about it?

Another theory has been proposed by Liu Hui. He speculates that the date "*jiaxu*" in the preface to the *Ruyijun zhuan* may refer to the year 1514; he adds that it "definitely" could not refer to the year 1574.[15] The source of his confidence is hard to ascertain, however, as he provides no credible evidence to support either speculation. Instead he embarks on a curious attempt to date the work itself. He notes that the *Ruyijun zhuan* is one of nine works mentioned in the preface to the *Jin Ping Mei* and that some of these works date to the Chenghua (1465–1488) and Hongzhi (1488–1506) reign periods and are also mentioned in the *Baichuan shuzhi* (Catalog of the hundred streams) by Gao Ru (fl. sixteenth century).[16] Liu Hui notes that some of these works are listed in approximate chronological order, and indeed some of them are. As the *Ruyijun zhuan* is mentioned next to last in this list, he surmises that it must have been "printed" during the Zhengde reign period (1506–1522). The *Ruyijun zhuan* is not, of course, mentioned in the *Baichuan shuzhi;* but even if it were, the preface of this work is dated 1540. And the earliest extant edition of the *Jin Ping Mei* was published in 1618 or shortly thereafter, although it appears to have circulated in manuscript form for some time before it was published. (Apparently the earliest printed edition of the *Ruyijun zhuan* was published in Japan in 1763, although it doubtless circulated in manuscript form for some time as well.) In any event, the fact that the *Ruyijun zhuan* is mentioned in the preface of a novel that was first published in 1618—and is not mentioned in a catalog of books whose preface is dated 1540—is not convincing evidence that the *Ruyijun zhuan* or its preface was printed between the years 1506 and 1522.

But there is a more serious defect in this analysis: it is based on a false premise. Liu Hui assumes that the preface, the work itself, and the postscript were all written at approximately the same time, an assumption that is simply not substantiated. The *Ruyijun zhuan* was quoted extensively in many works soon after it was written, as can be seen in the notes to my critical edition in Part Two of this book. Although quotations from the *Ruyijun zhuan* are quite common, I cannot find a single line of Huayang Sanren's preface referred to in any way during the sixteenth century. While this fact alone does not prove that this preface does not date to the early sixteenth century, it is an important piece of circumstantial evidence—particularly when one considers the wide range of works that quoted the *Ruyijun zhuan* and even copied lengthy passages from it verbatim.

Ōta Tatsuo and Iida Yoshirō do not believe that the preface to the *Ruyijun zhuan* dates to the sixteenth century. They contend that Wang Rumei's conclusions are "bold speculations." Yet they are not averse to engaging in some rather adventuresome speculations themselves.[17] As the colophon to the Japanese edition of the *Ruyijun zhuan* is dated 1763, they argue that a logical way to date the preface is to assume that its "*jiaxu*" date refers to 1754—an assumption which takes for granted the very question that is in dispute. As the simple logic of their method is not capable of telling them anything else, they conclude that Huayang Sanren must have been the pen name of an unidentified and anonymous Japanese author who lived during the eighteenth century.[18] While the authors of this theory claim that its simplicity is one of its strong points, it might be observed that it is so simple that it is not supported by any evidence. Nor is it clear why the adherents of this theory do not even mention the contents of the preface. To conclude that it was probably written by an unnamed person about whom absolutely nothing is known—based on a two-character date that could refer to the year 1514 or to any number of other dates as easily as it could refer to the year 1754—is indistinguishable from simply admitting that they have no idea who wrote it.

The process of dating the preface should be based on an examination of the text itself and an investigation into the life and works of anyone said to have written it. It is, for example, significant that the pen name Huayang

Sanren is also associated with at least two other prefaces which assert that in dangerous times irregular methods are necessary to cure a society of its ills—a conclusion similar to that of the preface of the *Ruyijun zhuan*. His introduction to the second story of the *Yuanyang zhen* also contains a brief but significant quotation from the *Ruyijun zhuan* suggesting he knew of this work and was capable of perceiving its subtle irony.

Huayang Sanren's Preface to the Yuanyang zhen

Huayang Sanren's preface to the *Yuanyang zhen* is, by turns, a historical anecdote, a Buddhist metaphor, a fanciful explanation of traditional Chinese medicine, and an encomium on the morally persuasive powers of fiction:[19]

> 醫王活國、先工針砭、後理湯劑。迨針砭失傳、湯劑始得自專爲功。然湯劑灌輸肺腑、針砭攻刺膏肓。世未有不知膏肓之愈于肺腑也。世人黑海狂瀾、滔天障日、總泛濫名利 二 關。智者盜名盜利。患者死名死利。甚有盜之而死、甚有盜之而生、甚有盜之出生入死、甚有盜之轉死回生、搏挽空輪、撐持色界、突[20]奧于玄扃絳府、而曰:膏之下肓之上。[21]是扁鵲 之望而卻走者也。古德 拈一 詩云: 鴛鴦 繡出 從君看、不把金針度與人。[22]道人不惜和 盤托出、痛下頂門毒棒。此針非彼針、其救度一 也。使世 知千針萬針、針針相投。一 針兩針、針針見血。上拔梯緣、下焚數[23]宅。二 童子環而向泣: 斯世有瘳乎?
>
> 獨醒道人漫識于蚓天齋。[24]

To treat the king and save the life of the country, at first stone acupuncture needles were implemented, and later liquid prescriptions were devised. When [the art of using] stone acupuncture needles was no longer transmitted, liquid prescriptions first began to be used exclusively. But liquid prescriptions are poured into the *feifu* [region between the lungs and abdomen while] stone acupuncture needles prick the *gaohuang* [region between the heart and diaphragm].[25] Nobody in this world does not know that the *gaohuang* is more vital than the *feifu*. People in this bitter ocean of turbulent waves that fill the heavens and occlude the sun eventually drift to the two passes of fame and fortune. Those who are clever steal fame and steal fortune. Those who are infected die for fame and die for fortune. There are even those who steal them and die; there are even those who steal them and live; there are even those who steal them, flourish, and then die; there are even those who steal them and transform death into life, grasp at the wheel of emptiness, and hold fast to the ephemeral world [that is] profoundly secluded beyond the mysterious gate of the crimson district [that is, the region around the heart], or as it has been described: "under the heart and above the diaphragm."[26] This [ability to treat illnesses infecting this region] was a goal that Bian Que did not attain.[27] An ancient worthy wrote a poem on adhering to the One that says: "Once the mandarin ducks have been embroidered, you may enjoy them as you will, but do not pass the golden needle to anyone."[28] I am not unwilling to be completely explicit, to strike the top of the head forcefully with a merciless club.[29] This needle [of fiction] is not that needle [of acupuncture], yet the manner in which they liberate is one and the same.[30] Let the world know that of a thousand needles or ten thousand needles, every needle will hit its mark; one needle, two needles, every needle will see blood. Above, the ladder has been removed; below, the dwellings of the pulse are burned.[31] The two children wander in circles and sob to each other: "Can this world be cured?"[32]

Casually written by the only sober man of the Way in the Earthworm Heaven Studio

In traditional Chinese medicine the term "*gaohuang*" refers to an area beneath the heart and above the diaphragm. As liquid medications cannot reach this spot and acupuncture needles cannot penetrate it, illnesses that infect this region are incurable. The locus classicus of this term is a famous passage in the *Zuo zhuan*.[33] In 581 B.C. a duke fell gravely ill and dreamed that his illness had assumed the likeness of two small boys. The boys knew that a skilled physician would be summoned so they repaired to the *gaohuang* region where all attempts to eradicate them would prove futile. When the physician learned that the illness had infected this region, he informed the duke that he knew of no way to treat it, and the duke soon died. The two children who wander in circles at the end of this preface are an allusion to this passage.

To Huayang Sanren, this allusion is a metaphor for the mortal illness that infects the society in which he lives. He wrote the preface to the *Yuanyang zhen* after the Ming dynasty had fallen and the traditional means of acquiring fame and fortune, an education in the Confucian classics, had been supplanted by what he regarded as the petty pursuit of business and profit. Not only were unlettered commoners becoming obscenely rich, but scholars who had mastered the Confucian classics—and had thereby acquired the personal virtue that only such studies were thought capable of inculcating—were no longer appreciated by the government. Most of the *Yuanyang zhen* describes melancholy variations on this theme: the first story tells the tale of a poor scholar who endures years of lonely tribulation while society, which would have benefited from his wisdom and virtue, is content to remain depraved and ignorant; the second story describes the pitiful fate of another poor scholar who suffers at the hands of corrupt and incompetent officials; the third story details the exasperating successes of a rich and uneducated merchant who is constitutionally incapable of perceiving his own vulgarity;

the final story laments another petty merchant's preoccupation with the pursuit of wealth.

Huayang Sanren suggests that the traditional methods used to treat serious illnesses in the past have been lost forever. Moreover, society has become so ill that even the old methods, had they survived, might still have proved ineffective. In his day, the pursuit of fame and fortune is equivalent to an illness that infects the region between the *gao* and the *huang*. Even though this disease is usually fatal, he hopes that under these desperate circumstances the bold application of the golden needle of fiction might succeed where all other treatments have failed. A golden needle has many connotations: it is another name for an acupuncture needle; it is a traditional Buddhist metaphor for the key to a problem; and it figuratively describes the techniques of art. Huayang Sanren makes use of all of these meanings—in fact, they are all contained in the title of this work: *A Needle for Embroidering Mandarin Ducks*. In the *Yuanyang zhen*, Huayang Sanren employs a golden needle to embroider a pair of mandarin ducks, a work of art that he assumes will delight the reader. But the needle itself, the way in which his art is produced, is not as important as the final result: Huayang Sanren intends to employ the moral power latent in fiction to address his sick society. Thus as he prepares to wield this metaphorical needle, the two small boys wander in circles and sob. Unlike the story in the *Zuo zhuan*, they now fear they are vulnerable.

Huayang Sanren's view of his role in society is suggested by the way he signs the preface: "Casually written by the only sober man of the Way in the Earthworm Heaven Studio." This is an allusion to a story in Mencius that describes a man who is honest and self-reliant to a fault. When this man's brother obtains wealth in a manner that violates his highly refined morals, he finds that he can no longer live with him. At length his moral sense develops in such a fashion that, upon learning that a goose his mother prepared for a meal one day had been provided by his brother, he vomits in a display of ostentatious scrupulosity. Mencius, unimpressed by such regurgitations of virtue, concludes that "pushed to the utmost limits, his way of life would only be possible if he were an earthworm."[34] By naming his studio the "Earthworm Heaven Studio," Wu Gongchen describes an uncompromising yet perfectly useless manifestation of virtue that was, perhaps, not in short supply after the Ming dynasty had fallen and many members of its official class refused to serve the new regime. The line of poetry quoted in the preface to the *Yuanyang zhen*, "Once the mandarin ducks have been embroidered, you may enjoy them as you will, but do not pass the golden needle to anyone," was in fact thought to have been written by a loyalist who refused to serve a new dynasty after the old one had fallen.[35]

Huayang Sanren's claim that fiction has unique persuasive powers was often made during the late Ming. Editors like Feng Menglong (1574-1646) describe fiction as an enterprise whose purpose is to warn society of the ills that afflict it. This is evident in the titles of three of his short-story collections: *Yushi mingyan* (Illustrious words to instruct the world), *Jingshi tongyan* (Comprehensive words to admonish the world), and *Xingshi hengyan* (Lasting words to awaken the world).[36] To Feng Menglong and many others, fiction had become an instrument for discussing, diagnosing, and even treating the ills that had insinuated themselves into all levels of society during the late Ming.

The Fiction of Huayang Sanren

It is not easy to find fault with Wang Rumei's conclusion that Wu Gongchen is probably the author of the preface to the *Ruyijun zhuan*. Certainly his analysis of Wu Gongchen's career (or lack of one) and his examination of historical sources mentioning Wu are more persuasive than arguments with less stringent evidentiary standards. Although Wang Rumei seems to have identified the author of the preface, he does not compare the text of the *Ruyijun zhuan* to the *Yuanyang zhen*. Such a comparison nevertheless suggests that the author of the latter was quite familiar with the former: the *Yuanyang zhen* briefly alludes to the *Ruyijun zhuan* on one occasion in a manner suggesting that Wu Gongchen, like the author of the preface, perceived the irony of the *Ruyijun zhuan* and could indeed have viewed it as a moral work.[37]

The preface to the second story of the *Yuanyang zhen* describes the corruption of the central government. Thievery had become endemic, Wu Gongchen protests, for hunger and destitution had driven otherwise honest citizens to desperate lengths. Not only was the government incapable of addressing such problems, but it was in the habit of selecting officials according to criteria that undermined the completion of their official duties.[38] This had become a conspicuous problem during the late Ming, and it is also a central theme of the *Ruyijun zhuan*.

The preface to the second story of the *Yuanyang zhen* repeats only one fragment of a sentence from the *Ruyijun zhuan,* but it is an important one: "I have known many men."[39] This is part of a line spoken by Wu Zetian when she first beholds the endowment of her new lover Xue Aocao. Although I have already discussed this passage in the introduction, I have not come close to explaining its full significance:

> The empress held it fast in both hands as if she had just received a treasure and said: "How monumental! It is not of this world. I have known many men, but there has never been one like this. In the past, Wang Yifu had a chowry with a handle of white jade; it was uniquely transparent and lustrous. For this reason I name it 'chowry handle': the ultimate of beauty."[40]

In the preface to the second story of the *Yuanyang zhen*, Wu Gongchen had exactly this appraisal of Xue Aocao in mind as he makes precisely the opposite point: when a government official is confronted with a superior human specimen who is not acting in a moral fashion, he should stop and teach, whatever the consequences. In this preface an honest government official named Lu Ji (261–303) finds himself in this situation.[41] Instead of shirking his responsibility, he bravely remonstrates with a bandit leader named Dai Yuan who is, in fact, committing armed robbery:[42]

> I have known many men, but as I observe your appearance and manner, it is a pity that such a giant should be mired in this path. Why not abandon it, study some books, nurture a scholarly calling, do some work for the court, and then you would not be wasting your great endowment?[43]

As the story goes, Lu Ji was a high official traveling to the capital by boat, but one day it was commandeered by bandits. The leader of the bandits, Dai Yuan, had always led a life of crime. Now he stood on the bank of the river and directed everyone under his command to execute his orders with dispatch. Lu Ji was fascinated with Dai Yuan's criminal efficiency. Indeed he was so struck by his imposing stature and natural leadership abilities that he placed his own life in jeopardy, confronted Dai Yuan, and said: "Your talent is such, and yet you still commit robbery?"[44] Dai Yuan had never heard of the difference between right and wrong. Upon hearing Lu Ji's remarks, he broke down in an epiphany of moral compunction and wept and abandoned the life of crime. Lu Ji took him under his wing, provided for his education, and eventually recommended him to the court. Dai Yuan proved worthy of Lu Ji's recommendation and at length became a general who served the state with great distinction.

By choosing the story of Lu Ji, the author has not only selected an official whose method of appraising human talent is conspicuously more sensible than that of Wu Zetian; he has selected a contemporary of Wang Yan whose biography is in the *Jin shu*. And while it appears that the author consulted one of the versions of this story that is found in the *Jin shu* and the *Shishuo xinyu*, there is a crucial difference: he also includes a brief line that occurs in the *Ruyijun zhuan* but not in the original versions of this story.[45] Moreover, the language used to describe Dai Yuan is more reminiscent of Wu Zetian's appraisal of Xue Aocao than the descriptions of him in the *Jin shu* and *Shishuo xinyu*. As Huayang Sanren was a connoisseur of improbable moral tales, no doubt he was attracted to the story of Xue Aocao. While the story of Xue Aocao is perhaps even more implausible than the story of Dai Yuan, Huayang Sanren argues that he was faithful to the state and his irregular remonstrations, while obscene, were nevertheless effective.

As well, the author of the *Ruyijun zhuan,* in turn, appears to have found the line "I have known many men, but there has never been one like this" in the biography of the famous Tang minister and historian Fang Xuanling (578-648).[46] Fang Xuanling was known for his literary abilities when he was but a teenager; he was also famous for his precocious criticism of Emperor Sui Yangdi's immorality. When he passed the *jinshi* examination at the tender age of eighteen, an official remarked:

> I have known many men, but I have never seen a man like this. He will surely become a man of great accomplishment. I only regret that I will not see him leap from the valley straight into the clouds.[47]

It is an inflexible maxim of the *Ruyijun zhuan* that whenever Wu Zetian quotes a classical text, its transmission through her lewd intelligence inexorably renders it absurd or obscene—and this example is both. Some might find it sacrilegious that a line used to describe a famous Tang official known for his probity could be used by Wu Zetian to describe a new lover.

The author of the *Ruyijun zhuan* almost certainly had the biography of Fang Xuanling in mind as he composed Wu Zetian's first impression of Xue Aocao. And it is probably no coincidence that Fang Xuanling is the author of the *Jin shu*—the history containing the story of Wang Yan's chowry handle that is mentioned in the very next line. When the *Yuanyang zhen* and its prefaces are compared to the *Ruyijun zhuan,* it is not unreasonable to take Huayang Sanren at his word when he claims that Xue Aocao is a loyal subject who, in the most difficult of situations, acts in a controversial yet moral fashion. While there is reason to suspect that the author of the *Yuanyang zhen* might have found the graphic descriptions in the *Ruyijun zhuan* excessive, his preface to this brief work is as serious as the work itself.[48]

Postscript and Colophon

The postscript and the preface to the *Ruyijun zhuan* have little in common. While Huayang Sanren knows quite a bit about this work, the author of the postscript betrays no special understanding. The postscript is little more than an advertisement for the supposedly erotic parts of the novella—probably because it was written by the Japanese publisher himself.

Ōta Tatsuo and Iida Yoshirō argue that Yanagi Hyakusei, the name attached to the postscript, was the pen name of Ogawa Hikokurō, the proprietor of a bookstore located in Nihonbashi from 1727 to 1784.[49] The postscript mentions that its author "published it in my shop in order to provide a topic of conversation for the inquisitive." As this Ogawa Hikokurō dates the colophon "the thirteenth year of the Hōryaku reign period," or 1763, it is assumed that the *kanoe tatsu* date of the postscript is 1760. The title page of this Japanese edition of the *Ruyijun zhuan* also states that it was published in the Eastern Capital by the publishing house Seihikaku; Ōta and Iida contend this is another reference to the bookstore run by Ogawa Hikokurō in Tokyo. The calligrapher who copied the preface to the *Ruyijun zhuan* and styled himself the "Eremite of the Portal of Pander," or something like that, also hailed from the Eastern Capital; most likely he too was associated with this bookstore. In any event, it does not appear that the author of the preface was also the calligrapher, as two lines of the preface were transposed and it is difficult to make sense of it as written.

Clearly the author of the postscript regards the *Ruyijun zhuan* as a dirty little book that might make him some money. He does not reveal that he knows anything about its rhetorical techniques. He emphasizes what he calls its "pleasurable" character—a characterization ill suited to a work containing so many grotesque, ironic, and lewd descriptions whose purpose seems to be to shock and disgust the reader, not gratify his sensual appetites.

Dating the Text of the *Ruyijun zhuan*

Evidence suggests that the preface to the *Ruyijun zhuan* was written in 1634, that the postscript was written in 1760, and that the colophon was written in 1763. But dating the text itself is a much more speculative endeavor.

As we have seen, the earliest work to mention the *Ruyijun zhuan* was the *Dushu yide* by Huang Xun. The preface to this work is dated 1562; but as Huang Xun probably died in 1540, his appraisal of this work could not, of course, have been written after that date. In Chapter 4 I examine his life and works in some detail and discuss evidence that leads me to believe that he himself might well have been the author of the *Ruyijun zhuan*. Moreover, an analysis of the relationships between the text, Huang Xun's appraisal of it, and a poem he wrote about Wu Zetian's lovers suggests that he might have written this work before he passed the *jinshi* examination in 1529. And if the speculations presented in Chapter 6 are accurate and the *Ruyijun zhuan* does indeed allude to the Great Ritual Debate that occurred at the beginning of the reign of the Jiajing emperor (r. 1522–1567), it could not have been written before approximately 1521. The text of the *Ruyijun zhuan* would thus appear to have been written sometime between 1521 and 1529. But the only thing we can say with certainty is that it was written before Huang Xun died in about 1540.

8

Later Works

The most wonderful things are brought about in many
instances by means the most absurd and ridiculous; in the
most ridiculous modes; and, apparently, by the most
contemptible instruments.

—Edmund Burke, *Reflections on the Revolution in France,* p. 154

Contemporaries recognized that the *Ruyijun zhuan* was, if nothing else, a novel creation for Chinese literature: a unique combination of history and fiction that described sexual relations in weird and unprecedented detail. Quite a few authors paid it the dubious compliment of copying its most licentious passages straight into their own works. And until the *Jin Ping Mei* was published approximately ninety years later, easily eclipsing it in terms of size, sophistication, and importance, the *Ruyijun zhuan* was the most influential work of its kind. There can be little doubt that it left a permanent mark—some might say an indelible stain—on Chinese literature.

Although the *Ruyijun zhuan* is most famous for its novel descriptions, it undermines many of them with references to the classics and standard histories. There is reason to suspect that its earliest extant appraisals, the "Du *Ruyijun zhuan*" and the preface of 1634, appreciate this aspect, but few other texts take its ironic references seriously. Nevertheless, the examination of such works is still useful: a comparison of the passages they copy demonstrates that the earliest extant edition of the *Ruyijun zhuan,* printed in Japan in 1763, is probably quite close to the original manuscript that was most likely written during the 1520s.

And it is just as useful to consider the parts that were cut. With few exceptions, later works that quote the *Ruyijun zhuan,* even works that copy most of the text verbatim, almost always cut its references to the classics, its condensed yet accurate portrayal of Tang history, and its historical poetry. Virtually every work eliminates all traces of Xue Aocao's moral remonstrations. Later authors found that they interfered with the description of sex. When such passages are cut, the descriptions are not only placed in a context that is much more conducive to flights of carnal fancy, but their meaning is ineluctably transformed. They become pornographic in a way they could not have been otherwise. In Bakhtin's terms, a dialogical work that contains many divergent voices becomes a monological one in which voices that express regret, doubt, disgust, and even outrage are silenced, leaving only the monotonous, depraved spectacle that these voices scoffed at in such a subtle fashion.

In this chapter I examine four works that copy significant passages from the *Ruyijun zhuan:* the *Wu Zhao zhuan* (Story of Empress Wu Zhao [Wu Zetian]), the *Nongqing kuaishi,* the *Sui Tang liangchao shizhuan* (Historical record of the Sui and Tang dynasties), and the *Jin Ping Mei.*[1] Each of these works tells us something different about the text of the *Ruyijun zhuan* and its influence on later works. The author of the *Jin Ping Mei* not only copies many of its descriptions, but he seems to be one of the few authors to appreciate its sophisticated rhetorical technique. The *Sui Tang liangchao shizhuan* is significant because it copies a few pages from the *Ruyijun zhuan* almost verbatim. The *Wu Zhao zhuan* and the *Nongqing kuaishi* are significant because of the manner in which they simplify the text of the *Ruyijun zhuan.* Like many erotic works, they delete its ironic allusions not because they think their readers will not be able to understand them but precisely because they are afraid they might.

The *Wu Zhao zhuan*

The *Wu Zhao zhuan* is a short abridgment of the *Ruyijun zhuan* found in a work whose preface is dated 1587. Whereas the *Ruyijun zhuan* describes Tang history in surprisingly accurate detail before introducing the first graphic descriptions at about its midpoint, the *Wu Zhao zhuan* is little more than a stupid series of sexual acts. It gets right to the point in the first few lines: as the ever more feeble exertions of Xue Huaiyi, Zhang Yizhi, and Zhang Changzong fail to satisfy the empress' insatiable desire, Xue Aocao is introduced in an attempt to provide perfect satisfaction. A deluge of graphic description follows. In a few pages both the plot and the protagonists are exhausted and the story ends as abruptly as it began.

The *Wu Zhao zhuan* deletes almost all of the history found in the original text. Emperors Taizong and Gaozong are not mentioned. More than forty other characters are omitted. All of the poetry is cut. The elaborate descriptions of clothing and meals are cut. There is no discussion of politics, of the demotion or reinstatement of the legitimate crown prince, or of virtuous ministers. Xue Aocao, quite content to accommodate his sovereign as she sinks

insensibly into a state of lewd oblivion, does not utter a single line of remonstration. And almost all of the obvious ironic allusions have been deleted—
such as the reference to Wang Yan's chowry handle and the story of Jin
Xiangong's infatuation with his concubine Li Ji.[2] The author simply copies
the *Ruyijun zhuan*'s most graphic descriptions and deletes everything that
might detract from them. Yet even a crude little work like the *Wu Zhao zhuan*
can tell us something important about the *Ruyijun zhuan*. If nothing else, it
reminds the reader that when everything but the most graphic parts are cut,
there is, in fact, scarcely anything left.[3]

The *Nongqing kuaishi*

The *Nongqing kuaishi* is a Qing-dynasty novel published in 1712 that expands
the length of the *Ruyijun zhuan* severalfold.[4] One of the few texts that quotes
the bulk of the earlier work, it includes most of its poetry, letters, and memorials to the throne. It does not omit references to famous ministers and other
historical figures, and in some instances it purports to relate a more complete
version of incidents that are barely mentioned in the original. The story of Wu
Zetian's lover and spiritual adviser Xue Huaiyi, for example, now occupies a
few pages and is embellished with additional details found in standard
sources like the *Zizhi tongjian*. But in the *Nongqing kuaishi* the description of
sex is more important than the history, and the empress' relations with figures
like Xue Huaiyi are described in the kind of graphic detail that, in the original, is reserved for her relationship with Xue Aocao. While the *Nongqing
kuaishi* contains a great deal of history, most of the sophisticated references
to the historical record found in the *Ruyijun zhuan* are deleted. Thus the
reader is delivered from the irksome task of having to think very hard about
what he is reading. He is also protected from allusions that might cause him
to question his own response to descriptions that, in the original, are meant
to be obscene.

And in the *Nongqing kuaishi* the role of Wu Zetian is completely transformed. As we have seen, the earliest extant appraisal of the *Ruyijun zhuan* argues, in the manner of Zhu Xi's *Zizhi tongjian gangmu*, that Wu Zetian is not
to blame for the moral degradation of the Tang dynasty.[5] The author of the
Nongqing kuaishi, however, blames Wu Zetian for everything. From the very
beginning she harbors the intention of usurping the throne. It is her idea that
she should be made an imperial consort.[6] She is the one who seduces two feckless emperors. And she is the one who must ultimately be blamed for the corruption and decline of the Tang. While standard historical sources do not say
that Wu Zetian engaged in improper intimate contact, those who find their

descriptions evasive, incomplete, misleading, or even maddening will find what they are looking for in the pages of the *Nongqing kuaishi:* most of the graphic descriptions in the *Ruyijun zhuan* are copied straight into this novel. Wu Zetian is lewdly indolent yet brutally vicious, devoted to hedonism yet destitute of taste, preoccupied with her posterity yet constitutionally incapable of acting accordingly. While some considered her one of the most resourceful politicians of her age, anything could be imputed to an empress who was so perversely erratic, who was crafty enough to usurp the throne, and who was brazen enough to transform her murderous past into proof that she was a reincarnation of the Buddhist messiah—only in the end to turn her reign into a profane spectacle that would disgust her rivals, exasperate her allies, and excite the indignation of historians.

Xue Aocao's role is transformed as well. In the *Ruyijun zhuan* many of his encounters with Wu Zetian are attended by his inappropriate moral remonstrations; these are all deleted. At the beginning of their relationship he does express, or affects to express, concern that his unworthy endowment might pollute the imperial constitution; but such scruples are rare and of short duration. He does not mention the improper demotion of the crown prince or the necessity of reinstating him. In contrast to other erotic novels that borrow from the *Ruyijun zhuan,* many of these remonstrations can still be found in the pages of the *Nongqing kuaishi*—but they have now been transferred to the mouths of worthy officials like Di Renjie. They are never allowed to intrude upon the lewd relationship between the empress and her favorite (who now appears incapable of even conceiving such sentiments). And while this novel contains a fair amount of history that is not found in the work which inspired it, its author does not come close to matching the standard of historical accuracy that was quite remarkably set by the author of the *Ruyijun zhuan.*[7]

One feature of the text of the *Nongqing kuaishi* deserves special mention: it ends with a historical poem about the Tang dynasty written by Zhu Xi.[8] As the author of this novel is not interested in the career of Wu Zetian except as it relates to her carnal appetites, an erudite poem of this sort seems out of place. Furthermore, as the author conspicuously disagrees with Zhu Xi's minority view that Wu Zetian's misbehavior is ultimately due to the immoral example set by Emperor Taizong, it does not make sense that he would end his novel with such a poem. And the poem as it is found in this novel contains several errors, so it seems unlikely that it was copied directly from the collected works of Zhu Xi.[9] I suspect that the author of the *Nongqing kuaishi* copied this poem from an edition of the *Ruyijun zhuan* that was more complete than the edition published in 1763. I say this because part of this very same poem was quoted almost two centuries earlier by Huang Xun in his "Du *Ruyijun zhuan.*" This is quite a coincidence—particularly as there is no evidence to suggest that the author of the *Nongqing kuaishi* knew of Huang Xun's appraisal or that he understood the provenance or true import of this poem. I therefore think that this poem by Zhu Xi was probably found near the end of the original text of the *Ruyijun zhuan* and was omitted in subsequent versions.

The *Sui Tang liangchao shizhuan*

The *Sui Tang liangchao shizhuan* is a long historical novel, consisting of 122 chapters, that was first published in 1619. It is very rare: a unique copy survives in the Sonkeikaku Bunko in Tokyo. It has never been reprinted—a fact that is unlikely to amaze anyone who has read it, as it is far from being the most compelling historical novel to relate the events of the Sui and Tang dynasties. So far as I am aware, no one has previously noted that the author of the *Sui Tang liangchao shizhuan* was quite familiar with the text of the *Ruyijun zhuan*. It is, in fact, one of the rare works containing extended verbatim quotations that are not graphically sexual in nature.[10] It also contains a few of its historical poems, all cited in the notes to my critical edition of the *Ruyijun zhuan* in Part Two.

There are two prefaces to this novel. The first, which has been described as inane, is attributed to Yang Shen (1488-1559); the second, assumed to be spurious, is attributed to Lin Han (1434-1519).[11] As the earliest extant edition of this novel was published in 1619, even if a version of it did date to the middle of the sixteenth century it is impossible to prove how close this later edition might have been to it. Hence it is impossible to date the text of the *Ruyijun zhuan* based on the occurrence of quotations found in this work. But the passages copied into the *Sui Tang liangchao shizhuan* at least suggest that the 1763 edition of the *Ruyijun zhuan* is probably quite similar to a version in circulation near the end of the sixteenth century.[12]

A poem found in the *Sui Tang liangchao shizhuan* and the *Nongqing kuaishi*—but not in the 1763 edition of the *Ruyijun zhuan*—deserves special attention. Like the poem by Zhu Xi that appears at the end of the *Nongqing kuaishi*, the occurrence of this poem in these two works suggests that it might have been contained in an earlier version of the *Ruyijun zhuan,* a speculation that appears more likely when we examine the text of the poem itself:

> Amidst the thirty-six peaks of Mount Wu,
>   there is a rendezvous of rain and clouds;
> The sordid conduct in the innermost chambers
>   is disseminated more widely each day.[13]
> A phoenix and her mate turn topsy-turvy,
>   their love in true harmony;
> A title is bestowed as he is gloriously invested
>   as the Lord of Perfect Satisfaction.[14]

The references to Mount Wu, clouds and rain, and phoenixes tumbling in amorous delight are all stock descriptions. The second line, however, contains a glimmer of sophistication. It incorporates a line from the *Shu jing* that casts an ominous shadow over the banal descriptions of love that surround it. The entire passage, of which the last line is quoted in this poem, is as follows:

> I have heard that the good man, doing good, finds the day insufficient, and that the evil man, doing evil, likewise finds the day insufficient. Now Show, the king of Shang, with strength pursues his lawless way. He has cast away the time-worn sires, and cultivates intimacies with wicked men. Dissolute, intemperate, reckless, oppressive, his ministers have become assimilated to him; and they form parties, and contract animosities, and depend on *the emperor's* power to exterminate one another. The innocent cry to Heaven. The odour of such a state is plainly felt on high.[15]

The last line of this passage, which Legge does not translate as literally as I have done, is used in this poem to condemn Wu Zetian's conduct. It is similar to other allusions to classical texts that are scattered throughout the *Ruyijun zhuan*. While the second line of this poem would still be condemnatory even if the reader did not recognize its provenance, the identification of its source makes the condemnation all the more censorious. It is indeed a central point of the *Ruyijun zhuan* that Wu Zetian is "dissolute, intemperate, reckless, [and] oppressive," that her "ministers have become assimilated" to her, that they "form parties, and contract animosities, and depend on *the emperor's* power to exterminate one another." Like so many other passages in the *Ruyijun zhuan*, this poem draws the reader's attention in opposite directions simultaneously: its descriptions of love, if that is what the licentious fury of Wu Zetian should be called, are often punctuated by erudite references designed to prevent the educated mind from insensibly dissolving into an erotic stupor. Authors who blindly copy passages from the *Ruyijun zhuan*, like the author of the *Sui Tang liangchao shizhuan*, never add allusions of this sort.[16] I therefore suspect that, like the poem by Zhu Xi at the end of the *Nongqing kuaishi*, this brief poem appeared in the original manuscript of the *Ruyijun zhuan*.

The *Jin Ping Mei*

At first glance, the *Ruyijun zhuan* and the *Jin Ping Mei* seem to have little in common. One barely amounts to forty-five pages and is written in condensed classical Chinese; the other is several thousand pages long and written in a subtly modulated vernacular. The *Ruyijun zhuan* has not been celebrated for the sophistication of its rhetorical technique; the *Jin Ping Mei,* by contrast, is widely considered one of the most stylistically advanced novels to have appeared in Chinese or perhaps any language. And while the *Jin Ping Mei* copies much of the graphic vocabulary coined by the author of the *Ruyijun zhuan,* one might assume that an occasional verbal parallel comprises the full extent of their relationship. Yet when we compare the rhetorical strategies of these two works, it appears that the *Ruyijun zhuan* not only inspired the *Jin Ping Mei*'s graphic descriptions but was also an unlikely example, perhaps even the source, of rhetorical techniques that were new to Chinese fiction and worthy of emulation.

The Sex

Patrick Hanan notes that the *Ruyijun zhuan* is one of the most significant sources of the *Jin Ping Mei*.[17] The *Jin Ping Mei* mentions the *Ruyijun zhuan* in its preface, and it cites Wu Zetian and Xue Aocao by name in chapter thirty-seven.[18] The erotic imagery employed by the two works and many of their sensuous situations are strikingly similar:

> A good many of the erotic situations . . . are also to be found in the short story. Both the parallel incidents quoted above take place out of doors, in the *Chin P'ing Mei's* case, by an arbour, and in the story's case, in a summer-house. There is an episode in each work in which the man begins to copulate with the woman while she is still in a state of drunken slumber. There is a scene in the story, and several in the *Chin P'ing Mei,* in which the practice of inflicting "love-burns" is described. The empress sees birds mating, and then thinks of her own situation; this is reminiscent of Chin-lien on several occasions. Furthermore, the main fact of the story's pornographic description, its *raison d'être,* is the size of Hsüeh Ao-ts'ao's genitals; it is precisely for this property that he has been recommended to the Court in the first place. The erotic passages in the story are largely occupied with the pleasure and pain which the empress has to endure. This is the same aspect of erotic description which is stressed in the *Chin P'ing Mei,* at least from the point in Chapter 49 at which Hsi-mên Ch'ing obtains the itinerant priest's magic medicine.[19]

The *Ruyijun zhuan*'s influence on the *Jin Ping Mei* is particularly evident in chapter twenty-seven, one of its more notorious chapters, whose second half is titled "Pan Jinlian Engages in a Drunken Orgy Under the Grape Arbor." In this chapter, Ximen Qing makes love to her with such sadistic ardor that she almost loses consciousness. This scene borrows heavily from the passage in the *Ruyijun zhuan* in which Xue Aocao's amorous enthusiasm almost causes the death of his sovereign and benefactress.[20]

When we compare the full text of the *Ruyijun zhuan* to the text of the *Jin Ping Mei,* it is clear that the latter regularly employs the vocabulary coined by the former. If even the slightest of linguistic parallels are included, about fifty quotations are used on almost eighty occasions; about a dozen of them are found clustered together in chapter twenty-seven. But the author of the *Jin Ping Mei* does not simply copy extended passages from the *Ruyijun zhuan;* even in chapter twenty-seven, the material he quotes comes from many different parts of the *Ruyijun zhuan.* And in only a few instances does he copy two or more consecutive phrases.

Another similarity between these two works is that their graphic descriptions, unlike those found in most other works reputed to be pornographic, are often interrupted by bizarre, irrelevant, and inappropriate materials. As noted in the introduction, the first graphic description in the *Ruyijun zhuan* occurs almost at its midpoint. It is the longest such description—it occupies about five pages—but it is interrupted with such regularity that one might almost forget that the empress and her lover are still locked in a carnal embrace.

One of the most notorious scenes in the *Ruyijun zhuan* that influenced equally notorious scenes in the *Jin Ping Mei* is the one in which Wu Zetian and Xue Aocao burn incense on their sexual organs to demonstrate their mutual devotion.[21] Wu Zetian explains her purpose to her ever more accommodating lover in the following fashion: "I hear that in love affairs among the people there is a custom of making a scar by burning incense on their private parts, a custom that has become a topic of conversation. Why should you and I not do this?"[22] Some modern commentators have noted in relation to this passage that sociological studies indicate it is not unusual for some people to remain sexually active until an advanced age; others have concluded that this passage in the *Ruyijun zhuan* could be viewed as a unique insight into sexual practices of the early sixteenth century. But the purpose of depicting Wu Zetian's dissolute desires in this work is not to celebrate the possibility of fulfilling senescent appetites or to describe the sometimes uncommon practices of the common folk.[23] Wu Zetian is at this juncture not only old; for the purposes of an erotic work, she is ancient. She is not only in her eighties; her hair and teeth are falling out. The author spares no repulsive detail. He does not describe Wu Zetian when she is a youthful beauty. He waits until she is as decrepit and corrupt as it is possible to imagine that an object of erotic description could be. This scene constitutes an extreme, sneering climax to what has already amounted to a most extreme work. By this point the intensity of Wu Zetian's emotional attachments has become mechanically proportional to the intensity and frequency of the physical acts in which she engages. Thus when she realizes that her relationship with Xue Aocao must finally come to an end, her unusually intense emotions are reduced to unusually intense sex.

While the author of the *Jin Ping Mei* copies much of the vocabulary found in this scene of inflamed passions, perhaps the manner in which Wu Zetian later recalls it is more important than the scene itself. As we noted earlier, the author of the *Ruyijun zhuan* subtly insinuates unidentified lines from *Shi jing* love poems into Wu Zetian's letter in order to depict the wide disparity between her beastliness and her sentimental conception of herself. This technique is also put to good use by the author of the *Jin Ping Mei* in many situations, most of which do not refer to sexual activity of any kind. Pan Jinlian in particular routinely sings of her tender, melancholic sentiments with a variety of popular songs that, like the materials quoted by Wu Zetian, are uniquely inappropriate to her present situation.

Pan Jinlian/Wu Zetian

While the characters of Pan Jinlian and Wu Zetian may not exemplify the heights to which the human spirit may aspire, the manner in which their carnal appetites are portrayed in the *Ruyijun zhuan* and the *Jin Ping Mei* is far from being destitute of artistic merit. And they have much in common. Both are stereotypes of the licentious concubine: Wu Zetian is said to have murdered her own child in order to incriminate a rival; Pan Jinlian murders the son of a rival wife in order to regain the affections of her fickle husband. And the mental states of both are portrayed with subtle allusions to poetry and song that are particularly ill suited to their violent natures. David Roy notes:

> The use the author makes of all this borrowed conventional material is neither careless nor accidental. One of the major themes of the narrative is the fatal consequences of self-deception. In passage after passage, beginning as early as the first chapter, P'an Chin-lien, whom the reader soon discovers to be a ruthless and depraved adulteress and murderer, is shown to identify herself almost completely with the personae of the sentimental popular lyrics that she sings, both to herself and to others. This is, therefore, on the one hand an economical and aesthetically effective way of demonstrating both the form and extent of P'an Chin-lien's self-deception, and on the other hand a telling exposure of the inadequacy of such traditional stereotypes to convey the complexity and problematic quality of human reality.[24]

Although this technique is not as readily apparent or artfully employed in the *Ruyijun zhuan* as in the *Jin Ping Mei,* suggestions of the latter's sophistication are scattered throughout the pages of the former. While the allusions uttered by Wu Zetian may be quite obscure and the reader must often identify them before he can determine their meaning, the ironic songs associated with Pan

Jinlian are more straightforward. One example is found in chapter eight: Pan Jinlian is, as usual, longing for Ximen Qing, whose roving eye is again spell-bound by another beauty. When she casts her red embroidered shoes in order to predict her fate—will he come to see her or not?—two songs testify to the delicacy of the sentiments that afflict her. One of them goes:

> Quietly taking down the bamboo blind,
> Leaving the door to creak,
> All I can do is lie underneath my quilt,
>   cursing his name.
> How can you care so much for "misty willows,"
> That you won't come to my place anymore?
> "My eyebrows have lost their color; who will
>   repaint them for me?"
> Before whose house has he tethered his horse
>   to the green willows?
> As for him,
> He is unfaithful to me;
> As for me,
> I am yearning for him.[25]

As Katherine Carlitz notes, loyalty and fortitude—hallmarks of lovesick maid-ens in popular Chinese verse—are not Pan Jinlian's most conspicuous vir-tues.[26] Lovesick creatures solemnly savor the bitter fruits of their pitiable condition; they are emotionally incapable of emulating the lewd genius with which Pan Jinlian wields her poisonous tongue. As soon as this song has been sung, Pan Jinlian manufactures a pretext so that she may better vent her spleen: she then savagely beats and lashes out at her own stepdaughter. Such a response to the pangs of unrequited love is not characteristic of the maiden of popular song submerged in a state of lonely torpor.

Another notable aspect of the *Ruyijun zhuan* is the role of its implied nar-rator and the manner in which ironic references to classical texts are incorpo-rated. Although a historian might employ the same allusions—indeed, many of the allusions found in this work are taken from the standard histories—the author of the *Ruyijun zhuan* alters the manner in which they function.[27] In the *Ruyijun zhuan* they are no longer the observations of an anonymous historical narrator: now they are spoken by the characters themselves. It is one thing for a historian to insert allusions into the biography of a historical figure. It is quite another for a writer of fiction to place the same allusion directly in the mouth of a central character who does not understand its implications—especially when the likes of Xue Aocao clearly do understand. When the implied narra-tor of the *Ruyijun zhuan* attempts to wipe his fingerprints off his most ironic ob-servations, for that is what he is doing, he makes the portrayal of the psychological states of his characters more complex and subject to a wider range of interpretation. His allusions, instead of functioning as summaries or preordained conclusions, must first be interpreted by other characters and then, in turn, by the reader. And the reader is clearly expected to note the incongruence between what is being said, who is saying it, the facts of the situation, and how other characters interpret the links between these elements. This is not how historical texts usually work.

If the rhetorical technique of the *Ruyijun zhuan* never rises to the level of sublimity found in the *Jin Ping Mei*, its author nevertheless subtly experiments with the historical materials he has copied into his novella and fashions a work of fiction whose techniques are very different from the texts he copies. I would be surprised if the author of the *Jin Ping Mei* did not think so too.

The *Ruyijun zhuan*'s Influence

The *Ruyijun zhuan* holds a unique position in the Chinese narrative tradition. It is a culmination of earlier pseudohistorical erotic works in the literary language, and it appeared just as much longer vernacular narratives began to develop. But what role did it play in the development of the Chinese novel? Apparently the author of the *Jin Ping Mei* is the only one who understood and improved upon the rhetorical techniques invented by the author of the *Ruyijun zhuan*. Virtually every other work influenced by the *Ruyijun zhuan* studiously ignores its most sophisticated techniques and copies only its descriptions of human sexuality. In this regard, the *Ruyijun zhuan* and the *Jin Ping Mei* are in a class by themselves.

9
The Moral

All criticism has its season, in which it lives, if it lives
at all, by a dazzle or minor radiance that cannot
be expected to last.

—Frank Kermode, "The Men on the Dump," p. 93

The last person who claimed to have perceived a moral in the *Ruyijun zhuan*—and had the temerity to put this opinion in writing—was Huayang Sanren. His preface of 1634 argues that this work illustrates, in an offensive fashion, a moral that is nevertheless worthy of consideration. His observations have not, however, gained many adherents over the past three and a half centuries. Indeed, they are ignored when they are not greeted with sneers of derision. How could a work that describes sexual promiscuity with such queer genius have anything to do with morality? The *Ruyijun zhuan* has instead become synonymous with everything that is vile. And its notoriety has stood what, in this instance, is a most dubious test of time. Few texts have attempted to erect such an ignominious monument to the licentious fury of Empress Wu Zetian. The *Ruyijun zhuan* is regarded, and rightly so, as the father of a new genre for Chinese fiction. Yet it can also be regarded as something of a victim of its own success. For at least the next century the vocabulary it coined was slavishly emulated by many authors who wrote what can only be called dirty books, few of which even pretend to aspire to the sophistication of the work that inspired them. The crudity of the *Ruyijun zhuan*'s degenerate posterity, with the conspicuous exception of the *Jin Ping Mei,* has merely obscured its original character. While the *Ruyijun zhuan* is perhaps the most influential work of its kind in the Chinese language, even its most strident critics have failed to demonstrate a familiarity with its rhetorical techniques or its use of historical texts.

A simple list of what was previously unknown about this work attests to the lack of serious scrutiny it has received. Its author was unknown—indeed, no one had even speculated in print as to his possible identity. Its time of composition was unknown. Its earliest appraisals, Huang Xun's "Du *Ruyijun zhuan*" and Huayang Sanren's preface of 1634, were not taken seriously and similarities between their rhetorical techniques and those employed by the *Ruyijun zhuan* were not noted. Nor was the history of the Tang dynasty that appears in the *Ruyijun zhuan* compared to standard historical sources. The existence of numerous quotations from the Confucian classics was not mentioned; nor was the sophistication with which they are employed. As its author was unidentified, its time of composition was unknown, and its meaning was left undetermined, little effort was made to compare its depiction of human desire to contemporary philosophical trends. The *Ruyijun zhuan* is one of those works that inspires strong opinions—the intensity of which, in my experience, stands in inverse proportion to the amount of effort the reader has put into it.

The close association between Huang Xun and the *Ruyijun zhuan* is one of the central discoveries of this book. A close analysis of his "Du *Ruyijun zhuan*" and a poem found near the end of his collected works titled "The Little Barbarian" reveals that Huang Xun knew much more about this work than could be expected of even the most assiduous reader. His intimate familiarity with the most arcane texts to which the *Ruyijun zhuan* alludes suggests that he might well be its author. When one reads the *Ruyijun zhuan* with Huang Xun's career in mind, everything contained in this work looks suspicious. The *Ruyijun zhuan*'s descriptions of sex are, of course, unlike previous depictions—not only more graphic but fundamentally different. The novella does not raise earlier descriptions found in poetry, drama, and short stories to a higher level. Traditional descriptions of sensuality and feminine beauty, such as those found in Han-dynasty *fu* poetry, invite the reader to entice himself. They rely on his complicity. In the *Ruyijun zhuan*, however, traditional descriptions of feminine beauty have lost their persuasive power. And to the central characters of the *Ruyijun zhuan*, desire has become a curiously quantifiable entity. The intensity of emotional attachments is directly related to the intensity and frequency of physical acts. When a relationship becomes more intimate, it is quite simply manifested by a new position or new technique.

Human desire has always been a central question of Chinese philosophy. Desire is the proper response of the disposition, which is the substance of nature, which is formed by heaven. Yet desire compromises reason and makes people misbehave. This is the ineluctable nature of human beings—weak and degenerate creatures who, left to their own devices and deprived of the wisdom imparted by ritual and education, would insensibly pursue their appetites until they led to their own destruction. But how seriously does the author of the *Ruyijun zhuan* view the regulation of human desire? Is he really interested in questions as ponderous as the disposition of the substance of nature, the proper response of the disposition, or the pursuit of what desire deems attainable? The answers to these questions are suggested by a remarkable little scene in which Wu Zetian spontaneously responds to the beauties of nature and, in her inimitably perverse fashion, alludes to a line from a famous classical text.

It is the first month of summer during the first year of the Shengli reign period, or 698. The rains have just ceased and the empress and her favorite are strolling through the rear garden hand in hand. In the midst of a grove of verdant willows she notes that secluded songbirds are mating with one another as they harmoniously warble their own names. But this is all the lewd empress can stand:

> Suddenly the empress' lecherous desires were aroused and she said with a sigh: "Even songbirds know the joy of mating with each other. Could it be that man is not the equal of a bird?"
>
> Quickly she ordered her female attendants to spread a cushioned comforter of Sichuan brocade in a secluded spot, then snickered as she said to Ao-cao: "You and I should today emulate the joy of the songbirds."[1]

The famous late-Ming-dynasty playwright Tang Xianzu (1550–1616) appreciated this unique scene. Indeed, he alludes to it at a crucial juncture of his *Mudan ting* (Peony pavilion), one of his most famous plays.[2] While this play is traditionally interpreted as a sensitive affirmation of untainted human sentiment, its young and innocent heroine Du Liniang quotes a line spoken by Wu Zetian at a particularly inopportune moment.[3] Her tutor, an insufferably dense pedant attempting to teach her the first poem found in the *Shijing*, emphasizes the traditional moral reading of this poem. But when his student contemplates the cry of the faithful birds, she inexplicably thinks about the physical aspects of love: "Could it be that man is not the equal of a bird?" Du Liniang's passions have just been stimulated by the beautiful spring scenery; she is planning to take a stroll through her rear garden; a willow tree figures prominently—all elements that parallel the scene in the *Ruyijun zhuan*. Du Liniang is even thinking of her future lover Liu Mengmei, whose surname means "willow."

It is not clear why Tang Xianzu places an observation of a degenerate empress in the mouth of what some consider the most innocent virgin of Chinese drama. But it is clear that he recognizes, as every educated reader of the day would have recognized, that this line—"Could it be that man is not the equal of a bird?"—is a line attributed to Confucius that is found, of all places, near the beginning of the *Daxue,* a text memorized by everyone who aspired to pass the imperial examinations.[4] In this passage Confucius too is interpreting a line of poetry found in the *Shi jing*:

> There is that little oriole, resting on a corner of the mound. The Master said: "When it rests, it knows where to rest. Is it possible that a man should not be equal to this bird?"[5]

It is, as ever, an inflexible maxim of the *Ruyijun zhuan* that every noble sentiment is rendered ludicrous or obscene when it enters Wu Zetian's consciousness. This line was originally the culmination of a parable of moderation. The little oriole knows when to stop, but humans do not. Confucius, a profound student of nature, laments that people are not always capable of emulating the natural moderation of even the most insignificant of creatures. But Wu Zetian is constitutionally incapable of moderating her lust. The contemplation of such a natural scene not only fails to elicit the proper response, it elicits its opposite; and after her lewd desires have been rekindled, there is no stopping them. Instead of heeding the wisdom of the portentous line that she herself quotes, she abandons herself yet again to the dictates of her ruling passion.

There can be no doubt that Huang Xun, if indeed he was the author of the *Ruyijun zhuan*, was intimately familiar with the provenance and significance of this line. Huang Xun had not only become intimately familiar with the *Daxue* during his preparations for the imperial examinations. He had also written a commentary to this work titled *Daxue yanyi fujian* (Superficial remarks on the *Daxue yanyi*).[6] Although this work appears to have been lost and we are not able to read what Huang Xun wrote about this line, we can be sure that the purpose of incorporating such an allusion was not to celebrate Wu Zetian's spontaneity. Even when her contemplations of nature give rise to an observation that is attributed to the most august of philosophers, she cannot help drawing the wrong conclusion. The incorporation of such an allusion, in such a manner, at such a time, in such a work, does not contribute to the creation of an erotic ambiance. Like so many other allusions scattered throughout the *Ruyijun zhuan*, it elicits in the mind of the educated reader a host of associations that sabotage such an atmosphere. There can be but little doubt that, in the estimation of the author of the *Ruyijun zhuan*, Wu Zetian is indeed not the equal of that bird.

PART TWO

Translation and Original Text

Annotated Translation

I have never seen anyone who loved virtue as much as sex.

Confucius, *Analects* 9.18

WRITTEN BY XU CHANGLING OF WUMEN[1]
The Story of Empress Wu Zetian's Lord of Perfect Satisfaction[2]
Eastern Capital, Seihikaku[3]

Preface to "The Lord of Perfect Satisfaction"

What is the *Ruyijun zhuan?* It is the story of Empress Wu Zetian's inner chamber.[4] Although it is told in an offensive manner, is it not still adequate to serve as an admonitory example? In the past, the fact that the four whitebeards assisted the crown prince and the fortunes of the Han were thereby made secure was really due to the efforts of the marquis of Liu.[5] As for the marquis of Liu, it can be said that he was faithful to the state. Empress Wu Zetian was violent beyond regulation and became more lecherous with each passing day. Even though she went so far as to depose the crown prince and usurp the throne, no one was able to rectify the situation. And the reinstatement of Zhong Zong was truly due to the efforts of Mr. Aocao.[6] Although he attained advancement through lascivious conduct, was he not also faithful to the state? At such a time, were the marquis of Liu to have worried about him and the four whitebeards to have fostered him, how could they have been effective? The *Book of Changes* says "simply handed in through a window"; Mr. Aocao used this method.[7] Viewing it in this fashion, even though

133

it is told in an offensive manner, is it not still sufficient to serve as an admonitory example?

Autumn of the year *jiaxu*.[8] Written by Huayang Sanren.[9]

Calligraphy by the Eremite of the Portal of Pander, Eastern Capital.[10]

The Story of Passion in the Boudoir

Empress Wu Zetian was the daughter of the commander in chief of Jing prefecture, Wu Shihuo; as a child her nickname was "Fair Flatterer."[11] When she reached the age of fourteen, the Erudite Emperor heard of her beauty and obtained her for the rear palace, bestowing upon her the title lady of talents.[12]

After much time had passed, the Erudite Emperor became ill. As crown prince, Gaozong attended upon him with liquid medications.[13] The Fair Flatterer waited to one side. Gaozong was delighted upon seeing her and wanted to have an affair, but he lacked the opportunity.[14] After a while Gaozong got up to go to the bathroom. The Fair Flatterer knelt as she served him with a golden pan of water. Gaozong playfully sprinkled her with the water and intoned:[15]

> Suddenly I recall on Mount Wu
>   that spirit in my dream;
> The road to Yang Terrace is obstructed,
>   and there is no entrée.[16]

The Fair Flatterer then matched his couplet and said:

> Before enjoying, behind the brocaded curtains,
>   a meeting of wind and clouds,
> I first bathe from the golden pan
>   in the rain and dew of imperial favor.[17]

Gaozong was ecstatic and led her to an assignation in a small, secluded chamber inside the palace where they were utterly entangled. When they were finished, the Fair Flatterer grasped the emperor's clothing and sobbed: "Although I am lowly, I have long served the emperor. By desiring to fulfill the passions of Your Majesty I have violated the regulation against illicit affairs. On the day when you become emperor, who knows where you will place me?"

Gaozong untied the nine-dragon mutton-lard jade belt hook he was wearing and gave it to her, saying: "Should the emperor die, you shall be elevated to empress." The Fair Flatterer kowtowed repeatedly and accepted it.[18]

After this time when they entered to wait upon the emperor's illness they often had secret relations.

The illness of the Erudite Emperor intensified. The Fair Flatterer was sent to Ganye Temple where her hair was shaved and she was made a nun. After Gaozong succeeded to the throne, he went to Ganye Temple to offer incense and secretly ordered the Fair Flatterer to let her hair grow.[19] When her hair was seven feet long she was conveyed to the palace and appointed lady of bright deportment of the left.[20]

After Miss Wu entered the Palace of Bright Deportment she competed with Empress Wang and Pure Consort Xiao for the emperor's favor.[21] At this time Miss Wu was thirty-two.[22] Sobbing, she told Gaozong: "Your Majesty occupies the throne. Do you not remember the memento of your jade belt?"[23]

Gaozong thought to himself that as Empress Wang and Pure Consort Xiao had both lost his favor, he intended to demote them and elevate another. The next morning as the emperor held court he summoned Zhangsun Wuji and asked: "Empress Wang does not have a son; Lady Wu of Bright Deportment does have a son.[24] I intend to demote the empress and promote a new empress. What is your opinion?"

Wuji did not dare speak.[25]

There was a close adviser named Chu Suiliang who said in remonstration: "Empress Wang was formally married to you.[26] When the deceased emperor neared death he grasped Your Majesty's hand and said to us: 'I have a good son and a good daughter-in-law. I entrust them both to you.' It is as if his words are still in my ears. I dare not forget them. Moreover, Empress Wang has never committed a transgression. On what basis would she be demoted? If Your Majesty must replace the empress, I humbly request that the new one be carefully selected from one of the famous families under heaven. Furthermore, Miss Wu served the deceased emperor and was dispatched to be a nun, something known by everyone. The ears and eyes of all under heaven cannot be covered. I have transgressed against Your Majesty. My offense merits death." He then removed his hat, kowtowed until his head bled, and said: "I return Your Majesty's ivory tablet of office and request permission to return to my fields and cottage."[27]

Empress Wu, who was hidden behind the standing screen and overheard this, then cried out: "Why don't you have this sharp-tongued bandit beaten to death?"[28]

Gaozong was furious and immediately had Chu Suiliang subjected to extreme torture and then commanded him to commit suicide. Zhangsun Wuji was demoted to commander in chief of Tan prefecture.[29] Later when an official historian read the historical record to this point he intoned a poem that said:

Despite all obstacles the emperor's loyal servant
    did not regard his own welfare;[30]
His direct remonstrances were truly
    in the manner of Bi Gan.[31]
The official tablet was returned on the imperial steps,
    in the end his heart was red-blooded;
His forehead kowtowed on the palace steps
    until the columns were red with blood.[32]
If the majestic phoenix lacks the heart
    to establish the ordinances of the state,[33]
Incestuous hinds will have something to say
    that may confuse the imperial intelligence.[34]
The present dynasty has generously instituted
    spring and autumn sacrifices in his honor,
Which for all eternity again make manifest
    his loyalty to the altars of earth and grain.[35]

Chu Suiliang was tortured and Zhangsun Wuji was demoted. The court was tied up like a sack and Miss Wu was fraudulently elevated to empress of bright deportment.[36]

At this time Wu Zhao arrogated and confounded the authority of the court, coming and going without regard for protocol.[37] She frequently joined Gaozong in the audience hall and he pampered and feared her. After this time all under heaven referred to them as the "two emperors."

Later, the emperor's eyes dried up and could not see clearly, and he was unable to attend to official business. When officials reported to the throne, the matter was often relegated to Empress Wu to decide.[38] The empress was intelligent of disposition and knowledgeable of events from ancient times to the present. She read literature and history widely, and all the matters that she decided satisfied the emperor's intentions.

Empress Wang and Pure Consort Xiao were framed and punished for crimes they did not commit. Each was flogged with a cane two hundred times, their hands and feet were cut off, and they were tossed into a wine crock. Their steeped bones were fished out and buried in the rear garden.[39] Her father Wu Shihuo was named the duke of Zhou and in addition was enfeoffed as the prince of Taiyuan.[40]

When Gaozong died, Crown Prince Li Zhe ascended the throne.[41] His temple name was Zhongzong. After the emperor had ascended the throne, Concubine Wei was elevated to empress.[42] Before a year had passed Li Zhe was demoted to prince of Luling by Empress Wu, who promoted her next son Li Dan to emperor.[43] After being a puppet for seven years he was then demoted to crown prince.[44] At this time she elevated herself to Empress Wu Zetian, constructed seven temples to the Wu family, and then dispatched a general to attack and kill the prince of Langya, Li Chong, and the prince of

Yue, Li Zhen.[45] Troops were again mobilized to massacre the Tang imperial family. She named herself Wu Zhao and was acclaimed as the August Emperor and Great Saint Zetian of the Golden Wheel.[46] The dynasty was named Zhou and her nephew Wu Sansi was elevated to crown prince.[47]

Prime Minister Di Renjie calmly remonstrated and said: "Your Majesty has elevated Crown Prince Wu. I sincerely fear that after Your Majesty's ten thousand years have expired and your nephew has become the son of heaven, it will be difficult for him to worship an aunt in the ancestral temple."[48]

Upon hearing this petition the empress immediately elevated Li Dan to emperor and changed his surname to Wu.[49] After this time people gradually developed the intention of overthrowing the Zhou dynasty and restoring the Tang. A poem says:

> One sentence calls back
>   the dream of the parrot;
> Snatched back from the highest heavens
>   he returns as a young phoenix.[50]

Empress Wu was herself aware that the hearts of the people were rebellious and that her personal conduct was not correct, but she slandered people by accusing them of disloyalty. The number executed could not be fully enumerated. She was inwardly lascivious and outwardly ruthless. Later an official historian chanted a poem to deride her. The poem says:

> With the crow of the hen
>   the purple palace was empty;
> It took but the fallen flowers from a few trees
>   and the ground was covered with red.[51]
> In that age the Fair Flatterer
>   resided in the Northern Palace;
> One morning the son of heaven
>   occupied the Eastern Palace.[52]
> The chambers of the empress engendered disorder
>   because of the Zhang brothers;
> The restoration of the state itself
>   depended upon Duke Di.[53]
> Before the events of man take shape
>   their fate is preordained;
> To this day is remembered
>   the story of Li Chunfeng.[54]

After the empress negligently followed the counsels of the Zhang brothers, she used the ruthless officials Lai Junchen, Suo Yuanli, and others and implemented unjust methods; none of the officials dared to offer remonstrations.[55] Fortunately, Di Renjie was at court and could be relied upon to maintain the government. But alas, a single man named Xue was presented to the throne and the sovereign gave free rein to her desires and indulged in lechery. The story scarcely bears retelling . . .

Originally, at the end of the Sui dynasty, Xue Ju mobilized troops in Longxi and arrogated the title "Emperor of the Qin."[56] His second son Renyue followed his elder brother Rengao and was defeated at Qianshui, surrendered, and was put to death in Changan.[57] Before this, Rengao's beloved concubine Suji committed adultery with a servant boy.[58] As soon as she became pregnant, Rengao angrily cast her out at Liushui. When his troops were defeated, she alone escaped.

She gave birth to a son and named it Yufeng. After he grew up he was fond of reading the military treatises of Sun Zi and Wu Qi.[59] In response to the difficulties of his family he did not pursue an official career and chose a wife from Cao. They had two sons; the elder was Xue Boying, the second was Xue Aocao. During the third year of the Yifeng reign period of Gaozong, Yufeng died.[60] Aocao and his elder brother moved to Changan. In the first year of the Yonglong reign period, Boying died.[61]

Aocao traveled to Luoyang and took up residence there. At this time Aocao was eighteen. He was more than seven feet tall and had a beautiful white face; his eyebrows and eyes were fine and bright; he was powerful, unusually fleet of foot, and widely versed in the classics and histories; and he excelled at the arts of calligraphy, painting, playing the *qin,* and the game of go. He could drink more than a peck of wine without getting drunk, thereby leading to many excursions in revelry. And his meaty implement was exceptionally great and unusually virile. All the ne'er-do-wells of the village knew of it, and every time they encountered Aocao drinking alcohol sought to get a peek at it and have a good laugh.

Aocao said: "I have been afflicted by this thing. I still have not experienced sexual relations. Whenever it has been aroused there is no place to employ it. This is a cause of distress to me. How can it be a fit subject for your mirth?"

They coerced him until he pulled out his meaty implement. When it became engorged its veins stood out and its head had four or five sunken furrows. When it became excited, the flesh in the furrows protruded like a snail oozing forth. From the tip to the base the sinews vigorously rippled like an earthworm. From head to tail it had more than twenty striations. It was red and lustrous, clear and unblemished. These characteristics were, no doubt, due to the fact that it had not yet been tainted by women. When the youths saw it they were all amazed and tested it by hanging a peck of grain from its head. It stayed erect with strength to spare. Everyone guffawed uncontrollably and fell into a heap.

From time to time they would accompany Aocao to houses of prostitution. When the inmates first saw this handsome youth who was proficient at singing songs and taking part in drinking games, everyone fell in love and yearned for him. But when they compelled him to reveal his meaty implement, everyone screamed and fled his presence. Among them was an experienced and lecherous one who by dint of a hundred stratagems guided him to the goal, but in the end he could not enter. After the fame of Aocao's meaty implement had spread, no one was willing to marry him. He sighed constantly and suffered from feelings of anguish.

At this time the empress was over sixty years old. Princess Qianjin recommended one Feng Xiaobao to the throne, and he received imperial favor.[62] Xiaobao had formerly been a mountebank who sold pharmaceuticals in the city of Changan. His meaty implement was very strong and stout; by applying aphrodisiacs he was able to copulate all night without getting tired. The empress loved him utterly. Claiming that he possessed technical skill, she shaved his hair and made him a Buddhist monk, changed his name to Huaiyi, from time to time summoned him into the palace to supervise construction, and thereupon fornicated with him. He was successively promoted to commander in chief and was enfeoffed as a duke of state.[63]

Afterward Huaiyi became wealthy and proud, kept many women on the outside, and also competed for favor with the imperial physician Shen Nanqiu.[64] In anger he burned the White Horse Temple and the Brilliant Hall.[65] The empress plotted with Princess Taiping and had strong women bludgeon him to death.[66] His corpse was conveyed back to the temple and it was fraudulently claimed that he had died of a sudden illness. Shen Nanqiu too received advancement due to his lecherous abilities. After much time had passed he could not overcome a disease of lust as his bone marrow was exhausted and he died.

At this time the empress was already seventy years old. But although she was of advanced age, her teeth and hair were not in decline and her ample flesh and attractive demeanor were just like those of a young woman. As a result of this cultivation her desires grew incandescent. Even veteran prostitutes and nymphomaniacs were not able to match her.

At this juncture, Zhang Changzong was recommended as a handsome youth who possessed a large meaty implement. He was summoned and, as expected, was captivating and beautiful. Changzong also recommended his fraternal cousin Yizhi as fair and possessed of capacities greater than his own.[67] When put to the test it proved to be true. These brothers both found favor, were promoted to the official positions of minister of the Bureau of Prisons and director of the Palace Library, and were enfeoffed as dukes of state.[68] Those in and out of the court feared them, calling Changzong Squire Six and

Yizhi Squire Five, furthermore saying that the countenance of Squire Six resembled a lotus blossom.[69]

During the first month of winter in the second year of the Tianshou reign period,[70] Empress Wu wanted to roam through the imperial garden with Yizhi and Changzong to take pleasure in the flowers. She promulgated an edict that said:

> Tomorrow morning I will roam the imperial garden;
> With great dispatch let spring be informed.
> The flowers must bloom overnight
> Without waiting for the morning zephyrs to blow.[71]

As soon as Empress Wu's decree had been issued, the next morning the one hundred flowers all bloomed. Today people call the tenth month "lesser spring" for this very reason. This also meant that heaven complied with Empress Wu's wish. A poem was chanted which said that Changzong had a body as fair as a flower and so forth. The poem said:

> After an audience with the Golden Wheel
>   they emerge from the palace gate;
> An edict is issued with fiery dispatch
>   commanding the warmth of spring.[72]
> Even if the flowers were replete with
>   a thousand varied hues,
> They would not match the lotus blossom
>   that resembled Squire Six.[73]

Also called the reincarnation of Wang Zijin, he was made to wear clothes decorated with bird feathers and ride a colorfully decorated wooden crane.[74] A man from the time wrote a poem that said:

> In the past he encountered Fuqiu Bo;
> Today he is like Ding Lingwei.[75]
> The palace attendant has talent and demeanor;
> But his name is not that of the archivist.[76]

Changzong and Yizhi would alternate evenings on duty. On evenings when they were off duty they usually abandoned themselves to mirthful drinking with beautiful women and would fornicate until dawn. When they copulated with the empress, their interest flagged and their virility frequently gave way, so that the passions of the empress were not fulfilled.

It was spring of the second year of the Zaichu reign period.[77] One day Empress Wu was meditating in the Garden of Harmonious Spring.[78] As she observed the serenity of the spring scenery and the profusion of scents and colors, fallen petals formed into piles and wafts of catkins cloaked her clothes.

Add to this birds on secluded perches warbling wildly, female and male meeting their match, and bees and butterflies rifling the flowers, wings overlapped above and below. In response to these surroundings her passions were aroused and she wanted to summon the likes of Changzong in order to bestow her favor, but fearing that their interest in her was depleted she inadvertently fell into deep thought and wept.

At this time the eunuch attendant Zong Jinqing ascended the steps and said: "What is Your Majesty thinking about today?[79] Could it not be that your beloved son the prince of Luling has long been separated from your presence?" Although Jinqing already knew the empress' intent, he said this intentionally in order to probe her.

The empress furiously replied: "Who made you say this? You're my family's old slave. How could you not know me?"

Jinqing kowtowed and begged to die, saying: "I do not wish to elude the executioner's axe.[80] I must dare to say something in addition."

The empress said: "Go ahead and say it. I won't hold it against you."

Jinqing said: "Your humble servant will presume to guess Your Majesty's sentiments. Is it not the case that the likes of Yizhi and Changzong are insufficient to meet Your Majesty's expectations?"

The empress snickered and said: "Yes. What a smart lad you are."

Jinqing said: "I observe that the likes of Yizhi and Changzong have reached the heights of wealth and distinction and yet they derisively say that Your Majesty is advanced in years. Only after they have been summoned several times do they comply with reluctance. They pretend to seek mutual pleasure with you, but their hearts are not in it. Therefore their energies are enfeebled and their strength impotent. They do not achieve consummate excitement but shrink halfway through. They are incapable of making Your Majesty obtain satisfaction. Instead I hear that in their outside residences they keep singing boys and dancing girls. Powder and mascara gather in droves. How then can they devote all their energies to Your Majesty?"

Upon hearing this statement the empress angrily cursed and said: "I have been betrayed by these lackeys. I thought there was a limit to their energy. I did not know they had relations with others. I'll dispose of them like a slab of meat on a table."[81]

Jinqing said: "Your Majesty, pray subdue your thunderous anger. The likes of these are not worth the trouble of staining the chopping block and headsman's axe. I have another suggestion. I hear that in the city of Loyang there is a handsome young man whose family name is Xue and given name is Aocao. This person is nearly thirty, his abilities and appearance are all that could be asked for, and furthermore his meaty implement is virile and strong. The likes of Yizhi and Changzong cannot match him. If Your Majesty were to issue an edict instructing me to summon him by imperial decree, he would certainly be able to satisfy the imperial passions and wait upon you eternally beside your table and mat."

The empress said: "Do you know this person?"

Jinqing said: "I do not know him but hear that young people from the same locality say: 'A hand cannot grasp it, a ruler cannot measure it. Its head resembles a snail, the body is like a skinned rabbit, and the sinews look like earthworms. Hang a peck of grain on it and it will not droop.'"

The empress leaned upon the standing screen and sighed: "No need to elaborate. I understand." Then she ordered the imperial treasury to provide two ingots of gold, one pair of white jade *bi*, four bolts of patterned brocade, and a covered carriage drawn by four horses.[82] She personally wrote the decree to Aocao. The decree said:

> In such intervals as occur while conducting the affairs of state there has long been an emptiness in the depths of my heart.[83] I have thought of obtaining a person of high moral standing with whom to converse and feast. I have heard that you entertain high aspirations and that your natural endowments are prodigious. I fervently wish to meet you to assuage my famished bosom. With regard to the further details, the emissary will be able to inform you fully. Do not obdurately maintain your purity as that would be a betrayal of my intentions.[84]

Jinqing received the decree and then, taking with him the gold and silk, paid a visit to Aocao. After a while he saw Aocao, and Aocao said: "My base qualifications pollute the imperial virtue. This is not appropriate for a subject. I dare not follow these orders."

Jinqing said: "If you do not wish to traverse the azure clouds to high official position, in the end you will find yourself in distress behind wretched village gates."

Aocao said: "There is an appropriate road to the azure clouds. To use a meaty implement as the stairway to advancement is assuredly disgraceful."

Jinqing whispered in his ear and said: "You can fly to the heights and ascend beyond heaven and earth. Furthermore you still have not experienced sexual relations. If not the current empress, who could accommodate you?"

Aocao had no alternative but to go. On the road he sighed and said: "The worthy should be able to progress because of their talents. What is the topic of today's examination?"

With flying speed Jinqing reported to the empress. The empress dispatched a series of eunuchs and attendants on horseback to hasten him on his way.[85] Upon arrival, Jinqing led Aocao into the rear palace to be presented. After paying obeisance he was instructed to sit. After the presentation of tea, the attendant concubines were instructed to lead him to a bath in the Chamber of Translucent Jade. They presented marrow unguent solution and bathed him, and furthermore shed their inner and outer garments in order to excite him. Aocao's meaty implement proudly exposed itself. The palace concubines covered their mouths and tittered. They withdrew saying: "Today the empress has found her man."

After the bath was completed he was dressed in a cloud-soaring crane-feather cape, girdled with a seven-treasure buckled belt, and capped with an ornately decorated emerald hat held in place by a raven sash. Upon inspection he was as elegant as an immortal. The empress was elated. Clapping her hands and saying, "An immortal has descended upon this place," she instructed the banquets office to prepare a repast.[86]

Jinqing sat with them in a threesome and, using large ruby lotus cups filled with grape wine from Western Liang prefecture, with both hands presented several rounds to Aocao. Just when Aocao wanted to start guzzling, the empress' desires were moved. Her countenance was slightly flushed, but certainly this was not because of the wine. With a twitch of her chin she instructed the attendants to arrange articles such as a soft quilt and delicate coverlet in the heated eastern chamber of the Huaqing Palace and ordered Jinqing to withdraw.[87]

The empress took Aocao by the hand, entered, and sat with him shoulder to shoulder. After a while two girl servants presented a golden pan of rose-perfumed water. The empress ordered them to leave and closed the golden phoenix door herself, bolting it with the nine-dragon crossbar. The imperial concubines strolled back and forth past the crack in the door in order to spy on them, and for this reason knew exactly what happened from beginning to end in great detail.

The empress washed her vagina with the rose-perfumed water and said to Aocao: "Jinqing says that you are still a virgin, that you have yet to experience sexual relations. Is this true?"

Aocao said: "I have been unfortunate. The body I have inherited is too large. I have stumbled along for several years, content to remain unmarried and alone. Today in complying with the imperial decree I do not know how to express my apprehension. I am of coarse constitution and unfit to minister to the imperial body. I request that the concubines first be instructed to look at it; based on whether the implement is acceptable or not, things should proceed or stop. If Your Majesty were to see it suddenly I am afraid it would startle the imperial passions and I would be deserving of ten thousand deaths."

Empress Wu said: "So your meaty implement is as large as that? I should examine it personally." She then had him remove his undergarments. The empress scrutinized it for a long time, observed it dangling with magnificent length, and said in sport: "Do not be hesitant and cause needless suffering."

At the time Aocao's meaty implement was still limp. The empress guided it with her hand and fiddled with it, then said: "The organ you have reared is as large as this and yet you have not experienced sexual relations!" Then she undid her clothes and revealed her vagina. The flesh around the vulva became tumid; it was ample and smooth without pubic hair. Aocao withdrew and did not dare advance. The empress led his hand and had him stroke it. Aocao's meaty implement gradually enlarged and abruptly it sprang up. The flesh in all the furrows of the glans filled out. Lateral sinews extended, firm and unyielding it sprang erect.

The empress held it fast in both hands as if she had just received a treasure and said: "How monumental! It is not of this world. I have known many men, but there has never been one like this.[88] In the past, Wang Yifu had a chowry with a handle of white jade; it was uniquely transparent and lustrous.[89] For this reason I name it 'chowry handle': the ultimate of beauty."

While Empress Wu was stroking it, her amorous desires were agitated and she laid her head on a Qiuci pillow decorated with a wandering fairy motif and used a crescent moon cushioned comforter to support her waist as she lay on her back.[90] Aocao lifted the empress' two feet with his hands and paused at the mouth of her vagina. The empress directed him with her two hands. At first it was so constricted that he could not penetrate. The empress said: "Enter gradually." Aocao wanted to penetrate quickly. The empress steeled herself to receive him, knit her brow, clenched her teeth, and endured the pain. The knob of the glans was completely submerged. Soon vaginal secretions seeped out and gradually it felt smoother. Then he again advanced slightly. The empress could not bear it, however, and urgently pulled out the band of her panties and fastened it halfway down the length of his organ. The empress said to Aocao: "Your chowry handle is extremely rigid and thick. My vagina is extremely sore and cannot endure it. It would be a good idea to slow down and resume after a short rest."

Before long, Aocao noticed that the empress' eyes were vacant and her palms hot. Her cheeks were flushed and her breathing accelerated. Vaginal fluids overflowed and the empress gradually began to respond to him with her own body. Aocao then began to thrust and retract. After two hundred times the empress unconsciously grasped Aocao's waist with her hands. She gave vent to abandoned cries, both eyes closed in exhaustion, perfumed perspiration flowed forth, and her four limbs lay inert upon the cushioned comforter. Aocao asked: "Is Your Majesty all right?"

The empress was not able to speak. Aocao wanted to pull out his chowry handle but the empress hurriedly embraced him, saying: "You truly are my son.[91] Don't ruin my excitement." Aocao again resorted to shallow retractions and deep thrusts several hundred times. A torrent of vaginal fluid saturated the band. The empress stroked Aocao's shoulder and said: "You satisfy me to perfection. But why did we meet so late?[92] I should bestow upon you the title 'Lord of Perfect Satisfaction.' Next year on your behalf I will change the name of the calendar year to 'First Year of Perfect Satisfaction.' "[93]

Aocao said: "Your Majesty's vital energies have not deteriorated and your appearance is ever more youthful. My inferior abilities are sufficient to be deployed. Why should you sigh that it is so late? In this mundane world I have not had a single encounter with a woman. Today I have first come to know the joy of sexual relations, which is a fulfillment of my personal aspirations. However, my crude form has affronted your jadelike body. Though I were to pluck out the hairs of my head they would not suffice to enumerate my crimes.[94] If you are gracious enough not to reject me, so that I can always attend you upon quilt and coverlet, even if I were to die it would seem like life."[95]

The empress said: "My Lord of Perfect Satisfaction, if you do not neglect me, how could I be willing to forget you for even a moment? From now on you should not refer to yourself as 'subject' or address me as 'Your Majesty.' I have feelings for you as deep as those of a husband and wife. The ceremonies appropriate to ruler and subject should be terminated."

Aocao said: "I live in fear of an unnatural death. How could I dare to suppress the noble and promote the lowly? It is only because Your Majesty favors me."[96]

Then after Aocao and the empress had copulated for a long time, during their unbridled jesting and joking the chowry handle softened slightly. The empress said: "Are you tired?"

Aocao said: "I have yet to know contentment; how could I know fatigue?"[97]

The empress added: "You have just experienced sexual relations for the first time but do not yet know how to make it more pleasurable. But there is still a day and a time for heights of passion and unrestrained desire. I must be rather remiss. We can stop here."

Aocao again grasped the empress' feet and said: "Wait just a minute." He hurriedly took a silk handkerchief and made use of the mouth of her vagina to rub his chowry handle. The more he rubbed the more rigid it became, so again he penetrated.

The empress said: "A famished man! How is it you are so insatiable?"

The empress had intended to rest for a while, but when she saw that Aocao's lewd excitement was fully rekindled, she let herself go and allowed him to retract and thrust as he pleased. The empress' passions were further delighted. She gripped and wriggled vigorously. Her liquid secretions overflowed. Her vaginal vapors were as hot as steam. The sound made by their grapplings seemed to continue incessantly.

Aocao raised his waist and screwed her. The empress embraced Aocao and in a coquettish manner said: "Lord of Perfect Satisfaction, your character is ruthless. Now I am dying of delight."

The two bodies were pasted together, and after a long time the empress said: "You can stop now. Passions cannot be allowed to reach the extreme."

Aocao said: "Why worry about the trouble entailed? If you intend to throw a party, why fear a man with a great belly?"

The empress said: "How much rice and tea are you able to consume?"

Aocao said: "The quantities I eat and drink could fill a great ravine or swell a vast river."

The empress said: "What the Lord of Perfect Satisfaction has said would entail a great waste of the host's materials."

Aocao said: "My passions have been aroused. I hope that Your Majesty will accommodate me." Then he surreptitiously unfastened two rounds of the band and again penetrated.

The empress, feeling the urgent pressure in her vagina and knowing that Aocao was taking advantage of her, then said: "You are committing the crime of lèse-majesté."

Aocao said: "If one looks out for faults it is only as a means of recognizing goodness.[98] I hope Your Majesty will be a bit more accommodating."

The empress said: "Tolerance is certainly a good thing, but it's just that pain and pleasure are in extreme imbalance."

Aocao did not listen and penetrated about two more inches. The empress could not prohibit him, so she let Aocao come and go, thrust and retract, to the point where his sperm was about to ejaculate. At first Aocao did not know that he was going to ejaculate, and he thrust forward until his chowry handle penetrated all the way to her cervix. The cervix is the innermost recess of a woman and its flesh is like a flower pistil enveloped by a calyx beginning to frondesce. When the head of the man's stalk penetrates to this point, he will feel a melting sensation the pleasure of which is indescribable.

The empress felt the head of his chowry handle rise vigorously as her cervix quickly contracted. She knew he had ejaculated and responded with abandon. Aocao had reached adulthood without having married so he ejaculated like a geyser. Vaginal fluids oozed forth and their bodies remained as though pasted together. After a while the empress said: "I'm exhausted," wiped her vagina with her panties, and got up.

After much time had passed she ordered that the doors be opened, saw that the sun was already setting, and dined with Aocao in the front chamber. The empress' emotions were completely gratified. She appointed Zong Jinqing general of the Left Palace Gate Guard and director of the Palace Domestic Service.[99] She bestowed on him one gold urn laden with pearls, two silver urns laden with gold, a thousand bolts of varicolored silk, and thirty thousand strings of cash to reward him, and said: "You are far more worthy than Wei Wuzhi.[100] Gold and jade are not to be compared to you. Tomorrow I will change the name of the calendar year to the First Year of Perfect Satisfaction."[101] An amnesty was made universal, exceeding customary regulations.

At this time the left vice-director of the Department of State Affairs, Yang Zhirou, directly presented a memorial to the throne and said: "All officialdom has accepted the imperial decree to change the name of the calendar year, but many do not comprehend the meaning of the term 'Perfect Satisfaction.'[102] As it does not designate an auspicious object and furthermore is unrelated to the way of governance, it is requested that you change it."

The empress replied: "How dare you disagree with a proposition that I myself have put forth!" Then she stripped Zhirou of his office. After that time everyone was fearful and did not dare to offer criticism.

The empress loved Aocao to such an extreme that she desired to snatch the offices away from the Zhang brothers and give them to him and furthermore wished to construct a magnificent residence for him. Aocao declined with resolution, saying: "Your Majesty has many favorites on the outside, and the harm caused to your imperial virtue is not insignificant. Why would you then make such a promotion? Furthermore I live by myself alone. Why would you need to build a residence for me?" The empress became even more enamored of him.

In the first year of the Changshou reign period, the crown prince's wives Liu and Dou after some investigation came to know the provenance of the term "Perfect Satisfaction" and thereupon discussed it together, saying: "Aocao's meaty implement is like a donkey's, and Empress Wu can accommodate it with room to spare."[103]

When the empress heard of this she was incensed: "How dare those vermin act thus!" She ordered them both to commit suicide.[104]

The empress had a suspicious and jealous nature. In the time of Gaozong, whenever she had misgivings about any of the female attendants she had them killed for minor infractions. Many such were protected by Aocao, and those who thereby escaped harm were legion.

From this time on the empress spent much time with Aocao. When they sat, their thighs were stacked upon one another; when they slept, their shoulders were connected. Their affections were expressed in myriad forms. The empress once said to Aocao: "When I read in the *Spring and Autumn Annals* that Jin Xiangong was infatuated with Li Ji to the point where he killed the crown prince Shensheng and banished his sons Yiwu and Chonger without regret, I thought in my heart that this was excessive.[105] But now I am so passionately in love that I have to laugh that Jin Xiangong's love of Li Ji was shallow in comparison."

Aocao rejected this imputation with great apprehension and said: "When I first entered the palace the crown prince had already been removed to Luling. If I am to be compared to Li Ji then I certainly have never interfered in the maternal relationship between Your Majesty and your sons. If the outer court were to hear of this it would not be to my advantage."

The empress said: "I am so utterly infatuated with you that I unconsciously alluded to this."

In the second month of the first year of the Yanzai reign period,[106] the empress had the Pavilion of Captured Fragrance constructed in the imperial garden. The empress feasted with Aocao in the pavilion. When the empress had imbibed to the point where she was half-intoxicated, her amorous desires got the better of her and she laughingly said to Aocao: "Although you and I have long had intimate intercourse, you have yet to insert your chowry handle all the way."

That day a set of drapes with exquisite gold filigree was hung up in the pavilion. The empress embraced Aocao and said: "Today we will attempt to deploy your chowry handle completely in order to augment our pleasure. But you cannot be reckless and cause me only to suffer pain."

Aocao said: "Usually when I have sexual intercourse with Your Majesty there is not much left that I can do. But when I devote myself wholeheartedly to serving Your Majesty's amorous pleasure, I sometimes unwittingly go a little further than before. To speak of pain today is to misinterpret my loyal heart."

The empress laughed and said: "That is not the case. It is only the hardness and sharpness of your advance that worries me. If you thrust and drive, come and go gradually, there will be nothing for me to fear."

The empress then reclined on her back with her head on a high pillow, a folded quilt supporting her waist. Aocao grasped his chowry handle and inserted it into the mouth of the empress' vagina. He massaged the head until it was lubricated but did not let it penetrate deeply.[107] The empress' desires were aroused and could not be withstood. She desperately desired that his chowry handle fathom the deep and mysterious depths. Aocao intentionally allowed it to penetrate only shallowly. Vaginal fluids exuded from the mouth of her vagina that were like the slime secreted by a snail. The empress told Aocao to penetrate more deeply, but Aocao suddenly pulled out. The empress made coquettish sounds and looked at Aocao and said: "You short-lived bandit, what are you doing?"

Aocao then drove it straight to the point where the band of her panties had been tied and said to the empress: "Isn't deep penetration sublime?"

The empress closed her eyes and said with a laugh: "Send it in slowly."

Aocao did not listen and inserted two or three more inches.

The empress said: "What recklessness!"

Aocao again squatted and with his two hands lifted the empress' haunches in order to savor the sight as it went in and out. Realizing that the empress was in ecstasy he again inserted two or three inches.

The empress said: "Fantastic! This is no ordinary condition. I am dying."

Thereupon her murmurs became tremulous and her accelerated panting coquettishly soft. She raised her two feet, propped them up on Aocao's back, and lifted herself in order to contend with him tens of times. Aocao gripped the empress' haunches, up and down, thrusting and retracting, coming and going with great urgency. Aocao sported with her and said: "I don't suppose that your vagina is hot and tingling, is it?"

The empress said: "The pleasure is indescribable. But may I ask how much remains?"

Aocao said: "More than two inches."

The empress said: "This part is unusually thick. As it is said: 'You're slowly getting to the best part,' and that is how it should be. But you cannot insert it completely."[108]

Aocao said: "Having come this far, the situation will not allow me to stop."

With a flatulent burble he penetrated straight to the root. There was not the space for a single strand of hair left between them.[109] The empress was highly aroused. Her entire body was pasted to Aocao. She raised her waist and writhed and wriggled several hundred times, then looked at Aocao and said in a low voice: "Don't move. My head feels so dizzy, I hardly know where I am."

Aocao's excitement was just then fully aroused. He withdrew his organ as far as the glans and then drove his chowry handle in over a hundred more times. Vaginal secretions flowed without ceasing. Empress Wu spontaneously cried out: "My own Daddy, you're killing me with pleasure. But stop for just a minute, such vigorous comings and goings are hard to endure."

Aocao did not listen as her vaginal secretions dribbled out. The sound resembled a throng of coolies plunging through the muck. After a while the empress' feet went limp, her eyes closed and teeth clenched, breathing through her nostrils was very faint, and her faculties were disoriented. Aocao was terrified. He immediately pulled out his chowry handle and raised the empress into a sitting position. Only after a long time did she come back to her senses. Aocao said: "What happened to Your Majesty? It terrified your humble servant and I did not dare continue."

The empress opened her eyes wide and gazed at Aocao. Then she embraced him and said with coquettish tears: "After this you should not be so reckless. If you had not paused for a moment I would have perished as a result. What would you have done then?"

Aocao said: "The fact that Your Majesty was unable to sustain it any longer has nearly shattered my courage and made it impossible for me to bring my delightful arousal to its completion. Because of the shock, my chowry handle has become flaccid."

The empress said: "For the time being let us forgo this. As long as I am fortunate enough to remain alive, you may have it whenever you want it."

Using Aocao's thigh as a pillow, the empress casually caressed his chowry handle with her face and said: "Since I have gotten along in years I have yearned for an exceptional man. Who would have thought that through Jin-qing's recommendation I could have obtained someone as well endowed as you? Although our meeting is late, truly it is the blessing of my old age. But you must not emulate the likes of Yizhi, who starts well but cannot finish."

Aocao said: "If I casually neglect Your Majesty, may the gods strike me dead. Your Majesty grasps the power of life and death. If I deviate from what I have said today, may knives and spears inflict ten thousand deaths upon me. But I do not know what Your Majesty intends to do in the future. I am of humble origins. If I had not met Your Majesty, how would I have known that the area below the skirt is so delectable?"

The empress said: "As for you, if it were not for me no one could accommodate you; as for me, if it were not for you no one could satisfy me. I often recall when I was fourteen and attended upon Taizong. Taizong's meaty implement was of average proportions. I was very young and still felt a pain that I could not endure. After attending upon him in bed for half a year, I still did not develop a taste for it.

"When I was twenty-six or seven I attended upon Gaozong. Gaozong's meaty implement was large and virile, but the inception of arousal and its consummation were all his to have. I was not able to enjoy myself as I wished.

"Fortunately, upon his death I met the monk Huaiyi.[110] His meaty implement did not at first equal Gaozong's. But after it was inserted into the furnace it gradually grew larger and longer until it was extremely stiff and hot and could last the entire night without fatigue.[111]

"Shen Nanqiu too was large and virile. He risked his life to please me, ejaculating endlessly until he contracted an illness.

"Now the brothers Changzong and Yizhi are both beautiful young men. Yizhi's meaty implement is particularly large. Changzong's is six or seven inches long and sufficient to provide for my pleasure. But after only one ejaculation it is no longer willing to elevate and is even stricken with paralysis. I despise it. The meaty implements of these several men are the choicest selections from all of humanity, but they are not even remotely comparable to the endowment of my Lord of Perfect Satisfaction. After today there is no need to insert the stalk and submerge the head completely, just insert half and that will be sufficient."

At this time the empress had become quite elevated in years.[112] Her appearance was ever more attractive and her teeth and hair had not changed. But for the old female and the young male, inevitably one wanes as the other waxes, and Aocao's strength was somewhat enervated.

On one occasion they relaxed in the Florid Flower Pavilion. In front of the balcony the crabapple trees were in full bloom. The empress plucked a sprig and stuck it on one side of her cloudy locks. Her creamy breasts were half exposed and her demeanor was bewitching. She leaned on the turquoise standing screen and cast a sidelong glance at Aocao. Suddenly Aocao's amorous desires sprang up. Shoulder to shoulder they stood with their mouths united. Then they spread out a soft comforter on which to copulate, insisting upon the consummation of their pleasure. They did this so many times that it is impossible to enumerate them fully.

After this day, whenever the empress held court and Zhang Changzong and Zhang Yizhi were in attendance, she could not even bear to turn her head to look at them. The imperial favor she showed to them gradually diminished, and after she retired from court she no longer summoned them.

The Zhang brothers were secretly alarmed and suspicious and could not fathom the reason. One day the empress went to the Luxurious Forest Garden and summoned the academicians of the North Gate to a feast.[113] Changzong and Yizhi were there.

The empress saw that their cheeks were like peach blossoms, their laughter captivating, their eyes brilliant. Spontaneously her amorous desires were aroused, and she had both offer jade cups of wine to her long life. Changzong slightly exposed his wrist. It was the same color as white jade. The empress pinched it with her fingernail. When the wine was finished, she summoned them into the palace and Changzong said: "We are to receive the imperial favor once again."

When they reached the door the empress came to a halt. Her eyes like autumn rivulets conveyed her passion. After a long pause she said: "I cannot help it. I do not mean to slight you." She signaled to the eunuch attendants and had them present Changzong with a thousand catties of yellow gold, and Yizhi with a thousand ounces of gold, and then ordered them to leave.

The Zhang brothers' suspicions increased, and when they learned upon inquiry that Aocao was monopolizing the empress' favor in the palace, they could only sigh deeply. Privately the empress too felt regret and often went to the North Gate Academy to solace and succor Changzong and Yizhi. They imbibed and jested as before, and gifts were presented in incalculable abundance, but it did not lead to debauchery.

In the first month of summer in the first year of the Shengli reign period, when the rains had just ceased, the empress held Aocao's hand and strolled through the rear garden.[114] In the midst of a green grove of willows, secluded songbirds mated with each other and warbled their names. Suddenly the empress' lecherous desires were aroused and she said with a sigh: "Even songbirds know the joy of mating with each other. Could it be that man is not the equal of a bird?"[115]

Quickly she ordered her female attendants to spread a cushioned comforter of Sichuan brocade in a secluded spot, then snickered as she said to Aocao: "You and I should today emulate the joy of the songbirds."

After they had each removed their undergarments, the empress knelt face-down on a cushion, reared up her haunches, and had Aocao enjoy her by inserting his chowry handle into her from behind. His hands caressed her breasts as if he were a calf attempting to suckle. They made numerous burbling noises; in fact, the details of their delight would be quite difficult to describe.

One day the empress said to Aocao: "Today at dawn I saw Squire Six shine in the first sunlight like a lotus blossom on the water. Squire Five also looked quite fresh and pure."

Aocao said: "A gentleman does not appropriate the source of another's pleasure.[116] Why does Your Majesty not call them in to divide up the nights and wait upon you with quilt and pillow?"

The empress snickered and said: "Once you have eaten the lichees of the South Sea, green plums are like chewing wax. Once you have seen the ocean, it is difficult for other bodies of water to compare.[117] I am at that point!"

Aocao said: "I would not feel sour about it."

The empress said: "Of course, you are not sour. But I cannot stand how sweet they are." They both clapped their hands and guffawed.

That year in the sixth month on a hot summer evening the empress went to the Pavilion of the Balmy Breezes and with a golden pan poured water on an iridescent South Seas dragon-scale stone. The cool vapors exuded by this stone assailed the beholder. She spread out a blue-green dust-repellent raw silk soft comforter from Quxu, placed a Korean "dragon beard" rush mat on top, and burned Cambodian camphor incense.[118] Then the empress laid naked upon the mat.

When she was in a state of slumbering oblivion, Aocao suddenly showed up at her side. At the time the moonlight was as bright as broad daylight and the empress' body was as lustrous as jade, alternately illuminated and shadowed in the wavering luminescence. As Aocao's lecherous desires were suddenly aroused, he raised his chowry handle and slowly inserted it into her vagina. While in a dream state the empress made an anguished sound and then awoke. By the time her starry eyes flashed open with surprise, Aocao had already thrust and retracted several tens of times.

The empress said: "You have not waited for the ruler's mandate![119] Penetrating deep into the forbidden quarters, what should be your punishment?"

Aocao said: "Your humble servant braved death to enter Hongmen and thought only of loyalty to my ruler."[120]

The empress guffawed. Raising her body, she abandoned herself to his thrusting and driving. Aocao draped the empress' arms and wrists around his shoulders and neck, propped up her feet, then lifted her torso up and thrust into it. The empress laughed sarcastically and said: "Even singing girls and wanton sluts wouldn't do this. Only you and I can be utterly debauched and do everything that can be done."

Afterward, on the evening of the Mid-Autumn Festival, Aocao and the empress were enjoying the moonlight in the Pavilion of Assembled Fairies in the Palace of the Upper Yang.[121] Wine goblets were plied in mutual toasts to the tune of subtle strains of music resembling intimate whispers. But mirth and laughter before we know it give way to sighs. Generally speaking, pleasure in the extreme leads to sorrow.[122] This is the nature of man.

Among the palace concubines, the one who was most clever, the Lady of Handsome Fairness Shangguan, understood the intentions of the empress.[123] She offered a goblet to her long life accompanied by a song that went:

> The autumn wind is crisp and clear, the myriad pipes are silent;
> Fallen pearls of dew are luxuriant, the moon is like a disk of jade.
> On such a beautiful evening as this, offer up the jade cups;
> The empress embraces an immortal youth, for a thousand years of
> ardent flight.
> Still there is regret, there is no enchantment.
> When the goddess of the moon laments her loneliness, what
> should be done?

The empress was delighted and instructed Shangguan to sing Aocao into a state of arousal. As she stepped forward, Shangguan sang:

> The moon is brilliant, as the winds arise in the Jianzhang Palace,
> Fragrance permeates the air, a fine night has not ended in the
> Weiyang Palace.[124]
> A pair of phoenixes in ardent flight, quavering and quivering in
> harmony;
> Youthful years do not return, bit by bit they flow away;
> We hope you apply yourself diligently, attending to our celestial
> empress.[125]

When Aocao had finished drinking, he lifted his cup to the empress and sang:

> On the Jasper Terrace in the Ninth Heaven, the divine scenery is vast;
> As distant as clouds and mud are we, how would I dare to forget?
> May you live as long as the heavens, forever and without end;
> Passing in and out of the Milky Way, we will soar about together.

After he finished singing, Aocao took the opportunity of his inebriation and, without further observing the rites for ruler and subject, pulled the empress to his bosom. He saturated her breasts with wine. Aocao drank half himself and had the empress drink the remainder. The empress complied with utter delight, and in a while she led him by the hand to the Palace of Supreme Tranquillity to rest.[126]

The empress took off all her outer clothes and wore only a short Lingnan "tube cloth" chemise.[127] She and Aocao embraced, and she called for a Guilin small-world fragrant pastry.[128] The empress masticated it finely and with her tongue driveled it into Aocao's mouth. The empress lifted one leg to the side. Aocao stroked his chowry handle and thrust it toward the mouth of her vagina at an angle. They abandoned themselves to lechery. Suddenly it entered her and the empress raised her body and leaned to one side to receive it until it went all the way in to the base. They came and went, thrust and drove, and there was no longer any sign of painful hesitation.

Then she had young servant girls hold candles and stand in attendance at their side. With her delicate hand she pulled at the chowry handle and made Aocao lie down on his back. The empress received Aocao's chowry handle with the mouth of her vagina then mounted him like a horse and straddled him. With each hop and dip the chowry handle gradually entered her. Only three or four inches of the base were left. Aocao raised his body and drove.

The empress laughed and said: "You're just too merciless! You want to be the end of me. But don't move, I want to observe the virtuosity of its comings and goings." The empress placed her hands on the bed and dangled her head to savor the sight.

Amorous arousal convulsed her. Vaginal fluids flowed so copiously that, in all, the handkerchiefs had to be changed five times. It was already the third watch, and by this time the empress' four limbs could no longer move. Aocao feared that the empress' strength had been depleted so he shifted her to the bottom and with maximum force thrust and retracted, came and went, several hundred times. He drove straight to the base and then thrust all the way to her cervix over a hundred more times.

The empress' eyes grew dim and her voice quavered constantly as she said to Aocao: "The pleasure of this rendezvous sets it apart from the others. I am truly excited to death. Use all your force and toy with me a while longer. Even if I should die it wouldn't matter."

For a long time the empress made no sound at all. Aocao knew he was about to ejaculate, so he raised himself up and with maximum force thrust and retracted as he drove it in. The empress clenched her teeth, her face reddened and her nose turned blue, then suddenly she gasped and cried out: "You are truly my son. I really am dying."

He ejaculated like a geyser. Aocao's strength had been somewhat dissipated, so he pulled out his chowry handle in order to give it a rest. The empress' passions had not yet subsided. She used a silk handkerchief to wipe clean the chowry handle, lay her head on Aocao's thigh and caressed his chowry handle with her face, then used her mouth to suck on it. She looked back and saw the young servant girls to one side holding the candles. Feeling quite embarrassed she then ordered the servant girls: "You use your mouths to suck on it too."

The head of the chowry handle was enormous and their mouths could not accommodate it, so they could only nibble and suck on it. The empress then said: "Only I am able to accommodate the organ Aocao has raised, though it has nearly been the death of me on numerous occasions. As for the likes of you, you'd be long dead."

The servant girls laughed but did not respond. Before she had finished speaking, the empress embraced Aocao tightly. Aocao's chowry handle again grew stiff and again they copulated. He thrust and drove several hundred times with all his might. The empress' body was exhausted, so once their desires were satisfied they stopped.

One day it was reported from the rear garden that the peonies were in bloom. The empress provided some wine and with Aocao went to enjoy the flowers. When she was half intoxicated, the empress said: "You are very vigorous and possess great strength. Can you embrace me, walk, and do battle at the same time?"

Aocao said: "Of course."

They took off their lower garments and he had the empress embrace his neck and place her legs around his waist. He inserted his chowry handle into her vagina, circled the peony balustrade, then continued several paces and temporarily came to a halt as singing girls played the new tune "Red Peonies Fluttering on the Stairs."[129]

They sipped from soft gold cups and dribbled into each other's mouths. In the yard there were two white deer and dancing cranes that became so stimulated by the sight that they all copulated as well.[130] Of those who were present, there were none who did not cover their mouths in shock. The empress, however, maintained perfect composure.

On another evening the empress and Aocao had partied to excess. Shoulder to shoulder they slept embracing one another, and by midday they had still not arisen. The empress said to Aocao: "Even if you had studied, passed the imperial examinations in the top grade, and reached the position of prime minister you could never have received such special treatment. Your devotion to me can be called complete. Your food, drink, and clothing are of imperial quality. Nor is the way in which I have treated you neglectful. I would like to entitle you and distinguish you, but if you persist in so strenuously declining such honors, I could enrich your brothers and your whole clan. I will not go back on my word."

Aocao said: "As I have said before, I am all by myself. Has Your Majesty forgotten? I have not advanced by way of talent and truly have no expectation of riches or honor. I only have a hoard of sincerity that I have cultivated for a long time. I do not wish to elude the executioner's axe in saying this, but Your Majesty will certainly not listen. If Your Majesty does happen to listen, even if it were the day of my death it would seem like the era of my rebirth."[131]

The empress said: "Pshaw! My Lord of Perfect Satisfaction, what are you saying? I have already presented my body to you, how could you have something to say that I wouldn't listen to?"

Aocao said: "Since Your Majesty has permitted me to speak, I should dare to speak. For what offense has the crown prince been demoted to prince of Luling and banished to Fang prefecture? Furthermore, recently I heard that he has corrected his previous errors and has become a new man.[132] All under heaven say that Your Majesty intends to usurp the Tang. I fear that after your thousand autumns and ten thousand years have expired, the calamity that befell the Lü clan may occur.[133] The hearts of the people do not yet despise the Tang.[134] Your Majesty should summon the prince of Luling immediately and place him on the throne. Your Majesty could then preside in the palace with folded arms. What pleasure could equal this?"

The empress looked perturbed.

Aocao said: "If Your Majesty does not accede, I request that my male member be cut off to propitiate the people of the empire." Suddenly he raised a small dagger, turned it toward his chowry handle, and attempted to sever it. The empress vigorously struggled to seize it, but the head of the chowry had already been cut to a depth of about half an inch and blood flowed in a torrent.

The empress got up and used a clean silk cloth to wipe it dry, then blew on it. She alternately wept and cursed, saying: "Silly child, how could you bring yourself to do such a thing?"

Aocao said: "As for my being your child, I am only a temporary child. Your Majesty has an imperial child who is Your Majesty's own flesh and bone. How can you stand to reject him?"

The empress' heart was moved. From this time on Aocao often exhorted her along the same lines, and afterward, having obtained the similar counsel of Di Renjie, she summoned the prince of Luling to again be crown prince.[135] Those inside and outside the court said that Aocao had long sullied the inner chambers in the imperial palace, and all had wanted to seize an opportunity to kill him. When they heard that he had rendered internal assistance to the Tang, however, they praised him.

In the second year of the Shengli reign period, the empress was seventy-six years old.[136] She was often ill and the amount she ate and drank had decreased. One day she said to Aocao: "You and I are quite compatible. For the past several years we have been just like birds with wings overlapped or branches growing entwined.[137] But fine things are not durable, and the road to happiness is never smooth.[138] I feel that my spirits are not nearly what they used to be. What do you think?"

Aocao said: "Had Your Majesty not spoken I would not have dared to open my mouth. Your Majesty is advanced in years and overindulgence in the bedchamber does not seem to be the way to maintain good health. But should you die one day, I would not be concerned about being entombed to follow you to the underworld. My only fear is that my gross constitution would leave a blemish on your imperial virtue."

The empress said: "Yes, I will think about that for you." After several more days had passed she said: "I have a plan. Of all my nephews only the prince of Wei, Wu Chengsi, is most virtuous.[139] I love him dearly. He can take care of you in his home. Wait until you hear news of my death. Then change your name and you can be a very rich man in the area between the old states of Wu and Shu."[140]

The next day she summoned Chengsi and said: "I have favored Xue Aocao, as you know, and I have loved you more than any of my sons. Today I am consigning him to your home. Take good care of him. Do not inquire into his comings and goings. If outsiders should learn of this, it would certainly cause you trouble in the future."

Chengsi was petrified, and he said in response: "I would not dare contravene your orders."

That evening the empress ordered that wine be prepared in order to bid farewell to Aocao. All such rarities as leopard placenta, camel hump, red sheep tail, preserved green dragon meat, and the most precious delicacies from water and land from the western extremes of Xiliang to as far south as Siam were prepared, along with the most famous wines.[141] The empress poured Aocao a seven-jeweled gold cup to bid him farewell. With each cup they spoke several words and then sobbed and wept profusely for a long time. Aocao drank as much as he could until he was inebriated. Then he wept and said: "After this time I will no longer hear the reverberation of your jade girdle pendants. Your Majesty must eat well and take good care of yourself. If after your ten thousand years have expired my humble debt of gratitude has not yet been repaid, I hope that your fragrant spirit will descend into my dreams. Then I could enjoy the illusion of serving you."

When the empress heard this she wept even more bitterly. After some time she forced herself to speak and said: "My Lord of Perfect Satisfaction is still healthy, do not be enamored of someone as decrepit as myself." She said to Aocao: "I hear that in love affairs among the people there is a custom of making a scar by burning incense on their private parts, a custom that has become a topic of conversation. Why should you and I not do this?"

Then she ordered that ambergris incense cakes be produced, and after they had repeatedly bowed to heaven and pledged a vow, she burned a whole cake on the head of Aocao's chowry handle. The empress burned a cake on her vulva as well and then said: "My relationship with you began in pain, why should it not end with pain?"[142]

After they went to bed she said to Aocao: "Not even the great termination of death itself surpasses this level of pain. Even if I were to die tonight I would be a contented spirit."

Then she ordered Aocao to recall in sequence all the positions for sexual intercourse that they had tried in the past and ordered him to reenact them one by one. Each was performed over ten times. By daylight they both lay exhausted on the dragon comforter. That day he was given three hundred catties of yellow gold, one peck of pearls, equivalent amounts of coral, precious jade, and fifty sets of clothing that were conveyed with him to the home of Chengsi. She and Xue wept and bid each other farewell.

The empress then turned to Chengsi and said: "Serve Mr. Xue as you would serve me." After this time Chengsi served Aocao day and night very assiduously. At every banquet he had his favorite concubine Wen Boxiang sing to cheer him up.[143] Boxiang was a famous singing girl of Changan who later became Chengsi's concubine. She had always admired Aocao's good looks, demeanor, and endowments, and began to make eyes at him. In the middle of the night she surreptitiously sought out Aocao and endeavored to copulate with him. No matter what he did, though, he could not succeed in penetrating her but only managed to moisten the head of his organ. Boxiang's passions were fully aroused, but all she could do was bite his shoulder and then take her leave.

The empress' incense-burning sores healed and her illness gradually stabilized. She attended a party in the rear garden and noticed the talent and beauty of the Zhang brothers. Involuntarily beset by a longing for their youth, she summoned them into the palace and said to Changzong: "For the past several years it is as if someone had cast a spell on me. Only today did I again become aware of your existence."

Changzong did not dare ask any questions. But in the midst of copulation this one was shocked that the other was so small, and that one was shocked that the other was so vast. They did their best to bring things to a fair conclusion, but in the end they were not satisfied.[144] Next she summoned Yizhi, but it was just the same.

More than a month later she then sent a young eunuch to the home of Chengsi with a single lustrous pearl, ten red love beans, one hundred pieces of ambergris incense, and a pair of golden mandarin ducks and had them secretly delivered to Aocao together with a letter written on a piece of gold-flecked imperial dragon phoenix paper that said:

In the past we hurriedly bid farewell.[145] To think about this carefully, it causes distressing sighs.[146] Every time I drink by myself on a fine spring day, and sleep by myself on a moonlit night, I realize that, though surrounded by beauties, I lack a soul mate and glistening tears appear on my gown and table. The days gone by were so happy, today is so sad. The nights gone by were so short, tonight is so long. In the blink of an eye we were as far apart as heaven and earth, in no time at all we were suddenly as distant as Hu and Yue. What is man's allotted span that he should endure living separation? Today I have sent a letter to communicate that on a night in which there is a full moon, I am sending a small oxcart to convey you through the Gate of Expectant Spring so that you may stay a few days in order to complete our yet unfulfilled fate and furthermore make a tryst to be lovers in the life to come. Do not say "How could there not be other men?"[147] I can see you if I stand on the tips of my toes.[148] The purport of the works I have quoted is such that I need say no more.

At the bottom of the letter was also appended a poem that said:

> Seeing vermilion turn into emerald,
>   my thoughts are in confusion;
> Made haggard by this separation,
>   I often think of you.
> If you don't believe that of late
>   my tears fall constantly;
> Open the chest and examine
>   my pomegranate red skirt.[149]

Aocao wept as he read. He wrote a response to the empress and gave it to the young eunuch. After he had left, Aocao sighed and said: "If I enter the palace again I will certainly never leave. When you see an opportunity you should seize it and not wait an entire day, isn't that right?[150] Now I have escaped the burning house."[151] At night, without letting Chengsi know, he assembled a small amount of gold and other valuables and then appropriated his host's thousand-*li* horse and left through the western gate.

Chengsi was petrified. He dispatched horsemen to search in all four directions, but they could not locate him. This was explained completely in a memorial to the throne that pleaded for mercy. The empress could only sigh with anguish. Changzong understood the empress' intentions and parted with ten thousand pieces of gold to search the South Seas for a unique medicine. He consumed it and along with Yizhi cultivated his turtle stalk. After one month they were again presented and regained their great favor.

In the empress' final year they were killed beside the imperial curtains by the crown prince and Prime Minister Zhang. Then their limbs and bodies were butchered and torn to pieces.[152]

After the crown prince ascended the throne he was grateful to Aocao and tried to locate him, but was unsuccessful.

Afterward, in the middle of the Tianbao reign period,[153] people in the city of Chengdu saw him. Dressed in bird feathers with a yellow cap, he had a child's face and black hair like someone about twenty years old. People say that he had found the *way*, and so forth. Afterward, nothing was known of his ultimate fate.

End of The Story of Passion in the Boudoir

[POSTSCRIPT]

Is not the relationship between the histories and novels similar to that between the classics and their commentaries? What is latent in the classics is made manifest by the commentaries, as in the case of the inner and outer stories of Emperor Wu of the Han dynasty and Zhao Feiyan.[154] It is as if the secret circumstances of the inner chambers were made visible before us today and suffice to make manifest what is latent in the histories; this is of course like the classics having commentaries. Recently I obtained the *Story of Empress Zetian's Lord of Perfect Satisfaction*. It relates events very circumstantially and the words are polished and uniquely colorful. Compared to these other tales it is more pleasurable by far. Therefore I have published it in my shop in order to provide a topic of conversation for the inquisitive.

Spring of the year *kanoe tatsu*,
Sōyō, Yanagi Hyakusei[155]

[COLOPHON]

The rabbit garden collection of books[156]

Thirteenth year (*mizunoto hitsuji*) of the Hōryaku reign period[157]

Nihonbashi south road, 3rd street[158]
Ogawa Hikokurō[159]
Eastern Capital bookstore   Dōshōshichi

Critical Edition

吳門徐昌齡著
則天皇后如意君傳
東都　　清閟閣[1]

如意君傳序

如意君傳者何? 則天武后中冓之言也。[2] 雖則言之醜也、亦足以監[3]
乎? 昔者四皓翼太子、漢祚以安、實賴留侯之力。如留侯、可謂社稷[4]
忠矣。則天武后強暴無紀、荒淫日盛。[5] 雖乃至廢太子而自立、衆莫
之能正焉。而中宗之復也、實敖曹氏之力也。此雖以淫行得進亦非
社稷忠耶? 當此之時、留侯慮之、四皓翼之、且焉能乎? 易曰: 納約自
牖;[6] 敖曹氏用之。由是觀之、雖則言之醜也、亦足監[7]乎? 甲戌[8]秋。華
陽散人題。

華陽散人題。

東都牛門隱士書

[1a] 閫娛情傳

武則天宮后者、荊州都督士彠女也、幼名媚娘。年十四、文皇聞其
美麗、納之后宮、拜爲才人。久之、文皇不豫。高宗以太子入奉湯藥。

媚娘侍側。高宗見而悅、[9] 欲私之、未得便。會、高宗起如廁。媚娘奉金盆水跪進。高宗戲以水洒[10]之、且吟曰：

> 乍憶巫山夢裏魂；
> 陽臺路隔奈無門。[11]

媚娘即和、曰：

> 未承[12]錦帳風雲會；
> 先沐金盆雨露恩。[13]

高宗大悅、遂相攜交會於宮內小軒僻處、極盡繾綣。[1b]既畢、媚娘執御衣而泣曰：妾雖微賤、久侍至尊。欲全陛下之情、冒犯私通之律。異日居九五、不知置妾身何地耶？高宗解所佩九龍羊脂玉鉤、與之曰：即不諱、當冊汝爲后。媚娘再拜而受。[14]自是入侍[15]疾、輒私通焉。文皇病大漸。出媚娘於感業寺、削髮爲尼。高宗嗣大位、幸感業寺行香、私令媚娘長髮。髮後長七尺、載之入宮、[16]拜爲左昭儀。武氏入昭儀宮、與王皇后蕭淑妃爭寵。[17]時、武氏年三十二歲。泣訴高宗曰：陛下位居九五、不念玉[18]帶之記乎？[19]高宗心思王皇后蕭淑妃二人失寵、有廢立之意。次早臨朝、宣長孫無忌、問曰：王皇[2a]后無子、武昭儀有子。朕欲廢后立后。卿意何如？無忌不敢言。有近臣褚遂良諫曰：王皇后表禮所聘。先帝臨崩、執陛下手、謂臣等曰：朕佳兒佳婦、咸以付卿。言猶在耳。不敢忘也。況王后未嘗有過。何以廢之？陛下必欲易后、伏請妙選天下名族。且武氏經事先帝、又出爲尼、人所共知。天下耳目不可掩也。臣逆陛下。臣罪當誅。遂免冠、叩頭流血、曰：臣還陛下牙笏官、請願歸田里。武后隱在屏後聽見、厲聲言曰：何不撻死這利口賊？[20]高宗大怒、即將褚遂良加極刑賜死。[21]長孫無忌貶[22]爲潭州都督。後史官讀史至此、有詠曰：[2b]

> 蹇蹇王臣既匪躬；[23]
> 直言眞有比干風。
> 笏還螭陛心終赤；
> 額叩龍墀血柱[24]紅。[25]
> 威鳳無情建國紀；
> 聚麀[26]有語亂宸聰。
> 聖朝厚賜春秋祀；
> 千古重昭社稷忠。[27]

褚遂良加刑、無忌被貶。[28]朝廷括囊、[29]而詐立武氏爲昭儀皇后。時武曌僭亂朝權、出入無忌。每與高宗同殿、高宗燮而畏之。緣是天下謂之二聖。[30]後、帝兩目枯眩、不能票本。百官奏事、或令武后決之。[31]后性質聰敏、博通古[32]今、涉獵文史、處事皆稱旨意。將王皇后與蕭淑妃誣陷坐罪。各杖二百、斷去二人手足、投酒甕中。[33]浸撈³⁴骨殖、埋於後苑。贈父武士彠爲周國公、加封太原 [3a]王。高宗崩、太子李哲即位。號爲中宗主。皇帝旣即位、立韋妃爲皇后。未及一³⁵年、被武后廢爲廬陵王、立次子李旦³⁶爲帝。虛位七年、又被廢爲皇嗣。是時自立爲則天武后、立武氏七廟、遣將擊殺琅琊王李沖、及越王李貞。又舉兵殺戮唐朝宗室。自名武曌、稱爲則天大聖金輪皇帝。國號周、立姪武三思爲太子。宰相狄仁傑從容諫曰: 陛下立武太子。誠恐陛下萬歲後、姪爲天子、難以祔³⁷姑於太廟。³⁸太后聞奏、遂以立李旦³⁹爲皇帝、改姓武。元元⁴⁰由是漸有反周爲唐之意。詩云:

> 一語喚回鸚鵡夢;
> 九霄奪得鳳雛還。⁴¹

[3b]武后自知人心不服、內行不正、以反逆誣人。誅殺不可勝計。中淫外酷。後、史官詠詩一首嘲之。詞曰:

> 牝雞聲裡紫宸空;
> 幾樹飛花滿地紅。
> 當代媚娘居北闕;
> 一朝天子寓東宮。
> 椒房倡亂由張氏;
> 社稷中興賴狄公。
> 人事未形先有數;
> 至今追憶李淳風。⁴²

自太后聽信二張、用酷吏來俊臣索元禮等、行不正之法、百官俱不敢諫。幸賴狄仁傑在朝維持國政。惜乎一薛進而遑欲恣淫矣。可勝道哉! 初、隋末、薛舉稱兵於隴西、僭號秦帝。次子仁越⁴³從其兄仁杲⁴⁴戰敗淺水、降、殛死於長安。先是、仁杲⁴⁵之愛妾素姬與家僮姦。[4a]方孕矣、仁杲⁴⁶怒而出之於六水地。兵敗獨得免。生一子、名曰玉瑲。長、好讀孫吳兵法。感家難不仕、娶於曹。有二子。長薛伯英、次即薛敖曹也。高宗朝儀鳳三年、玉瑲卒。敖曹兄弟徙居長安。永隆元年、伯英卒。敖曹遊於洛陽、遂僑居焉。時敖曹年十八。長七尺餘、白皙⁴⁷美容顏、眉目秀朗、有膂力、趫捷過人、⁴⁸博通經史、善書畫琴弈⁴⁹諸藝。飲酒至斗餘⁵⁰不醉、以故多輕俠之遊。而肉具特壯大異常。里中少年好事者俱知之、每遇敖曹飲酒、求一觀、以爲戲笑。敖曹曰: 予以此物累。不知人道。時有所感、無地可施。方用爲苦。何足供諸君歡 [4b]也? 強之、乃出其肉具。麥闊稜跂、其腦有坑窩四五處。及怒發、坑中之肉隱起若蝸牛湧出。自頂至根筋勁起如蚓⁵¹蚺之狀。⁵²首尾有二十餘條。紅⁵³瑩光彩、洞徹不昏。蓋未曾近婦人之漸漬也。少年見之、咸驚異、試以斗粟挂其莖首。昂起有餘力。無不大笑絕倒。間與敖曹遊娼家。初見其美少年、歌謳酒令、無不了了、愛而慕之。稍與迫觀肉具。無不號呼避去。間有老而淫者、勉強百計導之、終不能入。敕曹肉具名既彰、無肯與婚者。
居時常歎嗟、有悲生之感。時太后年已 ⁵⁴ 六十餘。千金公主 進馮小
寶⁵⁵者、得幸。小寶⁵⁶素無賴、賣藥長安 [5a]市。其肉具頗堅而粗。⁵⁷
以淫藥敷⁵⁸之、每接通霄不倦。⁵⁹太后絕愛之。⁶⁰托言其有巧思、⁶¹髡其
髮爲僧、改名懷義、時時召入宮督工作、因而淫接。累官至大總管、
封國公。後懷義富貴 而驕、⁶²多蓄女子於外、⁶³又與御醫沈南⁶⁴璆爭寵。
怒燒白馬寺及⁶⁵明堂。太后與太平公主謀、使健婦撲殺之。載其屍
還寺、詐云暴卒。南⁶⁶璆亦以善淫進。久之、不勝慾病、髓竭而死。⁶⁷
時后已七十。春 秋雖高、齒髮不衰、豐肌艷 態、宛若 少年。頤養之
餘、慾心轉熾。⁶⁸雖宿娼淫婦、莫能及之。會有薦張昌宗美而少、其
肉具大者。召見之、果嫣然佳麗也。昌宗又薦其從兄易之[5b]白 晳⁶⁹
且器用過臣。⁷⁰試之良是。兄弟俱有寵、官至司僕卿、麟臺監、爵
封國公。中外畏之、稱昌宗爲六郎、易之爲五郎、且謂六郎面似蓮
花⁷¹之態。天授二年孟冬、武后同易之昌宗欲遊上苑翫花。出詔旨
曰:

> 明朝遊上 苑;
> 火速報春知。
> 花須連夜發;
> 莫待曉風吹。⁷²

武后詔旨一出、次早百花俱開。今人謂十月小陽春、正此故也。是
亦天從武 后之意。詠詩止道 昌宗有花容之身云爾。其詩曰:

> 朝罷金輪出 正陽;
> 詔 書火急報春 光。
> 花中護有千[6a]紅紫;
> 不及蓮花似六郎。⁷³

又稱爲王子晉後身。使披羽衣、乘彩裝木鶴。時⁷⁴人有詩云:

> 昔遇⁷⁵浮丘伯、
> 今同丁令威。
> 中郎⁷⁶才貌是;
> 藏史姓⁷⁷名非。⁷⁸

昌宗易之更一夕入直。出 直之夕、多縱美人歡飲、淫媾⁷⁹達旦。⁸⁰至
與太⁸¹后接、心乏、往往中衰、后情不愜。時載初⁸²二年春。一日、武后
宴坐融春園。觀風光駘蕩、香色旖旎、落花結⁸³砌、飛絮霑衣。加
以幽禽亂呼、雌雄相敵、蜂蝶侵花、差池上下。感物觸情、欲召昌宗
輩幸之、懼 [6b]其興盡、不覺沈 吟欷歔。時宦官⁸⁴宗⁸⁵晉卿⁸⁶歷階而
上、奏曰:陛下今日何念? 得非爲愛 子廬⁸⁷陵王久違膝下乎? 晉卿雖⁸⁸
已知后意、故爲是言探之。后艴然曰:誰令汝爲此言? 汝我家老奴。
寧不知我者? 晉卿⁸⁹叩頭 請死曰:臣不避斧鉞。⁹⁰敢別有所陳。后

曰：卿試言之、吾不罪汝。晉卿[91]曰：微臣仰探聖情。莫非易之昌宗
輩不足以當陛下意？后微哂曰：然。大聰明兒。晉卿[92]奏曰：臣觀易
之昌宗輩富貴極、笑[93]言陛下有年紀。至數召、不得已勉爾承奉。虛
情交樂、非中所好。是以氣衰力瘁。不盡興而中縮。不能使陛下暢美。
且[94]聞其外宅歌兒舞女。粉[7a]黛成群。寧肯盡心竭力於陛下耶？后
聞奏、忿忿罵曰：朕爲此奴輩所賣。謂其精力有限。不知其有他遇也。
朕棄之如几[95]上肉耳。[96]晉卿[97]曰：陛下少息雷霆之怒。[98]此輩不足以
污礧斧。臣更有所獻。臣聞洛陽城中有一美少年者、姓薛名敖曹。
其人年近三十、才貌兼全、且肉具雄健。非易之昌宗輩可及。陛下
下尺一之詔、使臣銜命召之、必能暢美聖情、永侍几席。后曰：汝識
其人乎？晉卿[99]曰：臣未識其人、聞鄉中少年言：手[100]不能握、[101]尺不
能量。頭似蝸牛、身如剝兔、[102]勃若蚯蚓之狀。掛斗粟而不垂。[103]后
倚幃屏而嘆曰：不必言、已[104]得之矣。乃出 [7b]內帑黃金二錠、白
璧[105]一雙、文錦四端、安車駟馬。手詔敖曹。其詔曰：

　　朕萬機[106]之暇、久曠[107]幽懷。[108]思得賢士、以接譚讌。聞卿[109]抱負不凡、
　　標資偉異。急欲一見、慰朕饑渴之懷。其諸委曲、去使能悉。毋專潔
　　身、[110]有孤朕意。

晉卿[111]奉詔乃[112]齎金帛訪敖曹。會[113]見敖曹、敖曹曰：下賤之資、汙[114]
瀆聖德。非臣所宜。不敢奉命。晉卿[115]曰：足下不欲行於青雲之上、
乃終困於閭閻之下。敖曹曰：青雲自有路。今以肉具爲進身之階、[116]
誠可恥也。晉卿[117]耳語曰：足下能高飛遠舉、出于[118]乾坤之外。且汝
尚不知人[8a]道。非今聖上、誰可容者？敖曹不得已而行。在道嘆曰：
賢者當以才能進。今日之舉、是何科目？晉卿[119]飛報太后。后連遣宮[120]
奴侍郎、馳騎促之。旣至、晉卿[121]引敖曹入見後殿。拜畢命坐。賜茶
訖、命侍嬪導之浴於瑩玉室。賜膩髓湯沐浴、且脫內外服以誘之。
曹肉具昂然自露。宮嬪掩口而笑。退曰：聖上今日得人矣。浴罷、衣
以雲翹鶴氅之服、束以七寶鉤[122]條、戴以九華碧玉之冠、韜以烏[123]
巾。望之、翩翩如神仙中人也。后大悅、撫掌而語曰：仙降於吾所、
促大官具膳。晉卿[124]三人者坐、用紅玉大蓮花杯、酌以西涼州葡[125]
萄酒、捧賜敖曹、凡數行。[8b]曹方欲大釂、而后意動。面色微紅、殊
不在酒。頤指左右、於華清宮東暖閣[126]設軟衾細褥之類、敕晉卿[127]
且退。后自攜敖曹手、入、與之並肩而坐。俄、兩小鬟捧金盆薔薇水
進。后麾之出、自闔金鳳門、橫九龍鎖。諸嬪御往來於門隙窺視之、
故得始末甚詳。后以薔薇水澡其牝、謂敖曹曰：晉卿言汝尚童身、未
識人道、有諸？敖曹曰：臣不幸、遺體過大、蹉跎數載、甘守鰥孤。今
奉聖詔、惶懼不知所出。臣粗猥之質、不足以任聖體。乞先令嬪御試
觀之、具可否、取進止。陛下暴見、恐驚動聖情、臣當萬死。武后曰：
肉具大至此邪？朕當親覽焉。遂 [9a]令脫去中裾。[128]后睥睨良[129]久、
見其纍垂偉長、[130]戲曰：卿勿作逗遛、徒忍人也。[131]時、[132]敖曹肉具尚

柔。后引手撫弄曰：畜物許[133]大、尚未識人道！乃自解衣、出其牝。
顧肉隆起、豐膩無毳毛。[134]曹避不敢前。后引其手、令撫摩之。曹肉
具漸壯、俄然而蹺。腦窩中肉皆塊滿。橫筋張起、堅勁挺崛。[135]后捧
定如獲寶、曰：壯哉！非世間物。[136]吾閱人多矣、未有如此者。[137]昔、王
夷甫有白玉麈[138]柄、[139]瑩潤不啻類。因名麈[140]柄、美之極也。武后撫
弄之際、情思紛蕩、乃枕龜茲遊仙枕、[141]用偃月墩褥[藉][142]其腰仰
臥。敕曹以手提后雙足、[143]置于牝口。后以兩手導之。初甚艱澀、不
能進。后曰：[9b]徐徐而入。敕曹欲急進。后勉強承受、[144]蹙眉嚙齒
忍其痛。[145]僅沒龜稜。[146]既而淫水浸出、[147]漸覺滑落。[148]遂[149]又進少許。
后不能當、急以手牽其褌帶、纏中之半。后謂敕曹曰：麈[150]柄甚堅硬
粗大。陰中極疼痛不可忍。宜緩往來、少息再爲之。未久、敕曹覺后
目慢掌熱、[151]頰赤氣促。淫水溢下、[152]后漸以身就。曹遂稍用抽拽。至
二百回、后不覺以手攀敕曹腰。颯聲顫語、[153]雙眸困閉、香汗浸出、四
肢軃然於墩褥之上。[154]敕曹曰：陛下無恙乎？后不能言。曹欲抽出
麈[155]柄、后急抱曰：真我兒也。無敗我興。曹又淺抽深送[156]者數百
回。淫水汪汪濕透褌帶。后撫敕曹肩[10a]曰：卿甚如我意。[何相見
之晚也？][157]當加卿號如意君也。[158]明年爲卿改元如意矣。[159]敕曹曰：
陛下血氣未衰、容姿轉少。臣之駑才足可展力。何歎晚[160]也？臣在閤
浮間未獲一遇婦人。今日始知人道之樂、於臣私計遂矣。但臣猥
陋之形、冒犯玉體。擢髮不足數其罪。[161]倘承不棄、使得常侍衾褥、
雖死猶生也。[162]后曰：如意君、汝若不怠於我、我豈肯頃刻忘汝乎？
自今勿稱臣、勿呼陛下。我與汝夫婦情深。君臣之禮當[163]絕。曹曰：
臣嘗懼不測之死。安敢抑尊就賤？惟陛下愛臣故耳。然曹與后交
接之久、於其諧[164]謔笑語之間、麈[165]柄少緩。后曰：倦乎？敕曹
[10b]曰：未知足、焉知倦？后又曰：汝乍然人道、未知所以快樂。然
極情恣欲尚有日時。必我少怠。斯可止矣。曹亦握起后足曰：且稍
停。[166]急取繒巾、藉[167]其牝口、拭麈[168]柄。愈拭[169]愈勁、因復進之。后
曰：饑餓士也。何無厭飽如此？后意欲少息。見敕曹淫心正熾、[170]縱
身任其抽送。[171]后情悅益、[172]扳搖甚急。[173]淫水滂溢。牝中氣熱如
蒸。[174]往來聲滋滋不絕。[175]曹舉腰幹之。[176]后抱定曹作嬌態曰：如意君、
汝爲人毒害。今我快活死也。[177]兩體[178]猥貼、[179]久之、后曰：可休矣。
情不可極[180]也。敕曹：奚爲憚煩？有心請客、寧畏大腹漢耶？后曰：
君能吃得多少茶飯？敕曹曰：臣食若填巨[11a]壑、飲若灌大川。后
曰：如意君之言大費主人物料。敕曹曰：臣情興已[181]發。望陛下優
容、乃密解褌帶兩匝、又進之。后覺牝中逆急、知敕曹有所欺、乃
曰：卿甚罔[182]上耶？曹曰：觀過斯知仁矣。[183]望陛下少加容納。后曰：
容忍固是好事、但苦樂不均之甚耳。敕曹不聽、又進二寸許。后不
能禁拒之、[184]任敕曹往來抽拽、[185]至精欲洩之際。[186]曹初不知精[187]來、
乃置麈[188]柄直抵牝屋之上。牝屋乃婦人深極之處、有肉如含苞花
蕊[189]微柝。男子莖[190]首至其處、覺其翕翕然、暢美不可言。[191]后覺敕
曹麈[192]柄首昂健、牝屋急蹲。知其洩、怡然感之。[193]敕曹盛年久曠、一

洩 [11b] 如注。[194] 淫水湧起、以身貼定。移時、后曰: 我置矣。以 褌衣
拭牝而起。良久、乃敕開扉、視日已[195] 晡矣、與曹宴於前軒。后情大悅。
拜宗[196] 晉卿爲左監門衛將軍、知內使[197] 省事。賜金甕一、實以珠、銀
甕二、實以金、綵帛千段、錢三萬緡、勞之曰: 汝賢於魏無知遠矣。
于[198] 金玉[199] 不足比也。明日改元如意元年。肆赦覃被、過於常制。
時、右僕射楊執柔 特[200] 奏、曰: 百官奉詔改元、多不喻如意之旨。既
非瑞物、又無關治道、請更之。后曰: 我所出 豈敢他議。罷執柔官。
自是眾惕息不敢議矣。后愛敖曹之極、欲奪二 張官爵與之、且爲治
大第。敖曹固辭、曰: 陛下外 [12a] 多寵、聖德 所損非 細。奈何復有此
舉? 且臣孑然一身、治第何爲? 后益憐之。長壽元年、皇嗣妃 劉
氏竇[201] 氏詢知如意之絲、因相與爲言曰: 敖曹肉具如驢、武后容受
有餘。后聞之大怒: 鼠輩敢爾! 俱賜自盡。后性多猜忌。高宗時、嬪
御凡所疑者、后輒以 細故殺之。曹多所護持、得免者眾。自是常與
曹、坐則疊股、寢則連肩。情愛萬狀。后常謂曹曰: 我讀春秋、晉獻公
惑于驪姬、至殺太子申生、逐公子夷吾重耳而不悔、我心以爲太過。
今我得情愛深溺、如笑晉獻公之愛驪姬 尚淺 也。曹惶謝曰: 臣初入
宮、皇太子已 遷於廬陵。若以驪姬 [12b] 比、臣實未嘗有間於陛下子
母之間。使外 廷聞之、非臣之福也。后曰: 我寵愛君太切、[202] 不覺言
至此。

延載元年二 月、后於內苑構挹香亭。后與敖曹宴樂於亭上。后酒至
半酣、情思恍惚、笑謂曹曰: 我雖與君久相交狎、未嘗全入塵柄。是
日、陳設玲瓏銷金帳於亭中。后與曹摟[203] 抱、曰: 今日 試與君盡著
塵柄以 暢 其美。[204] 但不可倉卒、[205] 令人受苦楚 耳。敖曹曰: 臣與陛下
尋交感、所餘不多。但盡心奉承陛下 情興美快、不覺有所增益也。
今日[206] 苦楚、豈不負臣忠心乎? 后笑曰: 不然。但畏其堅硬銳進耳。
君若 緩緩抽送往來、[207] 誠所不懼 [13a] 也。后乃仰臥高枕、以疊褥藉
其腰。曹乃 握塵柄、投后 牝口。[208] 研摩濡首、[209] 不令深入。[210] 后情動不
能禁。急欲塵柄進深奧處。曹故淺淺 進送。淫津流牝口若 蝸牛之吐
涎。[211] 后令曹深入、曹忽然抽出。后作嬌聲、顧曹曰: 短命賊、何爲爾?
曹乃直送至嘗縛褌帶處、且謂后曰: 深入妙乎? 后瞑目笑曰: 款款送
進。曹不聽、又進二 三寸。后曰: 倉卒! 曹復蹲踞、以兩手扶后 股起、
看其出入之勢。[212] 知后美暢、復進二 三寸。后曰: 異哉! 此境[213] 界非
凡。吾其死矣。[214] 於是 聲囀顫嬌軟氣促。[215] 乃 蹺兩足、架於曹背、扳
抗者數十番。曹扶后股、上下抽拽、往來甚急。[216] 曹戲之 [13b] 曰: 牝中
可熱癢否? 后曰: 美不可言。[217] 且問、[218] 所餘幾何? 曹曰: 二 寸餘。后曰:
此處 猶麗。所謂漸入佳境[219] 唯可也。更不可盡入。曹曰: 到此地位、
勢不容已。戞戞然 而進直至根、[220] 間不容髮。[221] 后歡甚。通体[222] 著曹。舉
腰搖蕩掀騰者數百回、乃視曹低 語曰: 且勿動。我頭目森森然、莫
知所之。[223] 曹之 興方作。伸徹至腦、復送塵柄百餘度。[224] 牝口淫氣流綿
不絕。[225] 武后失聲大呼曰: 好親爹、快活殺我也。[226] 且少住片時、往來

迸急難禁。曹不聽、則牝中之津[227]滴滴而下。[228]其聲猶數夫[229]行泥淖中。[230]俄而、后兩足舒寬、目閉齒緊、鼻孔息微、神思昏迷。敖曹大驚、即取出塵[14a]柄、扶后起坐、久而方甦。曹曰：陛下何故如此？驚懼微臣、不敢爲之。后瞪目視曹、遂抱曹、作嬌泣聲[231]曰：茲復不宜如此粗率。倘若不少息、我因而長逝矣。汝則奈何？曹曰：陛下不耐事、險驚破臣膽、不得畢佳興也。塵柄因驚[232]漸痿。后曰：姑舍是。幸我一身未死、儘令君有受用處。后枕曹股、以面猥擦塵柄、曰：我年大思一奇漢子。不意因晉卿薦得子如此之大。相遇雖晚、實我後福。切不可效易之輩、有始無終也。曹曰：若輕舍[233]陛下、神明共殛之。陛下執生殺之柄。臣若渝今日之言、刀鎗萬死可也。但不知陛下日後何如耳？臣本賤人。[14b]不遇陛下、豈知裙帶之下有如此美味乎？[234]后曰：汝非我不能容、我非汝無以樂。常憶我年十四侍太宗。太宗肉具中常。我年幼小、尚覺痛楚不能堪。侍寢半年、尚不知滋味。二十六七時侍高宗。高宗肉具壯大、但興發興盡但由他。我不得恣意爲樂。幸彼晏駕得懷義和尚。其肉具初不如高宗。入爐之後、漸大漸長、極堅而熱、通夜不休。沈南[235]璆亦壯大。捨命陪我、連泄不已、以致得病。今昌宗易之兄弟、兩美麗少年。易之肉具頗大。昌宗長至六七寸、亦足供我快樂。而一泄後、再不肯舉、甚至中痿。我甚恨之。此數人肉具皆極人間[15a]之選、然不如我如意君遠矣。自今以後、不必盡根沒腦、[236]但入其半亦足矣。太后是時年已彌高、[237]姿容愈艷、齒髮不改。然老陰少陽、不無一損一益、曹筋力頗倦。偶少憩錦芳亭。軒前[238]海棠盛開。后折一枝、舉插雲鬟[239]之傍。[240]酥[241]胸半露、[242]體態妖嬈。[243]乃倚翠屏、斜視於曹。曹情思躍然而起。[244]兩肩並立、兩口相猥。即布軟褥交會、必盡其歡。如此數回、不可勝紀。后自是日臨朝、張昌宗張易之在列、不堪[245]顧盼。恩賜漸稀、退朝之後、亦無宣召。二張竊自驚疑、不審其故。一日、后幸華林園、召北[246]門學士宴。昌宗易之在焉。后見其兩頰如桃花、巧[15b]笑美盼。[247]不覺情動、令各進一玉厄酒爲壽。昌宗微露手腕、與玉同色。后以指甲搯之。既罷酒、召入宮、昌宗謂：且見幸矣。及門、后卻立、秋波送情。良久、乃曰：無奈何。我非薄子也。顧宦[248]者、賜以黃金千斤、并賜易之金千兩、令出。二張益疑之、訪知敖曹在宮中擅恩寵、惟洪[249]歎而已。[250]后亦內自愧、時時幸北門慰撫昌宗易之。飲讌如故、賞賚不貲、惟不及亂。

聖曆[251]元年初夏、霖雨方霽、后攜曹手遊於後苑。綠柳叢中幽禽相偶呼名。后淫情頓發、[252]歎曰：幽禽尚知相偶之樂。可以人而不如鳥乎？[253]促命諸嬪女鋪蜀錦墩[16a]褥於幽密之處、笑謂敖曹曰：朕與君今日當效禽鳥之樂。各去下衣、后乃伏於裀褥之上、兩股豎起、令曹以塵柄從牝口後插入牝中[254]取樂。手摸[255]兩乳、似犢之欲乳者。汩汩數聲、[256]其歡樂之情有難以形容者。[257]后一日謂曹曰：朝來見六郎、映初日如出水[258]芙蓉。[259]五郎亦自鮮潔。曹曰：君子不奪人

之歡。²⁶⁰陛下何不宣²⁶¹入、分夕奉衾枕？后微笑、曰：食南海生荔枝、
覺青李如嚼蠟也。²⁶²觀于海者難爲水。²⁶³吾其已²⁶⁴夫。曹曰：臣不敢
作酸。后曰：君自不酸、我不奈他²⁶⁵甜也。相與撫掌大笑。是歲六月
暑夕²⁶⁶后如清風閣、以金盆浸南海龍鱗石。其石涼氣襲[16b]人。鋪
渠胥國碧綃辟塵軟褥、上設高麗龍鬚席、²⁶⁷焚扶南瑞龍腦香。后祖²⁶⁸
臥於席上。睡思正酣、²⁶⁹敖曹奄至其傍。時月明如畫、后體玉瑩、輝
彩掩²⁷⁰映。²⁷¹敖曹淫思頓發、²⁷²遂揭麈柄、徐徐插入牝口。²⁷³后於夢魂
中作痛苦聲乃覺。星眸驚閃之際²⁷⁴被曹已²⁷⁵抽拽²⁷⁶數十次矣。²⁷⁷
后曰：不俟君命！²⁷⁸深入禁闥、²⁷⁹汝當何罪？曹曰：微臣冒死入鴻門、²⁸⁰
惟思忠於主耳。后大笑。縱身任其抽送。²⁸¹敖曹又將后臂腕架著肩
項、扶起兩足、兜而行之。后訕笑曰：彼娼妓淫婦尚未如此。惟吾
與汝二人心狂意蕩、無所不爲耳。後、中秋夜、曹於上陽宮集僊²⁸²
殿玩月。觸斝酬酢、切[17a]切私語。²⁸³歡笑之際、不覺欷歔。大抵樂
極悲生、人之常情也。宮嬪中最敏慧者上官婕妤知后意、乃捧觴上
壽、侑以歌、曰：

    金風澄澄兮萬籟寂；
    珠露湛湛兮月如璧。
    當此良霄兮奉玉卮；²⁸⁴
    至尊擁僊郎²⁸⁵兮千載于飛。
    猶復惆悵兮不自愉；
    彼月中僊子孤怨兮當何如耶？

后悅、令上官歌歡曹。進上官歌曰：

    月皎皎兮風生建章；
    芬襲襲兮良霄未央。
    鳳凰于飛兮和鳴鏘鏘；²⁸⁶
    少年不再兮冉冉流光；
    願子努力兮奉我天皇。

[17b]曹飲訖、舉杯奉后、歌曰：

    瑤臺九重兮僊²⁸⁷景茫茫；
    雲泥有間兮何敢相忘？
    願聖壽齊天兮永無疆、
    出入雲漢兮相翶翔。²⁸⁸

歌罷、曹乘酒興、無復君臣之禮、攜后于懷。以酒浸漬其乳。曹自飲
其半、餘半使后飲之。后欣然承受、已而攜手歸於大安宮²⁸⁹少息。
后悉去衣裳、止着嶺南筒布短襦。與曹猥抱、命取桂林小天香餅。
后細嚼之、以舌送沁曹口。后乃舉一足傍、曹乃擦麈柄斜投牝口。兩
相淫²⁹⁰蕩。忽已入牝、后舉身側而就之、至盡其根。往來抽送、無
復切切疼痛之態矣。於是令小嬪持燭立侍[18a]於傍。后以纖手拽

麈柄、令曹仰臥。后以牝口就曹麈柄、遂跨馬而坐。[291]一舉一落麈
柄漸入牝。惟根尚餘三四寸。曹仰身送之。后笑曰:汝爲人太毒害、欲
便了我。且勿動、我欲看其往來之妙耳.

后以兩手據榻、[292]垂其首而瓵之。情興搖蕩。淫水淋漓、[293]凡五換巾
帕。[294]且三鼓矣、后當斯時、[295]四肢不能舉動。曹恐后力乏、轉后在下、
極力抽拽往來數百回。[296]直送至根、復抽至牝屋、又百餘回。后目
瞑[297]聲顫不絕、謂敖曹曰:此一交會取樂比往常不同。眞快活死我
也。[298]與我着力多耍[299]一時。我便死也不妨。后良久不作聲。曹覺精
欲洩、聳身極力抽[18b]拽送之。后口齒相嗑、臉紅鼻青、忽失聲大
呼曰:眞我兒。我實死也。一洩如注。[300]敖曹力少倦、抽出麈尾、爲
之息。后情尚未休、用繒巾拭淨麈柄、頭枕曹股、以臉猥麈柄、以口
吮之。[301]回顧小嬪在傍秉燭。覺有慚色、即令小嬪曰:汝等亦口吮
之。麈柄頭闊、口不能容、惟咬哂而已。[302]后又謂曰:此畜物、獨我
能當之、然幾死者數。若汝等、死已久矣。小嬪笑而不答。言未
已、[303]后緊抱定曹。曹麈柄復硬、再與交合。盡力抽送數百回。[304]后乃
體疲、興盡而止。一日、後苑奏芍藥開。后置酒與敖曹賞之。半酣、
后曰:卿多健[305]膂力。能抱我、且行且戰乎? 敖曹曰: [19a]善。俱
脫下衣、使后抱其項、置兩足於腰間。插麈柄於牝內、遶芍藥欄、[306]
再行[307]數步則小立、伎樂奏紅藥當階翻[308]新詞。以口吸軟金杯、相
令吐而飲。庭有兩白鹿舞鶴。感之、亦皆孳尾。[309]左右無不掩口者。
后行之自若。復一夕、后與敖曹歡會過度。聯臂相猥而寢、至日高
猶未起。后謂敖曹曰:卿若讀書、登甲第、位至宰輔、不能有如此奇
遇。子之盡心於我可謂至矣。子飲食衣服與至尊等。我之待子、亦
不薄矣。我欲爵汝、貴汝。汝又懇辭、當取汝兄弟宗族富貴之、決不
爽信。敖曹曰:臣嚮者云、子然一身。陛下忘之耶? 臣非以才進身、
臣誠[19b]無所希富貴。第有積誠悃中畜之久矣。臣今[310]不避斧鉞
言之、陛下必不聽。陛下幸而聽、臣雖死之日、猶生之年。[311]后曰:吁!
如意君何言也? 我一身已付君、豈有言而不聽者乎? 敖曹曰: 陛
下旣已許臣言、臣當敢言。皇太子何罪廢爲盧陵王、遠謫房州? 況
聞比來改過自新。[312]天下但謂陛下欲削唐社稷。臣恐千秋萬歲後、
呂氏之禍及矣。人心未厭唐、[313]陛下宜速召盧陵王來、付以大位。陛
下高拱九重、何樂如之? 后有難色。敖曹曰:陛下如不從、臣請割
去陽事以謝天下。遽起小匕首向麈尾欲自裁。后急爭奪之、麈首
已傷入半寸許、血[20a]流涔涔。后起、用淨帛拭乾、以口呵之。且
泣且罵曰:癡兒、何至此也? 敖曹曰:臣之爲兒、乃片時兒耳。陛下
自有萬歲兒、係陛下親骨肉。何忍棄之? 后心動。敖曹自是每以爲
勸、後得狄梁公言、召盧陵王復爲皇太嗣。中外謂曹久穢宮掖、咸
欲乘間殺之。及聞內助于唐、反德之矣。

聖曆[314]二年后春秋七十有六。時每不豫、飲食減少。一日謂敖曹曰：我與汝好合。數年以來、比翼連枝[315]之不啻。[316]但好物不堅、[317]好事多磨。[318]我覺精神大不如前矣。其若汝何？敖曹曰：陛下不言、臣亦不敢啓齒。陛下春秋[20b]高、房慾過度、似非頤養之道。且一旦[319]不諱、臣從殉九原非所恤、第恐粗醜之質、遺穢聖德耳。后曰：然、吾爲汝思之。又數日、乃曰：吾得計矣。吾諸姪中、惟魏王武承嗣最良善。吾所鐘愛、可養汝彼第中。俟吾有凶問、即變姓名、吳蜀間作一大富人可也。次日、召承嗣、謂曰：吾之幸薛敖曹、汝所知也。吾愛汝異諸子、今[320]留寄汝第。[321]汝善待之。勿問[322]其出入、如外人知之、必爲汝後患。承嗣驚懼、荅[323]曰：敢不如命。是夕、后命置酒、與敖曹爲別。凡[324]豹胎、駝峰、紅羊尾、蒼虯脯、極水陸珍品、西極西涼、南至暹[325]羅、名酒悉備。后以七寶金叵羅酌送敖[21a]曹。每一杯敘數語、嗚咽汍[326]瀾久之。敖曹盡量痛飲至醉、泣而言曰：臣自此以後不復聞環珮之聲矣。陛下強玉食自愛、倘萬歲後、臣犬馬之報未盡、願降芳魂於夢寐。臣尚得彷彿以侍也。后聞言、愈加號慟。良久、強發聲曰：如意君健[327]在、勿[328]戀我衰朽[329]之人也。后謂敖曹曰：我聞民間私情、有於白肉中燒香疤者、以爲美譚。我與汝豈可不爲之？因命取龍涎香餅、對天再拜、設誓訖、於敖曹麈[330]柄頭燒訖一圓。后亦于牝顅上燒一圓、且曰：我爲汝以痛始、豈不以痛終乎？既就寢、謂敖曹曰：人生大限[331]亦不過如此苦耳。今夕死亦作樂[21b]鬼可也。因命歷記作過風流解數、[332]逐一命曹爲之。各過十餘度。至天明、俱奄然龍褥之上矣。是日、齎黃金三百斤、珠一斗、珊瑚、寶玉稱是、衣服五十襲與之、同載至承嗣家。[與][333]薛涕而別。且顧承嗣曰：事薛君如事我也。承嗣自是日夕侍敖曹惟勤。每宴使寵姬溫柏香歌以歡之。柏香乃長安名娼也、後爲承嗣妾。素慕敖曹丰姿、儀采、[334]器用、目色相授。中夜奔就曹、與之交接。百計不能入、濡首而已。[335]柏香情極、嚙曹臂而去。后火瘡愈、病亦漸安。遊後苑宴、見二張才色。不覺後生愧愛、召入宮、謂昌宗曰：吾數年來如爲人魘者。今日始[22a]知有卿耳。昌宗亦不敢問。然與交媾之際、此訝其小、彼訝其寬。勉爾苟完、[336]終不歡暢。[337]次召易之、亦然。更月餘、乃以明珠一顆、紅相思荳十粒、龍涎餅百枚、紫金鴛鴦一雙、遣小璫至承嗣第、密授敖曹。內銷金龍鳳箋一紙、書曰：

前者草草與子言別。[338]靜言思之、[339]殊是傷歎。每每至花朝獨飲、月夜獨眠、粉黛滿側、無一知己、[340]淚光淡淡[341]時在衫几。昔日何樂、今日何苦。昔夕[342]何短、今夕何長。一刹那頃、便作人天、咫尺間、頓成胡越。人生有幾、堪此生離？今遣信相聞、於月圓之夕、用小犢[22b]車載子從望春門入、少留數日、以修未了之緣、且結來生之好。勿云豈無他人。[343]跂予[344]望之。[345]引書指不多及。

箋尾又附一詩云：

看朱[346]成碧思紛紛;
憔悴支離爲憶君;
不信比[347]來長下淚;
開箱驗取石榴裙。[348]

敖曹讀之下淚。作 奏與小璫。去訖、旣而嘆曰: 再入必不出矣。見機
而作、不俟終日、[349]此[350]言非歟? 吾今已[351]脫火宅者。夜不令承嗣知、
輕齎金寶、竊其千里馬、從西門而去。承嗣大驚。遣騎 四布尋覓、
不知所在。具由奏聞 [23a]請罪。后惟悲歎而已。昌宗知后旨、乃捐[352]
萬金覓南海奇藥。服之、與易之養龜。彌月而後進御、復大有寵。至
后末年、爲
皇太子、張丞相所誅於御幄[353]之傍、肢體屠裂。
皇太子即位、德敖曹、問訪不獲。後、
天寶中、人於成都市見之。羽衣黃冠、童顏紺髮、如二十許。[354]人謂
其得道、云。以後竟不知其所終。

閨娛情傳^終

[跋][355]

[23b]史之有小說猶經有注解乎? 經所薀、注解發[356]之、迺如漢武飛
燕内外之傳。閨閣密 款猶視之于今、而足以發史之所薀; 則果猶
經有注解耳。頃得則天后如意君傳。其敘事委悉、錯言奇彩。[357]比
諸諸傳、快活相倍。因刊于家、以與 好事之人云。

庚辰春[358]   相陽柳伯生

兔園藏書[359]

寶曆十三癸未[360]年

日本橋南通三町目
小川彦九郎

東都書舖   同庄七

Notes

Introduction

1. Xu Changling, *Zetian Huanghou Ruyijun zhuan*, in *Siwuxie huibao*, 24.15-75. Although a good introduction to the various editions of this work and the state of current scholarship is found on pp. 15-20, this book will demonstrate that some of its conclusions are in error. A facsimile of the 1763 edition is found in Ōta and Iida, *Chūgoku hiseki sōkan;* vol. 3 contains an analysis of the *Ruyijun zhuan* and a table of suggested textual emendations; see pp. 11-41; a table of editions is found on pp. 193-195. An abridged version of the *Ruyijun zhuan* titled *Wu Zhao zhuan* may be found in Ye Rubi, *Zazuan xingshui bian.* The preface is dated 1587; a copy exists in the National Palace Museum in Taiwan; for a modern reprint see *Wu Zhao zhuan*, in *Siwuxie huibao waibian*, 1.85-89. The 1763 and late-nineteenth-century editions of the *Ruyijun zhuan* are reprinted in Xu Changling, *Ruyijun zhuan.* For further information about the *Ruyijun zhuan* see Sun Kaidi, *Zhongguo tongsu xiaoshuo shumu*, pp. 153-154; Hanan, "The Erotic Novel"; and Hanan, "Sources of the *Chin P'ing Mei*." Summaries of the plot and preliminary analyses of the *Ruyijun zhuan* are found in the following sources: Li Shiren, "*Ruyijun zhuan*," p. 48; Liu Hui, "*Ruyijun zhuan*," pp. 422-423; Zhang Peiheng, "*Ruyijun zhuan*," pp. 312-314; Zhong Wen, *Sida jinshu yu xingwenhua*, pp. 142-223; and Kang Zhengguo, *Chongshen fengyuejian*, pp. 55-61. A detailed analysis is found in Liu Hui, "*Ruyijun zhuan* de kanke niandai ji qi yu *Jin Ping Mei* zhi guanxi," pp. 47-59. To my knowledge, no other scholar has speculated in print as to the identity of the author of this work.

2. For the biography of Wu Zetian (624-705) see Liu Xu, *Jiu Tang shu*, 1.6.115-134; Ouyang Xiu and Song Qi, *Xin Tang shu*, 1.4.81-114 and 11.76.3474-3485; see also Fitzgerald, *The Empress Wu;* Twitchett, *Sui and T'ang China;* and Wang Diwu, *Wu*

Zetian shidai. For a discussion of the conflicting and incomplete accounts of her early career in standard historical sources see Guisso, *Wu Tse-t'ien*, pp. 11–25.

3. For the biography of Tang Taizong, Li Shimin (597–649), see *Jiu Tang shu*, 1.2.21–38, and *Xin Tang shu*, 1.2.23–49.

4. For a description of this title see Hucker, *Dictionary of Official Titles*, 515.6830.

5. For the biography of Tang Gaozong, Li Zhi (628–683), see *Jiu Tang shu*, 1.4.65–113, and *Xin Tang shu*, 1.3.51–79.

6. When Gaozong died in 683, Crown Prince Li Zhe ascended the throne; within a year he was demoted and another of Wu Zetian's sons, Li Dan, was made emperor. Li Dan was a puppet for seven years until Wu Zetian proclaimed herself emperor in 690. For the biography of Tang Zhongzong, Li Xian (name later changed to Li Zhe) (656–710), see *Jiu Tang shu*, 1.7.135–151, and *Xin Tang shu*, 1.4.106–114; for the biography of Tang Ruizong, Li Dan, see *Jiu Tang shu*, 1.7.151–163, and *Xin Tang shu*, 1.5.115–120.

7. For a discussion of the promulgation of the *Dayun jing* (Classic of the great cloud) see note 98 in Chapter 4.

8. See Sima Guang, *Zizhi tongjian*, 6482.6.

9. Ibid., 6553.12.

10. Xiaoxiao Sheng, *Jin Ping Mei cihua*. For a brief discussion of the textual relations between the *Jin Ping Mei* and the *Ruyijun zhuan* see Liu Hui, *Jin Ping Mei lunwen ji*, pp. 57–59; see also Hanan, "Sources of the *Chin P'ing Mei*," pp. 43–47. The intertextual relations between the *Ruyijun zhuan*, its historical sources, and many later novels are examined in the notes to my critical edition of the *Ruyijun zhuan* in Part Two.

11. *Sengni niehai*, 24.153–339; Lü Tiancheng (1580–1618), *Xiuta yeshi; Nongqing kuaishi*.

12. Kang Zhengguo, *Chongshen fengyuejian*, p. 55.

13. Huang Xun, "Du *Ruyijun zhuan*," in *Dushu yide*, 2.27a–28a. Huang Xun obtained the degree of *jinshi*, or metropolitan graduate, in 1529. This degree is conferred upon successful candidates in the highest level of the civil service examinations and qualifies them for appointment to government office; see Hucker, *Dictionary of Official Titles*, 167.1148.

14. Zhu Xi, "Zhaiju ganxing ershi shou," 66.18a.

15. Huayang Sanren wrote the preface found in the 1763 edition of the *Ruyijun zhuan;* this preface is dated *jiaxu*, which I believe is 1634. Huayang Sanren is probably an alias for a Ming loyalist named Wu Gongchen (c. 1610–c. 1662; *juren* 1636). The identity of Huayang Sanren, his preface to the *Ruyijun zhuan*, and its date of composition are discussed in more detail in Chapter 7.

16. *Ruyijun zhuan*, preface.

17. For the biography of Zhang Liang, the marquis of Liu, see Sima Qian, *Shi ji*, 6.55.2033–2049.

18. Kang Zhengguo, *Chongshen fengyuejian*, p. 55.

19. The term "pornography" and its application in Chinese and Western contexts is discussed at length in Chapter 1. In general, the word is used in this book to describe a narrative technique; it does not denote the legal or moral status of works that contain descriptions of sex. Pornographic technique is the marriage of banality, obscenity, and repetition; the pornographic novel contains only the rudiments of plot and characterization because they are irrelevant. Style and structure are replaced with simple, direct stimulation.

20. *Han Wudi neizhuan* (attributed to Ban Gu [32–92] but probably written during the fifth or sixth century), pp. 9–22; Ling Xuan, *Zhao Feiyan waizhuan*, 6.1a–9b; Wang Shifu, *Xixiang ji*. For a translation of the *Han Wudi neizhuan* see Schipper, *L'Empereur Wou*.

21. Birrell, *New Songs from a Jade Terrace*.

22. Liu Xu, *Jiu Tang shu;* Ouyang Xiu and Song Qi, *Xin Tang shu;* Sima Guang, *Zizhi tongjian*.

23. Sima Qian, *Shi ji;* Zuo Qiuming, *Zuo zhuan huijian;* Ban Gu, *Han shu; Maoshi yinde; Zhouyi yinde; Mengzi yinde; Lunyu yinde.*

24. The relation between the *Ruyijun zhuan* and the *Nongqing kuaishi* is examined in greater detail in Chapter 8.

25. For the Chinese text see *Ruyijun zhuan*, p. 9a. A chowry is a kind of whisk usually made from an animal's fur or tail; the handle is often intricately carved, as the chowry was also used as a fashion accessory.

26. For the biography of Wang Yan, *zi* Yifu, see Fang Xuanling, *Jin shu*, 43.1235–1239.

27. Mather, trans., *Shih-shuo Hsin-yü*, p. 433; Yu Jiaxi, *Shishuo xinyu jianshu*, p. 834. The author of the *Ruyijun zhuan* is familiar with the *Shishuo xinyu* and refers to anecdotes contained in it on more than one occasion.

28. Although the term "chowry handle" and the name Wang Yan are not found together in the *Jin Ping Mei*, this reference to Wang Yan in the *Ruyijun zhuan* did make an impression on the author and he includes a famous quotation from Wang Yan on the very first page. The descriptions of human sexual activity in the *Jin Ping Mei* are often based on those found in the *Ruyijun zhuan;* moreover, these two works often describe sexual activity in an ironic fashion. The reference to Wang Yan and the manner in which the *Jin Ping Mei* borrows from the *Ruyijun zhuan* are discussed in more detail in Chapter 8.

29. [Li Yu (1610–1680)], *Rou putuan*, in *Siwuxie huibao*, vol. 15. For an interesting discussion of the many levels of parody found in the *Rou putuan* see Hegel, *Novel in Seventeenth Century China*, pp. 171–187; for a translation see Hanan, *Carnal Prayer Mat.*

Chapter 1: Pornography and the West

1. Kendrick, *Secret Museum*, pp. 1–32.

2. For an illustrated description of many of the artifacts found in Pompeii see Grant, *Eros in Pompeii*.

3. Kronhausen and Kronhausen, *Pornography and the Law*.

4. The manner in which certain recent works discuss the question of pornography is controversial in its own right. The first paragraph of *Only Words* by Catharine MacKinnon, for example, begins thus: "Imagine that for hundreds of years your most formative traumas, your daily suffering and pain, the abuse you live through, the terror you live with, are unspeakable—not the basis of literature. You grow up with your father holding you down and covering your mouth so another man can make a horrible searing pain between your legs. When you are older, your husband ties you to the bed and drips hot wax on your nipples and brings in other men to watch and makes you smile through it. Your doctor will not give you drugs he has addicted you to unless you suck his penis." See MacKinnon, *Only Words*, p. 3. In a devastating review of this work, Judge Richard Posner notes: "The book is a verbal torrent that appeals, much like pornography itself

as MacKinnon conceives it, to elemental passions (fear, disgust, anger, hatred) rather than to the rational intellect. There is no nuance, qualification, measure or sense of proportion." See Posner, "Obsession," p. 31. An even more damaging criticism of her work is that her central assumption—pornography causes men to commit sex crimes against women—is debatable despite her protestations to the contrary. As Ronald Dworkin writes in another scathing review of *Only Words:* "No reputable study has concluded that pornography is a significant cause of sexual crime: many of them conclude, on the contrary, that the causes of violent personality lie mainly in childhood, before exposure to pornography can have had any effect, and that desire for pornography is a symptom rather than a cause of deviance." See Dworkin, "Women and Pornography," p. 38. Judge Posner's review of *Only Words* also contains a succinct appraisal of the assertion that pornography harms women: "MacKinnon's treatment of the central issue of pornography as she herself poses it—the harm that pornography does to women—is shockingly casual. Much of her evidence is anecdotal, and in a nation of 260 million people, anecdotes are a weak form of evidence. She does not acknowledge the limited scope of the scientific evidence that she does cite; this evidence, which concerns the attitudinal and behavioral effects of pornography, is largely limited to the violent kind, but she wants to forbid the nonviolent kind as well. She also does not consider the counterevidence, which is extensive. It includes such facts as that Denmark, which has no law against even hard-core pornography, and Japan, in which pornography is sold freely and is dominated by rape and bondage scenes, have rates of rape far lower than the United States; that the rate of rape in the United States has been falling even as the amount of hard-core pornography has undoubtedly increased because of the videocassette; and that women's status tends to be lower in societies that repress pornography (such as those of the Islamic nations) than in societies that do not (such as those of the Scandinavian nations)." See Posner, "Obsession," p. 34. For a collection of scientific articles on this subject see Malamuth and Donnerstein, *Pornography and Sexual Aggression;* see also Donnerstein et al., *The Question of Pornography.* For a refreshingly rational and erudite discussion of legal and moral issues related to sex and pornography see Posner, *Sex and Reason.* Catharine MacKinnon and Andrea Dworkin purport to offer indisputable evidence in the form of first-person accounts of the harm caused by pornographic materials; these accounts are transcripts of public hearings held in Minneapolis, Indianapolis, Los Angeles, and Massachusetts from approximately 1983 to 1992. MacKinnon and Dworkin claim that these materials have been "suppressed" and "censored" for almost fifteen years; a close reading of the footnotes, however, reveals that they hold this opinion because it took them a long time to find a publisher willing to publish them; see MacKinnon and Dworkin, *In Harm's Way,* p. 1, n. 1.

5. Kronhausen and Kronhausen, *Pornography and the Law,* p. 18.

6. Rabelais, *Gargantua et Pantagruel,* pp. 2–891; Joyce, *Ulysses.*

7. Bakhtin, *Dialogic Imagination.* For a discussion of Bakhtin's analysis of the novel as it relates to the *Jin Ping Mei* see Roy, "Introduction," *Plum in the Golden Vase,* pp. xliii–xlv.

8. Bakhtin, *Dialogic Imagination,* p. 35.

9. As Jean Marie Goulemot puts it: "Pornography is, after all, a strategy of writing. Or rather, for the pornographic text to fulfil its function, which is to produce a desire for physical pleasure and release in the reader, then it must put into operation a writerly strategy that is capable of producing that result and that result alone. That is to say that erotic literature is univocal, produces one meaning and is hostile to any attempt at interference or blurring." See Goulemot, *Forbidden Texts,* p. 62.

10. Kronhausen and Kronhausen, *Pornography and the Law,* p. 178. Another fa-

mous definition of pornography was written by Vladimir Nabokov in a postscript to his novel *Lolita* after he discovered that many readers considered it pornographic; his definition is indebted to the Kronhausens: "In pornographic novels, action has to be limited to the copulation of clichés. Style, structure, imagery should never distract the reader from his tepid lust. The novel must consist of an alternation of sexual scenes. The passages in between must be reduced to sutures of sense, logical bridges of the simplest design, brief expositions and explanation, which the reader will probably skip but must know they exist in order not to feel cheated. . . . Moreover, the sexual scenes in the book must follow a crescendo line, with new variations, new combinations, new sexes, and a steady increase in the number of participants . . . and therefore the end of the book must be more replete with lewd lore than the first chapters." See Nabokov, *Lolita*, pp. 284-285.

11. For the biography of Wang Huanghou see *Jiu Tang shu*, 7.51.2169-2170, and *Xin Tang shu*, 11.76.3473.

12. See *Ruyijun zhuan*, p. 2b; for a fully annotated version of this translation see Part Two.

13. Kang Zhengguo, *Chongshen fengyuejian*, p. 55.

14. See *Ruyijun zhuan*, p. 4b.

15. Ibid., p. 11a.

16. Foucault, *Sexuality*, 1.103. If the description of human sexuality as "an especially dense transfer point for relations of power" does not describe the plot of the *Ruyijun zhuan*, it is certainly close. In the *Ruyijun zhuan* the relationship between sex and the loss of imperial power is direct: Emperor Taizong dies soon after he becomes enamored of Wu Zetian; his son Emperor Gaozong becomes ill and dies after committing incest with her; and Wu Zetian herself becomes ill and loses the throne after becoming infatuated with Xue Aocao. The chronology of historical events is condensed to illustrate this point. But the observation that sexual relations in the *Ruyijun zhuan* revolve around the issue of power is, of course, merely one small step in the process of interpreting this difficult work: while it could be said that power is a factor of many scenes found in the *Ruyijun zhuan*, it is never the only factor and rarely seems to be the principal one. The implied author often sets Wu Zetian's desires in a context that is heavily laden with historical and classical allusions; these allusions serve as a sophisticated commentary for the educated reader who is fortunate enough to recognize them. And while it can be shown that the implied author is addressing complicated questions with sophisticated means, it is often difficult to determine what his ultimate point might be. Thus while the concept of power as discussed by Foucault can tell us something important about the plot of the *Ruyijun zhuan*, it is not particularly well suited to discussing the aspects of this work that make it truly unique.

17. Foucault, *Sexuality*, 1.68.

18. Hunt, *Invention of Pornography;* Hunt, *Eroticism and the Body Politic;* see also Michelson, *Speaking the Unspeakable*.

19. Hunt, *Invention of Pornography*, p. 11.

20. Ibid., p. 18; see also Darnton, *Edition et sédition*, pp. 13-16.

21. Frappier-Mazur, "Truth and the Obscene Word," pp. 203-221.

22. Hunt, *Invention of Pornography*, p. 10. Foucault does discuss the East, but he is brief. In any event, his observations are controversial: "China, Japan, India, Rome, the Arabo-Moslem societies . . . endowed themselves with an *ars erotica*. . . . Truth is drawn from pleasure itself, understood as a practice and accumulated as experience; pleasure is not considered in relation to an absolute law of the permitted and the forbidden, nor

by reference to a criterion of utility, but first and foremost in relation to itself; it is experienced as pleasure, evaluated in terms of its intensity, its specific quality, its duration, its reverberations in the body and the soul. . . . On the face of it at least, our civilization possesses no *ars erotica*. In return, it is undoubtedly the only civilization to practice a *scientia sexualis*." See Foucault, *Sexuality*, 1.57-58. Foucault evidently never heard of Daoist physiological alchemy. Its practitioners are supposed to focus not on pleasure but on the regulation of the vital energies of the body; it cannot be claimed that they understand pleasure in relation to itself: it would be more accurate to say that this is precisely the kind of attitude that physiological alchemy is meant to regulate. This is but one objection that could be raised regarding just one of the countries that Foucault names in his list; inhabitants of the other countries are also likely to view with some skepticism his description of their understanding of what he calls the "truth of sex." Foucault's attempt to contrast the *ars erotica* of China, Japan, and India to the *scientia sexualis* of the West bears a striking resemblance to what Edward Said calls "orientalism." In any event, stereotypical comparisons of East and West tell us very little worth knowing about either; see Said, *Orientalism*. Nadine Strossen challenges the notion that pornography is harmful, that it constitutes a violation of the civil rights of women, and that it leads to sexual aggression; see Strossen, *Defending Pornography*. She also notes that some recent critics of pornography lament its extreme and graphic style while simultaneously emulating those very features; see pp. 19 and 205.

23. Goulemot, *Forbidden Texts*, p. 40.

Chapter 2: Precursors

1. *Maoshi zhengyi*. For analyses of traditional commentaries that discover politics and morality behind the love poems of the *Shi jing* see Yu, *Reading of Imagery*, pp. 44-83, and Watson, *Early Chinese Literature*, pp. 202-230; see also Li, *Enchantment*, pp. 17-23.

2. Early Western attitudes toward allegorical and metaphorical readings of the *Shi jing* are summarized in Yu, *Reading of Imagery*, pp. 45-46. Yu argues that the terms "allegorical" and "metaphorical" do not adequately describe how poems of the *Shi jing* were meant to be interpreted; she contends that "the process is one of *contextualization*, not allegorization, and one that proved to be the dominant tradition in later criticism as well, which preferred to read a poet's work as literal records of actual experience, from which a biography could be constructed. Thus the moral lesson is not accidental or arbitrary, but one that arises from a specific context, and for a specific historical reason." See p. 76.

3. Ibid., pp. 69-70.

4. Watson, *Early Chinese Literature*, p. 211.

5. Zhu Xi's Song-dynasty edition of the *Shi jing* disposes of many of the most improbable political interpretations of the love poems. He recognizes that some of the poems are simply about love, which he styles licentiousness. But he does not completely reject political interpretations of the love poems; he admits they could serve as metaphors for the concerns of the state; see Zhu Xi, *Shi jizhuan*, p. 3.

6. Li, *Enchantment*, pp. 17-23.

7. For the Chinese text see Sima Xiangru, "Shanglin fu," pp. 66-67; for the translation see Li, *Enchantment*, p. 20.

8. Li, *Enchantment*, p. 20.

9. One of the earliest extended erotic descriptions found in the Chinese lan-

guage is contained in the "Meiren fu" (Rhapsody on the beauty), a work sometimes attributed to Sima Xiangru. Although this attribution is of questionable authenticity, its descriptions of seductive feminine beauty are similar to those found in the "Shanglin fu." There is much more detail in the "Meiren fu," however, even after the participants have become intimate, and the author does not divert the reader's attention to a moral of any sort. Instead he concludes with references to terms commonly used in Daoist descriptions of the beneficial effects of sexual relations. In this case the apotheosis of pleasure is a prelude to the calming of conscience. Daoist attitudes toward sex are discussed in more detail later in this chapter. For a brief discussion of the "Meiren fu" see van Gulik, *Sexual Life*, pp. 68-69; for the Chinese text see Sima Xiangru, "Meiren fu," in *Quan Han fu*, pp. 97-99. Many *fu* have been accused of presenting seduction under the guise of moral instruction; that examples like the "Meiren fu" lack such instruction shows that it was quite possible to write purely erotic *fu*. Thus the passages of moral instruction we do find in works like the "Shanglin fu" cannot be dismissed lightly.

10. In Chinese literature, feelings of loneliness and confusion often overwhelm a character at the precise moment of maximum sexual fulfillment. At the climax of the *You xianku* (Journey to the dwelling of the goddesses), a novelette from the late seventh century written in parallel prose, the lovers are awakened by the cries of a sick magpie and a crazed cock; they dress and then burst into tears. See Zhang Zhuo, *You xianku*, pp. 27-28; see also Zhang Zhuo, *You xianku*, in *Siwuxie huibao waibian*, 1.19-51.

11. Ling Xuan, *Zhao Feiyan waizhuan*, 6.1a-9b. For a modern typeset edition see Ling Xuan, *Zhao Feiyan waizhuan*, in *Siwuxie huibao waibian*, 1.59-67. For the biography of Zhao Feiyan see Ban Gu, *Han shu*, 12.97b.3988-3999. A few versions of this story appeared over the centuries under various titles. The Tang-dynasty version was particularly popular, and several elements from this story, such as the murder of a rival concubine's child and the death of the male protagonist through an overdose of aphrodisiacs, were incorporated into the late-Ming novel *Jin Ping Mei cihua*; see also Qin Chun, *Zhao Feiyan biezhuan*. For a modern edition see Qin Chun, *Zhao Feiyan biezhuan*, in *Siwuxie huibao waibian*, 1.73-79. A more erotic version of the story, complete with woodcut illustrations, appeared in 1621 under the title *Zhaoyang qushi* (The captivating history of Zhaoyang Palace); this version enters the realm of the supernatural, as Zhao Feiyan and her sister are reincarnations of fox and swallow spirits; see *Zhaoyang qushi*. For a brief discussion of the *Zhao Feiyan waizhuan* and *Zhao Feiyan biezhuan* see Xu Yimin, "*Zhao Feiyan waizhuan*," p. 745, and Xue Hongji, "*Zhao Feiyan biezhuan*," pp. 744-745. For a discussion of the text and authorship of the *Zhao Feiyan waizhuan* see Zhang Xincheng, *Weishu tongkao*, pp. 680-681. For a discussion of the text and authorship of the *Zhao Feiyan biezhuan* see Li Jianguo, *Songdai zhiguai chuanqi xulu*, pp. 160-163.

12. For the biography of Han Cheng Di, Liu Ao (51-7 B.C.), see *Han shu*, 1.9.301-331.

13. *Han Wudi neizhuan*, pp. 9-22; see also van Gulik, *Sexual Life*, pp. 136-137, and Xu Yimin, "Hanwu neizhuan," pp. 149-150.

14. For the biography of Emperor Wu, Liu Che (157-87 B.C.), see *Han shu*, 1.6.155-215.

15. See Yan Shigu, *Daye shiyi ji*, in *Tang Song chuanqi ji*, 6.201-209; for a discussion of this text and its attribution to Yan Shigu see Li Jianguo, *Tang Wudai zhiguai chuanqi xulu*, 2.555-563; *Milou ji*, in *Tang Song chuanqi ji*, 6.226-231; for a discussion of this text and its attribution to Han Wo see Li Jianguo, *Tang Wudai*, 2.897-900; see also Liu Yinbai, "*Milou ji*," p. 340. Yue Shi, *Yang Taizhen waizhuan*, 2.1.1a-11b and 2.2.1a-11b;

for a discussion of this text see Xue Hongji, "Yang Taizhen waizhuan," p. 665; for a detailed discussion see Li Jianguo, *Songdai zhiguai chuanqi xulu,* pp. 27-30.

16. For the biography of Lao Ai see *Shi ji,* 1.6.227; see also *Shi ji,* 8.85.2512, and *Zizhi tongjian,* 1.213-214.

17. For the biography of Lü Buwei see *Shi ji,* 8.85.2505-2514. This sentence is technically anachronistic: as Emperor Qin Shihuangdi had not yet proclaimed himself emperor, the empress dowager was still in reality a queen dowager.

18. See *Zizhi tongjian,* 1.213-214.

19. See *Shi ji,* 8.85.2508 and 2513.

20. Martin Huang, however, believes that Xue Aocao's "giant penis, normally a powerful symbol of supreme masculinity, results in his emasculation and forces him to assume a submissive role usually played by a female (as Wu Zetian did when she was a palace lady). In this situation of gender role reversal, castration becomes the only means for him to reclaim his lost masculinity." See Huang, *Desire and Fictional Narrative,* p. 122. While I disagree with this observation, Huang's exploration of desire in the Chinese context remains one of the most insightful works written on this topic to date.

21. See Needham and Lu, *Physiological Alchemy;* van Gulik, *Sexual Life,* pp. 70-115; Maspero, "Les procédés"; Schipper, "Science, Magic," pp. 14-20; Robinet, *Introduction;* Kohn, *Taoist Meditation.* For a discussion of "common misconceptions" about Daoist sexuality see Schipper, *Taoist Body,* pp. 144-155; see also Fang Fu Ruan, *Sex in China.*

22. Needham and Lu, *Physiological Alchemy,* pp. 29-30.

23. van Gulik, *Sexual Life,* p. 70.

24. Needham and Lu, *Physiological Alchemy,* p. 217.

25. Ibid. Needham coined the term "anablastemic enchymoma" to translate the Chinese term *"neidan";* anablastemic refers to the restoration of youth, and enchymoma refers to the elixir within; see pp. 27-28. For a detailed description of inner alchemy, as well as a short history, see Robinet, "Original Contributions," pp. 297-330.

26. For the Chinese text see *Quan Han fu,* p. 98; for the translation see van Gulik, *Sexual Life,* p. 69.

27. Schipper takes issue with the suggestion that in Daoism sexual activity was natural, spontaneous, or practiced freely. He cites the proliferation of sexual handbooks in the second century B.C. as evidence that sexual activity could not have been "natural"; see Schipper, *Taoist Body,* pp. 145-147.

28. *Han shu,* 6.30.1778-1779.

29. For the Chinese text see *Han shu,* 6.30.1779; for the translation and a discussion of this section of the *Han shu* see van Gulik, *Sexual Life,* pp. 70-71.

30. For a description of the medical texts found at Mawangdui see Harper, "Translation and Prolegomena," pp. 2-42; for a list of the medical texts see pp. 7-8. For a description of the tomb and other manuscripts see Riegel, "Summary." For a discussion and partial translation of one of the sex manuals entitled *He yinyang* see Harper, "Sexual Arts." For the original texts see *Mawangdui Hanmu boshu,* vol. 4. For another translation of *He yinyang* and for a translation of another Mawangdui sex manual titled *Tianxia zhidao tan* (Discourse on the ultimate way under heaven) see Wile, *Art of the Bedchamber,* pp. 77-83. For a discussion of the technical terminology found in the Mawangdui texts see Li and McMahon, "Contents and Terminology." For a revised and expanded version of Harper's study of early medical texts see Harper, *Early Chinese Medical Literature.*

31. Harper, "Sexual Arts," p. 197.

32. For the Chinese text and the translation see Harper, "Sexual Arts," pp. 204-

205. A translation of the *He yinyang* is also found in Wile, *Art of the Bedchamber*, pp. 78-79. On p. 222 (n. 4), Wile discusses the translation of the term "stove frame"; this passage makes the unusual difficulties of translating this type of literature abundantly clear: "Harper explores the possibilities for *tsao-kang* quite resourcefully, but in the end cannot definitively decipher the metaphor, let alone its referent. Because it lies somewhere between armpit and neck in our itinerary, Harper's 'Perhaps *tsao kang* refers to the thorax or to some part thereof' seems a safe assumption. The use of the word [*kang*] in anatomical nomenclature can be seen in *yang-kang*, an acupuncture point on the bladder meridian, and *mu-chih-kang*, the ends of the eyelids."

33. See Schipper, *Taoist Body*, pp. 103-108.

34. *Ishimpō*, comp. Tamba Yasuyori.

35. For a discussion of the texts found in the *Ishimpō* see Hsia et al., *Essentials of Medicine*, 1.1-26; van Gulik, *Sexual Life*, pp. 135-169; Wile, *Art of the Bedchamber*, pp. 83-113; and Harper, "Sexual Arts," pp. 218-219.

36. See *Shuangmei jingan congshu*. The titles of the sex handbooks that Ye Dehui found in the bibliography of the *Sui shu* were interspersed among the titles of various medical texts; see *Sui shu*, 4.34.1040-1050. See also van Gulik, *Sexual Life*, pp. 122-123, and Wile, *Art of the Bedchamber*, pp. 83-84.

37. Sun Simiao, *Beiji qianjin yaofang*.

38. Ibid., p. 489.

39. Unschuld, *Medicine in China*, pp. 101-116; Porkert, *Theoretical Foundations*, pp. 57 and 109.

40. van Gulik, *Sexual Life*, p. 313.

41. For the Chinese text see *Jin Ping Mei cihua*, 2.176-177; for the translation see Roy, *Plum in the Golden Vase*, 2.145.

42. For a discussion of this technique see van Gulik, *Sexual Life*, pp. 194-200. The technique is also discussed in Sun Simiao, *Beiji qianjin yaofang*, p. 489, and Wile, *Art of the Bedchamber*, pp. 36-43. For a similar analysis of this passage see Satyendra, "Metaphors of the Body," p. 91.

43. The sun and moon as symbols of male and female principles figure prominently in the meditation techniques of the Shangqing sect of Daoism; see Bokenkamp, *Early Daoist Scriptures*, pp. 283-289.

Chapter 3: Desire in the Ming Dynasty

1. For a discussion of human desire in the late Ming dynasty see Huang, *Desire and Fictional Narrative*, pp. 5-22; Epstein, "Beauty Is the Beast," pp. 109-180; Cheng, "Reason, Substance, and Human Desires," pp. 469-509; Li, *Enchantment*, pp. 47-88; and de Bary, "Individualism," pp. 181-225.

2. Chan, *Instructions*, pp. xix-xx. The Four Books are the *Analects*, *Great Learning*, *Doctrine of the Mean*, and *Book of Mencius;* the Five Classics are the *Book of History*, *Book of Odes*, *Book of Changes*, *Book of Rites*, and *Spring and Autumn Annals*.

3. The influence of Wang Yangming's predecessors on his philosophy should not be overlooked. His views concerning the moral nature of the mind and its self-sufficiency, for example, are foreshadowed in the philosophy of Lu Xiangshan (Lu Jiu-yuan, 1139-1193). Lu Xiangshan holds that the investigation of things is the same as the investigation of the mind; he questions the devotion of philosophers to what he considers isolated external details that are not central to life. The idealism of Wang

Yangming and Lu Xiangshan is often referred to as the "Lu-Wang school" and is contrasted to the rationalism of the "Cheng-Zhu school" of Cheng Yi, to a lesser extent his brother Cheng Hao (Cheng Mingdao, 1032–1085), and Zhu Xi. Wang Yangming also develops some of Zhu Xi's ideas concerning the problem of moral cultivation; for a brief discussion of Wang Yangming's concept of the mind (and his predecessors) see Tang, "Concept of Moral Mind." Although their views of individuality and the nature of human desire exerted great influence on the fiction written during the latter sixteenth century, various schools based on the philosophy of Wang Yangming that flourished after the *Ruyijun zhuan* was written, such as the Jiangyou, Zhezhong, and Taizhou schools, are not examined here. For more information concerning the philosophy of Wang Yangming, the influence of his predecessors on his thought, and other late-Ming philosophers see Chan, *Instructions;* de Bary, "Individualism," pp. 145–247; Li Zehou, "Ming-Qing Neo-Confucianism," pp. 551–569; Chan, *Source Book;* Tu Wei-ming, *Neo-Confucian Thought in Action;* Tu Wei-ming, *Humanity and Self-Cultivation;* and Ching, *To Acquire Wisdom.*

4. Wang Yangming's criticism of contemporary society and philosophy is summarized in a letter he wrote to his friend Gu Lin (Gu Dongqiao, 1476–1545); one section is particularly important and has often been treated as a separate essay titled "Baben saiyuan" (Pulling up the root and stopping up the source). See Wang Yangming, *Wang Yangming quanji,* 1.53–57; for a translation see Chan, *Instructions,* pp. 117–124.

5. Chan, *Wang Yangming Chuanxi lu,* p. 94.

6. "For all his emphasis on personal intuition of truth, he retains a faith in the fundamental rationality of man, and for all his insistence on discovering right and wrong for oneself, it does not even occur to him that there could be any essential conflict between subjective and objective morality, or that genuine introspection could lead to anything other than the affirmation of clear and common moral standards." See de Bary, "Individualism," p. 156.

7. Ibid., p. 150.

8. Rawski, "Economic and Social Foundations"; see also Elvin, *Pattern of the Chinese Past,* p. 203.

9. de Bary, "Individualism," pp. 175–176; see also Plaks, *Four Masterworks,* p. 19; and Brokaw, *Ledgers.*

10. For the Chinese text see *Wang Yangming quanji,* p. 968; for the translation see Chan, *Source Book,* p. 660.

11. For a translation of *Xiyou ji,* attributed to Wu Chengen, see Yu, *Journey to the West;* for a translation of *Shuihu zhuan* see Shapiro, *Outlaws of the Marsh;* for a translation of the first forty chapters of Xiaoxiao Sheng (pseud.), *Jin Ping Mei cihua,* see Roy, *Plum in the Golden Vase,* vols. 1 and 2; for a translation of the remainder see Egerton, *Golden Lotus;* for a translation of *Sanguo yanyi,* attributed to Luo Guanzhong or Shi Naian, see Roberts, *Three Kingdoms.*

12. Yu, *Journey to the West,* 3.220–237.

13. *Shuihu quanzhuan,* 3.1222; see also Shapiro, *Outlaws of the Marsh,* 3.1186–1191.

14. *Shuihu quanzhuan,* 2.461–475; see also Shapiro, *Outlaws of the Marsh,* 2.502–505.

15. For an examination of the misogyny and gratuitous violence found in the *Shuihu zhuan* see Hsia, "Water Margin," pp. 75–114.

16. Mote, "Yüan and Ming," pp. 248–249.

17. For two of many examples see Plaks, *Four Masterworks,* pp. 423 and 464.

18. *Sanguo zhi tongsu yanyi,* 10.62a; see also Plaks, *Four Masterworks,* p. 412.

19. This was from 1400 to 1575, but especially from 1450 to 1550; see Hanan, *Vernacular,* p. 54.

20. Hanan, *Chinese Short Story,* pp. 149-150; see also Hanan, *Vernacular,* pp. 60-68.

21. "Wenjing yuanyang hui," pp. 154-169; Hong Pian published this story in approximately 1550. For an annotated French translation see Lévy, *Études,* pp. 195-210. The *Jin Ping Mei* refers to the prologue of the "Wenjing yuanyang hui" at the very beginning of the novel; see Roy, *Plum in the Golden Vase,* 1.465, n. 6, and 466, n. 7.

22. For the Chinese text see Wang Xianqian, *Xunzi jijie,* 22.694; for the translation and a discussion of this passage see Yu, *Rereading the Stone,* p. 58.

23. For the Chinese text see *Xunzi jijie,* 23.704; for the translation and a discussion see Yu, *Rereading the Stone,* p. 63.

24. See Kline and Ivanhoe, *Virtue, Nature, and Moral Agency;* Goldin, *Rituals of the Way.*

25. Epstein, "Beauty Is the Beast," p. 143; see also Epstein, *Competing Discourses,* pp. 78-79.

26. Yu, *Rereading the Stone,* pp. 53-109.

27. Ibid., p. 108. Martin Huang argues that "the obsession with individual desire is an essential quality that defines traditional Chinese fiction as a narrative genre." See Huang, *Desire and Fictional Narrative,* p. 3; for a discussion of the liberation of desire in the late Ming and the anxiety it often caused, see pp. 5-22.

28. Huang Xun's education, his interest in the writings of Zhu Xi, and his discussions of human desire are examined in greater detail in Chapter 4.

29. For the Chinese text see Zhu Xi, *Zhongyong zhangju,* in *Sishu jizhu,* pp. 2a-2b; for the translation and a discussion of this passage see Ching, "Chu Hsi," p. 279.

30. For the Chinese text see *Jinsi lu,* 12.11; for the translation see Chan, *Reflections,* p. 272.

31. See Chan, *Source Book,* p. 631.

32. Chan, *Reflections,* p. 272.

33. If a person does not know how to regulate his passions, Zhu Xi says, the result could be the destruction of his nature: "The enlightened person controls his feelings so that they will be in accord with the Mean. He rectifies his mind and nourishes his nature. The stupid person does not know how to control them. He lets them loose until they are depraved, fetter his nature, and destroy it. In the way of learning, the first thing is to be clear in one's mind and to know where to go and then to act vigorously in order that one may arrive at sagehood." See Chan, *Reflections,* p. 36.

34. *Wang Yangming Chuanxi lu,* p. 104.

35. For the Chinese text see *Wang Yangming Chuanxi lu,* pp. 148-149; for the translation see Chan, *Instructions,* p. 82.

36. See Keqin, *Biyan lu,* no. 2003, 48.139a-292a; for a partial translation see Shaw, *Blue Cliff Records.*

37. For the Chinese text see *Wang Yangming Chuanxi lu,* p. 104; for the translation see Chan, *Instructions,* p. 52.

38. Ibid.

39. *Wang Yangming Chuanxi lu,* pp. 104-105.

40. Zhu Xi, *Zhongyong zhangju,* in *Sishu jizhu,* p. 2b.

41. For the Chinese text see *Wang Yangming Chuanxi lu,* p. 119; for the translation see Chan, *Instructions,* p. 60.

42. For the Chinese text see *Wang Yangming Chuanxi lu,* p. 120; for the translation see Chan, *Instructions,* p. 62.

43. For the Chinese text see *Wang Yangming Chuanxi lu*, p. 92; for the translation see Chan, *Instructions*, p. 44.

44. Liu Zongzhou (1578-1645), author of one of the most insightful commentaries to the works of Wang Yangming, puts it bluntly: "As soon as a single thought arises it is already desire." Quoted in *Wang Yangming Chuanxi lu*, p. 67.

45. For a discussion of the mirror as a Buddhist metaphor for the mind see Yu, *Rereading the Stone*, pp. 145-149.

46. *Wang Yangming Chuanxi lu*, pp. 37, 67, 83, and 105.

47. Ibid., p. 96; Chan, *Instructions*, p. 46.

48. For the Chinese text see *Wang Yangming Chuanxi lu*, pp. 217-218; for the translation see Chan, *Instructions*, p. 134.

49. The dating of the *Ruyijun zhuan* is discussed in Chapter 7.

50. This chapter is most concerned with the thought of Wang Yangming, as his philosophy was not only prominent but controversial at the time the *Ruyijun zhuan* was written. But the writings of philosophers like Wang Gen (1483?-1540) should not be overlooked. Wang Gen's ideas about the mind and the regulation of the body are quite different from those of Wang Yangming. As de Bary has noted, our understanding of the mind is quite different if approached from Wang Gen's vantage point: "Here then we observe a difference between Wang Ken and Wang Yang-ming which has important implications for those who follow them. Wang Ken's conception of the self is strongly physical—the bodily self or person (*shen*). Wang Yang-ming's emphasis in innate knowledge is on the mind (*hsin*), especially the identity of mind with principle or nature. Nature for Wang Ken is the physical self—not excluding, of course, the mind which was understood as of one substance with the body and which most often has the sense of 'heart.' Hence the terms 'School of the Mind' or 'Subjective Idealism' frequently used to designate the Wang Yang-ming school can be applied to Wang Ken and his followers only with substantial qualification. Liu Tsung-chou, a later 'revisionist' within the Yang-ming school, noted the crucial difference between Wang Ken and Yang-ming on this point, and asked whether it did not portend the abandonment of mind control and of the restraining influence of the mind over bodily desires." See de Bary, "Individualism," pp. 165-166. But even in the thought of Wang Yangming, the mind's control of the body appears to be an unresolved question.

Chapter 4: Authorship

1. Huang Xun, *Dushu yide*, 2.26b-28a.

2. Ibid., 2.27a.

3. For the biography of Zhang Yizhi (d. 705) see Liu Xu, *Jiu Tang shu*, 8.78.2706-2708, and Ouyang Xiu and Song Qi, *Xin Tang shu*, 13.104.4014-4016; for the biography of Zhang Changzong (d. 705) see *Jiu Tang shu*, 8.78.2706-2708, and *Xin Tang shu*, 13.104.4014-4016.

4. A brief summary of Huang's Xun's career is found in Liu Hui, "*Ruyijun zhuan* de kanke niandai," pp. 53-57.

5. *Jiaxing fu tuji*, 11.10a. This short biography of Huang Xun is also found, with minor textual variations, in *Jiaxing fu zhi*, 14.5b.

6. She district is today an area northwest of Xiuning district in Anhui province.

7. See Hucker, *Dictionary of Official Titles*, 183.1420 and 384.4691. It would probably have been more accurate to refer to Huang Xun's title as *bingbu lang*, or bureau

director in the Ministry of War; see Huang Xun, *Huang Tan Xiansheng wenji*, preface, p. 2b; for a description of this office see *Dictionary of Official Titles*, 384.4691 and 426.5278.

8. See Huang Xun, *Huang Tan Xiansheng wenji*, 3.13b and 5.18b. According to the *Huizhou fu zhi*, Huang Xun was from a place called Tandu in She district; this appears to be the reason why he is also referred to as Huang Tan; see *Huizhou fu zhi*, 18.16b.

9. *Huizhou fu zhi*, 13.31b.

10. 兼 was 樣; corrected per next occurrence found in the next line.

11. 唧 was written with the wrong radical on the right side; 唧同銜.

12. 望 was written with an incomplete and rare orthographic variant; see Morohashi Tetsuji, *Dai Kan-Wa jiten*, 7.21053.

13. *Huizhou fu zhi*, 18.16b. For another appraisal of the career of Huang Xun that appears to have been based on this passage in the *Huizhou fu zhi* see Liu Hui, "*Ruyijun zhuan*," pp. 53–54. Liu Hui lists the source of this biography as a local gazetteer called *Shexian zhi* from the Jiajing reign period. I have not located a local gazetteer of this title that dates to the Jiajing reign period; nor could I find this passage in the copy of the *Shexian zhi* that was published in 1609. Thus the ultimate source of this quotation is unclear. In any event, the version I quote here is clearly earlier; see *Shexian zhi*.

14. For a description of this title see *Dictionary of Official Titles*, 313.3733 and 421.5204. Jiaxing district is today an area to the east of Wuxing district.

15. The term *"dangdao"* is used to describe Huang Xun's superior; it is a circumlocution that allows the author of this biography to avoid using his title or real name. It could refer to the head of the Board of Personnel or even to the prime minister. For the Office of Scrutiny see *Dictionary of Official Titles*, 110.138.

16. See *Dictionary of Official Titles*, 157.965.

17. See *Dictionary of Official Titles*, 302.3573 and 384.4691.

18. Huang Xun, *Huang Ming mingchen jingji lu;* all four titles are also mentioned in *Shexian zhi*, 15.5a. The *Shexian zhi* notes that the *Daxue yanyi fujian* consisted of one *juan;* it appears to have been lost.

19. Huang Xun, *Huang Tan Xiansheng wenji*, 3.7b and 3.13a–b.

20. Ibid., 5.16a. He passed the provincial examination in 1525; see Huang Xun, *Huang Tan Xiansheng wenji*, 3.29b, and *Huizhou fu zhi*, 13.30b. He passed the *jinshi* examination in 1529; see Huang Xun, *Huang Tan Xiansheng wenji*, 3.3b, and *Huizhou fu zhi*, 13.31b.

21. Huang Xun, *Huang Tan Xiansheng wenji*, 3.13b and 5.18b.

22. Huang Xun, *Huang Tan Xiansheng wenji*, 3.25a and 7.17a. Huang Xun says he was made a *shi* to Jiangnan; this is an imprecise term that is usually translated as "commissioner"; see *Dictionary of Official Titles*, 421.5197. Jiangnan is a general term that refers to the region south of the Yangzi River; it includes the provinces of Jiangsu, Anhui, and Jiangxi.

23. Huang Zhijun, "Zhanyan," 19.26b. The precise title mentioned by Huang Zhijun is *ancha si fushi*, which appears to be an abbreviation for *tixing ancha shi si fushi*, or surveillance vice-commissioner in the Provincial Surveillance Commission. I suspect that Huang Xun might actually have been an assistant surveillance commissioner, or *ancha qianshi*. When he was district magistrate his rank was 7a; when he ended his career his rank was 5a. The rank of a surveillance vice-commissioner was 4a, while the rank of an assistant surveillance commissioner was 5a; if he were really surveillance vice-commissioner, a demotion would have been entailed when he was later named bureau director in the Ministry of War. I have not encountered any evidence to suggest

that Huang Xun was ever demoted, so the title ascribed to him by Huang Zhijun may be erroneous. The biography of Huang Xun quoted by Liu Hui lists his title as *jijian*, an unofficial reference to *jishizhong*, or supervising secretary; see Liu Hui, "*Ruyijun zhuan*," pp. 53–54. During the Ming dynasty, a supervising secretary was a member of the Six Offices of Scrutiny (Liuke); they were responsible for maintaining censorial surveillance over the Six Ministries and monitored the flow of documents between the emperor and the ministries. The rank of a supervising secretary fluctuated between 5a and 9a. At this point in his career, Huang Xun appears to have had surveillance or supervisory responsibilities, but his various biographies do not agree what title he held. For a discussion of these titles see *Dictionary of Official Titles*, 496.6446, 154.917, 130.539, 133.587, and 317.3793.2.

24. Huang Xun, *Huang Tan Xiansheng wenji*, 3.29b. For a discussion of this title see *Dictionary of Official Titles*, 452.5713.

25. Huang Xun, *Huang Tan Xiansheng wenji*, 5.19a.

26. Ibid., preface, p. 2b; *Jiaxing fu tuji*, 11.10a. For a description of this office see *Dictionary of Official Titles*, 384.4691 and 426.5278.

27. Huang Xun, *Huang Tan Xiansheng wenji*, 10.18b.

28. Ibid., preface, p. 3b. I have encountered only one significant discrepancy in the various descriptions of the career of Huang Xun. In the *Siku quanshu zongmu*, 502.2, he is said to have attained the position of *fu du yushi*, or vice-censor-in-chief; for a description of this title see *Dictionary of Official Titles*, 546.7335; the rank of a vice-censor-in-chief was 3a. I have not found this title associated with the name Huang Xun in any other work. I suspect that the author of this entry in the *Siku quanshu zongmu* simply misread the biography of Huang Xun that is found in the *Huizhou fu zhi*. When Huang Xun passed the *jinshi* examination in 1529, the title "district magistrate of Jiaxing" was recorded after his name; in the next column his colleague Wang Shangning, who passed the examination at the same time, was named vice-censor-in-chief. It appears that Wang Shangning's title in one column was erroneously applied to Huang Xun in the previous column; see *Huizhou fu zhi*, 13.31b. In any event, it appears that Huang Xun never became vice-censor-in-chief.

29. Huang Xun, *Huang Tan Xiansheng wenji*, preface, p. 4a.

30. Huang Xun discusses the nature of human desire in several passages; for some of the more significant see Huang Xun, *Huang Tan Xiansheng wenji*, 1.36b, 1.41a-b, 4.19a-b, 5.11b, 5.12b, and 6.5a-6b.

31. For a description of the Ziyang Shuyuan see *Huizhou fu zhi*, 9.19a-21b.

32. Huang Xun, *Huang Tan Xiansheng wenji*, 5.16b.

33. Ibid., 5.16b.

34. Ibid., 1.20a-22b.

35. Ibid., 1.21a-21b.

36. Ibid., 1.21b.

37. Ibid., 1.42a.

38. Ibid., 5.16a.

39. The *Dushu yide* specifically mentions the following dates: 1519 (3.42a), 1524 (3.44b), 1529 (4.32a), 1531 (1.4b), 1532 (4.20b), 1536 (2.26a, 3.34b), 1537 (4.8a), and 1538 (2.37b). Several historical events from the 1530s are mentioned, as well, such as the completion of the nine imperial temples in 1536 (3.35a) and the changing of the Yongle emperor's temple name in 1538 (2.37b); see Xia Xie, *Ming tongjian*, 2132.12, 2336.1, and 2150.2. It thus appears that much of the *Dushu yide* was written during the 1530s.

40. Huang Xun, *Dushu yide*, pp. 2.26a–37b. Liu Hui speculates that the "Du *Ruyijun zhuan*" might have been written before 1525 because that is the year in which Huang Xun took part in the provincial examinations. Liu Hui does not, however, attempt to explain how these examinations could have been related to the timing of Huang Xun's appraisal of this work; see Liu Hui, "*Ruyijun zhuan*," p. 56.

41. *Wenxuan*, 3.1405 (謝朓、始 出 尚書省): 宸景厭照臨。昏風淪繼體.

42. 已 was 巳.

43. Zhu Xi, *Zhuzi quanshu*, 66.18a: 晉陽啓唐祚、王明紹巢封、垂統已如此、繼體宜昏風。麈聚瀆天倫、牝晨司禍凶、乾綱一以墜、天樞遂崇崇。淫毒穢宸極、虐焰燔蒼穹、向非狄張徒、誰辦取日功。云何歐陽子、秉筆迷至公、唐經亂周紀、凡例孰此容、侃侃范太史、受說伊川翁、春秋二 三策、萬 古開群蒙. A corrupt version of this poem is found at the end of the *Nongqing kuaishi*: 晉陽啓唐祚、王明昭巢封、垂統尚如此、繼體宜昏風。麈聚瀆天倫、牝晨司禍凶、乾綱一以墜、天樞遂崇崇。淫毒況宸極、虐焰燔蒼穹、向非狄張徒、誰辦取日功。云何歐陽子、秉筆迷至公、唐經亂周紀、凡例熟比 容。侃侃范太史、受說伊川翁、春秋二 三策、萬 古開群蒙; see *Nongqing kuaishi*, pp. 449–450. The significance of this poem's appearance in the *Nongqing kuaishi* is discussed in Chapter 8.

44. Legge, *Chinese Classics*, 3.207: 天作孽、猶可違、自作孽、不可逭.

45. 褆同褆; see Morohashi, *Dai Kan-Wa jiten*, 10.34416.

46. *Shi ji*, 8.85.2506: 此奇貨可居.

47. Fan Ye, *Hou Han shu*, 7.62.2053.5: 以妻制夫、以卑臨尊、違乾坤之道、失陽唱之義. *Jiu Tang shu*, 3.22.857.15: 以明陽不獨運、資陰和 以助成；陰不孤行、待陽唱而方應.

48. Ban Gu, *Han shu*, 7.35.1903.5: 定 國禽獸行、亂人倫、逆天道、當誅. *Guanzi jiaozheng*, 5.76 (管子、八 觀): 倍人倫、而禽獸行、十年而滅.

49. 郎 was 即.

50. 已 was 巳.

51. Li Baiyao, *Beiqi shu*, 1.21.293; Li Yanshou, *Bei shi*, 4.31.1144: 姿體雄異.

52. *Bei shi*, 4.31.1144: 昂藏敖曹.

53. 毒 was 毒.

54. 已 was 巳.

55. Liu Hui, "*Ruyijun zhuan*," p. 53, changed 愛 to 受.

56. 云 was 雲.

57. 自 was 目.

58. 奔奔 was 奔之; corrected per *Maoshi yinde*, 10.49.1 (鄘風、鶉 之奔奔): 鶉之奔奔、鵲 之彊彊。人之無良、我以 爲兄。鵲 之彊彊、鶉 之奔奔、人之無良、我以爲君. See also Fang Xuanling, *Jin shu*, 3.28.863.14.

59. See note 44.

60. Huang Xun, *Dushu yide*, 2.27a.

61. For the biography of Tang Taizong, Li Shimin, see *Jiu Tang shu*, 1.2.21–38, and *Xin Tang shu*, 1.2.23–49. For the biography of the prince of Chao, Li Yuanji (602–626), the fourth son of Tang Gaozu and the younger brother of Tang Taizong, see *Jiu Tang shu*, 7.64.2420–2423, and *Xin Tang shu*, 11.79.3545–3547. According to the standard histories, Li Yuanji was not loved by the commoners under his command; he is said to have committed adultery with their women and to have used pedestrians for archery practice, taking delight in the spectacle of peasants running for cover as arrows rained down upon them. In 626 he persuaded the crown prince to join in a plot to assassinate Taizong; he claimed that Taizong was planning to usurp the position of crown prince

although that was what he was planning to do himself. When the plot was uncovered, they were put to death. Taizong then became crown prince and soon became emperor. The consort of Li Yuanji with whom Taizong committed adultery was surnamed Yang; her relationship with Taizong is mentioned in *Xin Tang shu*, 12.80.3579. Taizong had intended to elevate her to empress but was dissuaded by a senior minister; she gave birth to Li Ming, Taizong's fourteenth son. He was eventually named the prince of Cao; see *Jiu Tang shu*, 8.76.2666, and *Xin Tang shu*, 12.80.3579.

62. For the biography of Tang Gaozong, Li Zhi (628–683), see *Jiu Tang shu*, 1.4.65–113, and *Xin Tang shu*, 1.3.51–79. This line refers to Wu Zetian; for her biography see *Jiu Tang shu*, 1.6.115–134, *Xin Tang shu*, 1.4.81–114, and *Xin Tang shu*, 11.76.3474–3485. When Gaozong began his affair with Wu Zetian she was the lady of talents of his father, Emperor Tang Taizong. For a description of her title see *Dictionary of Official Titles*, 515.6830.

63. For the biography of Tang Xuanzong, Li Longji (685–762), see *Jiu Tang shu*, 1.7.165–238, and *Xin Tang shu*, 1.5.121–154. For the biography of the prince of Shou, Li Mao, the eighteenth son of Tang Xuanzong, see *Jiu Tang shu*, 10.107.3266–3267, and *Xin Tang shu*, 12.82.3613. Xuanzong committed adultery with Honored Consort Yang (Yang Guifei), one of the most famous women of the Tang dynasty; for her biography see *Jiu Tang shu*, 7.51.2178–2181, and *Xin Tang shu*, 11.76.3493–3496. When Gracious Consort Wu died, Xuanzong was disconsolate; his spirits did not revive until he met Yang Guifei, the consort of Gracious Consort Wu's son Li Mao. The manners and deportment of Yang Guifei were said to have reminded Xuanzong of Gracious Consort Wu.

64. This appears to be a quotation, but I have not been able to locate the source.

65. For the biography of Zhu Xi (1130–1200), one of the most famous philosophers of the Song dynasty, see Tuo Tuo et al., *Song shi*, 36.429.12751–12770. Jinyang is the name of the prefecture in which Tang Gaozu began the rebellion that ended with the founding of the Tang dynasty. The first half of this line refers to Taizong committing adultery with the consort of his younger brother Li Yuanji, the prince of Chao; see note 61. In the full text of Zhu Xi's poem, the seeds of the decline of the Tang dynasty are sown by Taizong and this affair; Zhu Xi also refers to Taizong and Gaozong committing adultery by sharing the same woman and, as well, to the impropriety of Wu Zetian's reign after she became emperor. Of course, Huang Xun's appraisal of the *Ruyijun zhuan* concludes that Taizong is ultimately responsible for the decline of the Tang.

66. This line contains a rare character for the word "evaded," *huan*, that is probably meant to call to mind a famous line from the *Shu jing*: "Calamities produced by Heaven may be avoided, but calamities of one's own making cannot be evaded." For the Chinese text and the translation see Legge, *The Shoo King*, p. 207.

67. This is a designation of one of the nine concubines; see *Dictionary of Official Titles*, 117.288. Wu Zetian was thirty-one in the year 655.

68. This encounter between Wu Zetian and Gaozong is mentioned briefly in *Zizhi tongjian*, 6284.7; Wu Zetian wept upon seeing Gaozong, and he wept in response. This encounter is also mentioned in Zhu Xi, *Yupi Zizhi tongjian gangmu*, 40.20b.

69. Gaozong's nickname was Zhinu, which literally means "pheasant slave"; see *Xin Tang shu*, 12.80.3571.14. I do not know why he was given this nickname. Huang Xun also refers to Gaozong as Zhinu in *Dushu yide*, 2.43a.6. The term "unique commodity" (*qihuo*) is an allusion to Lü Buwei, the famous prime minister of Emperor Qin Shihuangdi (r. 221–210 B.C.). When Lü Buwei was a merchant, he met a hostage princeling from the state of Qin named Zichu. Lü Buwei quickly perceived that if he

cultivated the friendship of this hostage he could "raise the status of his own gate"—or as the businessman in him put it, "This unique commodity can be stockpiled." Lü Buwei invested a tremendous amount of resources and brilliantly insinuated Zichu into the line of succession of the state of Qin. But this was just the beginning. Lü Buwei's favorite concubine soon caught the eye of Zichu, and he wanted her for his own. Lü Buwei was furious, but when he considered the investment he had already made in Zichu, he decided to give her up (although he knew she was pregnant with his own child at the time). She concealed this fact from Zichu and eventually gave birth to a boy named Zheng. This boy would eventually become Emperor Qin Shihuangdi, and Lü Buwei's initial investment paid handsome returns indeed: he was appointed prime minister and became one of the richest men in the country. But some time after Qin Shihuangdi had ascended the throne, his mother the queen dowager, with whom Lü Buwei was having an affair, inexplicably became quite lecherous; Lü Buwei feared that this affair would come to light, and in an unusual attempt to gratify the appetites of his former concubine, he introduced to her the lewd character Lao Ai, whose unique career is discussed at some length in Chapter 2. For the biography of Lü Buwei see *Shi ji*, 8.85.2505–2514.

70. The phrase "the female comes first and the male sings out" is an inversion of the principle behind the proverbial expression "the husband calls out and the wife follows" (*fu chang fu sui*). For an early discussion of this principle and the dangers inherent in a man following the example of a woman see Fan Ye, *Hou Han shu*, 7.62.2052–2053; see also *Jiu Tang shu*, 3.22.857.15. Early examples of the phrase used to describe incest, "the behavior of animals" (*qinshou xing*), are found in *Guanzi jiaozheng*, 5.76, and *Han shu*, 7.35.1903.5.

71. Wu Zetian's paramour Zhang Yizhi was named auxiliary to the director of imperial mounts in 699; this department was soon renamed and Zhang Yizhi became director of the palace corral; see *Jiu Tang shu*, 8.78.2706, and *Xin Tang shu*, 13.104.4014. For a description of Zhang Yizhi's titles see *Dictionary of Official Titles*, 297.3502 and 212.1958.

72. The names Squire Five and Squire Six refer to Zhang Yizhi and Zhang Changzong, respectively; Zhang Changzong's nickname Squire Six is a pun on the term *"liulang,"* another name for the lotus blossom; see Morohashi, *Dai Kan-Wa jiten*, 2.1453.577.3. Zhang Changzong was also the sixth son of his family.

73. The First Year of Perfect Satisfaction was 692.

74. For biographical information about Xue Huaiyi see *Jiu Tang shu*, 14.183.4741–4743.

75. Huang Xun is correct in asserting that standard historical sources do not contain explicit descriptions of Wu Zetian's amorous exploits with Xue Huaiyi. The *Jiu Tang shu* and the *Xin Tang shu*, in fact, never aver that Xue Huaiyi had become Wu Zetian's lover, although this is clearly the inference the reader is invited to make.

76. This description of Xue Aocao's physical constitution contains two brief yet significant quotations from the historical record; they are discussed in some detail later in this chapter.

77. The story of Lao Ai is discussed at length in Chapter 2.

78. I suspect that the original text may be corrupt at this point. This line might refer to Gaozong's meeting with Wu Zetian and Taizong's other former consorts in Ganye Temple.

79. This appears to be a quotation, but I have not been able to identify the source.

80. This is a quotation from a poem in the *Shi jing* that is traditionally interpreted

as criticism of improper sexual relations between the wife of a ruler and his brother: "Boldly faithful in their pairings are quails; Vigorously so are magpies. This man is all vicious, and I consider him my brother! Vigorously faithful in their pairings are magpies; Boldly so are quails. This woman is all vicious, and I regard her as marchioness!" For the Chinese text see *Maoshi yinde*, 10.49.1; for the translation see Legge, *Chinese Classics*, 4.80. See also *Jin shu*, 3.28.863.14.

81. The term "assembled female deer" (*ju you*) is an erudite term used to describe a father and son committing incest by sharing the same woman. An early example is found in the *Li ji* (Book of rites); it is also found in a poem quoted by the *Ruyijun zhuan*; see note 34 in my translation. The poem by Zhu Xi quoted earlier also uses this term to describe Taizong and Gaozong incestuously sharing Wu Zetian; see Zhu Xi, *Zhuzi quanshu*, 66.18a.

82. Huang Xun, *Dushu yide*, 2.27a.

83. Ibid.

84. Ibid., 2.27b.

85. Huang Zhijun, "Zhanyan," 19.26b. This text is also found in Sun Kaidi, *Tongsu xiaoshuo*, pp. 153-154.

86. Huang Xun, *Dushu yide*, 1.15b-17a and 2.22b-23b.

87. Ibid., 2.12b.

88. Zhaowang Ruyi is mentioned in Huang Xun, *Dushu yide*, 3.42b; Bi Gan is mentioned on p. 3.42a; Xue Rengao is mentioned on p. 2.9b.

89. 芯 was 苾; corrected per *Jiu Tang shu*, 4.37.1376: 垂拱已後、東都有契芯兒歌、皆淫豔之詞。後張易之兄弟有內嬖、易之小字契芯. See also *Xin Tang shu*, 3.35.919.10.

90. 芯 was 苾.

91. *Xin Tang shu*, 18.204.5801.10: 后最幼、姆抱以見、紿以男、天綱視其步與目、驚曰: 龍瞳鳳頸、極貴驗也; 若爲女、當作天子. See also *Jiu Tang shu*, 16.191.5094.1, and Huang Xun, *Huang Tan Xiansheng wenji*, 2.22b.

92. This poem is found in the collected works of Huang Xun; see *Huang Tan Xiansheng wenji*, 8.1b-8.2a.

93. The title and first line of this poem contain the nickname of one of Wu Zetian's lovers, Zhang Yizhi. The term *"qibi"* was originally the name of an ethnic tribe in the far western regions of the Tang empire; see *Xin Tang shu*, 19.217b.6142.1. It was then used as the name of a kind of lascivious song that was popular in the Eastern Capital soon after Wu Zetian ascended the throne. When Zhang Yizhi became one of her favorites, Qibi became his nickname; it appears to have been chosen for its lascivious overtones, and Zhang Yizhi is known to have sung bawdy songs of this type in the company of the empress. Zhang Yizhi and his brother reveled in their decadence, and with the assistance of the empress quickly became vulgarian spectacles who wore rouge, copious amounts of jewelry, and sometimes even bird feathers; see *Jiu Tang shu*, 4.37.1376.10, and *Xin Tang shu*, 3.35.919.10.

94. Wu Meiniang, or Fair Flatterer Wu, was the nickname of Wu Zetian. It also became the name of a song that was popular right before Wu Zetian became emperor; see note 11 in my translation.

95. One of the titles held by Zhang Yizhi was auxiliary to the director of imperial mounts; see note 71 above. The Mingtang, or Brilliant Hall, was renamed the Wanxiang shengong, or Palace of the Spirit of Myriad Forms, in 688 by Wu Zetian; see *Xin Tang shu*, 1.4.88.3. It was a magnificent three-story structure, three hundred feet tall, whose construction required the labor of tens of thousands of men; see *Jiu Tang shu*,

14.183.4742. The construction of this palace was supervised by Feng Xiaobao, whose name was later changed to Xue Huaiyi; for biographical information about Xue Huaiyi see *Jiu Tang shu*, 14.183.4741-4743. The Brilliant Hall was rarely referred to by its new name; see *Jiu Tang shu*, 14.183.4742-4743.

96. When Wu Zetian wanted to allow Xue Huaiyi greater access to her private quarters, she pretended that he was a monk and had his head shaved.

97. Shen Nanqiu, the imperial physician, supposedly had an affair with the empress. In the previous line, the metal blade appears to have had "lingering regrets" for him because, unlike Xue Huaiyi, as imperial physician he did not have to shave his head in order to gain special access to the empress. Shen Nanqiu's affair with Wu Zetian is mentioned briefly in *Jiu Tang shu*, 14.183.4743, *Xin Tang shu*, 11.76.3483, *Zizhi tongjian gangmu*, 41.30a.27, and *Zizhi tongjian*, 6499.1.

98. "Cries of the parrot" refers to a dream that Wu Zetian had immediately before she decided to reinstate her son Li Xian; the populace protested that he had been improperly deposed, and one of Wu Zetian's ministers took the occasion of her dream to remonstrate that the crown prince should be reinstated; see note 50 in my translation. The *Classic of the Great Cloud (Dayun jing)* is a Buddhist scripture published in 690 at the behest of Wu Zetian; one of the authors was her paramour Xue Huaiyi, although it is likely that most of the work was composed by more sophisticated exegetes. A central claim of this work is that Wu Zetian is a reincarnation of Maitreya, the Buddhist messiah. A copy of this text was purportedly placed in every temple in the empire, and all prefectures were ordered to build Great Cloud temples. Over a thousand men were made monks as part of this enterprise; the previous line of this poem that mentions the heads of three thousand men being shaved probably alludes to this event. For further information about the *Dayun jing* and its promulgation see *Jiu Tang shu*, 1.6.121.2 and 14.183.4742, *Xin Tang shu*, 1.4.90.6, and *Zizhi tongjian*, 6466.3 and 6469.4. Modern scholars have argued that the text of the *Dayun jing* existed before the reign of Wu Zetian and that Xue Huaiyi and others merely added a commentary; see Wang Diwu, *Wu Zetian shidai*, pp. 250-254. For a detailed analysis of this text and a partial translation see Guisso, *Wu Tse-t'ien*, pp. 36-50. Guisso argues that the promulgation of the *Dayun jing* and the construction of Great Cloud temples in every prefecture "were part of one of the most ambitious attempts in medieval China to mold men's minds, to use religious feeling to justify the very existence of a regime and even to rationalize its most unpopular acts."

99. The first half of this line might appear to contain one of the earliest references to the given name of Xue Aocao, hero of the *Ruyijun zhuan*. But the history behind this line and its syntax suggest that this is unlikely. The surname of the ruling house of the Tang dynasty was Li.

100. The surname Li literally means "plum blossom," so the plucking of plum blossoms figuratively describes Wu Zetian's slaughter of the Li family after she had assumed power; this is described in her biographies. The blossoming of the lotus refers to Wu Zetian's relationship with Zhang Changzong, brother of Zhang Yizhi. One of Zhang Changzong's nicknames was a pun on the word "lotus blossom."

101. The Zhang brothers were young men when they began their relationship with the empress; she was in her sixties.

102. "An old man from the family of Di" refers to Wu Zetian's prime minister, Di Renjie, one of the few officials at court who strenuously argued for the reinstatement of the legitimate crown prince; see *Zizhi tongjian*, 6526-6527. For the biography of Di Renjie (607-700) see *Jiu Tang shu*, 9.89.2885-2896, and *Xin Tang shu*, 14.115.4207-

4214. White Horse Temple refers to the death of Xue Huaiyi; his corpse was conveyed there after he was strangled by a group of women on the order of Wu Zetian; he had become proud, corrupt, and had burnt the Brilliant Hall to the ground; see *Jiu Tang shu*, 14.183.4743. To my knowledge, the Tang histories do not state that Xue Huaiyi ever had a child or that his spirit held a child and wailed in the White Horse Temple after he was murdered. One of the women who took part in his strangulation, however, had been a wet nurse earlier in her career. This line could possibly be a reference to this woman; see *Jiu Tang shu*, 14.183.4743.6.

103. The Changsheng dian, or Palace of Long Life, is probably a typo for Chang-sheng yuan, or Hall of Long Life. The Palace of Long Life was found in the Huaqing Palace; as the Huaqing Palace was not built until 723, this reference would be anach-ronistic; see note 87 in my translation. The Hall of Long Life, located on the palace grounds, was where Wu Zetian convalesced when she became ill late in her reign; see *Jiu Tang shu*, 8.78.2707, and *Xin Tang shu*, 13.104.4015. The line "there was still one bud" refers to Li Xian, the crown prince.

104. Li Xian was restored in 698; see *Zizhi tongjian*, 6534.6. Wu Zetian died in the Palace of the Upper Yang. The line "into whose house could she then descend?" prob-ably refers to the fact that Wu Zetian's spirit tablet would not be placed in the ancestral temple of the Tang; her spirit would therefore not have a home and would not receive the proper sacrifices.

105. The phrase "she has the pupils of a dragon and the neck of a phoenix" (*long-tong fengjing*) is from a description of Wu Zetian when she was a child. One day her nanny dressed Wu Zetian like a boy and brought her to a fortune-teller who observed the way she walked, noted the uniqueness of her eyes, then said in astonishment: "He has the pupils of a dragon and the neck of a phoenix, proof that he will be extremely distinguished; if he were a girl, he would become emperor." For the Chinese text see *Xin Tang shu*, 18.204.5801.10; see also *Jiu Tang shu*, 16.191.5094.1. Huang Xun also quotes this passage verbatim in *Dushu yide*, 2.22b.

106. The reference to Wang Yan is discussed in the introduction.

Chapter 5: Speculations About Contemporary Events

1. Huang Xun, *Dushu yide*, 1.33a-b.
2. Ibid., 2.27a.
3. For the biography of Ming Shizong, Zhu Houcong (1507-1567), the Jiajing emperor (r. 1522-1567), see Zhang Tingyu, *Ming shi*, 2.17.215-251; see also Lienche Tu Fang, "Chu Hou-ts'ung," pp. 315-322.
4. For the biography of Ming Wuzong, Zhu Houzhao (1491-1521), the Zhengde emperor (r. 1506-1522), see *Ming shi*, 2.16.199-214; see also Kwan-wai So, "Chu Hou-chao," pp. 307-315.
5. For the biography of Yang Tinghe (1459-1529) see *Ming shi*, 17.190.5031-5039; see also Chou Tao-chi, "Yang T'ing-ho," pp. 1542-1546.
6. For the Chinese text see Xu Jie, *Shizong Suhuangdi shilu*, 69.197.3681; for a translation of the entire text and a discussion see Fisher, *The Chosen One*, pp. 50-51.
7. For the biography of Ming Xiaozong, Zhu Youtang (1470-1505), the Hong-zhi emperor (r. 1488-1506), see *Ming shi*, 2.15.183-197; see also Chaoying Fang, "Chu Yu-t'ang," pp. 375-380.
8. For the biography of Zhu Youyuan (1476-1519), posthumously named Ming

Ruizong, see *Ming shi*, 12.115.3551-3555; for the biography of Ming Xianzong, Zhu Jianshen (1447-1487), the Chenghua emperor (r. 1465-1488), see *Ming shi*, 1.13.161-181; see also Chaoying Fang, "Chu Chien-shen," pp. 298-304.

9. For the biography of Ming Taizu, Zhu Yuanzhang (1328-1398), the Hongwu emperor (r. 1368-1399), see *Ming shi*, 1.1.1-57; see also Teng Ssu-yü, "Chu Yüan-chang," pp. 381-392; for the *Ancestral Instructions* see Zhu Yuanzhang, *Zuxun*.

10. *Shizong Suhuangdi shilu*, 70.1.3. The earliest occurrence of the phrase "When the elder brother dies, the younger brother succeeds" is found in the *Gongyang Commentary;* see *Chunqiu Gongyang zhuan*, p. 1116. Fisher notes: "The word 'brother' in the injunction did not refer to real brothers of the same parents, but to all males of the same family generation (*tang xiongdi*)"; see Fisher, *The Chosen One*, p. 50.

11. *Ming shilu*, 70.1.4; see also Fisher, *The Chosen One*, pp. 52-54.

12. For more information about the Great Ritual Debate see Fisher, *The Chosen One;* Lin Yanqing, *Jiajing Huangdi dazhuan*, pp. 53-116; Gu Yingtai, "Dali yi"; Li Xun, "'Dali yi' yu Mingdai zhengzhi"; Nakayama, "Min no Kaseichō no tairei mondai no hattan"; Nakayama, "Futatabi 'Kaseichō no tairei mondai no hattan' ni tsuite"; Ouyang Chen, "Wang Shouren yu Dali yi." A contemporary account of this debate was written under imperial auspices; see Yang Yiqing, *Minglun dadian;* see also Mote and Twitchett, *Ming Dynasty*, pp. 440-450.

13. *Yi li*, p. 374. See *Dushu yide*, 1.33b; Huang Xun also discusses the "Sangfu" chapter of the *Yi li* at some length in *Dushu yide*, 4.38a-40a.

14. For a brief discussion of the phrase "an adopted son recompenses his parents" and how it was related to an eleventh-century precedent that was often cited during the Great Ritual Debate, see Fisher, *The Chosen One*, p. 30. See *Ming tongjian*, 2.1836, 2.1839, 2.1842, 2.1846, 2.1853, and 2.1859. Huang Xun also discusses the term *"bensheng,"* or "natural," another key term in the Great Ritual Debate; see *Ming tongjian*, 2.1835-1846, 2.1852-1854, and 3.1896-1906.

15. See *Ming shilu*, 70.4.162-165.

16. *Dushu yide*, 1.13b.

17. For two examples of temple rearrangements and construction projects see *Dushu yide*, 2.37b and 3.35a; see also *Ming tongjian*, 3.2150, 3.2132, and 3.2336. For three discussions of the status of the crown prince see *Huang Tan Xiansheng wenji*, 2.28b, 3.2a, and 4.44b.

18. *Dushu yide*, 2.27a.

19. For a few examples see *Ming shilu*, 71.8.301-312, 72.37.929, 72.37.931-939, 72.41.1052, and 73.43.1112-1113. During the winter of 1997 I had the pleasure of meeting Carney Fisher, author of *The Chosen One*, one of the most important studies of the Great Ritual Debate. When I took the opportunity to show Dr. Fisher the text of the "Du *Ruyijun zhuan*," his first impression was that if this text could indeed be dated to the reign of Emperor Shizong, the line about fathers, sons, and elder brothers was quite likely a reference to the Great Ritual Debate, as I had suspected. Although similar phrases are found in the standard histories, there was a dramatic increase in discussions about fathers, sons, and elder brothers after Shizong assumed the throne; many are also found three years later when his relationships with his father and uncle had again become the topic of particularly contentious debates.

20. Shizong renamed his uncle Xiaozong "imperial deceased uncle" (*huang bokao*) in 1524; see *Ming shilu*, 73.43.1111.

21. The use of Tang Zhongzong as a precedent is described in many places, including *Ming shilu*, 72.38.0979, 72.39.1000, 72.40.1017, 72.40.1027, and 72.41.1060; see

also Fisher, *The Chosen One*, p. 126. Zhang Cong (1475–1539) wrote several memorials in which the precedent of Tang Zhongzong and the relationships between a father, a son, and an elder brother are discussed at some length; see *Ming shilu*, 71.8.300-313, for one of the more famous memorials to take the young emperor's side in the Great Ritual Debate. For the biography of Zhang Cong, whose name was later changed to Zhang Fujing, see *Ming shi*, 17.195.5173–5180; see also Chou Tao-chi, "Chang Fuching," pp. 67–70.

22. See *Jiu Tang shu*, 8.78.2707.7.

23. See Hucker, *Dictionary of Official Titles*, 372.4527 and 223.2154.

24. See *Ming shilu*, 72.40.1012–1014.

25. Ibid., 73.49.1236.

26. Fisher, *The Chosen One*, pp. 170–173.

27. Huang Zongxi (1610–1695) also notes that the Great Ritual Debate was, in one sense, a conflict between those who wished to base their arguments on external models and those who wished to use intuition as the ultimate criterion of moral action; see Huang Zongxi, *Mingru xuean*, p. 296; this passage is discussed in Fisher, *The Chosen One*, pp. 170–173. For criticism of Fisher's interpretation of the role of Wang Yangming's philosophy in the Great Ritual Debate see Chu, review of *The Chosen One*.

28. Zhang Cong's first memorial is found in *Ming shilu*, 70.4.162–165; it is discussed in Fisher, *The Chosen One*, pp. 57–60.

29. *Ming shilu*, 70.4.165; for the translation see Fisher, *The Chosen One*, p. 60.

30. Fisher, *The Chosen One*, p. 148.

Chapter 6: Sources

1. For the text of the "Du *Ruyijun zhuan*" and a translation see Chapter 4.

2. For the biography of Feng Xiaobao see *Jiu Tang shu*, 14.183.4741–4743.

3. Shen Nanqiu's affair with Wu Zetian is mentioned briefly in *Jiu Tang shu*, 14.183.4743, *Xin Tang shu*, 11.76.3483, *Zizhi tongjian gangmu*, 41.30a.27, and *Zizhi tongjian*, 6499.1. I have not found his name mentioned anywhere else in the sources I have consulted.

4. The Zhang brothers were functionally illiterate; see *Jiu Tang shu*, 8.78.2707.7. Nevertheless a few poems are attributed to them in the *Quan Tang shi*, pp. 867–869.

5. See Zhu Xi, *Yupi Zizhi tongjian gangmu*.

6. Three of the more obscure characters found in the *Ruyijun zhuan* are Zong Jinqing, Concubine Wei, and Wife Dou. Zong Jinqing (d. 710), who is found on p. 6b, is mentioned in *Jiu Tang shu*, 9.92.2971–2973, *Xin Tang shu*, 11.76.3483, and *Xin Tang shu*, 13.109.4102–4103; Concubine Wei, who is found on p. 3a, is mentioned in *Jiu Tang shu*, 7.51.2171–2175, and *Xin Tang shu*, 11.76.3486–3489; Wife Dou, who is found on p. 12a, is mentioned in *Jiu Tang shu*, 7.51.2176, and *Xin Tang shu*, 11.76.3489–3490. These characters are so obscure that even modern editions of the *Ruyijun zhuan* usually fail to correct typographical errors found in their names.

7. One unique object mentioned in the *Ruyijun zhuan* is a pillow from Qiuci, decorated with a wandering fairy motif, used by Wu Zetian during one of her encounters with Xue Aocao; see *Ruyijun zhuan*, p. 9a; such a pillow is mentioned in Wang Renyu, *Kaiyuan Tianbao yishi shizhong*, 68.4. Another rare object is a "dragon beard" rush mat upon which Wu Zetian had another tryst; see *Ruyijun zhuan*, p. 16b; a reference to such a mat is found in Cui Bao, *Gujin zhu*, 3.7a.8. I suspect that many of the rare objects de-

scribed in the *Ruyijun zhuan* may also be found in Tang historical sources; only a few have been identified in the notes to the annotated text and translation.

8. For the biography of Chu Suiliang see *Jiu Tang shu*, 8.80.2729-2739, and *Xin Tang shu*, 13.105.4024-4029.

9. For the three Chinese versions of this speech found in the *Ruyijun zhuan*, the *Jiu Tang shu*, and the *Xin Tang shu* see *Ruyijun zhuan*, p. 2a, and the notes to my critical edition in Part Two.

10. For the Chinese text see *Ruyijun zhuan*, p. 19b.

11. See *Xin Tang shu*, 14.115.4212; the Chinese text is found in the notes to my critical edition in Part Two.

12. For the Chinese text see *Xin Tang shu*, 14.115.4211.

13. For the Chinese text see *Ruyijun zhuan*, p. 3a.

14. For the biography of Tang Zhongzong, Li Xian (name later changed to Li Zhe), see *Jiu Tang shu*, 1.7.135-151, and *Xin Tang shu*, 1.4.106-114.

15. For the Chinese text see Zhang Zhuo, *Chaoye qianzai*, p. 60. Another version of this dream is found in *Xin Tang shu*, 14.115.4212.

16. For Wang Zijin's biography see *Le Lie-sien Tchouan*, p. 109. The historical record also states that Wu Sansi wrote a poem in which Zhang Changzong was called a reincarnation of Wang Zijin; Wu Sansi also ordered officials at court to write a response to his poem; see *Jiu Tang shu*, 14.83.4735, and *Xin Tang shu*, 19.106.5840.

17. For the Chinese text see *Ruyijun zhuan*, p. 6a.

18. Fuqiu Bo is mentioned in the biography of Wang Zijin in *Le Lie-sien Tchouan*, p. 109. A biography of Fuqiu Bo is found in *Liexian quanzhuan*, p. 119. The biography of Ding Lingwei is found in *Liexian quanzhuan*, p. 103, and Tao Qian, *Soushen houji*, p. 1.

19. See Hucker, *Dictionary of Official Titles*, 191.1580.

20. See *Zhuangzi yinde*, 35.13.46.

21. For the biography of Cui Rong see *Jiu Tang shu*, 9.94.2996-3000, and *Xin Tang shu*, 13.114.4195-4196; the text of the complete poem is found in *Quan Tang shi*, 68.767.

22. The four lines are also found in: *Jiu Tang shu*, 8.78.2706; *Lidai shihua*, 69.2; *Qing shi*, 512.24; and *Yanyi bian*, 145.21.

23. A barbarian general by the name of Sun Aocao is mentioned in the Tang histories. Although he was a contemporary of Wu Zetian, he does not appear to be related in any way to the character of Xue Aocao; see *Jiu Tang shu*, 16.199 lower 5350-5351, and *Xin Tang shu*, 20.219.6168.

24. See *Ruyijun zhuan*, p. 3b.

25. Perhaps the earliest example of the character *"ao"* used in the sense of "filthy" is found in the *Han shu;* more precisely, in this instance it is used to describe a "bloodbath"; see *Han shu*, 8.55.2479. The earliest example of the compound *"aozao"* that I have been able to locate is found in a commentary to this passage in the *Han shu;* Jin Zhuo, an official of the Jin dynasty (265-420), explains that the compound *"aozao"* was also used to describe a slaughter; see *Han shu*, 8.55.2480. This passage in the *Han shu* and the term *"aozao"* are also discussed in the *Chengzhai shihua*, where it is noted that *"aozao"* is a cognate for terms like *"angzang"* that simply mean "filthy"; see Yang Wanli, *Chengzhai shihua*, p. 145.

26. Variants of the term *"aozao"* are also found in *Zhuzi yulei*, 2.1129, 2.1208, and 5.2895. See also *Su Dongpo yishi huibian*, p. 109.

27. See Tao Zongyi, *Chuogeng lu*, p. 124; "Xinqiao shi Han Wu mai chunqing," 1.176; "Zhang Xiaoji Chenliu ren jiu," 1.931. The term *"aozao"* can also mean

"annoying"; see Tang Xianzu, *Zichai ji,* p. 1769. An interesting occurrence of the term *"aocao"* during the Ming dynasty is found in a sarcastic song to a meretricious prostitute that is attributed to the famous sixteenth-century poet Chen Duo; it is probably a reference to Xue Aocao. But as Chen Duo's precise dates are unknown and many songs attributed to him were not actually his, this allusion to Xue Aocao does not help us date the *Ruyijun zhuan.* See *Quan Ming sanqu,* 1.606.

28. *Xiuta yeshi,* pp. 325 and 490; this novel uses the term *"aoaozaozao"* on at least two occasions to describe anal intercourse; in both instances, Wu Zetian and the Zhang brothers are mentioned.

29. For the Chinese text see Chapter 4.

30. For the biography of Gao Ang see *Bei shi,* 4.31.1144–1148, and *Beiqi shu,* 1.21.293–296. His dates are discussed in *Beiqi shu,* 1.21.310, n. 6.

31. See *Bei shi,* 4.31.1144; see also *Beiqi shu,* 1.21.293.

32. See *Bei shi,* 4.31.1144; see also *Beiqi shu,* 1.21.293.

33. It is also possible that Huang Xun found the name Gao Ang amusing because one of its meanings is "erect," again demonstrating that Gao Ang's father had proved himself incapable of selecting names for his son that did not have ludicrous connotations.

34. Little, *Realm of the Immortals,* p. 51; see also Davidson, "Origin and Early Use," p. 242.

35. Yang Zhirou is mentioned in *Jiu Tang shu,* 7.62.2383, and *Xin Tang shu,* 13.100.3928.

36. See *Hailing yishi,* 54.4. As the *ruyi* possesses erotic connotations, perhaps it is no coincidence that the person who objects to Wu Zetian changing the name of the calendar year to Ruyi is named Yang Zhirou—a name that could easily be construed as a pun meaning something like "a male member that is adamantly soft." He would thus be the perfect person to object to Wu Zetian's use of the term *"ruyi,"* as his name has precisely the opposite connotation.

37. For the biography of Han Gaozu, Liu Bang, see *Shi ji,* 2.8.341–394.

38. For the brief biography of Emperor Hui, Liu Ying, see *Han shu,* 1.1b.85–93.

39. For the story of Zhaowang Ruyi and the unsuccessful attempt to make him crown prince see *Shi ji,* 2.8.395–397.

40. See notes 100 and 120 in my translation.

41. See *Ruyijun zhuan,* p. 19b.

42. Huayang Sanren's preface is discussed in more detail in Chapter 7.

43. Honored Consort Yang (Yang Guifei) was one of the most famous consorts of the Tang dynasty; for her biography see *Jiu Tang shu,* 7.51.2178–2181, and *Xin Tang shu,* 11.76.3493–3496.

44. See *Shi ji,* 5.39.1640–1660.

45. For an annotated version of the Chinese text see *Ruyijun zhuan,* p. 22a.

46. The full line from the *Shi jing* is: "To think about this carefully, I cannot spread my wings and fly away." For the Chinese text see *Maoshi yinde,* 5.26.4–5; see also *Maoshi yinde,* 13.58.5.

47. For an intelligent, but completely unannotated, discussion of masochism in a sexual context see Phillips, *Defense of Masochism.* Phillips notes: "The kind of sex we usually call sado-masochism is voluntary, consensual and, therefore, directed by masochistic rather than sadistic interests. Sadistic impulses are not collaborative ones, but rather test their effectiveness against the will of another person. Masochism needs collusion, because of the risk involved in submission. It cannot come into being without some form of relationship, a contractual bond or a mutual understanding, however

ephemeral"; see p. 13. Phillips also notes that sexual pain can be psychologically heal-
ing because it transforms "inner trouble into something that your body can take and
survive"; see p. 3.

48. The line "How could there not be other men?" is found in *Maoshi yinde*, 18.87.1;
see also *Maoshi yinde*, 24.119.1-2 and 25.120.1-2. The line "Who says that Song is far
away? I can see it if I stand on the tips of my toes" is found in *Maoshi yinde*, 13.61.1.

49. For the Chinese text see *Ruyijun zhuan*, p. 22b.

50. For the Chinese text see *Zhouyi yinde*, 47.4; for the translation see Wilhelm,
Book of Changes, p. 342.

51. For the biography of Gu Kaizhi see *Jin shu*, 8.92.2404-2406.

52. For the Chinese text see *Jin shu*, 8.92.2405. This quotation is also found, with
textual variations, in Yu Jiaxi, *Shishuo xinyu*, p. 686.

Chapter 7: Preface, Postscript, and Colophon

1. Liu Hui speculates that the preface to the *Ruyijun zhuan* was written in 1514;
see Liu Hui, "*Ruyijun zhuan* de kanke niandai," pp. 47-59. Wang Rumei believes it was
written in 1634 by a Ming loyalist named Wu Gongchen; see Wang Rumei, "*Yuanyang
zhen* ji qi zuozhe chutan," pp. 225-229; see also Wang Rumei, *Jin Ping Mei tansuo*, pp.
150-153. The editors of the preface to the Encyclopedia Britannica edition of the
Ruyijun zhuan speculate that the author of the preface was probably too young to have
been Wu Gongchen; see Xu Changling, *Zetian Huanghou Ruyijun zhuan*, pp. 16-18.
Ōta and Iida argue that the author of the preface was an unidentified Japanese figure
who must have written it in 1754; see Ōta and Iida, *Chūgoku hiseki sōkan*, pp. 11-15.

2. One exception is Wang Rumei, who has written a persuasive article about the
identity of Huayang Sanren; see Wang Rumei, "*Yuanyang zhen*," pp. 225-229. Unfor-
tunately, the only observation he makes about the preface to the *Ruyijun zhuan* is that
its style appears to differ from that of the novel, and he makes this observation in only
one sentence; see Wang Rumei, *Jin Ping Mei tansuo*, pp. 150-153. Another exception
is Kang Zhengguo, but he scarcely mentions the preface before concluding that it is
"obviously" preposterous; see Kang Zhengguo, *Chongshen fengyuejian*, p. 56.

3. See *Shi ji*, 2.9.395-412.

4. See *Maoshi yinde*, 10.46.1.

5. Cheng Yi, *Yi zhuan*, p. 147.

6. Wilhelm, *Book of Changes*, p. 117.

7. See Wang Rumei, *Jin Ping Mei tansuo*, pp. 170-181; Wang Rumei, *Yuanyang
zhen*, pp. 225-229. For more information about the *Yuanyang zhen* see Sun Kaidi,
Zhongguo tongsu xiaoshuo shumu, p. 99.

8. Wang Rumei, *Yuanyang zhen*.

9. Wang Rumei, *Jin Ping Mei tansuo*, p. 180; Wang Rumei, *Yuanyang zhen*, pp.
226-227.

10. Zhuo Erkan, *Ming yimin shi*, p. 608.

11. One example is the name Huayang Shanren; see Wang Rumei, *Yuanyang zhen*,
p. 228.

12. Wang Rumei, *Jin Ping Mei tansuo*, p. 181.

13. For the Chinese text see Wang Rumei, *Yuanyang zhen*, p. 227.

14. Xu Changling, *Zetian Huanghou Ruyijun zhuan*, pp. 16-18.

15. Liu Hui, "*Ruyijun zhuan* de kanke niandai," pp. 47-59.

16. Xiaoxiao Sheng, *Jin Ping Mei cihua*, 1.5. The title mentioned in the preface to the *Jin Ping Mei* is actually *Ruyi zhuan*, not *Ruyijun zhuan*, but there is little reason to suspect that the author of the preface is referring to a different work, as the *Jin Ping Mei* quotes the *Ruyijun zhuan* on several occasions. For a translation of the preface see Roy, *Plum in the Golden Vase*, 1.3–5. See also Gao Ru, *Baichuan shuzhi*, 6.90.

17. Ōta and Iida, *Chūgoku hiseki sōkan*, p. 14.

18. Ibid.

19. Wang Rumei argues that this preface is significant in the history of Chinese fiction; see Wang Rumei, *Jin Ping Mei tansuo*, pp. 171–183.

20. 突 was written with a rare orthographic variant; see Morohashi, *Dai Kan-Wa jiten*, 8.25495.

21. Zuo Qiuming, *Zuo zhuan*, 12.75: 肓之上、膏之下.

22. Yuan Haowen 元好問 (論詩三首): 暈碧裁紅點綴勻、一回拈出一回新。鴛鴦繡了從教看、莫把金針度與人; see Yuan Haowen, *Yuan Haowen shici ji*, p. 601; see also *Zhuzi yulei*, 104.2620: 鴛鴦繡出從君看、莫把金針度與人.

23. Wang Rumei amends 數 to read 藪; see Wang Rumei, *Yuanyang zhen*, preface.

24. Ibid.; I have changed the punctuation.

25. For a translation of this passage see Watson, *Tso chuan*, pp. 120–121. For a technical discussion of the medical terms *"gao"* and *"huang"* see Yu Yunxiu, *Gudai jibing minghou shuyi*, pp. 345–346.

26. "Under the heart and above the diaphragm" is a paraphrase of a famous line found in the *Zuo zhuan*: "above the diaphragm and below the heart"; for the Chinese text see Zuo Qiuming, *Zuo zhuan*, 12.75; for the translation see Watson, *Tso chuan*, p. 121.

27. Bian Que was a legendary physician; for his biography see *Shi ji*, 9.105.2785–2794.

28. A golden needle is a traditional Buddhist metaphor for the key to a problem. A poem containing this line has been attributed to Yuan Haowen (1190–1257), an official of the Jin dynasty (1115–1234). His biography is contained in *Jin shi*, 8.126.2742–2743. While Huayang Sanren appears to believe that Yuan Haowen was the original author of this line, it is also found in the *Zhuzi yulei* where it is quoted as proverbial; see *Zhuzi yulei*, 104.2620. As Yuan Haowen was only ten years old when Zhu Xi died, it is safe to assume that he did not write this line.

29. This clause is a variation of the proverbial expression "an acupuncture needle inserted into the top of the head" (*dingmen shang yi zhen*); it figuratively describes an argument that alerts its auditor to the error of his ways in a particularly striking fashion. In this instance Huayang Sanren transforms the diminutive acupuncture needle into a merciless club in an apparent attempt to make his point more obvious.

30. The word *"jiudu"* (to liberate) is a technical term often found in Buddhist and Daoist texts.

31. The precise meaning of this sentence eludes me. It appears to describe the manner in which Huayang Sanren plans to corner this illness, but the passage in the *Zuo zhuan* describing this illness does not mention a ladder or a dwelling. The word *"shu"* might refer to a technical term used in traditional Chinese medicine to describe one aspect of the pulse; see Guo Yong, *Shanghan buwang lun*, p. 18. As all avenues of retreat have been blocked, the illness has no alternative but to wander in circles and await the application of the metaphorical golden needle of fiction. This new treatment, if successful, would be the first that is capable of curing an illness infecting the vital *gaohuang* region.

32. In the original story contained in the *Zuo zhuan*, the illness assumes the form of two children who hide in the region between the *gao* and the *huang* so that the physician will be unable to kill them.

33. Zuo Qiuming, *Zuo zhuan*, 12.75-76.

34. For the Chinese text see *Sishu jizhu*, 6.15; for the translation see Lau, *Mencius*, p. 116.

35. See note 28.

36. Feng Menglong, *Yushi mingyan;* Feng Menglong, *Jingshi tongyan;* Feng Menglong, *Xingshi hengyan.* See also Wang Rumei, *Yuanyang zhen*, p. 231, and Wang Rumei, *Jin Ping Mei tansuo*, p. 183.

37. Wang Rumei, *Yuanyang zhen*, pp. 58-61.

38. Ibid., p. 59.

39. Ibid., p. 60; *Ruyijun zhuan*, p. 9a.

40. *Ruyijun zhuan*, p. 9a.

41. For the biography of Lu Ji see *Jin shu*, 5.54.1467-1481; see also Yu Jiaxi, *Shishuo xinyu*, p. 629.

42. For the biography of Dai Yuan, zi Ruosi, see *Jin shu*, 6.69.1846-1848.

43. Wang Rumei, *Yuanyang zhen*, p. 60.

44. Yu Jiaxi, *Shishuo xinyu*, p. 629.

45. See *Jin shu*, 6.69.1846, and Yu Jiaxi, *Shishuo xinyu*, p. 155.

46. For the biography of Fang Xuanling see *Jiu Tang shu*, 7.66.2459-2467, and *Xin Tang shu*, 12.96.3853-3858.

47. For the Chinese text see *Jiu Tang shu*, 7.66.2459.

48. The fourth story of the *Yuanyang zhen* contains descriptions of sexual activity that are reminiscent of those found in the *Ruyijun zhuan*, though not nearly so explicit. Only one small fragment is actually paraphrased: "deep thrusts and shallow retractions" (*shenchou qiansong*); see *Yuanyang zhen*, p. 207. The author's tone is overtly moralistic throughout this story; apparently the reader is not supposed to derive vicarious pleasure from such descriptions. Asserting that sexual immorality is a menace to society, the author illustrates his point with an attempted rape, an attempted suicide, a lecture on morals, and the public mortification of those who commit immoral acts.

49. Ōta and Iida, *Chūgoku hiseki sōkan*, pp. 13-14. For a discussion of minute textual attributes of this edition of the *Ruyijun zhuan* and aspects of later reprints see pp. 14-16; see also Xu Changling, *Zetian Huanghou Ruyijun zhuan*, pp. 17-19. It appears that the edition of the *Ruyijun zhuan* that Liu Hui consulted did not contain the Japanese colophon dated 1763; he therefore thinks the postscript should be dated 1520.

Chapter 8: Later Works

1. For a modern reprint of the *Wu Zhao zhuan* see *Siwuxie huibao waibian*, 1.85-89; see also Hanan, "The Erotic Novel." For the *Nongqing kuaishi* see *Siwuxie huibao*, vol. 21. The *Juan Yang Shengan pidian Sui Tang liangchao shizhuan* is generally known as the *Sui Tang liangchao shi* (or *zhi*) *zhuan.* This novel is very rare; I am indebted to Prof. Robert Hegel for lending me his personal copy which, in turn, is a reproduction of Liu Ts'unyan's photocopy of the microfilm made by Waseda University of the unique edition of this novel found in the Sonkeikaku Bunko in Tokyo. For more information about this novel see Sun Kaidi, *Riben Dongjing suo jian xiaoshuo shumu*, pp. 38-42; Sun Kaidi, *Zhongguo tongsu xiaoshuo shumu*, pp. 41-42; Hegel, *Novel in Seventeenth Century China*, pp. 194, 224, and 239; and Hegel, *"Sui T'ang yen-i,"* pp. 124-159. For the fourth work see Xiaoxiao Sheng (pseud.), *Jin Ping Mei cihua.*

2. Though a few of the ironic references remain, there is no reason to suspect that the author knew what they meant.

3. On occasion I have found it useful to consult the *Wu Zhao zhuan* when I suspected the text of the *Ruyijun zhuan* was corrupt; a few textual emendations based on the text of the *Wu Zhao zhuan* are found in the notes to my critical edition in Part Two. As the *Wu Zhao zhuan* is otherwise a vulgar little work that deletes almost everything that could be considered sophisticated in the *Ruyijun zhuan*, it does not appear to require further comment.

4. For a discussion of the dating of this novel see *Nongqing kuaishi*, preface, p. 15.

5. For the text, a translation, and a discussion of Huang Xun's "Du *Ruyijun zhuan*," see Chapter 4.

6. *Nongqing kuaishi*, p. 202.

7. In the *Nongqing kuaishi*, for example, Taizong is inaccurately said to have given Wu Zetian the name Zhao and the title Zetian; he is also said to have intended to elevate her to the rank of empress; see pp. 232–233. There are innumerable mistakes of this sort.

8. *Nongqing kuaishi*, pp. 449–450.

9. See Zhu Xi, *Zhuzi quanshu*, 66.18a. For the corrupt version of this poem found at the end of the *Nongqing kuaishi*, see *Nongqing kuaishi*, pp. 449–450. The Chinese text of both poems is found in note 43 in Chapter 4.

10. Xu Shuofang notes that the *Sui Tang yanyi* appears to paraphrase the opening of the *Ruyijun zhuan;* I think it is much more likely that it was paraphrasing the *Sui Tang liangchao shizhuan;* see Xu Shuofang, *Lun Jin Ping Mei de chengshu ji qita*, p. 78. The *Sui Tang liangchao shizhuan* was an important source for the *Sui Tang yanyi;* see Hegel, *Novel in Seventeenth Century China*, p. 194.

11. Sun Kaidi, *Riben Dongjing suo jian xiaoshuo shumu*, pp. 38–40.

12. Several passages of the *Sui Tang liangchao shizhuan* that echo passages in the *Ruyijun zhuan* are noted in my critical edition of the *Ruyijun zhuan* in Part Two.

13. The reference to Mount Wu and the phrase "rain and clouds," stock metaphors used to describe a sexual encounter, are found in a famous rhapsody attributed to Song Yu (third century B.C.) that describes a brief tryst between a king and a divine maiden; see Song Yu, "Gaotang fu," pp. 875–886. This line also incorporates a brief yet significant phrase from the *Shu jing:* "The sordid conduct is disseminated widely" (*huide zhangwen*). In context, Legge translates it as: "The odour of such a state is plainly felt on high"; see Legge, *Chinese Classics*, 3.290. For occurrences of this phrase in the Tang histories see *Jiu Tang shu*, 8.75.2643, and *Xin Tang shu*, 13.103.4001.

14. For the Chinese text see *Sui Tang liangchao shizhuan*, 10.97.42a; see also *Nongqing kuaishi*, p. 323.

15. For the Chinese text and the translation see Legge, *Chinese Classics*, 3.290.

16. When the author of the *Sui Tang liangchao shizhuan* meddles with the poems he copies, he tends to corrupt them rather than making them more sophisticated; one example is mentioned in note 33 in my translation in Part Two.

17. Hanan, "Sources," pp. 43–47.

18. *Jin Ping Mei*, preface, p. 5; the reference to the *Ruyijun zhuan* in the preface of the *Jin Ping Mei* is discussed in more detail in the notes to Chapter 7. For the reference to Wu Zetian and Xue Aocao in chap. 37 of the *Jin Ping Mei*, see *Jin Ping Mei*, 2.445.

19. Hanan, "Sources," pp. 45–46.

20. These are all noted in my critical edition of the *Ruyijun zhuan* in Part Two.

21. The burning of incense in this manner in the *Jin Ping Mei* and *Ruyijun zhuan* is discussed in more detail in note 142 in my translation.

22. For the Chinese text see *Ruyijun zhuan*, p. 21a.

23. Lu Ge and Ma Zheng, *Jin Ping Mei zongheng tan*, pp. 18–30.

24. Roy, *Plum in the Golden Vase*, 1.xlv–xlvi.

25. For the Chinese text see *Jin Ping Mei*, 1.167; for the translation see Roy, *Plum in the Golden Vase*, 1.150.

26. Carlitz, *Rhetoric of Chin p'ing mei*, p. 116.

27. Andrew Plaks argues that the distinction between historical and fictional narrative is "a question of content more than of form . . . the major observable difference that conspicuously separates the two branches of Chinese narrative is the simple fact that historiography (and historical fiction) deals primarily with affairs of state and *public life*—military, political, diplomatic, court-related—while fiction takes up the slack to cover the more individualized and intimate details of the *private lives* of figures of varying roles or status"; see Plaks, "Towards a Critical Theory," pp. 317–318. He later qualifies this statement: "We must also mention the easy readiness of the dynastic historian to step back from his pose of journalistic objectivity and into the role of commentator or judge. This salient feature of traditional historiography . . . not only points to the consistent emphasis on judgment over pure narration in the Chinese tradition, but also demonstrates the fact that a formal feature such as narrative stance does not coincide neatly with the generic categories of content. The very fact of the insistence on documentary evidence and full recording of dialogue—features carried over into fiction as well—often results in the rhetorical foregrounding of more than one point of view at the same time"; see p. 326. The first half of the *Ruyijun zhuan* is primarily public and relies on standard historical sources; the second half is primarily private and is the invention of the author. But the narrator of the *Ruyijun zhuan* plays games with his characters and with the reader in a manner that is quite unlike the standard historical texts which inspired his portrayal of Wu Zetian. For an excellent discussion of implied authors and the relationship between fiction and history in the Chinese context see Rolston, *Traditional Chinese Fiction*, especially pp. 105–165.

Chapter 9: The Moral

1. For the Chinese text see *Ruyijun zhuan*, p. 15b.

2. Tang Xianzu, *Mudan ting*, pp. 1805–2079.

3. Ibid., p. 1842.

4. See *Sishu jizhu*, 3.4a.

5. For the Chinese text see *Sishu jizhu*, 3.4a; for the translation see Legge, *Chinese Classics*, 1.362; for the text of the entire poem see Legge, *Chinese Classics*, 4.419.

6. This work by Huang Xun is mentioned in his biographies cited in Chapter 4.

Annotated Translation

1. Nothing is known about the name Xu Changling, though it might be a pseudonym of Huang Xun; his possible authorship of this work is discussed in Chapter 4. Wumen is present-day Suzhou.

2. For the biography of Wu Zetian see *Jiu Tang shu*, 1.6.115–134, *Xin Tang shu*, 1.4.81–114, and *Xin Tang shu*, 11.76.3474–3485.

3. The edition I have edited and translated was printed in the Eastern Capital (Tokyo) in 1763 by the publishing house Seihikaku, the proprietor of which was Ogawa

Hikokurō. It is the earliest extant edition of this work. There is also a movable-type edition believed to have been published in the late nineteenth century, a copy of which is in the Library of Congress. The best edition published to date is found in a collection of traditional Chinese erotica published by the Encyclopedia Britannica in Taiwan: Xu Changling, *Zetian Huanghou Ruyijun zhuan*, in *Siwuxie huibao*, 24.15–75. The editions of the *Ruyijun zhuan* and its preface and postscript are discussed in greater detail in Chapter 7.

4. The phrase "the story of the inner chamber" (*zhonggou zhi yan*) is a quotation from the *Shi jing*; see *Maoshi yinde*, 10.46.1: "The story of the inner chamber Cannot be told. What would have to be told Would be the vilest of recitals." For the translation see Legge, *Chinese Classics*, 4.74.

5. The four whitebeards are: Dongyuan Gong, Qili Ji, Xiahuang Gong, and Luli Xiansheng. The crown prince they assisted was Liu Ying; see *Shi ji*, 6.55.2045–2047. The Han dynasty lasted from 206 B.C. to A.D. 220. Its founding emperor, Liu Bang, had been persuaded by a favorite concubine named Qi Ji that his son Crown Prince Liu Ying was weak and not like his father; she proposed that Liu Ying be demoted and that her own son Zhaowang Ruyi be made crown prince. Empress Lü called upon Zhang Liang to assist her son Liu Ying; see *Shi ji*, 2.8.395–397 and 2.9.395–412. I discuss this incident in greater detail in Chapter 7. For the brief biography of Emperor Hui, Liu Ying, see *Han shu*, 1.1b.85–93.

6. For the biography of Tang Zhongzong, Li Xian (name later changed to Li Zhe) (656–710), see *Jiu Tang shu*, 1.7.135–151, and *Xin Tang shu*, 1.4.106–114.

7. The phrase "simply handed in through a window" (*na yue zi you*) is a quotation from the *Yi jing*. It is traditionally interpreted as a situation in which regular ceremonies and methods of exhortation are inappropriate. For the Chinese text see *Zhouyi yinde*, 19.29; for the translation see Wilhelm, *Book of Changes*, p. 117. This phrase is also found in one of the Tang histories; see *Jiu Tang shu*, 3.25.971.12.

8. I think the year *jiaxu* is 1634; the dating of the preface is discussed at some length in Chapter 8.

9. I think that Huayang Sanren is an alias for a Ming loyalist named Wu Gongchen. Huayang Sanren is also listed as the compiler of the early-seventeenth-century *Yuanyang zhen*, a collection of four short works of fiction depicting social and political problems of the late Ming. Wang Rumei argues that Huayang Sanren is an alias for Wu Gongchen; see "*Yuanyang zhen* ji qi zuozhe chutan," pp. 225–229; see also Wang Rumei, *Jin Ping Mei tansuo*, pp. 150–153. Huayang Sanren, his view of fiction, his prefaces, and his relationship to the *Ruyijun zhuan* are discussed in Chapter 7.

10. The identity of the calligrapher whose pen name is Gyumon Inshi is not known. In Japanese the word "ox" is homophonous with the word "pander" and is sometimes used in its stead; both are pronounced "*gyu*." The pen name could thus be rendered "Eremite of the Portal of Pander." See *Kōjien*, 605.1.

11. For the title commander in chief see Hucker, *Dictionary of Official Titles*, 544.7311. For the biography of Wu Shihuo see *Jiu Tang shu*, 7.58.2316–2318, and *Xin Tang shu*, 19.206.5835–5836. The nickname Wu Meiniang, or Fair Flatterer, was originally the name of a lascivious song that was popular during the late sixth century; see *Jiu Tang shu*, 7.62.2373. A song of this title was also popular right before Wu Zetian became emperor; see *Jiu Tang shu*, 7.51.2173.2.

12. Wu Zetian reached the age of fourteen in the year 637. For the biography of the Erudite Emperor, Tang Taizong, Li Shimin, see *Jiu Tang shu*, 1.2.21–38, and *Xin Tang shu*, 1.2.23–49. For the title "lady of talents" see *Dictionary of Official Titles*, 515.6830.

13. For the biography of Tang Gaozong, Li Zhi (628–683), see *Jiu Tang shu*, 1.4.65–113, and *Xin Tang shu*, 1.3.51–79.

14. A scene in which Gaozong is attracted to Wu Zetian even though he is attending to his dying father is also found in *Zizhi tongjian*, 7.6284, and *Zizhi tongjian gangmu*, 40.20b. In these accounts Gaozong's filial piety is applauded by his father; Gaozong attends him so assiduously that he does not leave his side or eat for several days.

15. This paragraph is also found in *Sui Tang liangchao shizhuan*, 10.91.1b–2a.

16. Mount Wu and Yang Terrace refer to a famous rhapsody attributed to Song Yu describing a sexual encounter between a king and a divine maiden; see *Wenxuan*, pp. 875–886.

17. This line of poetry is also found in *Sui Tang liangchao shizhuan*, 10.91.2a.

18. This scene is also found in *Sui Tang liangchao shizhuan*, 10.91.2a–2b.

19. In the year 649.

20. This is a designation of one of the nine concubines; see *Dictionary of Official Titles*, 117.288.

21. For the biography of Wang Huanghou see *Jiu Tang shu*, 7.51.2169–2170, and *Xin Tang shu*, 11.76.3473. For the biography of Xiao Liangdi see *Jiu Tang shu*, 7.51.2170, and *Xin Tang shu*, 11.76.3473; for her title see *Dictionary of Official Titles*, 435.5427. This scene is also found in *Sui Tang liangchao shizhuan*, 10.91.4b–5a.

22. In the year 655.

23. This sentence is also found in *Sui Tang liangchao shizhuan*, 10.91.5b.

24. For the biography of Zhangsun Wuji (d. 659) see *Jiu Tang shu*, 7.65.2446–2456, and *Xin Tang shu*, 13.105.4017–4022. Wu Zetian's son was Tang Zhongzong, Li Xian.

25. In the Tang histories, Zhangsun Wuji repeatedly states that Gaozong's plans are not acceptable. After bribery is delivered by the cartload and intense pressure is brought to bear by the emperor himself, Zhangsun Wuji no longer expresses his opinion but instead suggests that Chu Suiliang's opinion be solicited. See *Jiu Tang shu*, 7.65.2454–2455, and *Xin Tang shu*, 13.105.4020–4021.

26. For the biography of Chu Suiliang see *Jiu Tang shu*, 8.80.2729–2739, and *Xin Tang shu*, 13.105.4024–4029.

27. During the Tang dynasty, some officials bore an ivory tablet as a symbol of their authority; see *Dictionary of Official Titles*, 575.7859.

28. The scene that begins with Gaozong's inquiry into the feasibility of naming a new empress and ends with Wu Zetian's violent reaction to the advice of Chu Suiliang is also found, with minor textual variation, in *Sui Tang liangchao shizhuan*, 10.91.6a–6b. This passage appears to have been based on the standard histories; see *Jiu Tang shu*, 8.80.2739, *Xin Tang shu*, 13.105.4028–4029, *Zizhi tongjian*, 7.6290, and *Zizhi tongjian gangmu*, 40.22b; see also Liu Su, *Da Tang xinyu*, pp. 180–181.

29. In the Tang histories, Zhangsun Wuji is banished to Qian province on the pretext that he is plotting to overthrow the government; see *Jiu Tang shu*, 7.65.2456, and *Xin Tang shu*, 13.105.4021–4022. Chu Suiliang is demoted to commander in chief of Tan prefecture; although he is demoted repeatedly, he is not tortured or ordered to commit suicide; see *Jiu Tang shu*, 8.80.2739, and *Xin Tang shu*, 13.105.4029. By altering the fate of Chu Suiliang and having Gaozong order him to commit suicide, apparently the author of the *Ruyijun zhuan* is signaling that his story is entering the realm of fiction. In the *Sui Tang liangchao shizhuan*, Gaozong becomes very angry at Chu Suiliang but is persuaded that having him put to death would be a terrible mistake; see *Sui Tang liangchao shizhuan*, 10.92.7a–7b.

30. The phrase "despite all obstacles the emperor's loyal servant did not regard his

own welfare" (*jianjian wangchen ji feigong*) is a slightly modified quotation from the *Yi jing;* the phrase was originally "*wangchen jianjian feigong zhi gu.*" Wilhelm translates this line: "The king's servant is beset by obstruction upon obstruction, But it is not his own fault." The commentary to this line he translates as follows: "Ordinarily it is best to go around an obstacle and try to overcome it along the line of least resistance. But there is one instance in which a man must go out to meet the trouble, even though difficulty piles upon difficulty: this is when the path of duty leads directly to it—in other words, when he cannot act of his own volition but is duty bound to go and seek out danger in the service of a higher cause." For the Chinese text see *Zhouyi yinde,* 24.39; for the translation see Wilhelm, *Book of Changes,* p. 152. This phrase is also found in the standard histories; see *Jin shu,* 8.89.2303.7, *Jiu Tang shu,* 7.62.2391.11, and *Xin Tang shu,* 13.99.3919.13.

31. Bi Gan was the paternal uncle of the infamous King Zhou (r. 1086-1045 B.C.), the last emperor of the Shang dynasty (c. 1600-1045 B.C.). According to historical records, King Zhou was licentious and would not listen to counsel. Saying that a loyal subject should remonstrate with his ruler and not be concerned with the consequences, Bi Gan criticized King Zhou for three days and would not desist. Saying that he heard the heart of a virtuous man had seven apertures, King Zhou thereupon had Bi Gan's heart removed so that he could examine it; see *Shi ji,* 1.3.107-108. In this poem the reference to Bi Gan probably refers to an official named Zhou Jing who was implicated in a plot to kill Wu Sansi, the nephew of Wu Zetian. Zhou Jing and his accomplices thought that Wu Sansi's behavior had damaged the reputation of the court and extreme measures were necessary to remove him. When the plot was uncovered, Zhou Jing fled to the Bi Gan temple where he committed suicide in a final act of loyalty to the state. With his last words he praised the loyalty of Bi Gan and called upon the gods to revenge his death; see *Da Tang xinyu,* 75.1, and *Zizhi tongjian,* 6600.13. For the biography of Zhou Jing see *Jiu Tang shu,* 15.87 upper 4878-4879, and *Xin Tang shu,* 18.191.5507-5508.

32. Variations of this line are found in the Tang histories; see *Jiu Tang shu,* 2.17a.509.4, 13.54.4106.9, and *Xin Tang shu,* 17.175.5245.10.

33. The majestic phoenix (*weifeng*) is the name of a *fu* rhapsody that was written by Emperor Taizong and presented to Zhangsun Wuji as a description of his virtuous ability; see *Da Tang xinyu,* 141.6. A copy of this rhapsody is found in *Jiu Tang shu,* 7.65.2448-2449. An interlinear comment found in *Sui Tang liangchao shizhuan,* 10.92.8a, incorrectly identifies the phrase "*weifeng*" as the *zi* of Zhangsun Wuji; his real *zi* was "Fuji."

34. The term "assembled female deer" (*ju you*) is found in the *Li ji,* or *Book of Rites;* it refers to a father and son committing incest by sharing the same woman: "Brute beasts are without propriety, therefore father and son share the same hind." This is a pointed reference to Taizong and Gaozong sharing Wu Zetian. For the Chinese text see *Li ji yinde,* 1.6. This term is also used to describe Wu Zetian's relationship with Taizong in *Jiu Tang shu,* 8.67.2491.1.

35. This poem is also found, with minor textual variations, in *Sui Tang liangchao shizhuan,* 10.92.8a. For a discussion of historical poetry of this kind and authors who are often cited in historical fiction of the middle to late sixteenth century, see Zhang Zhenglang, "Jiangshi yu yongshishi."

36. The phrase "tied up like a sack" (*kuonang*) is found in the *Yi jing;* see *Zhouyi yinde,* 3.2. Wilhelm translates the commentary to this line as follows: "The strictest reticence is indicated here. The time is dangerous, because any degree of prominence leads either to the enmity of irresistible antagonists if one challenges them or

to misconceived recognition if one is complaisant. Therefore a man ought to maintain reserve, be it in solitude or in the turmoil of the world, for there too he can hide himself so well that no one knows him." See Wilhelm, *Book of Changes*, p. 14. Wu Zetian was elevated in the year 655.

37. Wu Zhao is the name Wu Zetian gave herself when she proclaimed herself emperor.

38. The three preceding sentences are also found in *Sui Tang liangchao shizhuan*, 10.92.11b.

39. The description of the fates suffered by Empress Wang and Pure Consort Xiao is a paraphrase of the historical record; see *Jiu Tang shu*, 7.51.2170, and *Xin Tang shu*, 11.76.3474. It is also found in *Sui Tang liangchao shizhuan*, 10.92.11b.

40. See *Jiu Tang shu*, 7.58.2317, and *Xin Tang shu*, 19.206.5835.

41. Gaozong died in 683. At one point the name of Tang Zhongzong, Li Xian, was changed to Li Zhe.

42. For the biography of Concubine Wei see *Jiu Tang shu*, 7.51.2171–2175, and *Xin Tang shu*, 11.76.3486–3489.

43. For the biography of Tang Ruizong, Li Dan, see *Jiu Tang shu*, 1.7.151–163, and *Xin Tang shu*, 1.5.115–120. He was made emperor in 684.

44. In the year 690.

45. During the Tang dynasty, Langya was a prefecture in Guangxi province. For the biography of Li Chong see *Jiu Tang shu*, 8.76.2663–2664, and *Xin Tang shu*, 12.80.3575–3577. For the biography of Li Zhen see *Jiu Tang shu*, 8.76.2661–2663, and *Xin Tang shu*, 12.80.3575–3576.

46. For a discussion of Wu Zetian's titles see Forte, *Propaganda and Ideology*, pp. 4–5 and 144–145. The empress was not actually given the title "Zetian" until the year 705, after she was deposed and near death; see *Zizhi tongjian*, 6582.1.

47. For the biography of Wu Sansi (d. 707) see *Jiu Tang shu*, 14.183.4734–4736, and *Xin Tang shu*, 19.206.5837–5842.

48. For the biography of Di Renjie see *Jiu Tang shu*, 9.89.2885–2896, and *Xin Tang shu*, 14.115.4207–4214. This passage is a paraphrase of *Xin Tang shu*, 14.115.4212; it is also found in *Sui Tang liangchao shizhuan*, 10.97.41a. As paraphrased by the *Ruyijun zhuan*, however, it is historically inaccurate. Wu Zetian was thinking about elevating Wu Sansi but did not actually do so. Di Renjie did not argue that Li Dan be elevated to emperor or that his name be changed; he argued that Crown Prince Li Xian (Li Zhe), the other son of Wu Zetian whom she had earlier demoted to prince of Luling, should be reinstated. Wu Zetian did in fact reinstate Li Xian in accordance with the counsel of Di Renjie.

49. Li Dan was made emperor in 684 after his brother Li Xian was demoted to prince of Luling; later that same year Li Dan was demoted to crown prince when Wu Zetian changed the name of the dynasty from Tang to Zhou and proclaimed herself empress.

50. This poem is also found in *Sui Tang liangchao shizhuan*, 10.97.41b, where it describes the reinstatement of the crown prince after the event has already taken place. In the historical record, however, this poem refers to a dream that Wu Zetian had before she decided to reinstate her son Li Xian. There are many versions of Wu Zetian's dream; the earliest I have identified occurs in *Chaoye qianzai*, p. 60; for a translation and discussion of this poem see Chapter 6. In the *Xin Tang shu*, Wu Zetian's dream is different but is interpreted in a similar manner by Di Renjie; see *Xin Tang shu*, 14.115.4212.

51. The expression "the hen heralds the dawn" (*pinji sichen*) is one of several describing a woman who has usurped the power of a man, leading to disaster; not coincidentally, this phrase is used to describe Wu Zetian in the standard histories; see *Jiu Tang shu*, 1.6.133.10, and *Zizhi tongjian*, 6585.5. The ultimate source of this expression is probably the *Shu jing;* see Legge, *Chinese Classics*, 3.302. The Zichen Palace, or Purple Palace, was frequented by Wu Zetian immediately after she assumed power; see *Jiu Tang shu*, 2.17a.508, and *Xin Tang shu*, 11.76.3477.

52. The Eastern Palace was the traditional abode of the crown prince. Wu Zetian was living in the emperor's palace, and the legitimate emperor was living in the crown prince's palace.

53. The Zhang brothers were Wu Zetian's lovers Zhang Yizhi and Zhang Changzong. Duke Di is Di Renjie.

54. This poem is also found in *Sui Tang liangchao shizhuan*, 10.97.40b–41a. Li Chunfeng (602–670) was a Daoist expert at interpreting portents. As an adviser to Taizong, he predicted that in thirty or forty years a woman then in court would use force to take over the dynasty and kill much of the ruling family. As this was already fated to take place, Li Chunfeng said that if Taizong attempted to kill this woman, his heirs would be annihilated; if he did nothing, his dynasty would survive. See *Jiu Tang shu*, 8.79.2717–2719, and *Xin Tang shu*, 18.204.5798. Li Chunfeng and his powers figure prominently just before Wu Zetian is introduced in *Sui Tang liangchao shizhuan*, 9.90.59b–60b.

55. For the biography of Lai Junchen (d. 697) see *Jiu Tang shu*, 15.186.4837–4842, and *Xin Tang shu*, 19.209.5905–5908. For the biography of Suo Yuanli (d. 691) see *Jiu Tang shu*, 15.186.4843–4844, and *Xin Tang shu*, 19.209.5904–5905.

56. The Sui dynasty lasted from 589 to 618. For the biography of Xue Ju see *Jiu Tang shu*, 7.55.2245–2247, and *Xin Tang shu*, 12.86.3705–3707. In 617 he proclaimed himself Hegemon of Western Qin (Xiqin bawang); see *Jiu Tang shu*, 7.55.2245, and *Xin Tang shu*, 12.86.3705.

57. Xue Renyue is mentioned in *Jiu Tang shu*, 7.55.2245, and *Xin Tang shu*, 12.86.3705. For the biography of Xue Rengao see *Jiu Tang shu*, 7.55.2247–2248, and *Xin Tang shu*, 12.86.3707–3708. The standard histories state that Xue Rengao was defeated at Qianshui but do not say that his brother Xue Renyue accompanied him; see *Jiu Tang shu*, 7.55.2248, and *Xin Tang shu*, 12.86.3707.

58. At this point the *Ruyijun zhuan* departs from the Tang histories. Xue Rengao's concubine is not mentioned in the histories; nor are her son Xue Yufeng or her grandsons Xue Boying and Xue Aocao, the hero of the *Ruyijun zhuan*. In the *Sui Tang liangchao shizhuan*, however, Prime Minister Di Renjie introduces Xue Aocao to Wu Zetian; see *Sui Tang liangchao shizhuan*, 10.97.41b–42a.

59. Sun Zi and Wu Qi wrote famous military treatises. For their biographies see *Shi ji*, 7.65.2161–2169.

60. In 678.

61. In 680.

62. Princess Qianjin is mentioned in *Jiu Tang shu*, 14.183.4741–4742. The name of Feng Xiaobao was changed to Xue Huaiyi by Wu Zetian; for his biography see *Jiu Tang shu*, 14.183.4741–4743. Princess Qianjin introduced him to Wu Zetian in *Xin Tang shu*, 11.76.3480.

63. See *Dictionary of Official Titles*, 298.3525.

64. The phrase used to describe Xue Huaiyi's wealth and pride is a quotation from the *Daode jing*. The full passage reads: "Wealth and place breed insolence That brings

ruin in its train. When your work is done, then withdraw! Such is Heaven's Way." For the Chinese text see *Laozi jiaogu*, 1.136; for the translation see Waley, *Way and Its Power*, p. 152. Shen Nanqiu, the imperial physician, supposedly had an affair with the empress; see *Jiu Tang shu*, 14.183.4743, *Xin Tang shu*, 11.76.3483, *Zizhi tongjian gangmu*, 41.30a.27, and *Zizhi tongjian*, 6499.1. I have not found Shen Nanqiu mentioned in any other historical sources.

65. He actually burned the Mingtang and the Tiantang and was transported to the Baimasi after he was strangled; see *Jiu Tang shu*, 14.183.4743.

66. For the biography of Princess Taiping see *Jiu Tang shu*, 14.183.4738–4740, and *Xin Tang shu*, 12.83.3650–3652. This particular event is related in *Jiu Tang shu*, 14.183.4743, and *Xin Tang shu*, 11.76.3483.

67. Zhang Yizhi was actually Zhang Changzong's brother, not his cousin. The description of Zhang Yizhi is a paraphrase of *Jiu Tang shu*, 8.78.2706.

68. For the minister of the Bureau of Prisons see *Dictionary of Official Titles*, 454.5748. For the director of the Palace Library see *Dictionary of Official Titles*, 313.3730. For the enfeoffment of the Zhang brothers see *Jiu Tang shu*, 8.78.2707, and *Xin Tang shu*, 13.104.4015.

69. Zhang Changzong's nickname, Squire Six, is a pun on the term *"liulang,"* another name for the lotus blossom; see Morohashi, *Dai Kan-Wa jiten*, 2.1453.577.3. Zhang Changzong was also the sixth son of his family.

70. In the year 691.

71. This poem is found in *Quan Tang shi*, 1.58.15; see also Yue Shi, *Guang Zhuoyi ji*, 235.21a.5–6.

72. In addition to referring to the sun, "Golden Wheel" (*jinlun*) was part of a title that Wu Zetian gave herself in the year 695; see *Jiu Tang shu*, 1.6.123.13. For a discussion of the religious significance of this title see Forte, *Propaganda and Ideology*, pp. 140–145.

73. The last line of the poem is also found in *Jiu Tang shu*, 9.2919.7; see also Liu Su, *Da Tang xinyu*, 143.6.

74. Wang Zijin was a famous immortal; for his biography see *Le Lie-sien Tchouan*, p. 109. The historical record also states that Wu Sansi wrote a poem in which Zhang Changzong was called a reincarnation of Wang Zijin; Wu Sansi also ordered officials at court to write a response to his poem; see *Jiu Tang shu*, 14.83.4735, and *Xin Tang shu*, 19.106.5840.

75. Fuqiu Bo, a famous immortal, is mentioned in the biography of Wang Zijin in *Le Lie-sien Tchouan*, p. 109. A biography of Fuqiu Bo is found in *Liexian quanzhuan*, p. 119. Ding Lingwei was a famous immortal whose biography is found in *Liexian quanzhuan*, p. 103, and Tao Qian, *Soushen houji*, p. 1.

76. For the palace attendant see *Dictionary of Official Titles*, 191.1580; this refers to Zhang Changzong. This poem, found in *Jiu Tang shu*, 8.78.2706, is an excerpt of a much longer poem found in *Quan Tang shi*, 68.767; for the full text of the poem see the notes to p. 6a of the critical edition in Part Two. The author is identified as Cui Rong; for his biography see *Jiu Tang shu*, 9.94.2996–3000, and *Xin Tang shu*, 13.114.4195–4196. The term "archivist" (*zangshi*) refers to Laozi; see *Zhuangzi yinde*, 35.13.46. In the unabridged version of the poem, *zangshi* is listed as an alternate reading for *zhushi*, which is an abbreviation of *zhuxiashi*, a more common reference to Laozi; for a description of this office see *Dictionary of Official Titles*, 181.1385. Laozi's surname, like that of the Tang ruling house that considered Laozi to be an ancestor, was Li. Wang Zijin was the son of Zhou Lingwang and also bore the royal name, but

Zhang Changzong did not. The poem may thus be interpreted as criticism of Zhang Changzong. In the *Benshi shi*, the first half of this poem is incorrectly attributed to Zhang Changling; see Meng Qi, *Benshi shi*, 23.9. The attribution to Cui Rong is also discussed in Wang Zhongyong, *Tangshi jishi jiaojian*, p. 205.

77. In the year 690.

78. The word used to describe Wu Zetian's relaxation, *"yanzuo,"* is a Buddhist term describing a kind of meditation; see Morohashi, *Dai Kan-Wa jiten*, 3.7166.30. It may also simply mean "to relax."

79. Zong Jinqing is mentioned in *Jiu Tang shu*, 9.92.2971–2973, *Xin Tang shu*, 11.76.3483, and *Xin Tang shu*, 13.109.4102–4103. The historical Zong Jinqing was not a eunuch; he was the son of Wu Zetian's female first cousin on the father's side; see *Xin Tang shu*, 3.35.905.3.

80. "Elude the executioner's axe" is a paraphrase of a common expression. An early example may be found in *Shi ji*, 8.87.2552.

81. The phrase "a slab of meat on a table" is found at least four times in the Tang histories; it is also the name of an unusual poem written by Yang Weizhen (1296–1370), an eccentric literary figure who was a minor official during the late Yuan dynasty. He was most famous for his controversial and influential poetic style, which was often unusual and ornate. Although his poems sometimes describe unorthodox subjects in weird detail, his poems about historical events were well known and respected during his lifetime. His poem about the slab of meat, a bizarre combination of history and strange description, includes a spoiled piece of meat that sprouts wings and flies into a grove of mulberry trees. This poem is found in a section of poems describing unusual events during the reign of Wu Zetian—including descriptions of Wu Zetian's affair with Xue Huaiyi and her dream of the parrot with broken wings, two events found in the *Ruyijun zhuan* as well. For references to the phrase "a slab of meat on a table" as it occurs in the Tang histories, and for the Chinese text of Yang Weizhen's poem, see the notes to p. 7a of the critical edition in Part Two. Yang Weizhen's other poems describing Tang historical events are found in Yang Weizhen, *Yang Weizhen shiji*, pp. 215–227. For biographies of Yang Weizhen see *Dictionary of Ming Biography*, pp. 1547–1553, and *Ming shi*, 24.285.7308–7309.

82. A *bi* is a jade disk with a circular hole in the middle.

83. "Conducting the affairs of state there has long been an emptiness" is a paraphrase of a line from a memorial to the throne written by Liu Kun (270–317). Liu Kun's memorial expresses concern about the health of the state and describes the dangers that often afflict the throne, especially the neglect of imperial affairs. See Liu Kun, "Quanjin biao," pp. 1701–1711. It is ironic that Wu Zetian would use this line to solicit a new lover.

84. Wu Zetian uses a loaded term to describe Xue Aocao's purity. In *Mencius* and many other works, the term *"jieshen"* refers to the conduct of sages who are attempting to keep their integrity intact: "I have never heard of anyone who can right others by bending himself, let alone someone who can right the Empire by bringing disgrace upon himself. The conduct of sages is not always the same. Some live in retirement, others enter the world; some withdraw, others stay on; but it all comes to keeping their integrity intact." For the Chinese text see *Mengzi yinde*, 37.7.10; for the translation see Lau, *Mencius*, p. 146. The philosophy of keeping oneself pure at all costs is challenged by the preface to the *Ruyijun zhuan*; this is discussed in Chapter 7.

85. For the term "attendants" see *Dictionary of Official Titles*, 426.5278.

86. The term *"daguan"* probably refers to the *daguan shu* (Banquets Office); see *Dictionary of Official Titles*, 467.5973.

87. The Huaqing Palace was not built until the year 723 and was not known by this name until 747. It was located not on the palace grounds but on Mount Li, famous for its Huaqing Springs where the famous concubine Yang Guifei took a celebrated bath immediately before her first romantic encounter with Emperor Tang Xuanzong. Xue Aocao's bath and presentation to Wu Zetian are obviously meant to parallel this later romantic occasion. For the biography of Yang Guifei see *Jiu Tang shu*, 7.51.2178–2181, and *Xin Tang shu*, 11.76.3493–3496; for the biography of Tang Xuanzong, Li Longji, see *Jiu Tang shu*, 1.7.165–238, and *Xin Tang shu*, 1.5.121–154.

88. During the reign of Wu Zetian, the word usually used to describe the imperial seal, *"xi,"* was replaced by the word *"bao,"* which I have translated as "treasure": "In the beginning Taizong carved the mandate-receiving mysterious imperial seal. It was made of white jade and had a hornless dragon sculpted on the top; the inscription read: 'The great mandate of heaven, those with virtue flourish.' Empress Wu changed [the names of] all of the *xi* into *bao*. When Zhongzong assumed the throne, they were again made *xi*." In the description of Xue Aocao's member that follows, Wu Zetian says that it is a unique item, not of this world, and compares it to a piece of white jade. As the imperial seal was unique and made of white jade, the author of the *Ruyijun zhuan* may have been aware of this special use of the word *"bao."* For the Chinese text see *Xin Tang shu*, 2.24.524. See also Wu Zeng, *Nenggaizhai manlu*, 1.80, for a detailed description. A slight variation of the sentence "I have known many men, but there has never been one like this" is also used in the Tang histories to appraise the famous minister and historian Fang Xuanling; this is discussed at some length in Chapter 7. For the Chinese text see *Jiu Tang shu*, 7.66.2459. Fang Xuanling was one of the authors of the *Jin shu*, the history containing the story of Wang Yan's chowry handle that is mentioned in the following line. For the biography of Fang Xuanling see *Jiu Tang shu*, 7.66.2459–2467, and *Xin Tang shu*, 12.96.3853–3858.

89. For the biography of Wang Yan, (*zi* Yifu, 255–311) see *Jin shu*, 43.1235–1239. The significance of this allusion is discussed in the introduction.

90. Qiuci was a country in Central Asia during the Han dynasty. During the Tang dynasty, the name was usually written with an alternate orthography. A pillow from Qiuci decorated with a wandering fairy motif is mentioned in Wang Renyu, *Kaiyuan Tianbao yishi*, 68.4.

91. While the phrase *"zhen wo er"* does not usually have incestuous connotations and can be translated as "you really are my darling" or its equivalent, I have chosen to translate it literally because Xue Aocao later objects to Wu Zetian's use of this appellation and protests that she has been neglecting her real son.

92. This sentence is also found in *Shi ji*, 9.2960.10, and Liu Su, *Da Tang xinyu*, 73.2.

93. The year 692.

94. Variants of this sentence are also found in *Shi ji*, 7.79.2414.5, *Yuanqu xuan*, 1217.9, and *Jin Ping Mei*, 1.391.11.

95. The last clause is also found in Wei Shou, *Wei shu*, 2.539.4.

96. Xue uses a loaded term to describe Wu Zetian's favor. *"Aichen"* literally means "the beloved subject." It is also the name of a famous essay written by the legalist philosopher Han Feizi (d. 233 B.C.) describing the problems that arise when a ruler is too partial to one of his subjects. Wu Zetian's description of her love for Xue is paradigmatically dangerous for the state and for Xue, and it is ironic that Xue clearly sees the danger while the empress does not. See Han Feizi, "Aichen," in *Han Feizi jijie*, p. 61.

97. The phrase Xue uses to say he is not yet "content" is reminiscent of the

philosophy of Laozi. In the *Daode jing*, the phrase *"zhizu,"* literally to "know contentment," describes an attitude of caution and moderation that leads to one's personal safety. Xue's use of this term to say he is not content highlights the dangerous nature of his relation with the empress. Arthur Waley translates a passage from the *Daode jing* that describes contentment as follows: "Be content with what you have and are, and no one can despoil you; Who stops in time nothing can harm. He is forever safe and secure." See Waley, *Way and Its Power,* p. 197.

98. This is a quotation from the *Analects:* "The Master said, Every man's faults belong to a set. If one looks out for faults it is only as a means of recognizing Goodness." For the Chinese text see *Lunyu yinde,* 6.7; for the translation see Waley, *Analects,* p. 103. This quotation is also repeated by Minister Di Renjie in the Tang histories; see *Jiu Tang shu,* 9.88.2885, and *Xin Tang shu,* 14.115.4207.

99. For the general of the Left Palace Gate Guard see *Dictionary of Official Titles,* 149.847. For the director of the Palace Domestic Service see *Dictionary of Official Titles,* 351.4249.

100. Wei Wuzhi (fl. 200 B.C.) is mentioned in the historical record because of an unusual recommendation he made to Liu Bang, founding emperor of the Han dynasty. Wei argued that a man named Chen Ping (d. 178 B.C.) would make a good general and suggested that Liu Bang hire him. Liu Bang did so, but Chen Ping was immediately vilified for his past history: he was accused of committing adultery with his sister-in-law; his fidelity was questioned because he had served many rulers; and he openly accepted bribes. Liu Bang summoned Wei Wuzhi and demanded an explanation. Wei did not aver that any of the accusations leveled against Chen Ping were untrue. Instead he said: "I introduced a man of unique stratagems; I only considered if his schemes were truly sufficient to benefit the country or not. And why should you doubt his ability merely because he committed adultery with his sister-in-law and accepted bribes?" Liu Bang then questioned Chen Ping himself, who said that he had indeed served many masters because none of them used his talent; he also admitted that he had accepted bribes because he needed the money. Liu Bang was impressed with his direct answers and thereupon promoted him. Chen Ping served with distinction and eventually became prime minister; he was known for his virtue and was credited with having saved the dynasty at several crucial moments. Wei Wuzhi was amply rewarded for having introduced Chen Ping. For the Chinese text see *Shi ji,* 6.56.2054. For the biography of Chen Ping see *Shi ji,* 6.56.2051-2063.

101. Wu Zetian actually did change the name of the calendar year to Ruyi in 692. Later that same year she again changed the name to Changshou. The historical records do not state why the empress chose these names, however.

102. For left vice-director of the Department of State Affairs see *Dictionary of Official Titles,* 394.4826. Yang Zhirou is mentioned in *Jiu Tang shu,* 7.62.2383, and *Xin Tang shu,* 13.100.3928. *"Ruyi,"* the term I have translated as "perfect satisfaction," also refers to a multipurpose backscratcher whose name was originally a transliteration of the Buddhist term *"anurubbha."* In this section of the *Ruyijun zhuan,* Yang Zhirou does not know that Wu Zetian has named the year after the perfect satisfaction provided by Xue Aocao's physical abilities; he thinks she is naming the year after a backscratcher, which of course would be equally inappropriate. As a *ruyi* is long and thin and can be said to resemble a phallus, the author of the *Ruyijun zhuan* has chosen an object that has obvious sexual overtones resonating with Xue Aocao's role. A *ruyi* is described in Wu Zeng, *Nenggaizhai manlu,* 36.8.

103. The first year of the Changshou reign period was 692. For the biography of

Wife Liu see *Jiu Tang shu,* 7.51.2176, and *Xin Tang shu,* 11.76.3489; for the biography of Wife Dou see *Jiu Tang shu,* 7.51.2176, and *Xin Tang shu,* 11.76.3489-3490. The crown prince to whom they were married was Li Dan.

104. Li Dan's wives Liu and Dou were put to death by Wu Zetian in the second year of the Changshou reign period (693), not the first year. Their biographies state they were put to death because a maidservant falsely accused them of having cast an evil spell on Wu Zetian. See *Jiu Tang shu,* 7.51.2176, and *Xin Tang shu,* 11.76.3489-3490.

105. For the story of Jin Xiangong, Li Ji, Yiwu, and Chonger see *Shi ji,* 5.39.1640-1660. Jin Xiangong's favorite concubine Li Ji requested that he demote his son the crown prince and elevate her own child in his stead. Crown Prince Shensheng committed suicide in a valiant attempt to save the state from the impending upheaval, but his replacement Xiqi was eventually murdered. This brought the state of Jin to the brink of civil war. It is curious that the empress has chosen a perfect example from the historical record to illustrate her dangerous obsession while remaining blithely ignorant of its moral; Xue Aocao, by contrast, immediately comprehends the devastating implications of the story and recognizes that it is uniquely applicable to his current situation and the succession struggles which are still unresolved.

106. In the year 694.

107. The term "wet head" (*rushou*) is an uncommon expression that usually means to drink until one is out of control. This phrase appears to have derived its meaning from the *Book of Changes.* The last line of the last hexagram of the book, *"weiji,"* reads: "There is drinking of wine In genuine confidence. No blame. But if one wets his head, He loses it, in truth. When one wets his head while drinking wine, it is because he knows no moderation." For the Chinese text see *Zhouyi yinde,* 39.64; for the translation see Wilhelm, *Book of Changes,* p. 718. The hexagram *"weiji"* has strong sexual connotations.

108. This proverbial expression, attributed to the famous Jin-dynasty (265-420) painter Gu Kaizhi, is discussed in Chapter 6. For the Chinese text see *Jin shu,* 8.92.2405. This quotation is also found, with textual emendations, in Yu Jiaxi, *Shishuo xinyu,* p. 686.

109. The unlikely source of this expression is a Han-dynasty work called the *Dadai liji* that describes the ritual foundations of order in the Chinese state: "The sages scrupulously maintained the disposition of the days and months in order to observe the motion of the stars, in order to apportion the alternations of the four seasons, this is called a calendar; they cut twelve tubes in order to differentiate between the high and low, pure and dissonant, of the eight kinds of musical sound, this is called music. Music dwells in *yin* but regulates *yang,* the calendar dwells in *yang* but regulates *yin,* music and the calendar alternate and regulate one another, there is not the space for a single strand of hair left between them." All of these ritual prescriptions for ordering the state have just been broken by Wu Zetian: she alters the calendar in ways that her ministers find capricious; she disrupts the seasons by ordering flowers to bloom out of season; and she confounds the order between high and low by sleeping with a commoner. As the order represented by the calendar is the same as the order of music, the music the empress makes with Xue Aocao is entirely inappropriate. The sounds of their lovemaking are described in unusual and even jarring detail; it does not reveal the mutual regulation of *yin* and *yang* but consists of flatulent burbling that resembles a throng of coolies plunging through muck. For the Chinese text see *Concordance to the Dadai liji,* 35.20-22. This phrase is also found in *Han shu,* 8.51.2359.

110. The word Wu Zetian uses to describe Gaozong's death, *"yanjia,"* is a technical term used only for emperors. Literally it means "the chariots leave late" and is meant

to describe the loss felt by the emperor's ministers immediately after he dies; when it is time for them to depart, they do so only after much hesitation and contemplation. It is interesting that Wu Zetian would use this term to recall the death of Gaozong while simultaneously viewing it as an opportunity to find a new and more sexually satisfying lover. She was fifty-nine years old when Gaozong died. See *Hanyu dacidian,* 5.713.

111. The term "furnace" *(lu)* is from Daoist physiological alchemy. See Needham and Lu, pp. 99–107. See also van Gulik, *Sexual Life,* pp. 79–80.

112. The phrase used to describe Wu Zetian's advanced age, *"migao,"* is rare. Perhaps the most famous use of this expression is found in the *Analects,* a work that would have been known, or more probably memorized, by every student of the traditional educational system. In this famous passage, Confucius' favorite student Yan Hui is describing the virtue of Confucius and the difficulty of attaining it. If called to mind by an educated reader of the *Ruyijun zhuan,* this passage could be read as a string of obscene double entendres that describe, in graphic detail, the current status of the physical relationship between Wu Zetian and Xue Aocao: "Yen Hui said with a deep sigh, The more I strain my gaze up towards it, the higher it soars. The deeper I bore down into it, the harder it becomes. I see it in front; but suddenly it is behind. Step by step the Master skillfully lures one on. He has broadened me with culture, restrained me with ritual. Even if I wanted to stop, I could not. Just when I feel that I have exhausted every resource, something seems to rise up, standing out sharp and clear. Yet though I long to pursue it, I can find no way of getting to it at all." For the Chinese text see *Lunyu yinde,* 16.11; for the translation see Waley, *Analects,* p. 140.

113. See *Dictionary of Official Titles,* 372.4527. This designation, which existed only during the Tang dynasty, referred to officials who were charged with drafting imperial pronouncements and various literary works upon imperial order. The Tang histories do not state that the Zhang brothers were ever appointed to such a post; in fact, they are described as functionally illiterate; see *Jiu Tang shu,* 8.78.2707.7.

114. The first year of the Shengli reign period was 698.

115. As the phrase "Could it be that man is not the equal of a bird?" is found in the *Daxue,* it is safe to assume that it would have been familiar to all educated persons. For the Chinese text see *Sishu jizhu,* 3.4a; for the translation see Legge, *Chinese Classics,* 1.362; for the text of the entire poem see Legge, *Chinese Classics,* 4.419. This allusion is discussed in detail in Chapter 9.

116. This is a proverbial saying; see *Yuanqu xuan,* 1682.6. It is also found in the *Gu zunsu yulu,* where it is attributed to the famous Zen monk Zhaozhou Congshen (778–897); see *Gu zunsu yulu* 13.228.6.

117. The phrase "Once you have seen the ocean, it is difficult for other bodies of water to compare" is a quotation from Mencius, who uses the perception of size as a metaphor to describe the stature of a sage. As in other instances, the *Ruyijun zhuan* puts such quotations in a context that readily leads to an obscene interpretation. D. C. Lau translates the entire passage as follows: "When he ascended the Eastern Mount, Confucius felt that Lu was small, and when he ascended Mount T'ai, he felt that the Empire was small. Likewise it is difficult for water to come up to the expectation of someone who has seen the Sea, and it is difficult for words to come up to the expectation of someone who has studied under a sage. There is a way to judge water. Watch for its ripples. When the sun and moon shine, the light shows up the least crack that will admit it. Flowing water is such that it does not go further forward until it has filled all the hollows. A gentleman, in his pursuit of the Way, does not get there unless

he achieves a beautiful pattern." For the Chinese text see *Mengzi yinde,* 52.24.1; for the translation see Lau, *Mencius,* p. 187.

118. Quxu guo is mentioned in Wang Jia (fourth century), *Shiyi ji,* p. 75.9.

119. The term Wu Zetian uses to describe how Xue Aocao has failed to wait for the ruler's mandate, *"siming,"* figures prominently in one of the most famous passages in the *Zhongyong:* "In a high position, he does not treat with contempt his inferiors. In a low situation, he does not court the favor of his superiors. He rectifies himself, and seeks for nothing from others, so that he has no dissatisfaction. He does not murmur against heaven, nor grumble against men. Thus it is that the superior man is quiet and calm, waiting for the appointments of Heaven, while the mean man walks in dangerous paths, looking for lucky occurrences. The Master said, 'In archery we have something like the way of the superior man. When the archer misses the centre of the target, he turns around and seeks for the cause of his failure in himself.'" For the Chinese text and translation see Legge, *Chinese Classics,* 1.395-396.

120. Hongmen is an allusion to the famous meeting between the Hegemon King Xiang Yu (232-202 B.C.) and the founding emperor of the Han dynasty, Liu Bang. Liu's faithful servant Fan Kuai (d. 189 B.C.) stormed into the room where Liu was being entertained by a sword dance that was meant to end with Liu's death. Fan successfully extricated Liu Bang and hastily they retreated; see *Shi ji,* 1.7.312-315. In the *Xiuta yeshi* an allusion is also made to this incident; see *Xiuta yeshi,* 2.194. "Hongmen" also puns with the term *"hongmen,"* which in this context alludes to the vagina.

121. The Shangyang gong was built by Gaozong; he often administered the government from this place; see *Xin Tang shu,* 4.38.982. Wu Zetian died in the Shangyang gong at the age of eighty-two; see Sima Guang, *Zizhi tongjian,* 6596.12.

122. This common expression exists in many forms.

123. This refers to a concubine whose full name was Shangguan Waner (664-710); for her biography see *Jiu Tang shu,* 7.51.2175-2176, and *Xin Tang shu,* 11.76.3488-3489. She was given the title "lady of handsome fairness" (*jieyu*) during the reign of Wu Zetian, a title given to concubines who assisted the emperor; see *Dictionary of Official Titles,* 144.780. During the reign of Zhongzong she was given the title "lady of bright countenance" (*zhaorong*), a designation of one of the nine concubines; see *Dictionary of Official Titles,* 117.289. She is said to have possessed unusual literary talent; in fact, Emperor Xuanzong had her poetry compiled into a work of twenty volumes. She also wielded great power in Wu Zetian's court and contributed to its dissolute reputation; see *Jiu Tang shu,* 7.51.2172. Thirty-two poems attributed to her are found in the *Quan Tang shi,* 1.60-64.

124. The Jianzhang Palace and Weiyang Palace were first built during the Han dynasty. The former was to the west of the latter, and both were outside the capital city of Changan. The Weiyang Palace was destroyed a couple of times, and during the Tang dynasty it was rebuilt in the center of the imperial garden; see *Hanyu dacidian,* 2.908 and 4.686. The phrase *"weiyang"* also has other connotations; it is perhaps most famous as a phrase in a poem found in the *Shi jing:* "What of the night? Vesper's still the hour." For the Chinese text see *Maoshi yinde,* 40.182.1; for the translation see Waley, *Book of Songs,* p. 191. This line from the *Shi jing* is the source of the name of the hero of the famous seventeenth-century erotic novel *Rou putuan,* Weiyang Sheng, or Vesperus: "Since the student was preoccupied with sex and favored the nighttime over the daytime and the earlier part of the night over the later part, he had, on seeing the lines 'What of the night? Vesper's still the hour' in the *Poetry Classic,* plucked a character or two out of context and taken the name Scholar Vesperus."

For the Chinese text see *Rou putuan*, 2.151; for the translation see Hanan, *Carnal Prayer Mat*, p. 20.

125. This line contains a quotation from the *Zuo zhuan*. The full text reads: "The male and female phoenix fly together, singing harmoniously with gem-like sounds. The posterity of this scion of the Gui will be nourished among the Jiang. In five generations they will be prosperous, and the highest ministers in Qi; in eight, there will be none to compare with them for greatness." For the Chinese text see *Chunqiu jingzhuan yinde*, 67.3.10; for the translation see Legge, *Chinese Classics*, 5.102–103. The first part of this line is, in turn, a quotation from the *Shi jing;* for the Chinese text see *Maoshi yinde*, 65.252.7.

126. It is an interesting coincidence that the Palace of Supreme Tranquility (Daan gong) is where the founding emperor of the Tang dynasty, Tang Gaozu, Li Yuan (565–635), died; see *Jiu Tang shu*, 1.3.45. Sometimes this palace is called the Taian gong; see *Jiu Tang shu*, 1.1.18.

127. The area called Lingnan is today the region around Guangdong and Guangxi. *Tong bu*, or *tongzhong bu*, is an ancient type of cloth so fine that it could be rolled up and inserted in a tube; see *Hanyu dacidian*, 8.1149.

128. I do not know what this is.

129. The term *"hong shaoyao,"* of which *hong yao* appears to be an abbreviation, is the name of a melody in *ci* and *qu* poetry. The entire line is also a quotation from a poem by Xie Tiao (464–494); for the Chinese text see *Wenxuan*, 3.1407–1408. For his biography see Xiao Zixian, *Nanqi shu*, 3.47.825–828.

130. The phrase used to describe animal copulation, *"ziwei,"* is rare. It is found at the very beginning of the *Shu jing:* "Birds and animals copulate." See *Shangshu tongjian*, 1.01.0170.

131. The last clause is also found in a love letter in one of the most famous Chinese love stories, the *Yingying zhuan;* see Yuan Zhen, *Yingying zhuan*, 133.5; see also *Dong Jieyuan Xixiang ji*, 145.7, Liu Su, *Da Tang xinyu*, 73.7, and Chen Shou, *Sanguo zhi*, 5.1366.7.

132. The expression "corrected his previous errors and has become a new man" occurs as early as the year 167 B.C.; see *Shi ji*, 2.427.13.

133. This refers to the extermination of the Lü clan after the death of Empress Lü in 180 B.C.; see *Shi ji*, 2.9.395–412. In the Tang histories, contemporaries also questioned Wu Zetian's legitimacy by comparing her to Empress Lü; see *Jiu Tang shu*, 3.25.957, 8.84.2796, and 9.87.2844; *Xin Tang shu*, 13.108.4084 and 14.117.4248.

134. This is a paraphrase of part of a speech by Di Renjie to Wu Zetian that argues precisely what Xue Aocao is arguing: "As I see it, neither heaven nor the people have yet come to despise the virtue of the Tang." See *Xin Tang shu*, 14.115.4212. This allusion is discussed in some detail in Chapter 6. This piece of advice from Di Renjie is important because it directly supports the argument made by Huayang Sanren in his preface to the *Ruyijun zhuan:* moral exhortation in difficult times can take peculiar if not repugnant forms.

135. The standard histories state that Di Renjie was the only person who argued that the legitimate crown prince should be reinstated; see *Jiu Tang shu*, 9.89.2895, and *Xin Tang shu*, 14.115.4214.

136. The second year of the Shengli reign period was 699.

137. The phrase "birds with wings overlapped or branches growing together" is a paraphrase of a famous line of poetry written by Bai Juyi (772–846): "In the heavens we shall be birds with wings overlapped, on the earth we shall be branches entwined together." For the Chinese text see *Quan Tang shi*, 7.4820.1.

138. The phrase "fine things are not durable" is found in a poem by Bai Juyi; see *Quan Tang shi*, 7.4822.12-13.

139. For the biography of Wu Chengsi (d. 698) see *Jiu Tang shu*, 14.183.4727-4729, and *Xin Tang shu*, 19.206.5837-5838. If Wu Zetian was seventy-six years old at this point, as the *Ruyijun zhuan* states, then Wu Chengsi would have been dead for over a year. He is said to have pined away because he was not made crown prince.

140. The states of Wu and Shu encompassed most of southern China during the Three Kingdoms period.

141. Xiliang is the name of a small country that existed from 400 to 421 in the far western regions of China. Today this area is part of Xinjiang.

142. Descriptions of the infliction of pain for erotic purposes are rare in Chinese literature; indeed this passage in the *Ruyijun zhuan* is the first detailed account I have encountered. This practice is mentioned in *Jin Ping Mei*, 1.187.8 and 1.279.4, and in more detail in 4.11.12-4.12.12 and 4.706.2-4.708.1. As described in the *Jin Ping Mei*, it involves the burning of dried moxa or incense on a woman's breasts, stomach, and mons veneris; the woman submits to this practice voluntarily, and it appears to heighten sexual pleasure, particularly for the man. In the *Jin Ping Mei* the man is not subjected to burning but instead engages in intercourse as the woman writhes involuntarily as her level of pain increases. For brief discussions of this practice see Roy, *Plum in the Golden Vase*, 1.500, n. 41, and van Gulik, *Sexual Life*, p. 161. A sixteenth-century author describes this practice in a song; see Feng Weimin (1511-1580), *Haifu shantang cigao*, 3.157.9-13. The Marquis de Sade also describes the burning of a woman's most sensitive parts for the production of sexual pleasure; see Sade, *Oeuvres*, 1.339; see also p. 1189.354, n. 1.

143. I have not found the name Wen Boxiang in the standard histories.

144. The compound that I translate as "fair conclusion" (*gouwan*) is not common. In the *Analects* it describes someone who is satisfied with his current position: "The Master said of the Wei grandee Ching, He dwelt as a man should dwell in his house. When things began to prosper with him, he said, 'Now they will begin to be a little more suitable.' When he was better off still, he said, 'Now they will be fairly complete.' When he was really rich, he said, 'Now I shall be able to make them quite beautiful.'" For the Chinese text see *Lunyu yinde*, 25.8; for the translation see Waley, *Analects*, p. 173.

145. This line is a paraphrase of a line in a poem by Mei Yaochen (1002-1062), a leading scholar-official and poet in the middle of the Northern Sung period. The original line reads: "In the past we hurriedly bid farewell, and were endlessly far apart for twenty years." For the Chinese text see *Mei Yaochen ji biannian jiaozhu*, 2.281. For the biography of Mei Yaochen see *Song shi*, 37.443.13091-13092; see also Liu, "Mei Yao-ch'en," pp. 761-770.

146. This line contains a quotation from the *Shi jing*. The full line reads: "To think about this carefully, I cannot spread my wings and fly away." For the Chinese text see *Maoshi yinde*, 5.26.4-5. This poem is traditionally interpreted as the lament of a woman who has been separated from her husband and longs for him.

147. This line is found three times in love poems in the *Shi jing*; see *Maoshi yinde*, 18.87.1, 24.119.1-2, and 25.120.1-2.

148. This line is a quotation from the *Shi jing*. The entire line reads: "Who says that Song is far away? I can see it if I stand on the tips of my toes." For the Chinese text see *Maoshi yinde*, 13.61.1. This poem is also traditionally interpreted as the lament of a woman who has been separated from her husband.

149. This poem, attributed to Wu Zetian, is found in the *Quan Tang shi*, 1.59.1. It also appears in *Yuefu shiji*, 4.1138.5. The attribution to Wu Zetian, however, is dubious; see Wu Zetian, *Wu Zetian ji*, p. 173.

150. This line contains a quotation from the *Xici zhuan* (Great commentary to the Book of Changes). For the Chinese text see *Zhouyi yinde*, 47.4; for the translation see Wilhelm, *Book of Changes*, p. 342. This quotation is discussed at length in Chapter 6.

151. The burning house is a Buddhist term for the troubles caused by the world of mundane affairs.

152. At this point the crown prince was Tang Zhongzong, Li Xian. Prime Minister Zhang was Zhang Jianzhi (625–706); for his biography see *Jiu Tang shu*, 9.91.2936–2942, and *Xin Tang shu*, 14.120.4321–4323. The deaths of Zhang Changzong and Zhang Yizhi are described in *Jiu Tang shu*, 8.78.2708, and *Xin Tang shu*, 13.104.4016. They were killed in the year 705.

153. The Tianbao reign period lasted from 742 to 755.

154. For the biography of Emperor Wu, Liu Che, see *Han shu*, 1.6.155–215. The *Han Wudi neizhuan* and *Zhao Feiyan waizhuan* are discussed at length in Chapter 2.

155. I think that *"kanoe tatsu"* refers to the year 1760 and that this postscript might have been written by the Japanese publisher; see Chapter 7. The preface to the 1995 edition of the *Ruyijun zhuan* suggests that the name Yanagi Hyakusei refers to the Japanese publisher; I am not certain this is how his name should be pronounced.

156. The term "rabbit garden" is perhaps an allusion to one of many historical anecdotes involving lowbrow educational materials or popular works associated with commoners; see Morohashi, *Dai Kan-Wa jiten*, 1.1368.8.

157. The Hōryaku reign period lasted from 1751 to 1764.

158. This is a district in the center of Tokyo; see *Kōjien*, 1841.3.

159. The preface to the 1995 edition of the *Ruyijun zhuan* states that Ogawa Hikokurō was a major publisher who had a bookstore in Nihonbashi from 1727 to 1784; see *Siwuxie huibao*, 24.18.

Critical Edition

1. This is the earliest extant edition of the *Ruyijun zhuan;* it was published by Ogawa Hikokurō in 1763 in Tokyo. My annotated and edited edition is based on the 1985 Tianyi chubanshe reprint of this edition. All emendations made to the text are noted in these notes, even if they are trivial; alternate orthographies of common characters, however, are not usually noted unless they are easily confused with other characters. The page numbers of this edition are enclosed in brackets. The *Chūgoku hiseki sōkan* (hereafter 1987) and *Siwuxie huibao* (hereafter 1995) editions of the *Ruyijun zhuan* make many changes based on a comparison of later editions and other works; when I think it is appropriate, I make the same changes and note the provenance. If later editions disagree with the edition of 1763, I always use the 1763 edition. The 1987 and 1995 editions introduce some errors; these are not noted unless they are significant. Historical events and characters are identified in the notes to the translation. Moreover, I have tried to identify quotations from other works and from works that quote from the *Ruyijun zhuan*. When a passage is quoted or adapted by more than one work, each quotation is arranged alphabetically according to the titles of the works in which the quotations are found. As much of the relevant text as possible is contained in the notes in order to provide the proper context; some of the

more significant quotations are discussed in the notes to the translation. As most of the *Ruyijun zhuan* is copied into the *Nongqing kuaishi,* and as the *Wu Zhao zhuan* is an abridged version of the *Ruyijun zhuan,* textual borrowing by these works is usually not noted. They are discussed in Chapter 8, however, because most of the ironic references to the historical record and the Confucian classics are removed by the authors of the *Nongqing kuaishi* and *Wu Zhao zhuan;* this casts light on the use of quoted materials by the *Ruyijun zhuan.* Furthermore, both the *Ruyijun zhuan* and the *Nongqing kuaishi* contain passages that parallel passages in the *Sui Tang liangchao shizhuan;* this work is also discussed briefly in Chapter 8. Finally, the proximate sources of other occurrences of unique or rare vocabulary are sometimes noted even though they might not be related to the *Ruyijun zhuan.*

2. Ban Gu, *Han shu,* 8.47.2216.10: 中冓之言. *Maoshi yinde,* 10.46.1 (鄘風、牆有茨): 中冓之言。不可道也。所可道也。言之醜也.

3. 監同鑒.

4. In the 1763 edition, a line of ten characters appears to have been written in the wrong column by the calligrapher. The column of characters 侯之力 如留侯可謂社稷 is inserted at this point; it originally came after the column 中宗之復也實敕曹氏之. The edition of 1995 corrects the mistake.

5. Li Yanshou, *Bei shi,* 7.57.2074.14; Wei Zheng, *Sui shu,* 3.25.709.15; Song Lian, *Yuan shi,* 11.38.3333.12; Linghu Defen, *Zhou shu,* 3.40.718.14: 荒淫日甚.

6. Liu Xu, *Jiu Tang shu,* 3.25.971.12: 納約自牖. Xia Xie, *Ming tongjian,* 1775.5: 三臣者、正宜納約自牖、憂形于色；乃徒以 疾求 去、冀以 感悟聖心、亦已迂矣. *Zhouyi yinde,* 19.29 (坎、六四): 樽酒簋貳。開缶。納約自牖。終無咎.

7. 監同鑒.

8. 戌 was 戊.

9. Zhu Xi, *Zizhi tongjian gangmu,* 40.20b: 貞觀十有一 年。書以 武氏爲才人。距 太宗之終。十有三 年。則武蓋十三年在宮中侍太宗矣。當高宗爲太子入侍之時。見而悅之. See also Zhu Xi, *Zizhi tongjian gangmu,* 40.17b; Sima Guang, *Zizhi tongjian,* 7.6267 and 7.6284.

10. 洒同灑.

11. 奈無門 was 豈 無 聞; 1995 corrected per *Nongqing kuaishi,* 237.10. As corrected, the characters 魂、門、and 恩 are in the same rhyme category: 元.

12. 承 was 羕; corrected per *Chipozi zhuan,* 127.10.

13. *Chipozi zhuan,* 127.10: 未承錦 帳風雲會。先沐 金盆雨 露恩.

14. *Sui Tang liangchao shizhuan,* 10.91.1b-2b:是 時帝苦於痾疾。一臥不起。太子入侍不離。左右見武氏扶帝於臥榻。極其妖態。太子悅慕其貌。將 欲私之。彼此以 目送情而未得其便。未幾 太子起身 往廁。武氏捧水跪進。太子灌手以 水洒之。武氏遂吟曰。未得君王寵、先沾雨 露恩。太子大喜。知其有意。遂 與武氏交會於宮門小軒。極盡繾綣。武氏執御衣而泣曰。妾雖微賤。久侍至尊。欲全殿下之情。冒犯私通之律。倘他日嗣登大寶。實妾身於何地邪。太子與之誓曰。俟宮車晏駕。即册汝爲后。有違此言。天厭絕之。武氏曰。出 語無憑。當留表記。太子即解碧玉寶帶。付之。武 氏頓首拜謝.

15. 侍 was 待.

16. *Zizhi tongjian gangmu,* 40.20b: 太宗崩。武氏出 爲尼。忌日。上詣寺行香。見之泣。后 聞 之。陰令 長髮。納之後宮. See also *Zizhi tongjian,* 7.6284.

17. *Sui Tang liangchao shizhuan,* 10.91.4b-5a:武氏出 居感業寺。爲尼數月。帝幸寺行香。因載之以 歸。納之後宮。遂得拜爲昭 儀。卻說武氏既得立爲昭儀。遂與王皇后蕭淑 妃 爭寵.

18. 玉 was 下; corrected per *Sui Tang liangchao shizhuan,* 10.91.5b.

19. *Sui Tang liangchao shizhuan*, 10.91.5b: 武氏泣訴曰。陛下尊居九五。獨不念玉帶之記乎.

20. *Jiu Tang shu*, 8.80.2739: 遂良曰: 皇后出自名家、先朝所娶、伏事先帝、無愆婦德。先帝不豫、執陛下手以語臣曰: 我好兒好婦、今將付卿。陛下親承德音、言猶在耳。皇后自此未聞有愆、恐不可廢。臣今不敢曲從、上違先帝之命、特願再三思審。愚臣上忤聖顏、罪合萬死、但願不負先朝厚恩、何顧性命。遂良致笏於殿陛、曰: 還陛下此笏。仍解巾叩頭流血。帝大怒、令引出. *Xin Tang shu*, 13.105.4028-4029: 遂良曰: 皇后本名家、奉事先帝。先帝疾、執陛下手語臣曰: 我兒與婦今付卿! 且德音在陛下耳、可遽忘之? 皇后無它過、不可廢。帝不悅。翌日、復言、對曰: 陛下必欲改立后者、請更擇貴姓。昭儀昔事先帝、身接帷笫、今立之、奈天下耳目何? 帝羞默。遂良因致笏殿階、叩頭流血、曰: 還陛下此笏、丐歸田里。帝大怒、命引出。武氏從幄後呼曰: 何不撲殺此獠? See also Liu Su, *Da Tang xinyu*, 180-181.

21. *Sui Tang liangchao shizhuan*, 10.91.6a-6b: 帝曰。今召卿等別無所言。為皇后無子。武昭儀有子。朕欲廢后而立昭儀。卿等以為何如。遂良對曰。陛下聖鑒錯矣。皇后乃名家之女。先帝曾為陛下六禮所聘。先帝臨崩之時執陛下手謂臣等曰。朕之佳兒佳婦。咸以付卿。言猶在耳。不敢忘也。皇后未聞有過。陛下何以廢之。陛下必欲立后。伏請妙選天下令族。何必武氏。且武氏經事先帝。人所共知。天下耳目不可掩也。萬代之後。謂陛下為何如。願留三思。臣今忤陛下意。罪當萬死。遂良奏罷。乃置笏於殿階。解巾叩頭流血曰。還陛下笏。乞放臣歸田里。骸骨得葬林下。臣之幸也。武氏在簾中聽聞。大呼曰。何不撲殺此獠。更待何時。帝大怒。急令引出便欲斬之.

22. 貶 was 眨.

23. Fang Xuanling, *Jin shu*, 8.89.2303.7; *Jiu Tang shu*, 7.62.2391.11: 王臣蹇蹇、匪躬之故. *Xin Tang shu*, 13.99.3919.13: 王臣蹇蹇. *Zhouyi yinde*, 24.39 (蹇、六二): 王臣蹇蹇。匪躬之故。象曰。王臣蹇蹇。終無尤也.

24. 1987 changed 柱 to 注.

25. *Jiu Tang shu*, 2.17a.509.4: 頭叩龍墀血流. *Jiu Tang shu*, 13.54.4106.9: 額叩龍墀出血. *Xin Tang shu*, 17.175.5245.10: 額叩龍墀、血被面.

26. 塵 was 麈; corrected per *Sui Tang liangchao shizhuan*, 10.92.8a.

27. *Sui Tang liangchao shizhuan*, 10.92.8a: 蹇蹇王臣既匪躬。直臣真有比干風。笏還螭陛心終赤。額叩龍墀血任紅。威鳳(無忌字)無情迷國紀。聚麀有語亂宸聰。聖朝厚賜春秋祀。千古重昭社稷臣.

28. 貶 was 眨.

29. *Zhouyi yinde*, 3.2 (坤、六四): 括囊、無咎無譽.

30. *Zizhi tongjian*, 6343.3: 中外謂之二聖.

31. *Sui Tang liangchao shizhuan*, 10.92.11b: 中外謂之二聖帝。時感風。眩目不能視。百司奏事。后獨臨朝決之.

32. 古 was 方; 1995 corrected per *Nongqing kuaishi*, 289.2.

33. *Sui Tang liangchao shizhuan*, 10.92.11b: 后命斷去手足。投酒甕中. See also Liu Su, *Da Tang xinyu*, 181.9; *Jiu Tang shu*, 7.51.2170; and *Xin Tang shu*, 11.76.3474.

34. 撈 was 榜.

35. 一 was 五.

36. 且 was 且.

37. 祔 was 附; corrected per *Xin Tang shu*, 14.115.4212.

38. *Sui Tang liangchao shizhuan*, 10.97.41a: 陛下若立子。則千秋萬歲後。配食太廟立姪。則未聞姪為太子而祔姑於廟者也. *Xin Tang shu*, 14.115.4212: 千秋萬歲後常享宗廟; 三思立、廟不祔姑.

39. 旦 was 且.

40. 元 was 人.

41. *Sui Tang liangchao shizhuan,* 10.97.41b: 元人有詩云。一 語喚回鸚鵡夢。九霄奪得鳳雛還.

42. *Da Tang Qinwang cihua,* 1019.7–9, *Sui Tang liangchao shizhuan,* 10.97.40b–41a: 牝雞聲裡紫宸空。幾樹飛花滿地紅。當代媚娘居北闕。一朝天子寓東宮。椒房倡亂由 (*Da Tang Qinwang cihua* was 皆) 張氏。社稷中興賴狄公。人事未形先有數。至今追憶李淳風.

43. 越 was 景; corrected per *Jiu Tang shu,* 7.55.2245, and *Xin Tang shu,* 12.86.3705.

44. 杲 was 果; corrected per *Jiu Tang shu,* 7.55.2247, and *Xin Tang shu,* 12.86.3707.

45. 杲 was 景; 1995 was 越.

46. 杲 was 景; 1995 was 越.

47. 晢 was 哲.

48. *Bei shi,* 3.22.817.2, 6.48.1764.5; Yao Silian, *Liang shu* 2.32.466.2; Li Yanshou, *Nan shi,* 5.61.1504.3; *Sui shu,* 5.51.1329.10: 趫捷過人.

49. 弈 was 奕.

50. 餘 was 余.

51. 蚯 was 丘.

52. *Hailing yishi,* 126.4: 其陽極壯健夯闊。自根至頂有筋勁起。如蚯蚓脈突.

53. 紅 was 江; 1995 corrected per printed edition.

54. 巳 was 已.

55. 寶 was 瑤; corrected per *Jiu Tang shu,* 14.183.4741.

56. 寶 was 瑤.

57. *Hailing yishi,* 158.10; *Sengni niehai,* 226.5: 其肉具頗堅而粗.

58. 敷 was 傅.

59. *Hailing yishi,* 126.9: 一接至通宵不倦.

60. *Sengni niehai,* 263.4: 以淫藥敷其肉具、一接至通宵不倦。后絕愛之.

61. *Qing shi,* 510.27; *Yanyi bian,* 143.16: 托言懷義有巧思. *Zizhi tongjian,* 6441.11: 太后託言懷義有巧思.

62. *Jin shi,* 8.132.2826.6: 凡人富貴而驕、皆死徵也. *Laozi jiaogu,* 1.136: 富貴而驕、自遺其咎。功成名遂而身退、天之道也. *Sengni niehai,* 263.12: 懷義富貴而驕.

63. *Sengni niehai,* 264.1: 多蓄子女於白馬寺.

64. 南 was 懷; corrected per *Jiu Tang shu,* 14.183.4743, and *Xin Tang shu,* 11.76.3482.

65. 及 was 延.

66. 南 was 懷.

67. *Hailing yishi,* 55.12: 髓竭而死. Liu Zongyuan, "Hejian zhuan," 1343.12; *Sengni niehai,* 203.6: 病髓竭而死.

68. *Bieyou xiang,* 229.7: 淫情正熾. *Chundeng mishi,* 43.10, 60.4, 72.1, 99.1: 慾火頓發, 47.9: 淫心勃動, 49.8, 87.9: 慾火難消, 58.6: 慾火委實難禁了, 67.5: 慾火頓起, 79.3: 慾火難禁, 84.2: 淫心勃勃, 86.11: 淫心陡 [起], 89.2: 慾火更發, 106.5: 慾火尚盛, 108.9: 慾火仍然未消, 114.6: 慾火大洩, 140.1: 慾火燄燄. *Chundeng mishi,* 98.10, 141.4; *Yaohu yanshi,* 173.8, 181.10; *Yiqing zhen,* 232.11, 236.7, 271.2: 慾火燒身. *Chundeng mishi,* 114.6; *Dengcao heshang zhuan,* 121.11; *Huanxi yuan,* 349.2: 慾心如焚. *Chundeng nao,* 263.4: 春心如熾, 293.3: 慾心火熾, 315.9: 興如火熾, 423.1: 淫心驟熾. *Dengcao heshang zhuan,* 41.12, 71.10; *Wushan yanshi,* 55.8, 70.11; *Zhulin yeshi,* 244.2: 慾心如火. *Dengcao heshang zhuan,* 136.9: 心如火焚. *Huanxi yuan,* 336.6: 淫興難過, 338.10: 淫 [興] 大發. *Huanxi yuan,* 350.2; *Yiqing zhen,*

308.12: 淫興大發. *Huanxi yuan*, 362.10, 377.10: 慾火如焚, 365.5: 慾火難焚, 389.5: 慾火上升.*Jin Ping Mei*, 2.184.10: 淫思益熾. *Qinghai yuan*, 245.3: 春心更熾. *Sengni niehai*, 203.3: 淫心彌熾, 221.5: 見婦心正熾, 226.7: 淫興勃發, 245.5: 淫興益熾. *Taohua yanshi*, 250.7; *Yaohu yanshi*, 176.4: 慾火難支. *Taohua yanshi*, 257.9: 慾火昌熾, 266.12: 淫心頓熄. *Wushan yanshi*, 35.12: 淫興復熾. *Wushan yanshi*, 87.4: 慾心愈熾. *Xinghua tian*, 124.8: 淫火大熾, 141.2: 淫情炭熾, 169.5: 情如火熾. *Yugui hong*, 324.1: 惹火燒身, 388.8: 慾火正熾. *Yaohu yanshi*, 175.9: 慾火奮發. *Yi-pian qing*, 266.11: 淫興正熾. *Zaihua chuan*, 184.8: 淫心甚熾. *Zhulin yeshi*, 256.5: 慾心如熾.

69. 晢 was 哲.

70. *Jiu Tang shu*, 8.78.2706: 臣兄易之器用過臣、兼工合鍊. *Qing shi*, 512.15; *Yanyi bian*, 145.12: 且器用過臣.

71. *Sui Tang liangchao shizhuan*, 10.97.40b; *Yanyi bian*, 147.9; *Zizhi tongjian*, 6572.6: 六郎面似蓮花.

72. Yue Shi, *Guang Zhuoyi ji*, 1.235.21a.5-6; *Lidai shihua*, 60.11; *Quan Tang shi*, 1.58.15: 明朝遊上苑。火速 (*Guang Zhuoyi ji* was 急) 報春知。花須連夜發。莫待曉風吹.

73. Liu Su, *Da Tang xinyu*, 143.6; *Jiu Tang shu*, 9.2919.7; *Zizhi tongjian*, 6572.7: 蓮花似六郎.

74. 時 was 眨; corrected per 1995.

75. 遇 was 偶; corrected per *Jiu Tang shu*, 8.78.2706.

76. 郎 was 即.

77. 姓 was 性; 1995 corrected per *Jiu Tang shu*, 8.78.2706.

78. *Jiu Tang shu*, 8.78.2706; *Lidai shihua*, 69.2; *Qing shi*, 512.24; *Yanyi bian*, 145.21: 昔遇浮丘 (*Qing shi* was 邱) 伯。今同丁令威。中郎才貌是。藏史姓名非. *Quan Tang shi*, 68.767 (崔融、和梁王衆傳張光祿是王子晉後身): 聞有沖天客。披雲下帝畿。三年上賓去。千載忽來歸。昔偶(一作遇)浮丘伯。今同丁令威。中郎才貌是。柱 (一作藏) 史姓名非。祇召趨龍闕。承恩拜虎闈。丹成金鼎獻。酒至玉杯揮。天仗分旄節。朝容間羽衣。舊壇(一作宮)何處所。新廟坐光輝。漢主存仙要。淮南愛道機。朝朝緱氏鶴。長向洛城飛. See also Wang Dang, *Tang yulin*, 163.11.

79. 媾 was 搆.

80. 旦 was 且.

81. 太 was 大.

82. 載初 was 延載; corrected per 1995.

83. 1987 speculates that 結 might be a mistake for 黏.

84. 宦官 was 官宦; 1995 corrected per printed edition.

85. 宗 was 牛; corrected per *Jiu Tang shu*, 9.92.2971, *Xin Tang shu*, 11.76.3483, and *Xin Tang shu*, 13.109.4102; *Nongqing kuaishi*, 315.12, and *Wu Zhao zhuan*, 85.3, were 牛.

86. 卿 was 鄉.

87. 盧 was 盧.

88. 雖 was 雅.

89. 卿 was 鄉.

90. *Han shu*, 9.69.2990.12; *Shi ji*, 8.87.2552: 不敢避斧鉞之誅. Tuo Tuo, *Liao shi*, 5.80.1280.7: 不避斧鉞言之. *Wei shu*, 5.77.1710.8: 不避斧鉞之誅.

91. 卿 was 鄉.

92. 卿 was 鄉.

93. 1987 changed 笑 to 矣.

94. 且 was 旦.

95. 1987 was 俎.

96. *Jiu Tang shu*, 14.178.4633.9: 其眾一 離、則巢賊几上肉耳、此所謂不戰而屈人兵 也. Tuo Tuo, *Song shi*, 26.157.8967.5: 机上肉爾. *Yang Weizhen shiji*, p. 224 (机上肉): 机上肉復有腊 毒、洛州長史明目人、已 識宮中遺產祿。机上肉、復何爲? 肉生兩翅桑中飛。小窗呼來博雙陸、夢中只愁鸚鵡 知。點籌 郎、無主決、老翁彈指空流血、黥面牝雞弄喉舌。老翁在瀧八十餘、一死幸逃紅血髏。葛荣不得裂腹胃、竹槎 不得完肌膚。儋州公、心業業。楊衛尉、髠長鬣. *Xin Tang shu*, 14.120.4312.1: 會日暮事遽、彥範不欲廣殺、因曰: 三 思机上肉爾、留爲天子藉手, 17.185.5402.15: 眾一 離、即巢机上肉耳、法謂不戰而屈人兵也, 17.186.5430.11: 以我爲机上肉乎?

97. 卿 was 鄉.

98. *Jiu Tang shu*, 3.19b.715.4, 16.200b.5396.1; Chen Shou, *Sanguo zhi*, 5.58.1350.12: 雷霆之怒.

99. 卿 was 鄉.

100. 手 was 乎.

101. *Sengni niehai*, 198.3: 手不能握.

102. *Bieyou xiang*, 305.6: 只見此物如剝皮兔子一 般. *Yichun xiangzhi*, 326.8: 露出把屌。形如剝兔.

103. *Rou putuan*, 372.9: 頭 如蝸牛。身如剝兔。掛斗粟而不垂.

104. 已 was 巳.

105. 璧 was 壁.

106. 機 was 幾; corrected per *Wenxuan*, p. 1707.

107. 曠 was 曠; corrected per *Wenxuan*, p. 1707.

108. *Wenxuan*, p. 1707 (劉 琨、勸 進表): 尊 位不可久虛、萬 機不可久曠。虛之 一日、則尊位以 殆; 曠 之浹 辰、則萬 機以 亂.

109. 卿 was 鄉.

110. *Mengzi yinde*, 37.7.10 (孟子、萬章上): 吾未聞枉己而正人者也。況辱己 以 正天下者乎。聖人 之行不同也。或遠或近。或去或不去。歸潔其身而已矣.

111. 卿 was 鄉 .

112. 乃 was 及; corrected per 1995.

113. 會was 金; corrected per 1987; 1995 changed to 尋 per *Nongqing kuaishi*, 319.4.

114. 汙 was 汗.

115. 卿 was 鄉.

116. 階 was 陛.

117. 卿 was 鄉.

118. 于 was 干.

119. 卿 was 鄉.

120. 宮 was 官; corrected per 1995.

121. 卿 was 鄉.

122. 鉤 was 劍; 1995 corrected per *Nongqing kuaishi*, 320.1.

123. 烏 was 鳥.

124. 卿 was 鄉.

125. 葡 was 蒲.

126. 1987 changed 東暖閣 to 東閣暖; *Wu Zhao zhuan*, 85.6, was 迎暉閣.

127. 卿 was 鄉.

128. *Sengni niehai*, 221.2: 脫去中裙.

129. 良 was 坐; 1995 corrected per *Nongqing kuaishi*, 320.9.

130. *Jin Ping Mei*, 2.184.1: 纍垂偉長.

131. *Sengni niehai*, 221.1: 勿逗遛作忍人也.

132. 時 was 眨.

133. 許 was 詐.

134. *Sengni niehai*, 199.12: 顱肉墳起、豐膩無毳毛.

135. 崛 was 掘.

136. *Huanxi yuanjia*, 503.4: 非人間世之比. *Sengni niehai*, 221.2: 堅壯勁崛。婦捧定、曰: 眞非世間物也.

137. Liu Su, *Da Tang xinyu*, 110.5: 僕閱人多矣、未見此賢. Ling Mengchu, *Erke Paian jingqi*, 8.163: 吾在此閱人多矣、無出君右者. *Huanxi yuanjia*, 502.1: 我閱人多矣。並無一個如你這般興趣. *Jiu Tang shu*, 7.66.2459: 僕閱人多矣、未見如此郎者. 必成偉器,但恨不睹其聳壑凌霄耳. *Xinghua tian*, 195.4: 奴在風塵閱過多人。惟你體不勞而運動自然. *Yichun xiangzhi*, 171.6: 吾閱人多矣。未有如子後庭之異者. Wu Gongchen, *Yuanyang zhen*, 60.7: 吾閱人多矣.

138. 塵 was 麈.

139. Wu Zeng, *Nenggaizhai manlu*, 36.5: 塵尾: 釋藏音義指歸云: 『名苑曰: 「鹿之大者曰麈。群鹿隨之、皆看麈所往、隨麈尾所轉爲準。」』今講僧執麈尾拂子、蓋象彼有所指麾故耳。王衍捉玉柄麈尾. Yu Jiaxi, *Shishuo xinyu*, 14.468.5: 昔王夷甫有白玉麈柄. See also *Shih-shuo Hsin-yü*, 310.8.

140. 塵 was 麈.

141. Wang Renyu, *Kaiyuan Tianbao yishi*, 68.4: 遊仙枕: 龜茲國進奉枕一枚、其色如碼瑙、溫溫如玉、其製作甚樸素。若枕之、則十洲三島、四海五湖、盡在夢中所見。帝因立名爲遊仙枕、後賜與楊國忠.

142. 藉 added per *Sengni niehai*, 221.3, and 1995.

143. *Sengni niehai*, 221.3: 用偃月墩自藉其腰仰臥。封以手提其雙足.

144. *Bieyou xiang*, 309.4; *Sengni niehai*, 200.1: 勉強承受.

145. *Jin Ping Mei*, 4.706.9: 蹙眉齧齒忍其疼痛.

146. 稜 was 褄; corrected per *Hailing yishi*, 58.11; *Jin Ping Mei*, 3.242.5, 3.279.10; *Yipian qing*, 160.3: 僅没龜稜. *Jin Ping Mei*, 3.281.5, 3.301.10, 4.560.2, 4.748.8, 4.753.7: 没稜露腦. *Sengni niehai*, 200.1: 僅没龜頭.

147. *Jin Ping Mei*, 4.560.2, 4.753.7; *Taohua ying*, 210.10: 淫水浸出.

148. *Hailing yishi*, 54.9: 便覺滑落有趣, 68.2: 漸覺陰中滑落. *Jin Ping Mei*, 3.242.5: 滑落.

149. 逐 was 遂.

150. 塵 was 麈.

151. *Sengni niehai*, 226.11: 目慢挈 (掌) 熱.

152. *Jin Ping Mei*, 4.230.1, 4.480.10: 淫水溢下.

153. *Sengni niehai*, 245.6: 颯聲顫語.

154. *Jin Ping Mei*, 2.178.1: 四肢舋然於枕簟之上, 2.180.6: 四肢收舋於衽席之上.

155. 塵 was 麈.

156. *Bieyou xiang*, 45.12, 239.9; *Chundeng mishi*, 141.7; *Jin Ping Mei*, 3.242.6, 3.301.10, 4.560.2, 4.748.8; *Wushan yanshi*, 99.6; *Zhulin yeshi*, 271.3: 淺抽深送. *Chundeng mishi*, 79.4; *Huanxi yuan*, 335.4, 338.8, 345.8, 377.4, 408.3: 大抽大送. *Chundeng nao*, 326.1; *Huanxi yuanjia*, 487.1; Wu Gongchen, *Yuanyang zhen*, 207.9: 深抽淺送. *Dengcao heshang zhuan*, 133.11: 輕抽慢送. *Huanxi yuan*, 338.9, 384.7: 一抽一送. *Zhulin yeshi*, 182.4: 淺抽深入.

157. The phrase 何相見之晚也 is added by 1995 per *Wu Zhao zhuan* because Xue later responds 何歡晚也. Liu Su, *Da Tang xinyu*, 73.2: 何見之晚也.

158. Wu Zeng, *Nenggaizhai manlu*, 36.8: 如意: 齊高祖賜隱士明僧紹竹根如意、

梁武帝賜昭明太子木犀如意、石季倫、王敦皆執鐵 如意。三者以竹木鐵 爲
之、蓋爪杖也。故音義指歸云:『如意者、古之爪杖也。或骨角竹木削作人手
指爪、柄可長三尺許。或脊有痒、手所不到、用以 搔抓、如人 之意。』然釋流
以文殊亦執之、豈欲搔痒耶? 蓋講僧尚執之、私記節文祀辭于柄、以備忽
忘。手執目對、如人之意。凡 兩意耳.

159. *Sui Tang liangchao shizhuan*, 10.97.41b-42a: 是時太后 淫心愈 盛。乃遍選
天下男子之強 徒者。入宮侍寢。少不如意。即捶殺之。狄仁傑乃 薦薛敖曹。
太后□□□□□□ 極盡淫樂。雖白晝亦無間焉。敕封敖曹爲如意君。賜
齎甚厚。

160. 晚 was 脫; 1995 corrected per *Nongqing kuaishi*, 322.1.

161. *Jin Ping Mei*, 1.391.11: 擢髮不足以 數京等之罪. Xia Xie, *Ming tongjian*,
1622.3: 劉瑾 罪惡貫盈、擢髮難數. *Quan Tang wen*, 3.1228.2.18 (高宗武皇后、
暴來俊臣罪狀制): 擢其髮不足以 數罪. *Shi ji*, 7.79.2414.5: 擢賈之髮以續賈
之罪、尚未足. *Wutong ying*, 103.4: 姦淫惡跡。擢髮難數. *Yuanqu xuan*, 1217.9: 擢
賈之髮不足數賈之罪. See also *Baichuan xuehai*, p. 79.

162. *Wei shu*, 2.539.4: 雖死猶生.

163. 當 was 常; 1995 corrected per *Nongqing kuaishi*, 322.4.

164. 諧 was 誰; 1995 corrected per printed edition. It might also be 誆 which
could more easily be misread as 誰.

165. 塵 was 麈.

166. 停 was 倞.

167. 藉 was 籍.

168. 塵 was 麈.

169. 拭 was 試.

170. See note 68.

171. *Huanxi yuan*, 356.12: 任情抽送. *Sengni niehai*, 202.4: 縱身任獻抽送.

172. *Sengni niehai*, 221.6: 婦情益悅.

173. *Sengni niehai*, 200.3: 扳搖之急.

174. *Sengni niehai*, 203.7: 而牝中氣覺蒸蒸然熱. *Nongqing mishi*, 345.5; *Xinghua
tian*, 254.12: 牝中如火炭相蒸.

175. *Sengni niehai*, 200.2: 往來聲滋滋不絕.

176. *Sengni niehai*, 221.6: 又挺腰幹之.

177. *Bian er chai*, 81.11; *Bieyou xiang*, 77.2; *Chundeng mishi*, 68.11; *Dengcao heshang
zhuan*, 47.11, 124.3, 134.1; *Sengni niehai*, 221.5, 226.11; *Yiqing zhen*, 236.9, 302.5: 快
活殺我. *Chundeng mishi*, 60.5, 114.7: 快活我也, 108.2: 真個快殺人也. *Chundeng
nao*, 343.6; *Xinghua tian*, 143.1: 我快活死也. *Chundeng nao*, 393.10: 令人快活殺也,
423.7: 不要快活殺了. *Chipozi zhuan*, 121.9; *Huanxi yuanjia*, 195.2; *Yichun xiangzhi*,
176.6: 快活死我也. *Dengcao heshang zhuan*, 59.11: 我便要如(死)去了, 67.4: 我也
死了。我也死了, 119.11: 快活死了也, 126.1: 快活快活殺也. *Huanxi yuan*, 408.8:
快活死了. *Lang shi*, 70.7, 104.6: 快活死人也. *Wushan yanshi*, 73.2; *Zhulin yeshi*, 246.2:
快活煞我也. *Xinghua tian*, 112.4: 快活死我了. *Xiuta yeshi* (*bencang ben*), 449.8: 快
活得死去了. *Xiuta yeshi* (*bencang ben*), 449.10; *Xiuta yeshi* (*zuimiange ben*), 253.5: 真個
是快活殺了. *Xiuta yeshi* (*zuimiange ben*), 277.1: 快活快活酸殺人了, 278.12: 快活
殺了我的親親的爹. *Yichun xiangzhi*, 98.7: 快活要死, 105.1: 快活欲死, 235.5: 我
要快活殺了. *Yiqing zhen*, 232.6: 我快活殺了. *Yiqing zhen*, 258.2, 274.12: 快活殺了.
Zhaoyang qushi, 105.1: 快活死也。快活死也, 164.7: 今番一定要快活死我哩.

178. 體 was 倦; 1995 corrected per *Nongqing kuaishi*, 322.10.

179. *Sengni niehai*, 221.7: 兩體偎貼.

180. *Sengni niehai*, 221.6: 情不可極.

181. 已 was 巳.

182. 岡 was 岡; 1995 corrected per printed edition and *Nongqing kuaishi*, 323.2.

183. Liu Su, *Da Tang xinyu*, 92.8: 仲尼云：觀過、斯知仁矣。足下可謂海曲明珠、東南遺寶. *Jiu Tang shu*, 9.88.2885: 仲尼云：觀過知仁矣. *Lunyu yinde*, 6.7 (里仁): 子曰．人之過也。各於其黨。觀過斯知仁矣. *Xin Tang shu*, 14.115.4207: 仲尼稱觀過 知仁、君可謂滄海遺珠矣.

184. *Sengni niehai*, 200.2: 又 進二 寸許、后 不能拒.

185. *Chundeng nao*, 304.4; *Hailing yishi*, 54.12; *Zhulin yeshi*, 174.4: 往來抽送. *Huanxi yuan*, 400.7: 來住(往)抽送. *Jin Ping Mei*, 2.179.6; *Sengni niehai*, 200.5: 往來抽拽. *Jin Ping Mei*, 4.480.8: 往來抽捲.

186. *Jin Ping Mei*, 4.276.9: 至精欲洩之際.

187. 精 was 及往; 1995 corrected per *Nongqing kuaishi*, 323.4.

188. 塵 was 塵.

189. 蕊 was 蓋; corrected per *Jin Ping Mei*, 2.180.3.

190. 莖 was 垂; corrected per *Jin Ping Mei*, 2.180.3.

191. *Chipozi zhuan*, 111.3: 又 有肉舌含花、花蕊微動、男子垂(莖)首至其處、覺便 翁翁然暢美. *Dengcao heshang zhuan*, 53.11: 妙不可言, 107.12: 甘美真不可言. *Jin Ping Mei*, 2.180.3: 直抵牝屋之上。牝屋者乃 婦人 牝中深極處、有屋如含苞花蕊。到此處 無折男子莖首覺翁然、暢美不可言, 3.242.6: 覺翁翁然、暢美不可言, 3.281.10, 4.479.11: 心中翁翁然、美快不可言也, 4.753.6: 覺翁翁然、渾身酥然、暢美不可言. *Sengni niehai*, 212.1: 更翁翁然動。暢美不可言. *Taohua ying*, 105.9: 婦人牝內有一 小竅。譬如花之含蕊一 般。故交合之際。必須陽物直頂其竅。方爲暢美. *Xinghua tian*, 79.12: 美不可言.

192. 塵 was 塵.

193. *Jin Ping Mei*, 2.166.2, 3.302.8: 怡然感之.

194. *Bian er chai*, 81.11; *Bieyou xiang*, 54.6; *Chundeng nao*, 295.9, 360.2; *Huan fuqi*, 81.10; *Huanxi yuan*, 349.7, 368.10, 384.11, 392.11, 406.11; *Huanxi yuanjia*, 149.4; *Jin Ping Mei*, 2.166.3, 2.461.8, 3.252.10, 3.302.8, 4.276.11, 4.666.9, 4.684.4, 5.222.3; *Lang shi*, 87.9; *Naohua cong*, 115.1; *Qinghai yuan*, 270.3, 282.1, 297.6; *Taohua ying*, 101.6; *Wushan yanshi*, 39.3, 87.11; *Xinghua tian*, 48.3, 95.2; *Yichun xiangzhi*, 235.11, 312.6; *Yipian qing*, 100.5, 275.4; *Zhulin yeshi*, 201.4: 一 洩如注. *Dengcao heshang zhuan*, 137.9; *Lang shi*, 146.8; *Sengni niehai*, 200.5: 大洩如注. *Dengcao heshang zhuan*, 171.10: 陰水如注. *Xinghua tian*, 95.11: 又 洩如注. *Yichun xiangzhi*, 183.5: 一 洩如傾, 192.11: 其洩如注.

195. 已 was 巳.

196. 宗 was 牛.

197. 使 was 侍; corrected per Hucker, *Dictionary of Official Titles*, 351.4249.

198. 于 was 千.

199. 玉 was 王.

200. 特 was 持; corrected per 1987 and *Nongqing kuaishi*, 323.12.

201. 寶 was 吳; corrected per *Jiu Tang shu*, 7.51.2176, and *Xin Tang shu*, 11.76.3489.

202. 切 was 功; 1995 corrected per printed edition.

203. 摟 was 樓.

204. *Jin Ping Mei*, 1.423.2, 2.184.10: 以暢其美.

205. 倉卒 was 愴悴; corrected per next occurrence on p. 13a.

206. 曰 was 日; corrected per 1987.

207. *Hailing yishi*, 59.5: 緩緩抽送.

208. *Jin Ping Mei*, 2.176.4: 執塵柄、抵牝口. *Sengni niehai*, 226.8: 以疊褥藉主腰下、握具投入牝口, 314.5: 握其肉具。投入牝中.

209. *Yichun xiangzhi*, 327.6: 屌方濡首. *Zhouyi yinde*, 39.64 (未濟、上九): 有孚于飲酒。無咎。濡其首。有孚失是。象曰。飲酒濡首。亦不知節也。

210. *Sengni niehai*, 200.1: 以肉具投入牝口。研濡漸漬。僅没龜頭.

211. *Jin Ping Mei*, 2.176.1, 4.749.3: 淫津流出。如蝸之吐涎. *Sengni niehai*, 202.4: 后牝中津流。若蝸牛之吐涎.

212. *Jin Ping Mei*, 2.179.6: 觇其出入之勢, 2.226.6: 兩手兜其股、極力而提之、垂首觀其出入之勢, 2.461.2: 扶起股觀其出入之勢, 3.302.1: 扶其股觇其出入之勢.

213. 境 was 界; corrected per *Sengni niehai*, 221.5.

214. *Sengni niehai*, 221.5: 境界非凡。眞快活殺我也.

215. *Sengni niehai*, 200.3: 聲顫氣促.

216. *Jin Ping Mei*, 3.281.6: 往來甚急.

217. *Jin Ping Mei*, 4.753.10: 美不可言.

218. 問 was 間.

219. *Bieyou xiang*, 84.10: 亦俱有漸入佳境之妙. Fang Xuanling, *Jin shu*, 8.92.2405: 愷之每食甘蔗、恒自尾至本。人或怪之。云: 漸入佳境.

220. *Lang shi*, 239.3: 將麈柄戛然而進.

221. Concordance to the *Dadai liji*, 35.20–22 (曾子天圓): 聖人慎守日月之數、以察星辰之行、以序四時之順逆、謂之曆;截十二管、以宗八音之上下清濁、謂之律也。律居陰而治陽、曆居陽而治陰、律曆迭相治也、其間不容髮. *Hailing yishi*, 68.2: 直盡至根。不留毫髮. *Jin Ping Mei*, 4.479.10: 盡没至根、間不容髮. *Jiu Tang shu*, 1.3.63.8: 當神堯任讒之年、建成忌功之日、苟除畏逼、孰顧分崩、變故之興、間不容髮、方懼毀巢之禍、寧虞尺布之謠? *Lang shi*, 69.7: 直至深底。間不容髮, 164.7: 直幹到根頭。間不容髮. *Sengni niehai*, 200.3: 戛戛然直抵至根。間不容髮. *Wushan yanshi*, 99.10; *Zhulin yeshi*, 271.6: 間不容髮. *Xinghua tian*, 94.12: 全身皆入至根。不容絲髮. *Yipian qing*, 105.5: 不容毫髮. *Zaihua chuan*, 193.10: 私以手探龜之入。穴已開(間)不容髮矣. *Zizhi tongjian*, 6314.5: 安危之機、間不容髮.

222. 体 was 休; 1995 corrected per *Wu Zhao zhuan*, 87.8.

223. *Jin Ping Mei*, 2.180.10: 我如今頭目森森然、莫知所之矣, 4.754.9: 我如今頭目森森然、莫知所矣.

224. *Sengni niehai*, 200.4: 伸徹至腦、復送至根、直頂琴弦者百餘度.

225. *Jin Ping Mei*, 2.176.5: 陰中淫氣連綿, 2.460.6: 牝中之津如蝸之吐涎、綿綿不絕. *Sengni niehai*, 245.6: 淫水流綿不絕.

226. See note 177.

227. *Jin Ping Mei*, 2.460.6: 牝中之津.

228. *Sengni niehai*, 202.4: 滴滴而下.

229. 1995 changed 夫 to 牛 per printed edition.

230. *Chundeng nao*, 325.11: 恰象鰍行泥淖. *Lang shi*, 195.12: 陰精淫滑。風聲如行泥淖中. *Jin Ping Mei*, 2.176.5: 數鰍行泥淖中. *Yichun xiangzhi*, 182.9: 如狗餂殘盤。鰍行泥濘.

231. *Jin Ping Mei*, 2.180.9: 作嬌泣聲.

232. *Jin Ping Mei*, 2.183.11: 那話因驚.

233. 舍 同 捨.

234. *Sengni niehai*, 201.2: 方知裙帶之下自有至味.

235. 南 was 懷.

236. *Hailing yishi*, 59.5, 107.4, 125.8; *Sengni niehai*, 221.4, 272.5; *Wumeng yuan*, 201.10; *Wushan yanshi*, 72.6; *Yipian qing*, 105.5: 盡根没腦. *Yiqing zhen*, 274.1: 没稜没腦, 274.2: 盡根頂抽. *Zhulin yeshi*, 247.5: 没頭没腦.

237. *Lunyu yinde*, 16.11 (子罕): 顏淵 喟然 歎曰。仰之彌高。鑽之彌堅。瞻之 在前。忽焉在後。夫子循循然 善誘人。博我以 文。約我以 禮。欲罷不能。既竭 吾才。如有所立卓爾。雖欲從之。末由也已.

238. 軒前 was 前軒.

239. 鬟 was 髮; corrected per *Jin Ping Mei*, 2.171.5.

240. *Jin Ping Mei*, 2.171.5: 盛開、戲折一枝、簪於雲鬟之傍.

241. An extra 酥 was deleted.

242. *Jin Ping Mei*, 2.183.10: 酥胸半露.

243. *Jin Ping Mei*, 2.432.7, 4.650.6: 體態妖嬈.

244. *Jin Ping Mei*, 4.753.3: 躍然 而起.

245. 1987 changed 堪 to 甚.

246. 北 was 非.

247. 盼 was 盻; corrected per *Maoshi yinde*, 12.57.2 (衛風、碩人): 巧笑倩兮、美 目盼兮.

248. 宦 was 官; 1995 corrected per printed edition.

249. 1987 changed 洪 to 浩.

250. 巳 was 已.

251. 聖曆 was 元統; corrected per 1995. The Yuantong reign period, near the end of the Yuan 元 dynasty, lasted from 1333 to 1334.

252. See note 68.

253. *Sishu jizhu*, 3.4a (大學三): 詩云。緡蠻黃鳥。止于丘隅。子曰。於止。知 其所止。可以人而不如鳥乎? *Tang Xianzu ji*, 3.1842.4: 關了的睢鳩、尚然有洲 渚之興、可以人而不如鳥乎?

254. *Jin Ping Mei*, 2.6.6, 2.225.9, 4.19.4, 4.424.10, 4.666.2: 插入牝中. *Sengni nie-hai*, 202.5: 插肉具於牝内. *Xinghua tian*, 252.8: 雙足豎起。悅生擧莖插入牝中. *Zhulin yeshi*, 251.11: 將那物插入牝中.

255. 摸 was 模.

256. *Chundeng nao*, 247.11, 293.12; *Naohua cong*, 59.3: 汩汩有聲. *Chundeng nao*, 325.11: 汩汩亂響. *Wushan yanshi*, 59.7: 汩汩其來.

257. *Sengni niehai*, 228.10: 有難以言語形容者.

258. 水 added per 1995.

259. *Chundeng mishi*, 99.1: 比一朵才出 水芙蓉.

260. *Gu zunsu yulu*, 13.228.6: 君子不奪人所好. *Yuanqu xuan*, 1682.6: 君子不奪 人之好.

261. 宣 was 宜, corrected per 1987.

262. *Sengni niehai*, 201.4: 豈肯棄甘而 嚼蠟乎.

263. *Chundeng nao*, 315.8: 正所謂曾經滄海難爲水. *Mengzi yinde*, 52.24.1 (盡心 上): 孔子登東山而小魯。登泰山而小天下。故 觀於海者難爲水。遊於聖人 之門者難爲言。觀水有術。必觀其瀾。日月有明。容光必照焉。流水之爲物 也。不盈科不行。君子之志於道 也。不成章不達.

264. 巳 was 已.

265. 1987 adds the character 不 at this point.

266. 夕 was 久.

267. Cui Bao, *Gujin zhu*, 3.7a.8: 孫興公問曰。世 稱黃帝錬丹於鑿 硯山乃得 仙。乘龍上天。群臣援龍鬚。鬚墜 而生草曰龍鬚。有之乎。答曰。無也。有龍 鬚草。一名緡雲草。故世人爲之妄傳至如今。有虎鬚草。江東亦織以 爲席。 號曰西王母席。可復是 西王母乘虎而墮其鬚也.

268. 祖 was 袓.

269. *Jin Ping Mei*, 2.225.6: 睡思正濃.

270. 掩 was 捲; corrected per *Jin Ping Mei*, 2.225.8.

271. *Jin Ping Mei*, 2.225.8: 玉體互相掩映.

272. *Jin Ping Mei*, 2.225.7: 淫思頓起. *Yugui hong*, 373.10: 淫心頓起. See also note 68.

273. *Jin Ping Mei*, 2.225.9: 塵柄徐徐插入牝口. *Sengni niehai*, 202.5: 插肉具於牝内.

274. *Jin Ping Mei*, 2.180.8: 星眸驚閃甦省過來, 2.225.9: 星眸驚欠(閃)之際.

275. 已 was 巳.

276. 拽 was 椛; corrected per *Jin Ping Mei*, 2.225.9.

277. *Jin Ping Mei*, 2.225.9: 已抽拽數十度矣.

278. Legge, *Chinese Classics*, 1.395-396 (中庸、14): 在上位。不陵下。在下位。不援上。正己而不求於人。則無怨。上不怨天。下不尤人。故君子。居易以俟命。小人。行險以徼幸。子曰。射有似乎君子。失諸正鵠。反求諸其身.

279. 闈 was written with a rare orthographic variant; see Morohashi, *Dai Kan-Wa jiten*, 11.41369; 1995 changed this character to 闈 per *Wu Zhao zhuan*, 88.8.

280. See *Shi ji*, 1.7.312-315.

281. *Sengni niehai*, 202.4: 縱身任獻抽送.

282. 僮 was 倦.

283. *Quan Tang shi*, 7.4821.12 (白居易、琵琶行): 大絃嘈嘈如急雨、小絃切切如私語.

284. 厄 was 后; 1995 corrected per *Nongqing kuaishi*, 390.2.

285. 郎 was 即.

286. *Chunqiu jingzhuan yinde*, 67.3.10 (左傳、莊廿二): 鳳皇于飛。和鳴鏘鏘。有嬀之後。將育于姜。五世其昌。並于正卿。八世之後。莫之與京. *Maoshi yinde*, 65.252.7 (生民之什、卷阿): 鳳凰于飛。翽翽其羽.

287. 僮 was 倦.

288. 翔 was 翱; 1995 corrected per *Nongqing kuaishi*, 390.9.

289. 宮 was 閣; corrected per *Jiu Tang shu*, 1.3.45.

290. 1987 changed 淫 to 搖.

291. *Sengni niehai*, 245.1: 跨馬而坐.

292. *Sengni niehai*, 226.9: 以兩手據榻.

293. *Fengliu heshang*, 118.3: 淫水淋淋流出. *Naohua cong*, 155.11; *Taohua ying*, 36.2, 166.10: 騷水淋漓. *Qiaoyuan yanshi*, 47.5; *Sengni niehai*, 200.2; *Yipian qing*, 100.4, 266.11; *Zhaoyang qushi*, 106.8: 淫水淋漓.

294. *Jin Ping Mei*, 4.753.10: 凡五換巾帕.

295. 時 was 眨.

296. *Sengni niehai*, 226.3: 恐主力乏、又轉主在下、極力抽送數百回. *Zhulin yeshi*, 186.11: 極力抽送。方才至根.

297. 瞑 was written with an orthographic variant that I have not located in any dictionary.

298. See note 177.

299. 要 was 要.

300. See note 194.

301. *Jin Ping Mei*, 2.184.7: 放在粉臉上、偎晃良久、然後將口吮之. *Lang shi*, 71.3: 婦人把玉柄偎在臉上。吮咂一回。咬嚼一回。不肯放下.

302. 已 was 巳. *Sengni niehai*, 227.2: 呼二女子以口吮之。二女子口不能容。只得咬咂一回.

303. 已 was 巳.

304. *Bieyou xiang*, 46.3; *Rou putuan*, 305.8; *Zhulin yeshi*, 247.5: 盡力抽送. *Chundeng*

nao, 264.1: 盡根抽送。一連就有數百. *Huanxi yuan*, 363.4: 恣意 抽送, 408.11: 竭
力抽送. *Sengni niehai*, 202.4: 縱身獻抽送數百回. *Yiqing zhen*, 232.2, 236.5; *Zhulin
yeshi*, 246.11: 儘力抽送.

305. 健 was 健.

306. 欄 was 攔

307. *Sengni niehai*, 202.5: 使后抱其頸。置 兩手[於] 腰間、插肉具於牝內。
遶殿巡行.

308. *Wenxuan*, 3.1407–1408 (謝朓、直中書省): 紫殿肅陰陰、彤庭赫弘敞。風
動萬年枝、日華承露掌。玲瓏結綺錢、深沈映 朱綱。紅藥當階翻、蒼苔依砌
上。茲言翔鳳池、鳴珮多清 響。信 美非吾室、中園思偃仰。朋 情以鬱陶、春
物方駘蕩。安得凌風翰、聊恣山泉賞.

309. *Shangshu tongjian*, 1.01.0170 (堯典): 鳥獸孳尾.

310. 今 was 令.

311. Liu Su, *Da Tang xinyu*, 73.7; *Dong Jieyuan Xixiang ji*, 145.7; Chen Shou, *Sanguo
zhi*, 5.1366.7; Yuan Zhen, *Yingying zhuan* 133.5: 雖死之日猶生之年.

312. Xia Xie, *Ming tongjian*, 1689.7: 伏望諭令寧王改過自新、無預有司之事.
Shi ji, 2.427.13: 改過自新.

313. *Xin Tang shu*, 14.115.4212: 臣 觀天人未厭唐德.

314. 聖曆 was 元統; corrected per 1995.

315. *Quan Tang shi*, 7.4820.1 (白居 易、長恨歌): 在天願作 比翼鳥、在地願 爲
連理枝.

316. 啻 was 苦; corrected per 1995; 1987 changed 苦 to 若.

317. *Quan Tang shi*, 7.4822.12–13 (白居 易、簡簡吟): 大都好物不堅牢.

318. 磨 was 魔.

319. 旦 was 且.

320. 今 was 令.

321. 第 was 弟.

322. 問 was 間; 1995 corrected per printed edition.

323. 荅同 答.

324. 凡 was 丸; corrected per 1995.

325. In the printed edition the character 暹 was written with an orthographic variant that I have not located in any dictionary.

326. 汍 was 汛; corrected per 1995.

327. 健 was 健.

328. 勿 was 忽; 1995 corrected per *Nongqing kuaishi*, 393.10.

329. 朽 was 柄.

330. 塵 was 塵.

331. 限 was 恨.

332. *Sengni niehai*, 226.12: 又以風流解數。與主大弄一番.

333. 與 added per 1995 and the printed edition.

334. 采 was 彩.

335. *Yichun xiangzhi*, 327.6: 屌方濡首.

336. *Lunyu yinde*, 25.8 (子路): 子謂衛公子荊善居室。始有。曰。苟合矣。少有。
曰。苟完矣。富有。曰。苟美矣.

337. *Sengni niehai*, 213.8: 先與婦交媾。婦訝其小。覺訝其寬。兩下苟完。默
然不暢.

338. *Mei Yaochen ji*, 2.281 (梅堯臣、令 狐秘丞守彭州詩): 前時草草別、渺漫
二十年.

339. *Maoshi yinde,* 5.26.4-5 (邶風、柏舟): 靜言思之、不能奮飛. See also *Maoshi yinde,* 13.58.5.

340. 已 was 巳.

341. Lu Cai, *Mingzhu ji,* 27.84.9: 淚光淡淡.

342. 夕 was 日; 1995 corrected per *Nongqing kuaishi,* 405.3.

343. *Maoshi yinde,* 18.87.1 (鄭風、褰裳): 子不我思。豈無他人. See also *Maoshi yinde,* 24.119.1-2, 25.120.1-2.

344. 1995 changed 予 to 足 per *Nongqing kuaishi,* 405.6.

345. *Maoshi yinde,* 13.61.1 (衛風、河廣): 誰謂宋遠、跂予望之.

346. 朱 was 來; corrected per *Quan Tang shi,* 1.59.1.

347. 比 was 此; corrected per *Quan Tang shi,* 1.59.1.

348. Wu Zeng, *Nenggaizhai manlu,* 161.9; *Quan Tang shi,* 1.59.1 (武則天、如意娘詩); *Yuefu shiji,* 4.1138.5: 看朱成碧思紛紛。憔悴支離爲憶君。不信比來長下淚。開箱驗取石榴裙.

349. 不俟終日 was 本雙太日; corrected per *Zhouyi yinde,* 47.4 (繫下、4): 子曰: 知幾其神呼。君子上交不諂。下交不瀆。其知幾乎。幾者動之微。吉之先見者也。君子見幾而作。不俟終日.

350. 此 was 比; corrected per 1995.

351. 已 was 巳.

352. 捐 was 指; corrected per 1987.

353. 幄 was written with the "standing heart" radical.

354. 許 was 計; corrected per 1987.

355. The character 跋 was added per the 1995 edition.

356. 1995 發 was 散.

357. 1995 彩 was 敘.

358. The Tianyi reprint has the character 陽 at this point, but it does not exist in the facsimile of the original postscript reprinted at the beginning of the 1995 edition.

359. This colophon is missing from the Tianyi reprint; it has been supplied by the facsimile of the original reprinted at the beginning of the 1995 edition.

360. 未 was 末.

Glossary

aichen 愛臣
ancha qianshi 按察僉(簽)事
ancha si fushi 按察司副使
angcang aocao 昂藏敖曹
angzang 骯臟
Anhui 安徽
anurubbha 阿那律
ao 鏖
aoaozaozao 鏖鏖糟糟
Aocao 敖曹
aocao 鏖糟
aozao 摮糟，奧糟，鏖糟 (dirty)
aozao 鏖糟 (slaughter)

Baben saiyuan 拔本塞源
Bai Juyi 白居易 (772-846)
Baimasi 白馬寺
Ban Gu 班固 (32-92)
bao 寶
beiyuan sima 備員司馬
bensheng 本生
bi 璧
Bian Que 扁鵲
Bi Gan 比干
bingbu lang 兵部郎

cairen 才人
Cao Cao 曹操 (155-220)
Cao, prince of 曹王
Changan 長安
Changsheng dian 長生殿
Changsheng yuan 長生院
Changshou 長壽 (692-694) reign
     period
Chao, prince of 巢王
Chen Do 陳鐸 (early 16th cent.)
Cheng Hao 程顥 (1032-1085)
Chenghua 成化 (1465-1488) reign
     period
Cheng Mingdao 程明道 (1032-1085)
Cheng Yi 程頤 (1033-1107)
Cheng Yichuan 程伊川 (1033-1107)
Chen Ping 陳平 (d. 178 B.C.)
Chonger 重耳
chung 中
Chunmei 春梅
Chu Suiliang 褚遂良 (596-658)
Cui Rong 崔融 (652-705)

Daan gong 大安宮
Dadai liji 大戴禮記

daguan 大官
daguan shu 大官署
Dai Yuan 戴淵
Dali yi 大禮議
Daming Gate 大明門
dangdao 當道
dao 道
Daode jing 道德經
Daxue wen 大學問
Daye 大業 (605-617) reign period
Dayun jing 大雲經
Ding Lingwei 丁令威
dingmen shang yi zhen 頂門上 一 針
Di Renjie 狄仁傑 (607-700)
Dongan Gate 東安門
Dongyuan Gong 東園公
Dou, Wife 竇氏
Du Liniang 杜麗娘

Eastern Capital 東都

Fang nei 房內
Fang Xuanling 房玄齡 (578-648)
Fang zhong 房中
Fan Kuai 樊噲 (d. 189 B.C.)
feifu 肺腑
fengjian 諷諫
Feng Weimin 馮惟敏 (1511-1580)
Feng Xiaobao 馮小寶
fu 賦
fu chang fu sui 夫唱婦隨
fu du yushi 副都御史
Fuji 輔機
fumu guan 父母官
Fuqiu Bo 浮丘伯

Gao Ang 高昂 (c. 500?-538)
gaohuang 膏肓
gewu 格物
gexin 格心
gongguo ge 功過格
gouwan 苟完
Guangdong 廣東
Guangxi 廣西
Guan Yu 關羽 (d.219)
Gu Dongqiao 顧東橋 (1476-1545)
Gu Kaizhi 顧愷之 (c. 344-c. 406)
Gu Lin 顧璘 (1476-1545)
Guofeng 國風

gyu 牛 (ox)
gyu 妓夫 (pander)
Gyumon Inshi 牛門隱士

Han Cheng Di 漢成帝
Han 漢 dynasty (206 B.C.-A.D. 220)
Han Gaozu 漢高祖
Han Wo 韓偓
Han Wudi 漢武帝 (r. 141-87 B.C.)
hao 號
ho 和
hongmen 紅門
Hongmen 鴻門
hong shaoyao 紅芍藥
Hongwu 洪武 (1368-1399) reign period
hong yao 紅藥
Hongzhi 弘治 (1488-1506) reign period
Hōryaku 寶曆 (1751-1764) reign period
hsin 心
huan 逭
huang bokao 皇伯考
Huang Zhijun 黃之雋
huanjing bunao 還精補腦
Huaqing Palace 華清宮
Huayang grotto 華陽洞
Huayang Sanren 華陽散人
Huayang Shanren 華陽山人
Hui, Emperor 惠帝
huide zhangwen 穢德彰聞

Jiajing 嘉靖 (1522-1567) reign period
Jiangnan 江南
Jiangsu 江蘇
Jiangxi 江西
Jiangyou 江右
jianjian wangchen ji feigong 蹇蹇王臣既匪躬
jiantang 鑑塘
Jianzhang Palace 建章宮
Jiaxing district 嘉興縣
jiaxu 甲戌
jieshen 潔身
jieyu 婕妤
jijian 給諫
Jin 晉 dynasty (265-420)
Jin 金 dynasty (1115-1234)
Jingzhou 荊州

jinlun 金輪
jinshi 進士
Jin Xiangong 晉獻公
Jinyang 晉陽
Jin Zhuo 晉灼
jishizhong 給事中
jiudu 救度
juren 舉人
ju you 聚麀

Kaiyuan 開元 (713-741) reign period
kanoe tatsu 庚辰
Keqin 克勤 (1064-1136)
konghe 控鶴
konghejian nei gongfeng 控鶴監內供奉
kuonang 括囊

Lady Sun 孫夫人
Lai Junchen 來俊臣 (d. 697)
Langya 琅邪
Lao Ai 嫪毐 (d. 238 B.C.)
Laozi 老子
Li 李
Liangxiang 良鄉
liangzhi 良知
Li Chong 李沖
Li Chunfeng 李淳風 (602-670)
Li Dan 李旦
Li ji 禮記
Li Ji 驪姬
Li Kui 李逵
Li Longji 李隆基 (685-762)
Li Mao 李瑁
Li Ming 李明
Lingnan 嶺南
lingzhi 靈芝
Lin Han 林瀚 (1434-1519)
Li Shimin 李世民 (597-649)
Li Shishi 李師師
Liu Ao 劉驁 (51-7 B.C.)
Liu Bang 劉邦 (256-195 B.C.)
Liu Bei 劉備 (161-223)
Liu Che 劉徹 (157-87 B.C.)
Liuke 六科
Liu Kun 劉琨 (270-317)
liulang 六郎
Liu, Marquis of 留侯
Liu Mengmei 柳夢梅
Liu, Wife 劉氏

Liu Ying 劉盈 (207-189 B.C.)
Liu Zongzhou 劉宗周 (1578-1645)
Li Xian 李顯 (656-710)
Li Yuan 李淵 (565-635)
Li Yuanji 李元吉 (602-626)
Li Zhe 李哲
Li Zhen 李貞
Li Zhi 李治 (628-683)
Li Zhi 李贄 (1527-1602)
longtong fengjing 龍瞳鳳頸
lu 爐
Lü Buwei 呂不韋 (d. 235 B.C.)
Lü, Empress 呂后
Lu Ji 陸機 (261-303)
Lu Jiuyuan 陸九淵 (1139-1193)
Luli Xiansheng 甪里先生
Lunyu 論語
Luo Guanzhong 羅貫中
Lü Tiancheng 呂天成 (1580-1618)
Lu Xiangshan 陸象山 (1139-1193)

Mao 毛 commentary
Mawangdui 馬王堆
Mei Yaochen 梅堯臣 (1002-1062)
Mengzi 孟子
migao 彌高
Ming Ruizong 明睿宗
Ming Shizong 明世宗
Ming Taizu 明太祖
Mingtang 明堂
Ming Wuzong 明武宗
Ming Xianzong 明憲宗
Ming Xiaozong 明孝宗
Mount Li 驪山
Mount Mao 茅山
mu-chih-kang 目之綱
Mudan ting 牡丹亭

na yue zi you 納約自牖
neidan 內丹
Nihonbashi 日本橋

Ogawa Hikokurō 小川彥九郎

Pan Jinlian 潘金蓮
pinji sichen 牝雞司晨
Pujing 普靜

qi 氣

Qian 黔 province
Qianjin, Princess 千金公主
qibi 契苾
qibier 契苾兒
Qibier xing 契苾兒行
qihuo 奇貨
Qi Ji 戚姬
Qili Ji 綺里季
qin 琴
Qin 秦
qing 情
Qing 清 dynasty (1644-1911)
Qin Shihuangdi 秦始皇帝 (r. 221-210 B.C.)
qinshou xing 禽獸行
Qiuci 龜茲 (modern orthography)
Qiuci 丘茲 (Tang orthography)
Queen Mother of the Western Paradise 西王母
Quxu guo 渠胥國

renqing 人情
renyu 人欲
Ruosi 若思
rushou 濡首
ruyi 如意
Ruyi 如意 (692) reign period
Ruyijun 如意君
Ruyi zhuan 如意傳

Sangfu 喪服
sanren 散人
Seihikaku 清閟閣
Shang 商 dynasty (c. 1600 B.C.-1045 B.C.)
Shangguan Waner 上官婉儿 (664-710)
Shangqing 上清
Shangyang gong 上陽宮
shanren 山人
shanshu 善書
She 歙 district
shen 身
shenchou qiansong 深抽淺送
Shengli 聖曆 (698-700) reign period
Shen Nanqiu 沈南璆
Shensheng 申生
shi 使
Shi dong 十動

Shi Naian 施耐庵
Shou, prince of 壽王
shu 數
Shu jing 書經
siming 俟命
Song Jiang 宋江
Song Yu 宋玉 (3rd cent. B.C.)
Sonkeikaku Bunko 尊經閣文庫
Sui Yangdi 隋煬帝 (r. 604-618)
Sun Aocao 孫敖曹
Sunü jing 素女經
Sun Zi 孫子
Suo Yuanli 索元禮 (d. 691)
Suzhou 蘇州

Taian gong 太安宮
Taiping, Princess 太平公主
Taizhou 泰州
Tandu 潭渡
Tang 唐 dynasty (618-907)
Tang Gaozong 唐高宗
Tang Gaozu 唐高祖
Tang Ruizong 唐睿宗
Tang Taizong 唐太宗
Tang Xianzu 湯顯祖 (1550-1616)
tang xiongdi 堂兄弟
Tang Xuanzong 唐玄宗
Tang Yin 唐寅 (1470-1524)
Tang Zhongzong 唐中宗
Tan 潭 prefecture
Tianbao 天寶 (742-756) reign period
tianli 天理
Tianshou 天授 (690-692) reign period
Tiantang 天堂
Tianxia zhidao tan 天下至道談
tixing ancha qianshi 提刑按察僉事
tixing ancha shi si fushi 提刑按察使司副使
tongbu 筒布
tongzhong bu 筒中布
tsao-kang 灶綱

wangchen jianjian feigong zhi gu 王臣蹇蹇匪躬之故
Wang Gen 王艮 (1483?-1540)
Wang Huanghou 王皇后
Wang Shangning 汪尚寧 (*jinshi* 1529)
Wang Yan 王衍 (255-311)
Wang Zijin 王子晉

Wanxiang shengong 萬象神宮
wei-fa 未發
weifeng 威鳳
weiji 未濟
Wei, Wife 韋
Wei Wuzhi 魏無知 (fl. 200 B.C.)
Weiyang Palace 未央宮
Weiyang Sheng 未央生
Wen Boxiang 溫柏香
Wencheng 文成
Wenhua Hall 文華殿
Western Jin dynasty 西晉 (265-317)
Wu 武
Wu Chengsi 武承嗣 (d. 698)
Wu, Emperor 武帝
Wu Gongchen 吳拱宸 (c. 1610-c.
    1662; *juren* 1636)
Wu, Gracious Consort 武惠妃
Wu Meiniang 武媚娘
Wumen 吳門
Wu Qi 吳起
Wu Sansi 武三思 (d. 707)
Wu Shihuo 武士彠
Wu Song 武松
Wu Yueniang 吳月娘
Wu Zetian 武則天 (624-705)

xi 璽
Xiahuang Gong 夏黃公
Xiang Yu 項羽 (232-202 B.C.)
Xiao Liangdi 蕭良娣
Xiaozong 孝宗 (r. 1488-1506)
Xici zhuan 繫辭傳
Xie Tiao 謝朓 (464-494)
Xiliang 西涼
Ximen Qing 西門慶
xing 性
Xiqi 奚齊
Xiqin bawang 西秦霸王
Xu Changling 徐昌齡
Xue Aocao 薛敖曹
Xuegu 學古
Xue Huaiyi 薛懷義
Xue Ju 薛舉
Xue Rengao 薛仁杲
Xue Renyue 薛仁越

Yanagi Hyakusei 柳伯生
Yang 楊

Yang Fei 楊妃
Yang Guifei 楊貴妃 (719-756)
yang-kang 陽綱
Yang Shen 楊慎 (1488-1559)
Yang Tinghe 楊廷和 (1459-1529)
Yang Weizhen 楊維楨 (1296-1370)
Yang Zhirou 楊執柔
yanjia 晏駕
Yan Shigu 顏師谷
Yanzai 延載 (694) reign period
yanzuo 宴坐
Yao Shun yindao 堯舜陰道
yeshi 野史
Yifeng 儀鳳 (676-679) reign period
Yifu 夷甫
Yi jing 易經
Yi li 儀禮
ying 應
Yiwu 夷吾
Yonglong 永隆 (680-681) reign period
yu 欲
yü 欲
Yuantong 元統 (1333-1334) reign
    period
Yuanwu 圜悟

Zaichu 載初 (690) reign period
zangshi 藏史
Zetian 則天
Zhang Changling 張昌齡
Zhang Changzong 張昌宗 (d. 705)
Zhang Cong 張璁 (1475-1539)
Zhang Fujing 張孚敬
Zhang Jianzhi 張柬之 (625-706)
Zhang Liang 張良 (d. 189 B.C.)
Zhangsun Wuji 長孫無忌 (d. 659)
Zhang Yizhi 張易之 (d. 705)
Zhao 璺
zhaorong 昭容
Zhaowang Ruyi 趙王如意
Zhaozhou Congshen 趙州從諗 (778-
    897)
Zheng 政
Zhengde 正德 (1506-1522) reign
    period
zhen wo er 眞我兒
Zhezhong 浙中
zhi 志
zhi 質

zhi liangzhi 致良知
Zhinu 雉奴
Zhizu 知足
zhonggou zhi yan 中冓之言
zhonglang 中郎
Zhongyong 中庸
Zhongyong zhangju 中庸章句
Zhou 周 dynasty (690–705)
Zhou Jing 周憬
Zhou, King 紂王 (r. 1086–1045 B.C.)
Zhou Lingwang 周靈王
zhubing 塵柄
Zhu Houcong 朱厚熜 (1507–1567)

Zhu Houzhao 朱厚照 (1491–1521)
Zhu Jianshen 朱見深 (1447–1487)
zhushi 柱史
zhuxiashi 柱下史
Zhu Youtang 朱祐樘 (1470–1505)
Zhu Youyuan 朱祐杬 (1476–1519)
Zhu Yuanzhang 朱元璋 (1328–1398)
zi 字
Zichen Palace 紫宸殿
Zichu 子楚
ziwei 葦尾
Ziyang shuyuan 紫陽書院
Zong Jinqing 宗晉卿 (d. 710)

Bibliography

Primary sources

*Baichuan xuehai*百川學海 [A sea of knowledge formed by a hundred streams]. Compiled by Zuo Gui 左圭. Changping: Zhongguo shudian, 1990.

Ban Gu 班固. *Han shu* 漢書[History of the Former Han dynasty]. 12 vols. Beijing: Zhonghua shuju, 1975.

Bian er chai 弁而釵 [Wearing a cap but also hairpins], by Zui Xihu Xinyue Zhuren 醉西湖心月主人 (pseud.). In *Siwuxie huibao* 思無邪匯寶[No depraved thoughts collectanea], vol. 6. Compiled by Chen Qinghao 陳慶浩 and Wang Qiugui 王秋桂. Taipei: Encyclopedia Britannica, 1995.

Bieyou xiang 別有香 [There is a special fragrance]. Compiled by Taoyuan Zuihua Zhuren 桃源醉花主人 (pseud.). In *Siwuxie huibao* 思無邪匯寶, vol. 8. Compiled by Chen Qinghao 陳慶浩 and Wang Qiugui 王秋桂. Taipei: Encyclopedia Britannica, 1995.

Biji xiaoshuo daguan 筆記小說大觀 [Great collectanea of note-form literature]. 17 vols. Yangzhou: Jiangsu Guangling guji kanxingshe, 1984.

Chen Shou 陳壽. *Sanguo zhi* 三國志 [History of the Three Kingdoms]. 5 vols. Beijing: Zhonghua shuju, 1973.

Cheng Yi 程頤. *Yi zhuan* 易傳 [Commentary on the Book of Changes]. Taipei: Xuesheng shuju, 1983.

Chipozi zhuan 癡婆子傳 [Story of a foolish woman]. Compiled by Furong Zhuren 芙蓉主人 (pseud.). In *Siwuxie huibao* 思無邪匯寶, vol. 24. Compiled by Chen Qinghao 陳慶浩 and Wang Qiugui 王秋桂. Taipei: Encyclopedia Britannica, 1995.

Chundeng mishi 春燈迷史 [Bewitching history of spring lanterns]. Compiled by

Qingyang Yeren 青陽野人 (pseud.). In *Siwuxie huibao* 思無邪匯寶, vol. 23. Compiled by Chen Qinghao 陳慶浩 and Wang Qiugui 王秋桂. Taipei: Encyclopedia Britannica, 1995.

Chundeng nao 春燈鬧 [Merriment amidst spring lanterns]. Compiled by Zuili Yanshui Sanren 檇李煙水散人 (pseud.). In *Siwuxie huibao* 思無邪匯寶, vol. 18. Compiled by Chen Qinghao 陳慶浩 and Wang Qiugui 王秋桂 Taipei: Encyclopedia Britannica, 1995.

Chunqiu Gongyang zhuan 春秋公羊傳 [Gongyang commentary to the Spring and Autumn Annals]. In *Shisan jing* 十三經 [Thirteen classics], vol. 2. Compiled by Wu Zhemei 吳哲楣. Beijing: Guoji wenhua chuban gongsi, 1995.

Chunqiu jingzhuan yinde 春秋經傳引得 [Concordance to the Spring and Autumn Annals and its commentaries]. Taipei: Chinese Materials and Research Aids Service Center, 1966.

A Concordance to the Dadai liji, ed. D. C. Lau and Chen Fong Ching. Hong Kong: Commercial Press, 1992.

Cui Bao 崔豹 *Gujin zhu* 古今注 [Notes on the old and new]. In *Gushi wenfang xiaoshuo* 顧氏文房小說 [Fiction from the library of Mr. Gu]. Compiled by Gu Yuanqing 顧元慶. 10 *juan*. Fac. repr., Shanghai: Shangwu yinshuguan, 1934.

Da Tang Qinwang cihua 大唐秦王詞話 [Prosimetric story of the prince of Qin of the great Tang]. 2 vols. Fac. repr. of early 17th-century ed., Beijing: Wenxue guji kanxingshe, 1956.

Dengcao heshang zhuan 燈草和尚傳 [Story of Monk Candlerush]. Compiled by Yunyou Daoren 雲遊道人 (pseud.). In *Siwuxie huibao* 思無邪匯寶, vol. 22. Compiled by Chen Qinghao 陳慶浩 and Wang Qiugui 王秋桂. Taipei: Encyclopedia Britannica, 1995.

Dong Jieyuan Xixiang ji 董解元西廂記 [Master Dong's Western chamber romance]. Edited and annotated by Ling Jingyan 凌景埏. Beijing: Renmin wenxue chubanshe, 1962.

Fan Ye 范曄. *Hou Han shu* 後漢書 [History of the Latter Han dynasty]. 12 vols. Beijing: Zhonghua shuju, 1973.

Fang Xuanling 房玄齡. *Jin shu* 晉書 [History of the Jin dynasty]. 10 vols. Beijing: Zhonghua shuju, 1974.

Feng Menglong 馮夢龍. *Jingshi tongyan* 警世通言 [Comprehensive words to admonish the world]. Taipei: Shijie shuju, 1958.

———. *Xingshi hengyan* 醒世恒言 [Lasting words to awaken the world]. Taipei: Shijie shuju, 1958.

———. *Yushi mingyan* 喻世明言 [Illustrious words to instruct the world]. Taipei: Shijie shuju, 1958.

Feng Weimin 馮惟敏. *Haifu shantang cigao* 海浮山堂詞稿 [Draft lyrics from Haifu Shantang]. Preface dated 1566. Shanghai: Shanghai guji chubanshe, 1981.

Fengliu heshang 風流和尚 [The romantic monk]. In *Siwuxie huibao* 思無邪匯寶, vol. 13. Compiled by Chen Qinghao 陳慶浩 and Wang Qiugui 王秋桂. Taipei: Encyclopedia Britannica, 1995.

Gao Ru 高儒. *Baichuan shuzhi* 百川書志 [Catalog of the hundred streams]. Preface dated 1540. Shanghai: Gudian wenxue chubanshe, 1957.

Gu Yingtai 谷應泰. *Mingshi jishi benmo* 明史紀事本末 [A history of the Ming dynasty arranged according to events]. 4 vols. Beijing: Zhonghua shuju, 1977.

———. "Dali yi" 大禮議 [The Great Ritual Debate]. In *Mingshi jishi benmo*, vol. 2, pp. 733-764.

————. "Shizong chong Daojiao" 世宗崇道教 [Emperor Shizong worships Daoism]. In *Mingshi jishi benmo,* vol. 2, pp. 783-799.

Gu zunsu yulu 古尊宿語錄 [Recorded sayings of eminent monks of old]. Compiled by Ze Zangzhu 賾藏主 [13th century]. 2 vols. Beijing: Zhonghua shuju, 1994.

Guanzi jiaozheng 管子校正 [Works of Guanzi edited and corrected]. Edited and annotated by Dai Wang 戴望 (1837-1873). In *Zhuzi jicheng* 諸子集成 [Corpus of the philosophers], vol. 5. Hong Kong: Zhonghua shuju, 1978.

Gudai wenyen duanpian xiaoshuo xuanzhu chuji 古代文言短篇小說選註、初集 [Annotated selection of classic literary tales, first collection]. Compiled by Cheng Boquan 成柏泉. Shanghai: Shanghai guji chubanshe, 1983.

Gujin xiaoshuo 古今小說 [Stories old and new]. 2 vols. Compiled by Feng Menglong 馮夢龍. Fac. repr., Shanghai: Shanghai guji chubanshe, 1993 .

Guo Yong 郭雍. *Shanghan buwang lun* 傷寒補亡論 [Treatise on cold lesions, with lacunae supplemented]. Beijing: Renmin weisheng chubanshe, 1994.

Gushi wenfang xiaoshuo 顧氏文房小說 [Fiction from the library of Mr. Gu]. 10 *juan.* Compiled by Gu Yuanqing 顧元慶. Fac. repr., Shanghai: Shangwu yinshuguan, 1934.

Hailing yishi 海陵佚史 [Unofficial history of Hailing]. Compiled by Wuzhe Daoren 無遮道人 (pseud.). In *Siwuxie huibao* 思無邪匯寶, vol. 1. Compiled by Chen Qinghao 陳慶浩 and Wang Qiugui 王秋桂. Taipei: Encyclopedia Britannica, 1995.

Han Feizi 韓非子. *Han Feizi jijie* 韓非子集解 [Works of Han Feizi with collected annotations]. Compiled by Wang Xianshen 王先慎. Taipei: Yiwen yinshuguan, 1974.

Han Wo 韓偓. *Milou ji* 迷樓記 [Tale of the tower of enchantment]. In *Tang Song chuanqi ji* 唐宋傳奇集 [Anthology of literary tales from the Tang and Song dynasties], *juan* 6. Edited by Lu Xun 魯迅. Beijing: Wenxue guji kanxingshe, 1958.

Han Wudi neizhuan 漢武帝內傳 [Intimate biography of Emperor Wu of the Han]. In *Gudai wenyen duanpian xiaoshuo xuanzhu, chuji* 古代文言短篇小說選注、初集 [Annotated selection of classic literary tales, first collection]. Compiled by Cheng Boquan 成柏泉. Shanghai: Shanghai guji chubanshe, 1983.

Huan fuqi 換夫妻 [Swapping husbands and wives]. Compiled by Yunyou Daoren 雲遊道人 (pseud.). In *Siwuxie huibao* 思無邪匯寶, vol. 13. Compiled by Chen Qinghao 陳慶浩 and Wang Qiugui 王秋桂. Taipei: Encyclopedia Britannica, 1995.

Huang Xun 黃訓. *Dushu yide* 讀書一得 [Trifles gleaned from reading books]. Xindu: preface dated 1562. Microfilm, University of Chicago Library, no. CBM 455.

————. *Huang Tan Xiansheng wenji* 黃潭先生文集 [Collected works of Mr. Huang Tan (Huang Xun)]. Xinan: preface dated 1559. Microfilm, University of Chicago Library, no. CBM 2100.

————, comp. *Huang Ming mingchen jingji lu* 皇明名臣經濟錄 [Record of the governance and assistance of famous ministers of the imperial Ming]. 53 *juan.* In *Wenyuange Siku quanshu* 文淵閣四庫全書, vols. 443-444. Taipei: Shangwu yinshuguan, n.d.

Huang Zhijun 黃之雋. "Zhanyan" 詹言 [Trifling words]. In *Zhaodai congshu, yiji* 昭代叢書、已集 [Collectanea of our dynasty, second series], *juan* 19. Fac. repr., n.d., pp. 1a-44a.

Huang Zongxi 黃宗羲. *Mingru xuean* 明儒學案 [Documentary history of Ming Confucianism]. Beijing: Zhonghua shuju, 1985.

Huanxi yuan 歡喜緣 [Fated pleasure]. In *Siwuxie huibao* 思無邪匯寶, vol. 23. Compiled by Chen Qinghao 陳慶浩 and Wang Qiugui 王秋桂. Taipei: Encyclopedia Britannica, 1995.

Huanxi yuanjia 歡喜冤家 [Adversaries in delight]. By Xihu Yuyin Zhuren 西湖漁隱主人 (pseud.). In *Siwuxie huibao* 思無邪匯寶, vols. 10 and 11. Compiled by Chen Qinghao 陳慶浩 and Wang Qiugui 王秋桂. Taipei: Encyclopedia Britannica, 1995.

Huizhou fu zhi 徽州府志 [Records of Huizhou prefecture]. Compiled by Wang Shangning 汪尚寧 et al. In *Mingdai fangzhi xuan* 明代方志選 [Selection of Ming-dynasty local gazetteers], vol. 2. Compiled by Wu Xiangxiang 吳相湘. Fac. repr., preface dated 1566; Taipei: Xuesheng shuju, 1965.

Ishimpō 醫心方 [Essence of medical prescriptions]. Compiled by Tamba Yasuyori 丹波康賴. Fac. repr. of 1854 ed.; Beijing: Renmin weisheng chubanshe, 1993.

Jiaxing fu tuji 嘉興府圖記 [Illustrated record of Jiaxing prefecture]. Compiled by Zhao Wenhua 趙文華 and Chao Ying 趙瀛. Microfilm of 1547-1549 ed., University of Chicago Library, no. CBM 419-20.

Jiaxing fu zhi 嘉興府志 [Records of Jiaxing prefecture]. Compiled by Liu Yingke 劉應珂 and Shen Yaozhong 沈堯中. Microfilm of 1610 ed., University of Chicago Library, no. CBM 410-11.

Jinsi lu 近思錄 [Reflections on things at hand]. Compiled by Zhu Xi 朱熹 and Lü Zuqian 呂祖謙. In *Zhuzi yishu* 朱子遺書 [Surviving works of Master Zhu]. Fac. repr. of Baogaotang edition, n.d.

Joyce, James. *Ulysses*. New York: Vintage Books, 1961.

Keqin 克勤 (*hao* Yuanwu 圓悟, 1064-1136), comp. *Biyan lu* 碧巖錄 [Blue cliff records]. 10 *juan*. In *Taishō shinshū daizōkyō* 大正新修大藏經 [Newly edited great Buddhist canon compiled in the Taishō reign period (1912-1926)], 85 vols. Tokyo: Taishō issaikyō kankōkai, 1922-1932, no. 2003, vol. 48, pp. 139a-292a.

Lang shi 浪史 [History of a debauchee]. By Fengyuexuan Youxuanzi 風月軒又玄子 (pseud.). In *Siwuxie huibao* 思無邪匯寶, vol. 4. Compiled by Chen Qinghao 陳慶浩 and Wang Qiugui 王秋桂. Taipei: Encyclopedia Britannica, 1995.

Laozi jiaogu 老子校詁 [Works of Laozi collated and with a commentary]. Compiled by Ma Xulun 馬敘倫. 3 vols. Beijing: Zhonghua shuju, 1974.

Li Baiyao 李百藥. *Beiqi shu* 北齊書 [History of the Northern Qi dynasty]. 2 vols. Beijing: Zhonghua shuju, 1973.

Lidai shihua 歷代詩話 [Talks on poetry chronologically arranged]. Compiled by He Wenhuan 何文煥. 2 vols. Beijing: Zhonghua shuju, 1981.

Lidai shihua xubian 歷代詩話續編 [Continuation of Talks on Poetry Chronologically Arranged]. 3 vols. Compiled by Ding Fubao 丁福保. Beijing: Zhonghua shuju, 1983.

Le Lie-sien Tchouan 列仙傳. [Biographies of the immortals]. Translated by Max Kaltenmark. Beijing: Université de Paris, Publications du Centre d'études sinologiques de Pékin, 1953.

[*Huitu*] *Liexian quanzhuan* [繪圖] 列仙全傳 [(Illustrated) complete biographies of the immortals]. Compiled by Wang Shizhen 王世貞. Taipei: Tailian guofeng chubanshe, 1974.

Li ji yinde 禮記引得 [Concordance to the Book of Rites]. Taipei: Chinese Materials and Research Aids Service Center, 1966.

Li Yanshou 李延壽. *Bei shi* 北史 [History of the northern dynasties]. 10 vols. Beijing: Zhonghua shuju, 1974.

———. *Nan shi* 南史 [History of the southern dynasties]. 6 vols. Beijing: Zhonghua shuju, 1975.

Linghu Defen 令狐德棻. *Zhou shu* 周書 [History of the Zhou dynasty]. 3 vols. Beijing: Zhonghua shuju, 1971.

Ling Mengchu 凌濛初. *Chuke Paian jingqi* 初刻拍案驚奇 [First collection of striking the table in amazement at the wonder]. Edited by Wang Gulu 王古魯. Shanghai: Gudian wenxue chubanshe, 1957.

———. *Erke Paian jingqi* 二刻拍案驚奇 [Second collection of striking the table in amazement at the wonder]. Edited by Wang Gulu 王古魯. Shanghai: Gudian wenxue chubanshe, 1957.

Ling Xuan 伶玄. *Zhao Feiyan waizhuan* 趙飛燕外傳 [Outer story of Empress Zhao Feiyan]. In *Gushi wenfang xiaoshuo* 顧氏文房小說, *juan* 6. Compiled by Gu Yuanqing 顧元慶. Fac. repr., Shanghai: Shangwu yinshuguan, 1934.

———. *Zhao Feiyan waizhuan* 趙飛燕外傳 [Outer story of Empress Zhao Feiyan]. In *Siwuxie huibao waibian* 思無邪匯寶外傳 [Supplement to the No Depraved Thoughts collectanea], vol. 1. *Dongfang yanqing xiaoshuo zhenben* 東方豔情小說珍本 [Rare editions of oriental erotic novels]. Compiled by Chen Qinghao 陳慶浩 and Wang Qiugui 王秋桂. Taipei: Encyclopedia Britannica, 1997.

Liu Kun 劉琨. "Quanjin biao" 勸進表 [A memorial recommending assumption of the throne]. In *Wenxuan* 文選. Compiled by Xiao Tong 蕭統. Shanghai: Shanghai guji chubanshe, 1992.

Liu Su 劉肅. *Da Tang xinyu* 大唐新語 [New anecdotes from the great Tang dynasty]. Edited by Xu Denan 許德楠 and Li Dingxia 李鼎霞. Beijing: Zhonghua shuju, 1984.

Liu Xu 劉昫. *Jiu Tang shu* 舊唐書 [Old history of the Tang dynasty]. 16 vols. Beijing: Zhonghua shuju, 1975.

Liu Zongyuan 柳宗元. "Hejian zhuan" 河間傳 [Story of (the woman from) Hejian]. In *Liu Zongyuan ji* 柳宗元集 [Collected works of Liu Zongyuan]. Edited by Wu Wenzhi. Beijing: Zhonghua shuju, 1979.

Long Wenbin 龍文彬. *Ming huiyao* 明會要 [Regulations of the Ming dynasty]. Taipei: Shijie shuju, 1960.

Lu Cai 陸采. *Mingzhu ji* 明珠記 [The luminous pearl]. Taipei: Kaiming shudian, 1970.

Lunyu yinde 論語引得 [Concordance to the Analects of Confucius]. Taipei: Chinese Materials and Research Aids Service Center, 1966.

Maoshi yinde 毛詩引得 [Concordance to the Mao version of the Book of Songs]. Tokyo: Japan Council for East Asian Studies, 1962.

Maoshi zhengyi 毛詩正義 [Correct annotations to the Mao version of the Book of Songs]. Edited by Kong Yingda 孔穎達. In *Shisanjing zhushu* 十三經注疏 [Thirteen classics with notes and commentaries]. Fac. repr., Taipei, 1963.

Mawangdui Hanmu boshu 馬王堆漢墓帛書 [The silk books from the Han tomb at Mawangdui]. Vol. 4. Beijing: Wenwu Press, 1985.

Mei Yaochen ji biannian jiaozhu 梅堯臣集編年校注 [Corrected and annotated collected works and chronological record of Mei Yaochen]. Edited by Zhu Dongrun 朱東潤. Shanghai: Guji chubanshe, 1980.

Meng Qi 孟棨. *Benshi shi* 本事詩 [Original incidents of poems]. Shanghai: Zhonghua shuju, 1959.

Mengzi yinde 孟子引得 [Concordance to the works of Mencius]. Taipei: Chinese Materials and Research Aids Service Center, 1966.

Nabokov, Vladimir. *The Annotated Lolita: Revised and Updated*. Edited by Alfred Appel, Jr. New York: Vintage Books, 1991.

Naohua cong 鬧花叢 [Merriment amidst the flowers]. By Gusu Chiqing Shi 姑蘇痴情士 (pseud.). In *Siwuxie huibao* 思無邪匯寶, vol. 19. Compiled by Chen Qinghao 陳慶浩 and Wang Qiugui 王秋桂. Taipei: Encyclopedia Britannica, 1995.

Nongqing kuaishi 濃情快史 [Heartthrobbing history of powerful passions]. Compiled by Jiahe Canhua Zhuren 嘉禾餐花主人 (pseud.). In *Siwuxie huibao* 思無邪匯寶, vol. 21. Compiled by Chen Qinghao 陳慶浩 and Wang Qiugui 王秋桂. Taipei: Encyclopedia Britannica, 1995.

Nongqing mishi 濃情秘史 [Secret history of powerful passions]. In *Siwuxie huibao* 思無邪匯寶, vol. 17. Compiled by Chen Qinghao 陳慶浩 and Wang Qiugui 王秋桂. Taipei: Encyclopedia Britannica, 1995.

Ouyang Xiu 歐陽修 and Song Qi 宋祁. *Xin Tang shu* 新唐書 [New history of the Tang dynasty]. 20 vols. Beijing: Zhonghua shuju, 1975.

Qiaoyuan yanshi 巧緣豔史 [Captivating history of fortuitous fate]. Compiled by Jianghai Zhuren 江海主人 (pseud.). In *Siwuxie huibao* 思無邪匯寶, vol. 12. Compiled by Chen Qinghao 陳慶浩 and Wang Qiugui 王秋桂. Taipei: Encyclopedia Britannica, 1995.

Qin Chun 秦醇. *Zhao Feiyan biezhuan* 趙飛燕別傳 [Alternate biography of Empress Zhao Feiyan]. In *Qingsuo gaoyi* 青瑣高議 [Remarkable opinions under the green latticed window]. Compilation attributed to Liu Fu 劉斧. Beijing: Zhonghua shuju, 1959.

———. *Zhao Feiyan biezhuan* 趙飛燕別傳 [Alternate biography of Empress Zhao Feiyan]. In *Siwuxie huibao waibian* 思無邪匯寶外編, vol. 1. *Dongfang yanqing xiaoshuo zhenben* 東方豔情小說珍本. Compiled by Chen Qinghao 陳慶浩 and Wang Qiugui 王秋桂. Taipei: Encyclopedia Britannica, 1997.

Qinghai yuan 情海緣 [Fate in a sea of passion]. By Deng Xiaoqiu 鄧小秋. In *Siwuxie huibao* 思無邪匯寶, vol. 19. Compiled by Chen Qinghao 陳慶浩 and Wang Qiugui 王秋桂. Taipei: Encyclopedia Britannica, 1995.

Qing shi 情史 [History of love]. Compiled by Zhanzhan Waishi 詹詹外史. Liaoning: Chunfeng wenyi chubanshe, 1986.

Qingsuo gaoyi 青瑣高議 [Remarkable opinions under the green latticed window]. Compilation attributed to Liu Fu 劉斧. Beijing: Zhonghua shuju, 1959.

Quan Han fu 全漢賦 [Complete *fu* poetry of the Han dynasty]. Compiled and edited by Fei Zhengang 費振剛, Hu Shuangbao 胡雙寶, and Zong Minghua 宗明華. Beijing: Beijing Daxue chubanshe, 1993.

Quan Ming sanqu 全明散曲 [Complete nondramatic song lyrics of the Ming]. Compiled by Xie Boyang 謝伯陽. 5 vols. Jinan: Qi-Lu shushe, 1994.

Quan Tang shi 全唐詩 [Complete poetry of the Tang dynasty]. 12 vols. Beijing: Zhonghua shuju, 1960.

Quan Tang wen 全唐文 [Complete prose of the Tang dynasty]. 20 vols. Kyoto: Chūbun shuppan-sha, 1976.

Rabelais, François. *Gargantua et Pantagruel*. Edited by Jacques Boulenger. Paris: Gallimard, "Pléiade," 1978.

Rou putuan 肉蒲團 [The carnal prayer mat]. [By Li Yu 李漁.] Edited by Chūsuirō shujin 傭翠樓主人. Japan: Seishinkaku, 1705.

Rou putuan 肉蒲團 [The carnal prayer mat]. [By Li Yu 李漁.] Compiled by Qingyin Xiansheng 情隱先生. In *Siwuxie huibao* 思無邪匯寶, vol. 15. Compiled by Chen

Qinghao 陳慶浩 and Wang Qiugui 王秋桂. Taipei: Encyclopedia Britannica, 1995.

Sade, Donatien-Alphonse-François Marquis de. *Oeuvres*. Vol. 1, *Les Cent Vingt Journées de Sodome ou L'École du Libertinage*. Edited by Michel Delon. Paris: Gallimard, 1992.

————. *Oeuvres*. Vol. 2, *Justine ou Les Malheurs de la Vertu*. Edited by Michel Delon. Paris: Gallimard, 1995.

————. *Oeuvres*. Vol. 3, *La Philosophie dans le Boudoir*. Edited by Michel Delon. Paris: Gallimard, 1995.

Sanguo zhi tongsu yanyi 三國志通俗演義 [Romance of the Three Kingdoms]. Attributed to Luo Guanzhong 羅貫中 or Shi Naian 施耐庵. Beijing: Renmin wenxue chubanshe, 1975.

Sengni niehai 僧尼孽海 [Monks and nuns in a sea of iniquity]. Compilation attributed to Tang Yin 唐寅. In *Siwuxie huibao* 思無邪匯寶, vol. 24. Compiled by Chen Qinghao 陳慶浩 and Wang Qiugui 王秋桂. Taipei: Encyclopedia Britannica, 1995.

Shangshu tongjian 尚書通檢 [Concordance to the Book of Historical Documents]. Compiled by Gu Jiegang 顧頡剛. Beijing: Guji xuandu congshu, 1982.

Shen Defu 沈德符. *Wanli yehuo bian* 萬曆野獲編 [Private gleanings of the Wanli reign period (1573–1620)]. Taipei: Xinxing shuju, 1976.

Shexian zhi 歙縣志 [Records of She district]. Compiled by Zhang Tao 張濤. Fac. repr. of 1609 edition, n.d.

Shih-shuo Hsin-yü: A New Account of Tales of the World. Translated by Richard B. Mather. Minneapolis: University of Minnesota Press, 1976.

Shisan jing 十三經 [Thirteen classics]. 2 vols. Compiled by Wu Zhemei 吳哲楣. Beijing: Guoji wenhua chuban gongsi, 1995.

Shisanjing zhushu 十三經注疏 [Thirteen classics with notes and commentaries]. Fac. repr., Taipei, 1963.

Shuangmei jingan congshu 雙梅景闇叢書 [Shadow of the double plum tree collection]. Compiled and edited by Ye Dehui 葉德輝. Changsha, 1914.

Shuihu quanzhuan 水滸全傳 [Variorum edition of the Outlaws of the Marsh]. Attributed to Luo Guanzhong 羅貫中 or Shi Naian 施耐庵. Edited by Zheng Zhenduo 鄭振鐸, Wu Xiaoling 吳曉鈴, and Wang Liqi 王利器. 3 vols. Beijing: Renmin wenxue chubanshe, 1954.

Shuofu 說郛 [Frontiers of apocrypha]. Compiled by Tao Zongyi 陶宗儀. 2 vols. Taipei: Xinxing shuju, 1963.

Sima Guang 司馬光. *Zizhi tongjian* 資治通鑑 [Comprehensive mirror for aid in government]. 10 vols. Beijing: Zhonghua shuju, 1976.

Sima Qian 司馬遷. "Lü Buwei liezhuan" 呂不韋列傳 [Biography of Lü Buwei]. In *Shi ji* 史記, vol. 8. Beijing: Zhonghua shuju, 1972.

————. *Shi ji* 史記 [Historical records]. 10 vols. Beijing: Zhonghua shuju, 1972.

Sima Xiangru 司馬相如. "Meiren fu" 美人賦 [Rhapsody on the beauty]. In *Quan Han fu* 全漢賦. Compiled and edited by Fei Zhengang 費振剛, Hu Shuangbao 胡雙寶, and Zong Minghua 宗明華. Beijing: Beijing Daxue chubanshe, 1993.

————. "Shanglin fu" 上林賦 [Rhapsody on Shanglin Park]. In *Quan Han fu* 全漢賦. Compiled and edited by Fei Zhengang 費振剛, Hu Shuangbao 胡雙寶, and Zong Minghua 宗明華. Beijing: Beijing Daxue chubanshe, 1993.

Sishu jizhu 四書集註 [Collected annotations to the Four Books]. Compiled by Zhu Xi 朱熹. Taipei: Yiwen shuju, 1980.

Siwuxie huibao 思無邪匯寶 [No depraved thoughts collectanea]. 45 vols. Compiled by Chen Qinghao 陳慶浩 and Wang Qiugui 王秋桂. Taipei: Encyclopedia Britannica, 1995-1997.

Siwuxie huibao waibian 思無邪匯寶外編 [Supplement to the No Depraved Thoughts Collectanea]. 2 vols. *Dongfang yanqing xiaoshuo zhenben* 東方豔情小說珍本 [Rare editions of oriental erotic novels]. Compiled by Chen Qinghao 陳慶浩 and Wang Qiugui 王秋桂. Taipei: Encyclopedia Britannica, 1997.

Song Lian 宋濂. Yuan shi 元史 [History of the Yuan dynasty]. 15 vols. Beijing: Zhonghua shuju, 1976.

Song Yu 宋玉. "Gaotang fu" 高唐賦 [Rhapsody on Gaotang]. In *Wenxuan* 文選. Compiled by Xiao Tong 蕭統. Shanghai: Shanghai guji chubanshe, 1992.

Su Dongpo yishi huibian 蘇東坡軼事匯編 [Collected anecdotes on Su Dongpo]. Compiled and annotated by Yan Zhongqi 顏中其. Changsha: Yuelu shushe, 1984.

[*Juan Yang Shengan pidian*] Sui Tang liangchao shizhuan [鐫楊升菴批點]隋唐兩朝史傳 [(Woodcut Yang Shengan annotated edition of the) Historical record of the Sui and Tang dynasties]. Attributed to Luo Guanzhong 羅貫中. 122 *juan*. Fac. repr. of 1619 ed. Tokyo: Sonkeikaku Bunko.

Sun Simiao 孫思邈. *Beiji qianjin yaofang* 備急千金要方 [Prescriptions worth a thousand pieces of gold for emergencies]. Fac. repr. of 1849 ed.; Taipei: Diqiu chubanshe, 1975.

Taishō shinshū daizōkyō 大正新修大藏經 [Newly edited great Buddhist canon compiled in the Taishō reign period (1912-1926)]. 85 vols. Tokyo: Taishō issaikyō kankōkai, 1922-1932.

Tan Qian 談遷. *Guoque* 國榷 [Evaluation of the events of our dynasty]. 6 vols. Beijing: Zhonghua shuju, 1988.

Tang Song chuanqi ji 唐宋傳奇傳 [Anthology of literary tales from the Tang and Song dynasties]. Edited by Lu Xun 魯迅. Beijing: Wenxue guji kanxingshe, 1958.

Tang Xianzu 湯顯祖. *Mudan ting* 牡丹亭 [The peony pavilion]. In *Tang Xianzu ji* 湯顯祖集 [Collected works of Tang Xianzu], vol. 3. Shanghai: Renmin chubanshe, 1973.

———. *Zichai ji* 紫釵記 [The purple hairpin]. In *Tang Xianzu ji* 湯顯祖集 [Collected works of Tang Xianzu], vol. 3. Shanghai: Renmin chubanshe, 1973.

Tao Qian 陶潛. *Soushen houji* 搜神後記 [Sequel to In Search of the Supernatural]. Beijing: Zhonghua shuju, 1981.

Tao Zongyi 陶宗儀. *Chuogeng lu* 輟耕錄 [Notes recorded during respites from the plow]. Beijing: Zhonghua shuju, 1980.

Taohua yanshi 桃花豔史 [Captivating history of peach blossoms]. In *Siwuxie huibao* 思無邪匯寶, vol. 23. Compiled by Chen Qinghao 陳慶浩 and Wang Qiugui 王秋桂. Taipei: Encyclopedia Britannica, 1995.

Taohua ying 桃花影 [Shadows of the peach blossom]. Compiled by Zuili Yanshui Sanren 檇李煙水散人 (pseud.). In *Siwuxie huibao* 思無邪匯寶, vol. 18. Compiled by Chen Qinghao 陳慶浩 and Wang Qiugui 王秋桂. Taipei: Encyclopedia Britannica, 1995.

Tuo Tuo 脫脫 et al. *Song shi* 宋史 [History of the Song dynasty]. 40 vols. Beijing: Zhonghua shuju, 1977.

———. *Liao shi* 遼史 [History of the Liao dynasty]. 5 vols. Beijing: Zhonghua shuju, 1974.

Wang Dang 王讜. *Tang yulin* 唐語林 [Forest of aphorisms from the Tang dynasty]. Shanghai: Gudian wenxue chubanshe, 1957.

Wang Jia 王嘉. *Shiyi ji* 拾遺記 [Gathering remaining accounts]. Beijing: Zhonghua shuju, 1981.

Wang Renyu 王仁裕. *Kaiyuan Tianbao yishi shizhong* 開元天寶遺事十種 [Anecdotes from the Kaiyuan (713-741) and Tianbao (742-756) reign periods]. Compiled and edited by Ding Ruming 丁如明. Shanghai: Shanghai guji chubanshe, 1985.

Wang Shifu 王實甫. *Xixiang ji* 西廂記 [Romance of the western chamber]. Fac. repr. of 1498 ed,; Taipei: Shijie shuju, 1963.

Wang Yangming 王陽明. *Wang Yangming Chuanxi lu xiangzhu jiping* 王陽明傳習錄詳註集評 [Thoroughly annotated collected commentary edition of Wang Yangming's Instructions for Practical Living]. Edited and annotated by Wing-tsit Chan 陳榮捷. Taipei: Xuesheng shuju, 1988.

———. *Wang Yangming quanji* 王陽明全集 [Complete works of Wang Yangming]. Compiled and edited by Wu Guang 吳光, Qian Ming 錢明, Dong Ping 董平, and Yao Yanfu 姚延福. 2 vols. Shanghai: Guji wenxue chubanshe, 1992.

Wang Zhongyong 王仲鏞. *Tangshi jishi jiaojian* 唐詩記事校箋 [Annotated edition of Recorded Occasions in Tang Poetry]. Chengdu: Bashu shushe, 1989.

Wei Shou 魏收. *Wei shu* 魏書 [History of the Wei dynasty]. 8 vols. Beijing: Zhonghua shuju, 1974.

Wei Zheng 魏徵. *Sui shu* 隋書 [History of the Sui dynasty]. 6 vols. Beijing: Zhonghua shuju, 1973.

"Wenjing yuanyang hui" 刎頸鴛鴦會 [Fatal attraction]. In *Liushijia xiaoshuo* 六十家小說. Compiled by Hong Pian 洪楩 and edited by Tan Zhengbi 譚正璧 under the title *Qingping shantang huaben* 清平山堂話本. Shanghai, 1957.

Wenxuan 文選 [Anthology of literature]. 3 vols. Compiled by Xiao Tong 蕭統. Shanghai: Shanghai guji chubanshe, 1992.

Wu Gongchen 吳拱宸. *Yuanyang zhen* 鴛鴦針 [A needle for embroidering mandarin ducks]. Edited by Wang Rumei 王汝梅. Shenyang: Chunfeng wenyi chubanshe, 1985.

Wu Zeng 吳曾. *Nenggaizhai manlu* 能改齋漫錄 [Random notes from the studio of one capable of correcting his faults]. 2 vols. Shanghai: Zhonghua shuju, 1960.

Wu Zetian 武則天. *Wu Zetian ji* 武則天集 [Collected writings of Wu Zetian]. Edited by Luo Yuanzhen 羅元貞. Shanxi: Shanxi renmin chubanshe, 1987.

Wu Zhao zhuan 武曌傳 [Story of Empress Wu Zhao (Wu Zetian)]. In *Zazuan xingshui bian* 雜纂醒睡編 [Miscellany compiled to ward off slumber]. Compiled by Ye Rubi 葉如璧. Preface dated 1587. Taipei, National Palace Museum.

———. In *Siwuxie huibao waibian* 思無邪匯寶外編, vol. 1. *Dongfang yanqing xiaoshuo zhenben* 東方豔情小說珍本. Compiled by Chen Qinghao 陳慶浩 and Wang Qiugui 王秋桂. Taipei: Encyclopedia Britannica, 1997.

Wumeng yuan 巫夢緣 [Fate in a dream of Mount Wu]. In *Siwuxie huibao* 思無邪匯寶, vol. 16. Compiled by Chen Qinghao 陳慶浩 and Wang Qiugui 王秋桂. Taipei: Encyclopedia Britannica, 1995.

Wushan yanshi 巫山豔史 [Captivating history of Mount Wu]. In *Siwuxie huibao* 思無邪匯寶, vol. 20. Compiled by Chen Qinghao 陳慶浩 and Wang Qiugui 王秋桂. Taipei: Encyclopedia Britannica, 1995.

Wutong ying 梧桐影 [Shadows of the *firmiana*]. In *Siwuxie huibao* 思無邪匯寶, vol. 16. Compiled by Chen Qinghao 陳慶浩 and Wang Qiugui 王秋桂. Taipei: Encyclopedia Britannica, 1995.

Xia Xie 夏燮. *Ming tongjian* 明通鑑 [Comprehensive mirror of the Ming dynasty]. 4 vols. Beijing: Zhonghua shuju, 1959.

Xiangyan congshu 香豔叢書 [Collection of erotic works]. Compiled by Chong Tianzi 蟲天子 (pseud.). 5 vols. Beijing: Renmin wenxue chubanshe, 1994.

Xiao Zixian 蕭子顯. *Nanqi shu* 南齊書 [History of the Southern Qi dynasty]. 3 vols. Beijing: Zhonghua shuju, 1972.

Xiaoxiao Sheng 笑笑生 (pseud.). *Jin Ping Mei cihua* 金瓶梅詞話 [The plum in the golden vase]. 5 vols. Tokyo: Dai An, 1963.

Xinghua tian 杏花天 [Apricot blossom heaven]. Compiled by Gutang Tianfang Daoren 古棠天放道人 (pseud.). In *Siwuxie huibao* 思無邪匯寶, vol. 17. Compiled by Chen Qinghao 陳慶浩 and Wang Qiugui 王秋桂. Taipei: Encyclopedia Britannica, 1995.

"Xinqiao shi Han Wu mai chunqing" 新橋市韓五賣春情 [Han Wuniang sells her charms at Newbridge Market]. In *Gujin xiaoshuo* 古今小說 [Stories old and new], vol. 1. Compiled by Feng Menglong 馮夢龍. Fac. repr., Shanghai: Shanghai guji chubanshe, 1993.

Xiuta yeshi (bencang ben) 繡榻野史 (本藏本) [Unofficial history of the embroidered couch (original edition)]. By Lü Tiancheng 呂天成. In *Siwuxie huibao* 思無邪匯寶, vol. 2. Compiled by Chen Qinghao 陳慶浩 and Wang Qiugui 王秋桂. Taipei: Encyclopedia Britannica, 1995.

Xiuta yeshi (zuimiange ben) 繡榻野史 (醉眠閣本) [Unofficial history of the embroidered couch (chamber of inebriated slumber edition)]. By Lü Tiancheng 呂天成. In *Siwuxie huibao* 思無邪匯寶, vol. 2. Compiled by Chen Qinghao 陳慶浩 and Wang Qiugui 王秋桂. Taipei: Encyclopedia Britannica, 1995.

Xiyou ji 西遊記 [Journey to the west]. Attributed to Wu Chengen 吳承恩. Beijing: Renmin wenxue chubanshe, 1972.

Xu Changling 徐昌齡. *Ruyijun zhuan* 如意君傳 [Lord of perfect satisfaction]. Taipei: Tianyi chubanshe, 1985.

———. *Zetian Huanghou Ruyijun zhuan* 則天皇后如意君傳 [Empress Wu Zetian's lord of perfect satisfaction]. Tokyo: Seishinkaku, 1763.

———. *Zetian Huanghou Ruyijun zhuan* 則天皇后如意君傳 [Empress Wu Zetian's lord of perfect satisfaction]. In *Siwuxie huibao* 思無邪匯寶, vol. 24. Compiled by Chen Qinghao 陳慶浩 and Wang Qiugui 王秋桂. Taipei: Encyclopedia Britannica, 1995.

Xu Jie 徐階. *Shizong Suhuangdi shilu* 世宗肅皇帝實錄 [Veritable records of the Majestic Emperor Ming Shizong]. Nangang: Academia Sinica, Institute of History, 1966.

Xu Xuemo 徐學謨. *Shimiao zhiyu lu* 世廟識餘錄 [Additional records of the paternal temple]. Taipei: Guofeng chubanshe, 1965.

Xunzi jijie 荀子集解 [Works of Xunzi with collected commentaries and annotations]. Edited by Wang Xianqian 王先謙. Fac. repr., Taipei: Yiwen yinshuguan, 1977.

Yan Shigu 顏師古. *Daye shiyi ji* 大業拾遺記 [Gathering remaining accounts of the Daye reign period (605–617)]. In *Tang Song chuanqi ji* 唐宋傳奇集, *juan* 6. Edited by Lu Xun 魯迅. Beijing: Wenxue guji kanxingshe, 1958.

Yang Wanli 楊萬里. *Chengzhai shihua* 誠齋詩話 [Sincerity studio talks on poetry]. In *Lidai shihua xubian* 歷代詩話續編. 3 vols. Compiled by Ding Fubao 丁福保. Beijing: Zhonghua shuju, 1983.

Yang Weizhen 楊維楨. *Yang Weizhen shiji* 楊維楨詩集 [Collected poetry of Yang Weizhen]. Edited by Zou Zhifang 鄒志方. Zhejiang: Zhejiang guji chubanshe, 1994.

Yang Yiqing 楊一清. *Minglun dadian* 明倫大典 [Great code to clarify relationships]. Microfilm of 1527 ed., University of Chicago Library, no. CBM 1150.

Yanyi bian 豔異編 [Compilation of rare beauties]. Compilation attributed to Wang Shizhen 王世貞. Chunfeng wenyi chubanshe, n.d.

Yaohu yanshi 妖狐艷史 [Captivating history of a fox spirit]. Compiled by Song Zhuxuan 松竹軒. In *Siwuxie huibao* 思無邪匯寶, vol. 23. Compiled by Chen Qinghao 陳慶浩 and Wang Qiugui 王秋桂. Taipei: Encyclopedia Britannica, 1995.

Yao Silian 姚思廉. *Liang shu* 梁書 [History of the Liang dynasty]. 3 vols. Beijing: Zhonghua shuju, 1973.

Yichun xiangzhi 宜春香質 [A fragrant constitution that befits the spring]. By Zui Xihu Xinyue Zhuren 醉西湖心月主人 (pseud.). In *Siwuxie huibao* 思無邪匯寶, vol. 7. Compiled by Chen Qinghao 陳慶浩 and Wang Qiugui 王秋桂. Taipei: Encyclopedia Britannica, 1995.

Yi li 儀禮 [Book of rites]. In *Shisan jing* 十三經 [Thirteen classics], vol. 1. Compiled by Wu Zhemei 吳哲楣. Beijing: Guoji wenhua chuban gongsi, 1995.

Yipian qing 一片情 [Expanse of passion]. In *Siwuxie huibao* 思無邪匯寶, vol. 14. Compiled by Chen Qinghao 陳慶浩 and Wang Qiugui 王秋桂. Taipei: Encyclopedia Britannica, 1995.

Yiqing zhen 怡情陣 [Battle of pleasing passions]. Compiled by Jiangxi Yeren 江西野人 (pseud.). In *Siwuxie huibao* 思無邪匯寶, vol. 22. Compiled by Chen Qinghao 陳慶浩 and Wang Qiugui 王秋桂. Taipei: Encyclopedia Britannica, 1995.

Yu Jiaxi 余嘉錫. *Shishuo xinyu jianshu* 世說新語箋疏 [Commentary edition of A New Account of Tales of the World]. Beijing: Zhonghua shuju, 1983.

Yuan Haowen 元好問. *Yuan Haowen shici ji* 元好問詩詞集 [Collection of Yuan Haowen's *shi* and *ci* poetry]. Edited and annotated by He Xinhui 賀新輝. Beijing: Zhongguo zhanwang chubanshe, 1986.

Yuan Zhen 元稹. *Yingying zhuan* 鶯鶯傳 [Story of Yingying]. In *Tang Song chuanqi ji* 唐宋傳奇集. Edited by Lu Xun 魯迅. Beijing: Wenxue guji kanxingshe, 1958.

Yuanqu xuan 元曲選 [Anthology of Yuan *zaju* drama]. Compiled by Zang Maoxun 臧懋循 (1550-1620). 4 vols. Beijing: Zhonghua shuju, 1979.

Yue Shi 樂史. *Guang Zhuoyi ji* 廣卓異記 [Expanded version of Records of Outstanding Achievement]. In *Biji xiaoshuo daguan* 筆記小說大觀, vol. 1. Yangzhou: Jiangsu Guangling guji kanxingshe, 1984.

———. *Yang Taizhen waizhuan* 楊太眞外傳 [Outer story of Yang Taizhen]. In *Gushi wenfang xiaoshuo* 顧氏文房小說, *ce* 2. Compiled by Gu Yuanqing 顧元慶. Fac. repr., Shanghai: Shangwu yinshuguan, 1934, *juan* 1, pp. 1a-11b, and *juan* 2, pp. 2.1a-11b.

Yuefu shiji 樂府詩集 [Collection of Music Bureau poems]. Compiled by Guo Maoqian 郭茂倩. 4 vols. Beijing: Zhonghua shuju, 1979.

Yugui hong 玉閨紅 [Rouge in the secluded jade chamber]. By Donglu Luoluoping Sheng 東魯落落平生 (pseud.). In *Siwuxie huibao* 思無邪匯寶, vol. 4. Compiled by Chen Qinghao 陳慶浩 and Wang Qiugui 王秋桂. Taipei: Encyclopedia Britannica, 1995.

Zazuan xingshui bian 雜纂醒睡編 [Miscellany compiled to ward off slumber]. Compiled by Ye Rubi 葉如璧. Preface dated 1587; National Palace Museum, Taiwan.

Zaihua chuan 載花船 [Boat laden with flowers]. By Xiling Kuangzhe 西泠狂者 (pseud.). In *Siwuxie huibao* 思無邪匯寶, vol. 9. Compiled by Chen Qinghao 陳慶浩 and Wang Qiugui 王秋桂. Taipei: Encyclopedia Britannica, 1995.

Zhang Tingyu 張廷玉. *Ming shi* 明史 [History of the Ming dynasty]. 28 vols. Beijing: Zhonghua shuju, 1974.

"Zhang Xiaoji Chenliu ren jiu" 張孝基陳留認舅 [Zhang Xiaoji discovers his brother-in-law in Chenliu]. In *Xingshi hengyan* 醒世恒言, vol. 1. Compiled by Feng Menglong 馮夢龍. Fac. repr., Shanghai: Shanghai guji chubanshe, 1993.

Zhang Zhuo 張鷟. *Chaoye qianzai* 朝野僉載 [Comprehensive record of affairs within and without the court]. Beijing: Zhonghua shuju, 1979.

———. *You xianku* 遊仙窟 [Journey to the dwelling of the goddesses]. In *Siwuxie huibao waibian* 思無邪匯寶外編, vol. 1. *Dongfang yanqing xiaoshuo zhenben* 東方豔情小說珍本. Compiled by Chen Qinghao 陳慶浩 and Wang Qiugui 王秋桂. Taipei: Encyclopedia Britannica, 1997.

Zhaoyang qushi 昭陽趣史 [Captivating history of Zhaoyang Palace]. By Guhang Yanyan Sheng 古杭艷艷生 (pseud.). In *Siwuxie huibao* 思無邪匯寶, vol. 3. Compiled by Chen Qinghao 陳慶浩 and Wang Qiugui 王秋桂. Taipei: Encyclopedia Britannica, 1995.

Zhouyi yinde 周易引得 [Concordance to the Book of Changes]. Taipei: Chinese Materials and Research Aids Service Center, 1966.

Zhu Xi 朱熹. *Shi jizhuan* 詩集傳 [Collected annotations to the Book of Poetry]. Fac. repr., Taipei: Yiwen yinshuguan, 1974.

———. *Yupi Zizhi tongjian gangmu* 御批資治通鑑綱目 [Comprehensive mirror for aid in government in outline and detailed form with imperial annotations]. 26 vols. Taipei: Shangwu yinshuguan, 1976.

———. *Yuzuan Zhuzi quanshu* 御纂朱子全書 [Complete works of Master Zhu compiled under imperial auspices]. 24 vols. Compiled by Li Guangdi 李光地. Fac. repr. of 1713 ed., n.d.

———. "Zhaiju ganxing ershi shou" 齋居感興二十首 [Twenty poems inspired by (historical) events while living in abstemious retirement]. In *Guxiangzhai xinke xiuzhen yuzuan Zhuzi quanshu* 古香齋新刻袖珍御纂朱子全書 [Old incense studio, newly cut, pocket edition, of The Complete Works of Master Zhu, compiled under imperial auspices], *juan* 66. Fac. repr., n.d., p. 18a.

———. *Zhongyong zhangju* [Commentary on the Doctrine of the mean, divided into chapters and sentences]. In *Sishu jizhu* 四書集注 [Collected annotations to the Four Books]. Fac. repr., Taipei: Yiwen yinshuguan, 1980.

Zhu Yuanzhang 朱元璋. *Zuxun* 祖訓 [Ancestral admonitions]. In *Mingchao kaiguo wenxian* 明朝開國文獻, vol. 3. Taipei: Xuesheng shuju, 1966.

Zhuangzi quangu 莊子詮詁 [Works of Zhuangzi with explanatory notes]. Edited by Hu Yuanjun 胡遠濬. Taipei: Taiwan Shangwu yinshuguan, 1980.

Zhuangzi yinde 莊子引得 [Concordance to Zhuangzi]. Cambridge, Mass.: Harvard University Press, 1956.

Zhulin yeshi 株林野史 [Unofficial history of the bamboo grove]. In *Siwuxie huibao* 思無邪匯寶, vol. 20. Compiled by Chen Qinghao 陳慶浩 and Wang Qiugui 王秋桂. Taipei: Encyclopedia Britannica, 1995.

Zhuo Erkan 卓爾堪. *Ming yimin shi* 明遺民詩 [Poems by Ming refugees]. Shanghai: Zhonghua shuju, 1960.

Zhuzi jicheng 諸子集成 [Corpus of the philosphers]. 8 vols. Hong Kong: Zhonghua shuju, 1978.

Zhuzi yulei 朱子語類 [Classified sayings of Master Zhu]. 8 vols. Compiled by Li Jingde 黎靖德. Taipei: Zhengzhong shuju, 1982.

Zuo Qiuming 左丘明. *Zuo zhuan huijian* 左傳會箋 [Collected annotations to the

Zuo documentary]. Edited by Takezoe Kōkō 竹添光鴻. Taipei: Mingde chubanshe, 1982.

Secondary Sources

Abramson, Paul R., and Haruo Hayashi. "Pornography in Japan: Cross-Cultural and
Theoretical Considerations." In *Pornography and Sexual Aggression,* Ed. by Neil M.
Malamuth and Edward Donnerstein. New York: Academic Press, 1984.
An Pingqiu 安平秋 and Zhang Peiheng 章培恒, comps. *Zhongguo jinshu daguan* 中
國禁書大觀 [Overview of Chinese banned books]. Shanghai: Shanghai wenhua
chubanshe, 1990.
Bakhtin, M. M. *The Dialogic Imagination: Four Essays.* Edited and translated by Caryl
Emerson and Michael Holquist. Austin: University of Texas Press, 1981.
Birch, Cyril, trans. *The Peony Pavilion.* Bloomington: Indiana University Press, 1980.
Birrell, Anne. *New Songs from a Jade Terrace: An Anthology of Early Chinese Love Poetry
Translated with Annotations and an Introduction.* Boston: Allen & Unwin, 1982.
Bloom, Irene. *Knowledge Painfully Acquired: The K'un-chih chi by Lo Ch'in-shun.* New
York: Columbia University Press, 1987.
Bokenkamp, Stephen R., with a contribution by Peter Nickerson. *Early Daoist Scrip-
tures.* Berkeley: University of California Press, 1997.
Brokaw, Cynthia J. *The Ledgers of Merit and Demerit: Social Change and Moral Order in
Late Imperial China.* Princeton: Princeton University Press, 1991.
Burke, Edmund. *Reflections on the Revolution in France.* Edited by J. C. D. Clark. Stan-
ford: Stanford University Press, 2001.
Butler, Judith. *Bodies That Matter: On the Discursive Limits of "Sex."* New York: Rout-
ledge, 1993.
Cameron, Vivian. "Political Exposures: Sexuality and Caricature in the French Revo-
lution." In *Eroticism and the Body Politic,* ed. Lynn Hunt. Baltimore: Johns Hop-
kins University Press, 1991.
Carlitz, Katherine. "Puns and Puzzles in the *Chin P'ing Mei.*" *T'oung Pao* 67, no. 3-5
(1981): 216-239.
———. *The Rhetoric of Chin p'ing mei.* Bloomington: Indiana University Press, 1986.
Chan, Wing-tsit. *Instructions for Practical Living and Other Neo-Confucian Writings by
Wang Yang-ming.* New York: Columbia University Press, 1963.
———, trans. *Reflections on Things at Hand: The Neo-Confucian Anthology Compiled by
Chu Hsi and Lü Tsu-ch'ien.* New York: Columbia University Press, 1967.
———, trans. and comp. *A Source Book in Chinese Philosophy.* Princeton: Princeton
University Press, 1963.
Cheng, Chung-Ying. "Reason, Substance, and Human Desires in Seventeenth-
Century Neo-Confucianism." In *The Unfolding of Neo-Confucianism,* ed. William
Theodore de Bary and the Conference on Seventeenth-Century Chinese
Thought. New York: Columbia University Press, 1975.
Ching, Julia. "Chu Hsi on Personal Cultivation." In *Chu Hsi and Neo-Confucianism,* ed.
Wing-tsit Chan. Honolulu: University of Hawai'i Press, 1986.
———. *To Acquire Wisdom: The Way of Wang Yang-ming.* New York: Columbia Univer-
sity Press, 1976.
Chou Tao-chi. "Chang Fu-ching." In *Dictionary of Ming Biography,* ed. L. Carrington
Goodrich and Chaoying Fang. New York: Columbia University Press, 1976.

———. "Yang T'ing-ho." In *Dictionary of Ming Biography*, ed. L. Carrington Goodrich and Chaoying Fang. New York: Columbia University Press, 1976.

Chu, Hung-lam. Review of *The Chosen One: Succession and Adoption in the Court of Ming Shizong*, by Carney T. Fisher. In *Harvard Journal of Asiatic Studies* 54, no. 1 (June 1994): 266–277.

Chu Hsi and Neo-Confucianism. Edited by Wing-tsit Chan. Honolulu: University of Hawai'i Press, 1986.

Clunas, Craig. *Superfluous Things: Material Culture and Social Status in Early Modern China.* Chicago: University of Illinois Press, 1991.

Darnton, Robert. *Edition et sédition: L'Univers de la littérature clandestine au XVIIIe siècle.* Paris: Gallimard, 1991.

———. *The Forbidden Best-Sellers of Pre-Revolutionary France.* New York: Norton, 1995.

Davidson, J. Leroy. "The Origin and Early Use of the Ju-i." *Artibus Asiae* 13, no. 4 (1950): 242–257.

de Bary, W. Theodore. "Individualism and Humanitarianism in Late Ming Thought." In *Self and Society in Ming Thought*, ed. W. Theodore de Bary. New York: Columbia University Press, 1970.

Dictionary of Ming Biography. 2 vols. Edited by L. Carrington Goodrich and Chaoying Fang. New York: Columbia University Press, 1976.

Donnerstein, Edward. "Pornography: Its Effect on Violence Against Women." In *Pornography and Sexual Aggression*, ed. Neil M. Malamuth and Edward Donnerstein. New York: Academic Press, 1984.

Donnerstein, Edward, Daniel Linz, and Steven Penrod. *The Question of Pornography: Research Findings and Policy Implications.* New York: Free Press, 1987.

Dreyer, Edward L. *Early Ming China: A Political History 1355–1435.* Stanford: Stanford University Press, 1982.

Dworkin, Ronald. "Women and Pornography." Review of *Only Words*, by Catharine MacKinnon. *New York Review of Books*, 21 October 1993, pp. 36–42.

Egerton, Clement, trans. *The Golden Lotus: A Translation, from the Chinese Original, of the Novel Chin P'ing Mei.* 4 vols. London: Routledge & Kegan Paul, 1972.

Elvin, Mark. *The Pattern of the Chinese Past.* Palo Alto: Stanford University Press, 1973.

Epstein, Maram. "Beauty Is the Beast: The Dual Face of Woman in Four Ch'ing Novels." Ph.D. dissertation, Princeton University, 1992.

———. *Competing Discourses: Orthodoxy, Authenticity, and Engendered Meanings in Late Imperial Chinese Fiction.* Cambridge, Mass.: Harvard University Asia Center, 2001.

———. "Inscribing the Essentials: Culture and the Body in Ming-Qing Fiction." *Ming Studies* 41 (1999): 6–36.

Eroticism and the Body Politic. Edited by Lynn Hunt. Baltimore: Johns Hopkins University Press, 1991.

Fang, Chaoying. "Chu Chien-shen." In *Dictionary of Ming Biography*, ed. L. Carrington Goodrich and Chaoying Fang. New York: Columbia University Press, 1976.

———. "Chu Yu-t'ang." In *Dictionary of Ming Biography*, ed. L. Carrington Goodrich and Chaoying Fang. New York: Columbia University Press, 1976.

Fang Fu Ruan. *Sex in China: Studies in Sexology in Chinese Culture.* New York: Plenum Press, 1991.

Fang, Lienche Tu. "Chu Hou-ts'ung." In *Dictionary of Ming Biography*, ed. L. Carrington Goodrich and Chaoying Fang. New York: Columbia University Press, 1976.

Fielding, Henry. *The History of Tom Jones.* New York: Knopf, 1991.

Fisher, Carney. *The Chosen One: Succession and Adoption in the Court of Ming Shizong*. Boston: Allen & Unwin, 1990.

Fitzgerald, C. P. *The Empress Wu*. Melbourne: F. W. Cheshire, 1955.

Food in Chinese Culture. Edited by K. C. Chang. New Haven: Yale University Press, 1977.

Forte, Antonio. *Political Propaganda and Ideology in China at the End of the Seventh Century: Inquiry into the Nature, Authors, and Function of the Tunhuang Document S. 6502 Followed by an Annotated Translation*. Naples: Instituto Universitario Orientale, 1976.

Foucault, Michel. *The History of Sexuality*. Translated by Robert Hurley. 3 vols. New York: Random House, 1980.

Frappier-Mazur, Lucienne. "The Social Body: Disorder and Ritual in Sade's *Story of Juliette*." In *Eroticism and the Body Politic*, ed. Lynn Hunt. Baltimore: Johns Hopkins University Press, 1991.

———. "Truth and the Obscene Word in Eighteenth-Century French Pornography." In *The Invention of Pornography*, ed. Lynn Hunt. New York: Zone Books, 1993.

———. *Writing the Orgy: Power and Parody in Sade*. Translated by Gillian C. Gill. Philadelphia: University of Pennsylvania Press, 1996.

Furth, Charlotte. *A Flourishing Yin: Gender in China's Medical History, 960–1665*. Berkeley: University of California Press, 1999.

Gibbon, Edward. *The Decline and Fall of the Roman Empire*. 8 vols. London: Folio Press, 1997.

Goldin, Paul Rakita. *Rituals of the Way: The Philosophy of Xunzi*. Chicago: Open Court, 1999.

Goulemot, Jean Marie. *Forbidden Texts: Erotic Literature and Its Readers in Eighteenth-Century France*. Translated by James Simpson. Philadelphia: University of Pennsylvania Press, 1994.

Grant, Michael. *Eros in Pompeii: The Secret Rooms of the National Museum of Naples*. New York: Morrow, 1975.

Guisso, R. W. L. *Wu Tse-t'ien and the Politics of Legitimation in T'ang China*. Bellingham: Western Washington University, 1978.

Halperin, David M., John J. Winkler, and Froma I. Zeitlin, eds. *Before Sexuality: The Construction of Erotic Experience in the Ancient Greek World*. Princeton: Princeton University Press, 1990.

Hanan, Patrick. *The Carnal Prayer Mat*. New York: Ballantine Books, 1990.

———. *The Chinese Short Story: Studies in Dating, Authorship, and Composition*. Cambridge, Mass.: Harvard University Press, 1973.

———. *The Chinese Vernacular Story*. Cambridge, Mass.: Harvard University Press, 1981.

———. "The Erotic Novel: Some Early Reflections." Conference paper. Indiana University, May 1983.

———. "Sources of the *Chin P'ing Mei*." *Asia Major*, n. s. 10, no. 1 (1963): 23–67.

———. "The Text of the *Chin P'ing Mei*." *Asia Major*, n. s. 9, no. 1 (1962): 1–57.

Hanyu dacidian 漢語大詞典 [Great dictionary of the Chinese language]. Compiled by Luo Zhufeng 羅竹風 et al. 12 vols. Shanghai: Hanyu dacidian chubanshe, 1993.

Harper, Donald. *Early Chinese Medical Literature: The Mawangdui Medical Manuscripts*. Sir Henry Wellcome Asian Series, vol. 2. London: Kegan Paul International, 1998.

———. "The Sexual Arts of Ancient China as Described in a Manuscript of the Second Century B.C." *Harvard Journal of Asiatic Studies* 47, no. 2 (1987): 539–593.

————. "The *Wu Shih Erh Ping Fang:* Translation and Prolegomena." Ph.D. dissertation, University of California, Berkeley, 1982.

Hegel, Robert. *The Novel in Seventeenth Century China.* New York: Columbia University Press, 1981.

————. "*Sui T'ang yen-i* and the Aesthetics of the Seventeenth-Century Suchou Elite." In *Chinese Narrative,* ed. Andrew Plaks. Princeton: Princeton University Press, 1977.

Hou Zhongyi 侯忠義 and Wang Rumei 王汝梅, eds. *Jin Ping Mei ziliao huibian* 金瓶梅資料匯編 [Collected material on the *Jin Ping Mei*]. Beijing: Beijing Daxue chubanshe, 1985.

Hsia, C. T. *The Classic Chinese Novel.* New York: Columbia University Press, 1968.

————. "The Water Margin." Chapter in *The Classic Chinese Novel.* New York: Columbia University Press, 1968.

Hsia, Emil C. H., Ilza Veith, and Robert H. Geertsma, trans. *The Essentials of Medicine in Ancient China and Japan: Yasuyori Tamba's Ishimpō.* 2 vols. Leiden: Brill, 1986.

Huang, Martin W. *Desire and Fictional Narrative in Late Imperial China.* Cambridge, Mass.: Harvard University Asia Center, 2001.

Huang, Ray. *1587, a Year of No Significance: The Ming Dynasty in Decline.* New Haven: Yale University Press, 1981.

Hucker, Charles O. *A Dictionary of Official Titles in Imperial China.* Stanford: Stanford University Press, 1985.

Hunt, Lynn, ed. *Eroticism and the Body Politic.* Baltimore: Johns Hopkins University Press, 1991.

————, ed. *The Invention of Pornography: Obscenity and the Origins of Modernity, 1500–1800.* New York: Zone Books, 1993.

Itzin, Catherine, ed. *Pornography: Women, Violence, and Civil Liberties.* New York: Oxford University Press, 1992.

Jacob, Margaret C. "The Materialist World of Pornography." In *The Invention of Pornography: Obscenity and the Origins of Modernity, 1500–1800,* ed. Lynn Hunt. New York: Zone Books, 1993.

Jin Ping Mei lunwen ji 金瓶梅論文集 [Collection of essays on the *Jin Ping Mei*]. Taipei: Guanya wenhua, 1992

Kang Zhengguo 康正果. *Chongshen fengyuejian: Zhongguo gudai xingwenxue juyu* 重審風月鑑: 中國古代 性文學舉隅 [Reexamination of the mirror of love: Examples of ancient Chinese erotic literature]. Taipei: Maitian chuban youxian gongsi, 1996.

Kendrick, Walter M. *The Secret Museum: Pornography in Modern Culture.* New York: Viking, 1987.

Kermode, Frank. "The Men on the Dump: A Response." In *Addressing Frank Kermode: Essays in Criticism and Interpretation.* Edited by Margaret Tudeau-Clayton and Martin Warner. Chicago: University of Illinois Press, 1991.

Kline, T. C., and Philip J. Ivanhoe, eds. *Virtue, Nature, and Moral Agency in the Xunzi.* Indianapolis: Hackett, 2000.

Kohn, Livia, ed., in cooperation with Yoshinobu Sakade. *Taoist Meditation and Longevity Techniques.* Ann Arbor: Center for Chinese Studies, University of Michigan, 1989.

Kōjien 廣辭苑 [Vast garden of Japanese phrases]. Compiled by Shinmura Izuru 新村出. 3rd ed. Tokyo: Iwanami shoten, 1988.

Kronhausen, Eberhard, and Phyllis Kronhausen. *Pornography and the Law: The Psychology of Erotic Realism and Pornography.* New York: Ballantine Books, 1959.

Lau, D. C., trans. *Mencius*. New York: Penguin Books, 1970.

Legge, James. *The Chinese Classics: With a translation, critical and exegetical notes, prolegomena, and copious indexes*. 5 vols. Taipei: SMC, 1991.

———, trans. *The Shoo King or Book of Historical Documents*. Hong Kong: University of Hong Kong Press, 1960.

Lever, Maurice. *Donatien Alphonse François, marquis de Sade*. Paris: Fayard, 1991.

———. *Sade: A Biography*. Translated by Arthur Goldhammer. New York: Farrar, Straus & Giroux, 1993.

Lévy, André. *Études sur le Conte et le Roman Chinois*. Paris: École Française d'Extrême-Orient, 1971.

Li Jianguo 李劍國. *Songdai zhiguai chuanqi xulu* 宋代志怪傳奇敘錄 [Commentary to Song-dynasty tales of anomalies and classical tales]. Tianjin: Nankai Daxue chubanshe, 1997.

———. *Tang Wudai zhiguai chuanqi xulu* 唐五代志怪傳奇敘錄 [Commentary to Tang-dynasty tales of anomalies and classical tales]. 2 vols. Tianjin: Nankai Daxue chubanshe, 1993.

Li Ling 李零. *Zhongguo fangshu kao* 中國方術考 [Studies on Chinese divinatory and medical arts]. Beijing: Renmin Zhongguo chubanshe, 1993.

Li Ling and Keith McMahon. "The Contents and Terminology of the Mawangdui Texts on the Arts of the Bedchamber." *Early China* 17 (1992): 145-185.

Li Shiren 李時人. *"Ruyijun zhuan"* 如意君傳 [The lord of perfect satisfaction]. In *Zhongguo tongsu xiaoshuo zongmu tiyao* 中國通俗小說總目提要 [Comprehensive bibliography and synopses of popular Chinese fiction]. Compiled by Yin Longyuan 尹龍元 and Li Jingfeng 李景峰. Beijing: Zhongguo wenlian chuban gongsi, 1991.

Li, Wai-yee. *Enchantment and Disenchantment: Love and Illusion in Chinese Literature*. Princeton: Princeton University Press, 1993.

Li Xun 李洵. "'Dali yi' yu Mingdai zhengzhi" '大禮儀'與明代政治 [The Great Ritual Debate and Ming-dynasty government]. *Dongbei Shida xuebao* 東北師大學報 (*zhexue shehui kexue ban*) 5 (1986): 48-62.

Li Zehou. "Thoughts on Ming-Qing Neo-Confucianism." In *Chu Xi and Neo-Confucianism*, ed. Wing-tsit Chan. Honolulu: University of Hawai'i Press, 1986.

Liang, Rachel L., Y. W. Ma, and Joseph S. M. Lau, trans. "Empress Chao Fei-yen." In *Traditional Chinese Stories: Themes and Variations*, ed. Y. W. Ma and Joseph S. M. Lau. New York: Columbia University Press, 1978.

Lin Yanqing 林廷清. *Jiajing Huangdi dazhuan* 嘉靖皇帝大傳 [Biography of the Jiajing emperor (r. 1522-1567)]. Shenyang: Liaoning jiaoyu chubanshe, 1993.

Little, Stephen. *Realm of the Immortals: Daoism in the Arts of China*. Cleveland: Cleveland Museum of Art, 1988.

Liu Hui 劉輝. *"Ruyijun zhuan"* 如意君傳 [The lord of perfect satisfaction]. In *Zhongguo gudai xiaoshuo baike quanshu* 中國古代小說百科全書 [Encyclopedia of traditional Chinese fiction]. Compiled by Liu Shide 劉世德 et al. Beijing: Zhongguo dabaike quanshu chubanshe, 1993.

———. *"Ruyijun zhuan* de kanke niandai ji qi yu *Jin Ping Mei* zhi guanxi" 如意君傳的刊刻年代及其與金瓶梅之關係 [The era in which the *Ruyijun zhuan* was published and its relationship to the *Jin Ping Mei*]. In *Jin Ping Mei lunwen ji* 金瓶梅論文集 [Collection of essays on the *Jin Ping Mei*]. Taipei: Guanya wenhua, 1992.

Liu, James. "Mei Yao-ch'en." In *Sung Biographies*, ed. Herbert Franke. Wiesbaden: Franz Steiner Verlag, 1976.

Liu Ts'un-yan. "Taoist Self-Cultivation in Ming Thought." In *Self and Society in Ming Thought,* ed. W. Theodore de Bary. New York: Columbia University Press, 1970.

Liu Yinbai 劉 蔭柏 "*Milou ji*" 迷樓記 [Tale of the tower of enchantment]. In *Zhongguo gudai xiaoshuo baike quanshu* 中國古代小說百科全書 [Encyclopedia of traditional Chinese fiction]. Compiled by Liu Shide 劉世德 et al. Beijing: Zhongguo dabaike quanshu chubanshe, 1993.

Lu Ge 魯歌 and Ma Zheng 馬征. *Jin Ping Mei zongheng tan* 金瓶梅縱橫談 [Discussion of the *Jin Ping Mei* in all directions]. Beijing: Yanjing chubanshe, 1992.

Lu Xun 魯迅. *Zhongguo xiaoshuo shilüe* 中國小說史略 [Short history of Chinese fiction]. Beijing: Dongfang chubanshe, 1996.

Ma, Y. W., and Joseph S. M. Lau, eds. *Traditional Chinese Stories: Themes and Variations.* New York: Columbia University Press, 1978.

Macaulay, Thomas Babington. *The History of England.* 5 vols. London: Folio Press, 1986.

MacKinnon, Catharine A. *Only Words.* Cambridge, Mass.: Harvard University Press, 1993.

———. "The Roar on the Other Side of Silence." In *In Harm's Way: The Pornography Civil Rights Hearings,* ed. Catharine MacKinnon and Andrea Dworkin. Cambridge, Mass.: Harvard University Press, 1997.

Malamuth, Neil M. "Aggression Against Women: Cultural and Individual Causes." In *Pornography and Sexual Aggression,* ed. Neil M. Malamuth and Edward Donnerstein. New York: Academic Press, 1984.

Malamuth, Neil M., and Edward Donnerstein, eds. *Pornography and Sexual Aggression.* New York: Academic Press, 1984.

Martinson, Paul Varo. "Pao, Order, and Redemption: Perspectives on Chinese Religion and Society Based on a Study of the *Chin P'ing Mei.*" Ph.D. dissertation, University of Chicago, 1973.

Maspero, H. "Les procédés de 'nourrir le principe vital' dans la religion Taoiste ancienne." *Journal Asiatique* 229 (1937): 353-430.

McMahon, Keith. "Causality and Containment in Seventeenth-Century Chinese Fiction." *T'oung Pao* 15 (1988).

———. *Misers, Shrews, and Polygamists: Sexuality and Male-Female Relations in Eighteenth-Century Chinese Fiction.* Durham: Duke University Press, 1995.

Michelson, Peter. *Speaking the Unspeakable: A Poetics of Obscenity.* Albany: State University of New York Press, 1993.

Morohashi Tetsuji 諸橋轍次. *Dai Kan-Wa jiten* 大漢和辭典 [Great Chinese-Japanese dictionary]. 13 vols. Tokyo: Taishūkan shoten, 1984.

Mote, Frederick W. "Yüan and Ming." In *Food in Chinese Culture,* ed. K. C. Chang. New Haven: Yale University Press, 1977.

Mote, Frederick W., and Denis Twitchett, eds. *The Ming Dynasty, 1368-1644,* Vol. 7, pt. 1, of *Cambridge History of China,* ed. Denis Twitchett and John K. Fairbank, 14 vols. Cambridge: Cambridge University Press, 1988.

Nabokov, Vladimir. "Vladimir Nabokov on a Book Entitled *Lolita.*" In *Lolita.* New York: Berkeley Medallion Books, 1966.

Nakayama Hachirō 中山八郎. "Futatabi 'Kaseichō no tairei mondai no hattan' ni tsuite" 再び '嘉靖朝の大禮問題の發端' に就いて [Origins of the Great Ritual Debate of the Jiajing reign period of the Ming dynasty revisited]. In *Shimizu Hakase tsuitō kinen Mindaishi ronsō* 清水博士追悼紀念明代史論叢 [Essays on Ming-dynasty history to commemorate Dr. Shimizu]. Tokyo: Daian, 1962.

———. "Min no Kaseichō no tairei mondai no hattan" 明の嘉靖朝の大禮問題の 發端 [Origins of the Great Ritual Debate of the Jiajing reign period of the Ming dynasty]. *Jimbun Kenkyū* 人文研究 8, no. 9 (1957): 39-63.

Needham, Joseph, and Lu Gwei-djen. *Science and Civilisation in China.* Vol. 5, pt. 5, *Spagyrical Discovery and Invention: Physiological Alchemy.* Cambridge: Cambridge University Press, 1983.

Ōta Tatsuo 太田辰夫 and Iida Yoshirō 飯田吉郎. *Chūgoku hiseki sōkan* 中國秘籍叢 刊 [Collection of clandestine Chinese books]. 3 vols. Tokyo: Kyūko shoin, 1987.

Ouyang Chen 歐陽琛. "Wang Shouren yu Dali yi" 王守仁與大禮議 [Wang Shouren (Wang Yangming) and the Great Ritual Debate]. *Xin Zhonghua* 新中華 12, no. 7 (1949): 27-33.

Pally, Marcia. *Sense and Censorship: The Vanity of Bonfires.* New York: Americans for Constitutional Freedom, 1991.

Phillips, Anita. *A Defense of Masochism.* New York: St. Martin's Press, 1998.

Plaks, Andrew H. *The Four Masterworks of the Ming Novel.* Princeton: Princeton University Press, 1987.

———. "Towards a Critical Theory of Chinese Narrative." In *Chinese Narrative: Critical and Theoretical Essays,* ed. Andrew Plaks. Princeton: Princeton University Press, 1977.

Pope, Alexander. "An Essay on Criticism." In *The Poems of Alexander Pope.* New Haven: Yale University Press, 1974.

Porkert, Manfred. *The Theoretical Foundations of Chinese Medicine: Systems of Correspondence.* Cambridge, Mass.: MIT Press, 1974.

Pornography and Sexual Aggression. Edited by Neil M. Malamuth and Edward Donnerstein. New York: Academic Press, 1984.

Posner, Richard A. "Obsession: *Only Words* by Catharine A. MacKinnon." *New Republic,* 18 October 1993, pp. 31-36.

———. *Sex and Reason.* Cambridge, Mass.: Harvard University Press, 1994.

Rawski, Evelyn. "Economic and Social Foundations of Ming and Ch'ing Culture." *Ming Studies* 2 (1978): 12-29.

Richlin, Amy, ed. *Pornography and Representation in Greece and Rome.* New York: Oxford University Press, 1992.

Riegel, Jeffrey. "A Summary of Some Recent *Wenwu* and *Kaogu* Articles: Mawangdui Tombs Two and Three." *Early China* 1 (1975): 10-15.

Roberts, Moss, trans. *Three Kingdoms: A Historical Novel Attributed to Luo Guanzhong.* Berkeley: University of California Press, 1991.

Robinet, Isabelle. *Introduction à l'alchimie intérieure taoïste: De l'unité et de la multiplicité.* Paris: Les éditions du cerf, 1995.

———. "Original Contributions of *Neidan* to Taoism and Chinese Thought." In *Taoist Meditation and Longevity Techniques,* ed. Livia Kohn, in cooperation with Yoshinobu Sakade. Ann Arbor: Center for Chinese Studies, University of Michigan, 1989.

Rolston, David L., ed. *How to Read the Chinese Novel.* Princeton: Princeton University Press, 1990.

———. *Traditional Chinese Fiction and Fiction Commentary: Reading and Writing Between the Lines.* Stanford: Stanford University Press, 1997.

Roy, David T. "The Case for T'ang Hsien-tsu's Authorship of the *Chin P'ing Mei.*" *CLEAR* 8, nos. 1-2 (July 1986): 31-62.

———. "Chang Chu-p'o's Commentary on the *Chin p'ing mei.*" In *Chinese Narrative: Critical and Theoretical Essays,* ed. Andrew H. Plaks. Princeton: Princeton University Press, 1977.

————, trans. "Chang Chu-p'o on How to Read the *Chin P'ing Mei*." In *How to Read the Chinese Novel*, ed. David L. Rolston. Princeton: Princeton University Press, 1990.

————. "A Confucian Interpretation of the *Chin P'ing Mei*." In *Proceedings of the International Conference on Sinology: Section on Literature*. Taipei: Academia Sinica, 1981.

————, trans. *The Plum in the Golden Vase or, Chin P'ing Mei*. Vol. 1, *The Gathering*. Princeton: Princeton University Press, 1993.

————, trans. *The Plum in the Golden Vase or, Chin P'ing Mei*. Vol. 2, *The Rivals*. Princeton: Princeton University Press, 2001.

Said, Edward. *Orientalism*. New York: Pantheon, 1978.

Sapolsky, Barry S. "Arousal, Affect, and the Aggression-Moderating Effect of Erotica." In *Pornography and Sexual Aggression,* ed. Neil M. Malamuth and Edward Donnerstein. New York: Academic Press, 1984.

Satyendra, Indira Suh. "Metaphors of the Body: The Sexual Economy of the *Chin P'ing Mei tz'u-hua*." *CLEAR* 15 (Dec. 1993): 85-97.

————. "Toward a Poetics of the Chinese Novel: A Study of the Prefatory Poems in the *Chin P'ing Mei tz'u-hua*." Ph.D. dissertation, University of Chicago, 1989.

Schipper, Kristofer, trans. *L'Empereur Wou des Han dans la Légende Taoiste; le "Han Wou-Ti Nei-Tchouan*." Paris: Maisonneuve, 1965.

————. "Science, Magic, and the Mystique of the Body." In *The Clouds and the Rain: The Art of Love in China,* ed. M. Beurdeley. London: Hammond & Hammond, 1969.

————. *The Taoist Body*. Translated by Karen C. Duval. Berkeley: University of California Press, 1993.

Self and Society in Ming Thought. Edited by W. Theodore de Bary. New York: Columbia University Press, 1970.

Shapiro, Sidney, trans. *Outlaws of the Marsh*. 4 vols. Beijing: Foreign Languages Press, 1988.

Shattuck, Roger. *Forbidden Knowledge: From Prometheus to Pornography*. New York: St. Martin's Press, 1996.

Shaw, Miranda. *Passionate Enlightenment: Women in Tantric Buddhism*. Princeton: Princeton University Press, 1994.

Shaw, R. D. M., trans. and ed. *The Blue Cliff Records: The Hekigan Roku*. London: Michael Joseph, 1961.

Siku quanshu zongmu 四庫全書總目 [General index to the complete library of the four treasuries]. Yong Rong 永瑢 et al. 2 vols. Beijing: Zhonghua shuju, 1992.

Sivin, Nathan. *Traditional Medicine in Contemporary China*. Ann Arbor: Center for Chinese Studies, University of Michigan, 1987.

So, Kwan-wai. "Chu Hou-chao." In *Dictionary of Ming Biography,* ed. L. Carrington Goodrich and Chaoying Fang. New York: Columbia University Press, 1976.

Stone, Charles R. "The *Ruyijun zhuan* and the Origins of the Chinese Erotic Novel." Ph.D. dissertation, University of Chicago, 1999.

Strossen, Nadine. *Defending Pornography: Free Speech, Sex, and the Fight for Women's Rights*. New York: Scribner, 1995.

Sun Kaidi 孫楷第. *Riben Dongjing suo jian xiaoshuo shumu* 日本東京所見小說書目 [Bibliography of works of Chinese fiction seen in Tokyo, Japan]. Beijing: Renmin wenxue chubanshe, 1991.

————. *Zhongguo tongsu xiaoshuo shumu* 中國通俗小說書目 [Bibliography of popular Chinese fiction]. Kowloon: Shiyong shuju, 1967.

Sung Biographies. Edited by Herbert Franke. Wiesbaden: Franz Steiner Verlag, 1976.

Tang Chun-I. "The Development of the Concept of Moral Mind from Wang Yangming to Wang Chi." In *Self and Society in Ming Thought,* ed. W. Theodore de Bary. New York: Columbia University Press, 1970.

Taoist Meditation and Longevity Techniques. Edited by Livia Kohn in cooperation with Yoshinobu Sakade. Ann Arbor: Center for Chinese Studies, University of Michigan, 1989.

Teng Ssu-yü. "Chu Yüan-chang." In *Dictionary of Ming Biography,* ed. L. Carrington Goodrich and Chaoying Fang. New York: Columbia University Press, 1976.

Tu Wei-ming. *Humanity and Self-Cultivation: Essays in Confucian Thought.* Berkeley: Asian Humanities Press, 1979.

———. *Neo-Confucian Thought in Action: Wang Yang-ming's Youth.* Berkeley: University of California Press, 1976.

Twitchett, Denis, ed. *Sui and T'ang China, 589–906 A.D.* Vol. 3 of *Cambridge History of China,* ed. Denis Twitchett and John K. Fairbank, 14 vols. Cambridge: Cambridge University Press, 1979.

———. *The Writing of Official History Under the T'ang.* New York: Cambridge University Press, 1992.

The Unfolding of Neo-Confucianism, ed. W. Theodore de Bary and the Conference on Seventeenth-Century Chinese Thought. New York: Columbia University Press, 1975.

U.S. Department of Justice. *Attorney General's Commission on Pornography, Final Report.* 2 vols. Washington, D.C.: Government Printing Office, 1986.

Unschuld, Paul U. *Medicine in China: A History of Ideas.* Berkeley: University of California Press, 1985.

van Gulik, R. H. *Sexual Life in Ancient China.* 1961. Reprint. Leiden: Brill, 1974.

Waley, Arthur. *The Analects of Confucius.* New York: Vintage Books, 1989.

———. *The Book of Songs.* New York: Grove Press, 1987.

———. *The Way and Its Power: A Study of the Tao Tê Ching and Its Place in Chinese Thought.* New York: Grove Press, 1958.

Wang Diwu 王滌武. *Wu Zetian shidai* 武則天時代 [The era of Wu Zetian]. Fujian: Xiamen Daxue chubanshe, 1991.

Wang, Richard. "Creating Artifacts: The Ming Erotic Novella in Cultural Practice." Ph.D. dissertation, University of Chicago, 1999.

———. "Liu Tsung-yüan's 'Tale of Ho-chien' and Fiction." *T'ang Studies* 14 (1996): 21–48.

Wang Rumei 王汝梅. *Jin Ping Mei tansuo* 金瓶梅探索 [Study of the *Jin Ping Mei*]. Changchun: Jilin Daxue chubanshe, 1990.

———. "*Yuanyang zhen* ji qi zuozhe chutan" 鴛鴦針及其作者初探 [Preliminary investigation of the *Yuanyang zhen* and its author]. In *Yuanyang zhen* 鴛鴦針. Edited by Wang Rumei. Shenyang: Chunfeng wenyi chubanshe, 1985.

Watson, Burton. *Early Chinese Literature.* New York: Columbia University Press, 1962.

———. *The Tso chuan: Selections from China's Oldest Narrative History.* New York: Columbia University Press, 1989.

Wile, Douglas. *Art of the Bedchamber: The Chinese Sexual Yoga Classics Including Women's Solo Meditation Texts.* Albany: State University of New York Press, 1992.

Wilhelm, Richard. *The Book of Changes.* Translated by Cary F. Baynes. Princeton: Princeton University Press, 1969.

Wright, Arthur F., and Denis Twitchett, eds. *Perspectives on the T'ang.* New Haven: Yale University Press, 1973.

Xu Shuofang 徐朔方. *Lun Jin Ping Mei de chengshu ji qita* 論金瓶梅的成書及其他

[Discussion of the composition of the *Jin Ping Mei* and other things]. Jinan: Qilu shushe, 1988.

Xu Yimin 許逸民. "Hanwu neizhuan" 漢武内傳 [Intimate biography of Emperor Wu of the Han]. In *Zhongguo gudai xiaoshuo baike quanshu* 中國古代小說百科全書 [Encyclopedia of traditional Chinese fiction]. Compiled by Liu Shide 劉世德 et al. Beijing: Zhongguo dabaike quanshu chubanshe, 1993.

———. "Zhao Feiyan waizhuan" 趙飛燕外傳 [Outer story of Empress Zhao Feiyan]. In *Zhongguo gudai xiaoshuo baike quanshu* 中國古代小說百科全書 [Encyclopedia of traditional Chinese fiction]. Compiled by Liu Shide 劉世德 et al. Beijing: Zhongguo dabaike quanshu chubanshe, 1993.

Xue Hongji 薛洪勣 "Yang Taizhen waizhuan" 楊太眞外傳 [Outer story of Yang Taizhen]. In *Zhongguo gudai xiaoshuo baike quanshu* 中國古代小說百科全書 [Encyclopedia of traditional Chinese fiction]. Compiled by Liu Shide 劉世德 et al. Beijing: Zhongguo dabaike quanshu chubanshe, 1993.

———. "Zhao Feiyan biezhuan" 趙飛燕別傳 [Alternate biography of Empress Zhao Feiyan]. In *Zhongguo gudai xiaoshuo baike quanshu* 中國古代小說百科全書 [Encyclopedia of traditional Chinese fiction]. Compiled by Liu Shide 劉世德 et al. Beijing: Zhongguo dabaike quanshu chubanshe, 1993.

Yu, Anthony, trans. *The Journey to the West.* 4 vols. Chicago: University of Chicago Press, 1980.

———. *Rereading the Stone: Desire and the Making of Fiction in Dream of the Red Chamber.* Princeton: Princeton University Press, 1997.

Yu, Pauline. *The Reading of Imagery in the Chinese Poetic Tradition.* Princeton: Princeton University Press, 1987.

Yu Yunxiu 余雲岫. *Gudai jibing minghou shuyi* 古代疾病名候疏義 [Detailed investigation into terms for illnesses in antiquity]. Beijing: Renmin weisheng chubanshe, 1955.

Zhang Peiheng 章培恒. *"Ruyijun zhuan"* 如意君傳 [The lord of perfect satisfaction]. In *Zhongguo jinshu daguan* 中國禁書大觀 [Overview of Chinese banned books]. Shanghai: Shanghai wenhua chubanshe, 1990.

Zhang Xincheng 張心澂. *Weishu tongkao* 僞書通考 [Comprehensive review of forged books]. Shanghai: Shangwu yinshuguan, 1957.

Zhang Zhenglang 張政烺. "Jiangshi yu yongshishi" 講史與詠史詩 [Professional storytelling and poetry on historical themes]. *Zhongyang yanjiuyuan lishi yuyan yanjiusuo jikan* 中央研究院歷史語言研究所季刊 10 (1948): 601–644.

Zhong Wen 鐘雯. *Sida jinshu yu xingwenhua* 四大禁書與性文化 [The four great banned books and sexual culture]. Harbin: Harbin chubanshe, 1994.

Zhongguo gudai xiaoshuo baike quanshu 中國古代小說百科全書 [Encyclopedia of traditional Chinese fiction]. Compiled by Liu Shide 劉世德 et al. Beijing: Zhongguo dabaike quanshu chubanshe, 1993.

Zhongguo tongsu xiaoshuo zongmu tiyao 中國通俗小說總目提要 [Comprehensive bibliography and synopses of popular Chinese fiction]. Compiled by Yin Longyuan 尹龍元 and Li Jingfeng 李景峰. Beijing: Zhongguo wenlian chuban gongsi, 1991.

Zito, Angela, and Tani E. Barlow, eds. *Body, Subject, and Power in China.* Chicago: University of Chicago Press, 1994.

Index

Production Notes for Stone/THE FOUNTAINHEAD OF CHINESE EROTICA

Interior design and composition by inari.

Jacket design by Timothy Mayer, inari.

Text and display type in Baskerville; Chinese type in Ming.

Printing and binding by The Maple-Vail Book Manufacturing Group.

Printed on 50 lb. Glatfeter Hi-Opaque, 440 ppi.